Family Deceptions

LORETTA GIACOLETTO

www.lorettagiacoletto.com

Copyright 2010 Loretta Giacoletto

Cover design by Caren Schlossberg-Wood

Cover photo © Carla F. Castagno/Dreamstime.com

ISBN: 13: 978-1469986708

Library of Congress Control Number: 2012907293

This book is a work of fiction. Names, characters, places, and incidents are either products of the author's imagination or used fictitiously. Any resemblance to actual events, locales, or persons, living or dead, is entirely coincidental. All rights reserved. No part of this publication can be reproduced or transmitted in any form or by any means, electronic or mechanical, without permission in writing from Loretta Giacoletto.

As an added bonus at the end of this novel

Check out the opening chapters of

THE FAMILY ANGEL

FAMILY DECEPTIONS

Book One—Chapter 1

Faiallo, Italy—1928

Pietro Rocca treasured those quiet moments on the alpine slope when he answered to no one but himself, a morning such as this that spread a blanket of solitude over the rugged terrain. He swept his long forked stick through decayed leaves, lifting and parting the undergrowth of early spring until he exposed a clump of mushrooms clinging to the base of a chestnut tree. Two more swipes uncovered the rest of the patch, sending up an earthy scent. He opened his knife and knelt to harvest the coveted delicacies when Tobi's distant barking interrupted his task. Pietro cocked his head toward the dense growth of trees and underbrush where Ugo had been kicking up rocks. *"Merda,"* he muttered, getting to his feet. Tobi didn't need to exert such effort on a fox or weasel since neither would've been foolish enough to attack the frolicking goat on his watch.

Pietro whistled; Tobi kept barking. Pietro whistled again and started walking uphill. Through the early morning haze he saw Tobi: feet grounded, body rigid, and head poised to attack. "Dammit, now what." Pietro grabbed a fallen limb and hurried toward the ruckus.

Tobi's hackles stood erect; his tail, unyielding. With lips curled and teeth bared, he was primed to defend his territory against any enemy: in this case a wild boar, the size of a young bull but with short, sturdy legs hugging the ground. As soon as the beast lowered its powerful head, Tobi lunged for the back feet. Swerving with an awkward grace, the porcine challenger raked Tobi with the curved tip of a long yellow tusk. Blood poured from Tobi's shoulder.

"Sonofabitch!" Pietro's financial investment in Tobi overruled his common sense. He jumped into the melee, delivering a solid whack to the boar's long snout. With a toss of its head, the boar sliced into Pietro's thigh, inflicting a gouge deeper than Tobi's. Pietro struck again before he fell back, reeling from the gushing wound. The boar staggered, blinked its beady eyes, and sensed fresh blood. Pietro scrambled to his feet and barely escaped the charging beast. Then Tobi leapt forward and sunk his teeth into its right ear, yanking sideways until the boar lost its footing and crashed to the earth.

As Pietro bounced away from the battle, his foot slid into a stony rut. His leg twisted with a loud snap. Pain shot from ankle to hip, so agonizing he nearly blacked out when it started back down his leg. He couldn't remember falling but felt the rocky soil cutting into his face. He heard snorting and yelping, smelled blood, and tasted the earth. Not even panic could help him up, but he did manage to roll a few meters away. For a brief moment he journeyed into the solace he treasured and when he returned, it was to the slurp, slurp of Tobi licking his face. The dog moved his velvet tongue down to the gash of warm blood on Pietro's thigh.

The leg was broken, that Pietro knew for sure. "Merda!" What stupidity, inexcusable for a farmer who'd spent his entire life mastering the foothills of the Alps. Biting his lip, he leaned on one elbow and blurted out a simple command. "Tobi, go home." The dog paused in its licking, gazed into Pietro's eyes, and then raced with the wind downhill toward a distant cluster of stone houses. The oldest had sheltered Rocca families for over three hundred years. Pietro knew Isabella would be churning butter. She seldom interrupted any chore, especially those involving her dairy products.

He sank back to the jagged earth, exhausted and cringing in pain. To his right lay the bristly-haired beast, its throat and belly ripped open to a swarm of buzzing flies. Beyond the steaming carcass, Ugo was shaking but still kicking up rocks while Vita and Fauna chewed on a patch of sparse greenery. For now the animals seemed content, but only time would tell. He sighed, uttering Isabella's name. If she even suspected his search for greener pastures and bigger mushrooms had led to the damn boar, and if all the commotion that followed had disturbed the precious milk of her livestock, there'd be hell to pay. Pietro's hell.

Meeting Isabella halfway might induce her sympathy. Pietro inched down a slope of rocky terrain that teased his aching ribs and dug into the exposed flesh of his thigh. He stopped to reconsider his strategy. Part way, he'd meet her part way instead. When the next unforgiving stone drew fresh blood, he rolled over and closed his eyes to the warm sun and chirping birds. His parents would've accepted Isabella, if only they had lived long enough to meet her. Damn the influenza for taking them in their prime. Damn the influenza for denying them the pleasure of grandchildren. Damn the influenza …

Pietro awoke to Tobi's happy barking, and his five-year old twins calling for their papa. He didn't open his eyes right away, even though he could sense Isabella's eyes boring through his. The hard ground barely acknowledged his wife of six years when she dropped to her knees. Her breath warmed his face as she issued her first order of the day. "Pietro, open your eyes."

He looked through heavy lids at the only woman he'd ever held or kissed. A triangle of paisley cloth tied behind her neck protected her dark, unruly hair from the sun. Her eyes, the color and shape of shelled almonds, registered no concern but he did catch the trace of a smile pass over her lips.

"Papa!" Riccardo and Gina shouted in unison. They knelt down, jockeying to plant wet kisses on his smooth-shaven face and to pat his stiff shoulder with their dimpled hands. What more could any man want: the unconditional love of adoring children.

Isabella sat back on her heels, waiting for an explanation before she started poking him. Pietro flipped his hand to the porcine carcass, its cavities inviting flies to deposit their eggs. "That damn *cinghiale* …"

"Could have made me a widow," Isabella said. "Bravo for Tobi, at last he proved his worth."

The cost of the pure bred had tested their willingness to compromise, one of the few times Pietro stood his ground.

"Nothing will go to waste," she said. "I'll do the butchering myself."

"Oh no, Mama," cried Gina. "Not Papa's leg."

"Silly," Riccardo said, pushing his sister aside. "Mama meant the damn cinghiale." He put his hand on Isabella's. "Don't worry, Mama. I'll be your helper."

"And I'll take care of Papa," the little girl said.

After a quick examination of Pietro's injuries, Isabella got up. "I need to go back for Aldo and the cart." She leveled her forefinger at the twins. "Stay here with Papa and don't leave his side. Understand?"

Two heads of black, curly ringlets nodded. The twins snuggled next to Pietro and watched their mama grow smaller as she distanced herself from them. She'd not yet disappeared when Gina began to wiggle and squirm, then she dug her wooden shoes into the dirt.

"You need to tinkle?" Pietro asked.

"No, Papa. I need to play."

Riccardo jutted out his lower lip. "But Mama said—"

"Go on, both of you. Take Tobi and don't wander beyond those trees." Pietro scooted his back against a small boulder and reveled in the sight of his children at play. Either the pain had subsided or the joy of his twins had muffled it. In any case he willed himself not to dwell on the impending remedy.

An hour passed before he heard Riccardo call out to his mama. Pietro leaned across one elbow and squinted into the sun, trying to make out his rescue unit. In the cart next to Isabella sat his neighbor and self-proclaimed mentor, Giovanni Martino. Aldo was fighting a valiant uphill battle, straining over the additional burden of Giovanni's weight, most of which centered on his massive belly. After a few meters the mule refused to go any further. Isabella slid off the cart and walked ramrod straight, her back refusing to bend with the incline. Aldo pulled a few more meters. He stopped again, this time not continuing until Giovanni climbed down and followed Isabella. Pietro couldn't help but chuckle, an indulgence his tender ribs quickly resisted

Giovanni's six-foot frame stooped to accommodate his fifty-three years. He took off his cap and wiped a red kerchief over his brow. Wisps of graying strands crisscrossed a bullet-shaped head, flanked by elongated ears sprouting patches of wiry hair. As he approached Pietro, his face softened to display a hodgepodge of crooked, stained teeth worn with age. "Ah, Pietro, Pietro," he said, shaking his head. "For one so agile, today you moved with the grace of an old woman."

"Old woman, hell, I backed into a damn rut."

"You fell into a load of *cacca*. You're a farmer, not a goat." Giovanni used the back of his hand to clear a droplet of clear mucus hanging from his bulbous nose. Grunting, he pushed his knees to the ground, and then tore the seam of Pietro's shredded trousers. "Next time—"

"Dammit, watch the leg." Pietro sucked in warm air, released it with a moan through his clenched teeth. He closed his eyes to stifle another moan. "*Mi dispiace*," he apologized. "Because of me Isabella took you away from your work."

"Giovanni insisted," Isabella called out from the cart as she wrapped a roll of muslin strips around two lengths of tree bark padded with hay. Holding up her sturdy hands, she wiggled long, bony fingers. "These are gifted, as were my nonna's—God rest her soul. Of course, I could work alone; but with help from Giovanni …"

"Just get the bones straight."

"Don't blame me for Mondo's limp," she said, referring to a neighbor whose leg she once set. "He got up when he should've stayed in bed."

"*Basta, basta,*" Giovanni said. "Who better to trust than your wife and me, your godfather?"

"And the godfather of our children," Isabella said.

Giovanni blew her a kiss. "Remember when you were a little *rigazzo*, Pietro, that day your *nonno* broke his leg?"

Pietro winced at the memory. Papa had ordered him outside, but he still heard all the yelling when the doctor arrived and yanked the old man's brittle bones back where they belonged.

Giovanni must've remembered too. He propped a kidney-shaped vessel to Pietro's shoulder and ordered him to drink with gusto. "To lessen the pain, my friend."

Pietro turned his head and let the wine trickle down his parched throat to warm and relax the blood sending sporadic chills through his body. Closing his eyes, he took a deep breath and gulped until the pouch went dry.

Isabella called for the twins and they came running. "See those flowers, way up there." She pointed to a sweep of yellow and blue. "Take Tobi and go pick some for your papa. And don't come back until I call you."

Riccardo headed uphill toward the meadow, stopping along the way to encircle his chubby fingers around a few stray plants while Gina skipped off in pursuit of tantalizing butterflies. When they'd gone far enough not to hear Pietro's pain but still within Isabella's sight, she nodded to Giovanni.

Standing behind Pietro, he eased down, straddling his bowed legs into a vise around Pietro's upper arms. "Chomp down," Giovanni said, shoving a length of chestnut over the patient's tongue.

Pietro sunk his teeth into the wood, releasing a bitter taste that masked the lingering warmth of wine. He forced his mind to concentrate on an overhead leaf where a motionless praying mantis stalked an unsuspecting grasshopper. Isabella's hands—gifted she called them, he had his doubts—were cradling the two sections of his leg. Overhead the mantis struck, immobilizing the grasshopper. Closer to earth, gently, ever so gently, Isabella lifted and extended, lifted and extended. As she maneuvered the bones into position, the mantis slowly devoured its prey. Pietro lost interest in the mysteries of nature and squeezed his eyes shut. *Blessed Mother, how much time do those gifted hands need to remarry my separated bones. Bravo!* The marriage was blessed when Giovanni loosened his grip. Only then did Pietro sail his mouthpiece into the air and let out a pent-up A-I-E-E!

"Louder, Pietro, maybe you'll bring rain," Giovanni said, wiping his brow again. He moved to help Isabella support the leg with a padded splint. "Relax, my friend. We're almost done."

"I'll never forget this, Giovanni."

"Nor will I, but it is your wife who deserves most of the credit. Treat her like the queen she is. Kiss the hem of her skirt and from there, work your way up."

Pietro waited for his queen to look up before he offered an impromptu comment, one bound to bring regret. "Isabella knows how I feel."

With the last muslin strip tucked in place, she leaned over to brush her lips across his cheek. "You were brave," she whispered, "but the pain from a leg getting set in no way compares to that of a woman giving birth."

*****

Two days later and at Isabella's request *Dottore* Ernesto Zucca made the one-hour automobile trek from Pont Canavese to the Rocca home. "Your wife's skills match that of any trained nurse I've encountered," he declared after a thorough examination of Pietro's injuries. "But the extent of this ligament damage still concerns me."

"Feeding my family concerns me," Pietro replied to Ernesto Zucca's backside.

The doctor and Isabella had their heads together and were

discussing Pietro's therapy as though he were in a coma. In spite of his protests Pietro wound up encased in plaster from upper thigh to lower ankle.

"Stay off that leg for at least two months," Dr. Zucca said while drying his hands with one of Isabella's immaculate linen towels.

"Easy enough for you to say," muttered Pietro from the bed he and Isabella had shared since their marriage. "My living depends on the produce markets in Pont Canavese and Cuorgnè."

"Only an idiot chooses his living over his limb, or his life." The doctor's tone softened when he turned to Isabella. "An injury such as this could still get infected. If gangrene sets in—

"It won't, Dottore. My husband will stay in bed."

"Merda," Pietro later grumbled when he and Isabella were alone. "What the hell does Ernesto Zucca know, him with his fancy suit and that Fiat 501."

"That Fiat enables him to see more patients in less time, some with broken legs and ungrateful tongues."

"You paid him?"

"With our best *tomino*."

All of Isabella's cheeses were the best. She babied the cows and goats more than their twins. Pietro turned his face to the wall. A man laid up was no better than a lame horse.

"I'll go to market," Isabella said.

"Women don't go to market alone."

"This one will."

"With everything else you have to do?"

"For now the weather is good, the roads are safe, it's only two days a week."

"We could send the twins to your sister."

"*Assurdità!* With four children my sister's hands are full."

"I thought she had three."

"You forget that no-good *caccata* she married."

"The twins can stay home with me."

"The twins will go to market."

"At four in the morning?"

"They'll sleep in the cart."

*****

On Monday the cock had not yet crowed when Isabella sat at the table, dunking the dry heel of Saturday's bread into fresh coffee. In that same all-purpose room Pietro stirred from the narrow bed Giovanni had set up, so the invalid wouldn't suffer the indignity of being confined to his bedroom.

Isabella had already loaded the cart with fresh milk and sweet butter, goat and cow cheeses, and dozens of large brown eggs. She prepared a soft pallet of warm blankets for the children still sleeping in their beds.

"Wait another thirty minutes," Pietro said. "By then Giovanni will pass by."

"Giovanni? Humph, as if I need that old goat showing me the way to Pont."

"I thought you liked him."

"I do, but not with his nose in our business. Besides, I want to be among the first to arrive." She leaned over and kissed his cheeks. "Serina offered to look in on you."

"Then leave the twins. She can help with them."

"Foist our little demons on Serina, her with a nursing baby?"

Pietro pressed her hands to his lips. "Mi dispiace, you work too hard and now this."

"And you worry too much. Now go back to sleep."

She carried the sleeping twins out the door, first Riccardo, and then Gina. The rooster—Isabella's, as were the hens since she ran the chicken house—began a cockle-doodle-do destined to continue past sunrise. Pietro didn't have to check his pocket watch to confirm the time; the damn rooster always crowed at four. Still, he stretched one arm to the bed stand and his papa's prized possession. Damn the influenza for making him an orphan before he became a man. And thank God for Giovanni who eased his pain then and ever since.

Pietro's godfather lived in the largest of eight houses sharing the same hillside with his. The Martino house, as it was now called, originated from the family of Giovanni's first wife. While Giovanni had been away fighting the Austrians, she died giving birth to their only child, a stillborn son. Had the boy lived, he would've been a few years older than Pietro's twenty-six.

Morning light filled the room while Pietro struggled with a dream about wild boars and deep ruts. He stumbled, lost his balance trying to bottom out. His leg jerked, as did his entire body, sending a surge of wake-up pain from ears to toes. He checked his watch, eight o'clock. Not that time mattered. For now, time would be measured by when Isabella left and when she returned. After relieving himself, Pietro slid the chamber pot under the bed. One hand over his rough face reminded him of the need to shave, a daily habit he seldom neglected.

"*Buon giorno*," a voice sang out with the opening door. In walked Serina Martino, with Baby Maria in her arms.

"You shouldn't have come," he said. "I don't need a nursemaid."

"Ah, but I promised Isabella." Serina set Maria down on the floor to play with her rattle. "So sorry I'm late but a hungry baby must be nourished."

She laughed, cradling her hands under heavy breasts. Serina's apron matched her eyes, the bluest Pietro had ever seen. No woman should have eyes as blue as a mountain lake washed with sun. The baby's eyes matched her mama's; the little head balder than Giovanni's.

"The bambina, who does she look like?"

Serina lifted her shoulders. "Who can say? At seven months I had but a single strand of hair." She laughed again and twisted one finger into the sienna curls piled on top of her head.

"How do you like your coffee?" She sniffed the enamel pot, shrugged, and put it on the stove to reheat. "With milk?"

"*Si*, but you don't have to …"

"Ah, but I must. Not a day passes without Giovanni talking about his beloved Pietro. You're the son he should've had. Does that make you my beloved stepson?"

"It makes you the wife of my good friend and godfather." He traded silly barbs with her until a whiff of foul air assaulted his nose. "What's that I smell?"

"It's your fault," she said.

After one sip of steaming milk and burnt coffee, Pietro screwed up his face. Isabella would've made a fresh brew. With food and drink Isabella never skimped.

"Too hot for your blood?" Serina asked.

"Too bitter."

He clanked the double-eared cup onto its saucer, making Baby Maria jump. She puckered her face and unleashed a splash of tears.

"Naptime," Serina sang out. She scooped up the wailer and headed to the twins' bedroom.

"You should go home. The bambina needs the comfort of her bed."

"This little angel sleeps wherever I put her."

Serina's soft lullaby grew softer until she backed out of the bedroom and closed the curtain. With a wink she circled her thumb and forefinger, then hurried to the sink and started priming the pump handle. Water gushed into the teakettle.

"What are you doing?" he asked when she put the kettle on the stove.

"Your face is growing whiskers."

He shook his head. "No, no. It can wait until Isabella returns."

"At three in the afternoon, don't be ridiculous. By then you'll have a beard and Isabella will still have her work and yours."

Pietro turned to the wall. He must've dozed off because when he shifted again, Serina was pouring hot water into an earthenware bowl. She set it on the bed stand along with his toiletries.

"Shall I hold or shave?" she asked, balancing a small mirror between her hands.

Scanning his reflected image, Pietro lowered his heavy eyebrows into a frown. Three days without sun had brought pallor to his olive complexion and emphasized an already prominent nose.

"Do not despair, Pietro," she said. "You're still the handsomest man in all of Faiallo."

Her patronizing words he didn't need.

"Maybe in the entire Canavese district," she went on. "But this I cannot say for certain since Giovanni never takes me anywhere."

Was it any wonder, Serina turned heads wherever they went. He lathered up and wielded the straightedge from side to side before finishing with the indentation in his chin. Quickly, he rinsed the remaining lather, dried his face, and ran a comb through his dark, obedient hair.

Serina's next move unnerved him as much as the perfume of her mother's milk. Until that moment only Isabella and his mama had touched the threadlike scar over his upper lip.

"The nature of man," she said, "is to inflict at least one flaw on an otherwise perfect canvas."

Pietro flinched, and lowered her hand with his.

*****

Three o'clock marked the return of Isabella and the twins. While Riccardo helped unload empty containers, Gina ran to Pietro's bedside. "Papa, Papa, everybody asked about you."

"Be careful," Isabella cautioned. "Remember Papa's leg."

"I won't let her forget it." Pietro removed Gina's elbow from his ribs as he eased over to make room for her.

"She held out a little sack of lemon drops. "Take one."

He asked for a kiss instead, and she obliged.

Riccardo pushed her aside to plant his own kiss. "We sold everything. Mama's cheese went first."

Isabella wiped her hands on her apron, leaned over, and exchanged kisses with Pietro. "Hm-m, you already shaved?"

"Serina heated up some water."

"Good. She gave you something to eat?"

He shrugged. "A little cheese, a little salami."

"A little nothing, I'll make polenta and sausage for supper."

"I don't need any more aggravation. Giovanni's bambino belongs at home, so does his wife."

"It's only for a while. Don't be such a *testa dura*."

"You're calling me a hard head," he said with a laugh that coaxed a smile from her. "The day, it went well?"

"A little trouble early this morning, Flavio tried to squeeze me out."

"Sonofabitch. Did Giovanni set him straight?"

"No, I did, before Giovanni got there."

*****

On Thursday Pietro's erratic breathing vibrated through the room while Isabella finished her market preparations. He didn't hear her load the cart or add extra wood to the stove or tiptoe out with the twins. Today they headed south, to the village of Cuorgnè in the valley below. By the time Aldo had pulled the creaking load around the first hairpin curve, Isabella's rooster welcomed the new dawn and a sluggish Pietro.

He flicked his thumb to a wooden match and lit the thin, Turkish cigarette gripped between his teeth. Cranking the window over his bed, he exhaled into the crisp, mountain air. He smoked until nothing but a paper fold of tobacco remained between his thumb and forefinger. After flipping the sliver outside, he closed his eyes and drifted off. When he awoke, it was to the milky scent of Serina. She towered over him, Baby Maria in her arms.

"You shaved," she said, feigning a pout.

"Last night, before I went to bed—I mean to sleep."

Her next words spilled in lyrical syllables, each beat matching the bouncing of Maria. "Poor Pietro, destined for a long, boring spring, cooped up like a rooster tied to its perch and with no reason to crow. You need a few distractions." Maria let out an impatient whine and started rooting at her mother's breast. "All right, my little one," Serina said, unbuttoning her blouse as she walked to his children's room. "I won't be long, Pietro. A full belly helps Maria sleep."

"Feed your baby at home," he called out. "I don't need you."

Her laugh grated on his nerves. "Oh, Pietro, of course you need me."

He enjoyed fifteen minutes of peace before she hovered over him, rubbing her hands like a sly purveyor. "Now, Pietro, what would you like?"

He rolled his eyes.

"I meant to drink, silly. Those sorry bones won't mend unless they're properly nourished."

No coffee, not after Monday's. "Perhaps a little wine."

She cracked two eggs into a goblet, beating them with a fork while adding wine from the jug. Handing him the thick potion, she said, "To your health and better times."

With four gulps he emptied the contents, ran his tongue over his lip, and returned the glass. "*Grazie*, you can leave now. I'm ready for a nap." He'd not lied; the wine made him groggy.

"No, no. Sleep now and you won't tonight." She feigned another pout. "And what about Maria? She'll turn into a little demon if I wake her." Serina pulled a chair beside his bed and sat. "Please indulge me. I have a favor to ask."

"For the wife of Giovanni—"

"Not for Giovanni's wife." She made a fist and tapped her breast. "For me, Serina." Her fingers slipped between the buttons of her bodice and produced a small package wrapped with string. "Friend to friend, Pietro, a safe place to keep this?"

He hesitated, thinking of Giovanni.

"Please, don't make me beg," she said. "Giovanni is generous but every woman needs her private nest egg."

Not Isabella. She held the purse strings tight enough for both of them. He motioned to their bedroom. "Tall chest, bottom drawer, metal box."

"This must be our secret, Pietro."

"Isabella respects what belonged to my parents."

He expected Serina to leave after disposing of her package. Instead she sat again.

"I won't forget your kindness, Pietro. If ever I can repay you—"

"Mi dispiace," he said, his voice less irritable. "But I don't want to keep you any longer. You have your own work at home."

"Life holds more than work. A man like you—"

Maria's crying interrupted her mama's next words, and relieved Pietro from having to hear them. Serina got up, stretched her arms to accent an hourglass figure. "Until next time, Pietro, pleasant dreams."

*****

The next time his family went to market Pietro didn't fall back to sleep. He figured this day would be Serina's last. He'd tell her after she fixed his eggs and wine, before she made a show of feeding her baby from those breasts that bounced with her every move. Two firm raps hit the door earlier than he expected; a third pushed it open. Pietro closed his eyes and faked deep sleep through a slack mouth. He heard petticoats rustle back and forth between the pump and stove, coffee grounds hit the bottom of the kettle, crusty bread snap as it separated.

"Pietro," a voice called out. "Wake up."

He opened his eyes to a tiny woman, her back arched into a shepherd's hook. Theresa Gotti balanced a tray of coffee and bread between her spindly arms. She wore widows black, her skirt skimming the tops of clunky black oxfords. Eyes set deep in their sockets empowered a face lined with the history of eighty years.

"Zia Theresa, I did not expect you." Pietro said, according the honorary title of aunt to his beloved mama's godmother and confidante.

"Serina could not come today. She asked me to stop by."

The old woman lived two houses away, and Pietro used to play with her grandchildren when they visited from Rivarola.

"You shouldn't have—"

"For the son of Madelena Rocca—God rest her soul—I would do anything." She bent over to put the tray down. With the measured effort of a mechanical toy, she straightened up, lifted her narrow shoulders, and squeezed until her face registered the pleasure of pain. "These aching bones cry out with each task I perform, even those in the name of love. Remember when I broke my collarbone?" Raising her left arm to shoulder height, she winced. "Growing old is God's revenge."

"Hm-m, the coffee is good, Zia."

"I added a little Frangelica—you look so pale. Dear Pietro, with that gamy leg prepare for the worse. No longer will you need a sniff of air to predict damp weather." She shook her head to the beat of a clicking tongue. "I pray your leg will walk straighter than my poor Mondo's. Not that I blame Isabella, you understand."

Mondo was her eldest, unmarried and with no prospects given his slow nature. Pietro patted her hand. "You are an angel, Zia."

"God chose not to bless my shriveled womb with daughters of my own. And those lazy wives of my sons …" She rolled her eyes. "At least your Isabella respects me." She dug into her apron pocket and pulled out a dainty jewelry case. "I always meant this for your mama."

Pietro caressed the lid before he opened it. Inside, red velvet cushioned the drop earrings and matching brooch, a gold filigree of emeralds and tiny diamonds. "Mama would've cried tears of joy."

"Don't expect such emotion from Isabella. But trust my words; these jewels will make her your queen. What's more, she will regard you as her king." Zia touched her skeletal finger to his forearm. "Learn from the mistakes of others, Pietro. Pleasure delayed is pleasure denied."

*****

On Thursday Serina went straight to the bedroom with her sleeping baby. "Poor Maria, she's teething so I gave her a touch of paregoric," she said, closing in on Pietro with that damnable scent. She asked if he missed her.

He shrugged. "Zia Theresa gave me fresh coffee."

"And what else?"

"A litany of complaints," he said with a grin.

"Ah-ha, you did miss me. Shall I fix the eggs and wine?"

"You should take your baby and go home." He waited for a snappy retort. Instead, she sniffled and rummaged in her pocket for a handkerchief. Serina pulled out the baby's bib and could've used it. But no, she grabbed the nearest kitchen towel and wiped her nose. Disrespecting Isabella's linens was akin to sneezing on an altar cloth.

"You listened to your Zia's problems. Can't you make room in that cold heart for mine?"

General aches and pains Pietro could abide, but miseries that brought women to tears embarrassed him. If Isabella experienced such miseries, which he doubted, she kept them to herself. He cleared his throat. "Perhaps you should talk with my wife."

Serina dropped to her knees, bent her head to the crook of his arm. "Forgive me for burdening you but I trust no one else. I've made certain mistakes, more than once."

"We all have, Giovanni too. But he is a forgiving man."

"He won't be after next week." She looked up, her face wet and blotched and begging for compassion. "When Giovanni returns from market, Maria and I will be gone, forever." Again she wiped her nose, this time on the bed sheet. "Please, you must help me."

"Don't talk like that. Giovanni loves you and the baby."

Sticking out her tongue, she blew a raspberry fart. "He's old and ugly and slobbers all over me until I want to throw up. Being with him feels like fornicating with my papa."

"Don't talk like that. Giovanni's your husband."

"And I am his whore. Did he tell you? I make him pay—before he touches me with those grubby paws that grope and fumble and rub me raw." She clutched Pietro's hand to her cheek. "I'm young. I need someone young, someone like you."

"But not me."

"Think of Giovanni. He lives each day for Maria and me. If we leave, he will surely die of a broken heart."

Pietro pulled his hand away. "Take your baby home."

"She'll sleep for hours."

He searched his mind for the right words. Those he pushed out sounded hollow. "I have a good marriage, one with no complications."

"And no excitement."

"Isabella would know."

"Not unless you tell her." She slipped her hand under the covers, trailing a warm finger across his rib cage and down his ribbon of hair. "I could teach you things."

Like what he wanted to ask, but that would seem like he condoned what she was about to do. "For god's sake, Serina, I can barely move."

"Pietro, Pietro. With me you won't have to move."

Chapter 2

Giovanni's wife engaged Pietro in an hour of lovemaking unlike any he'd known with Isabella. When Serina's primitive cry caused Baby Maria to let out one too, the bed quit shaking and Serina stretched to disengage herself from him. Preening naked on the rug Isabella had braided with care, Serina lifted her arms to receive the first of two petticoats.

"When you look at me, what do you see?" she asked.

"The body of Venus but much warmer, in fact, it simmers." She deserved the compliment but Pietro regretted the speed of his reply. He'd experienced a similar reaction to Isabella on their wedding night, one he'd reluctantly shared with her.

"Ah-h, a lover of fine art." Serina bent over to wet his face with her lips. "You've seen the museums of *Firenze*?"

"Only those in *Torino*. Your baby, she's crying again."

"Someday, you will take me to Firenze, si?"

He shook his head. "Impossible."

"Before today, I might have agreed." She hummed a lilting tune that didn't stop until she picked up Maria. "Shall I come back on Thursday?"

"No, I don't need you."

"Pietro, Pietro. First you cheat, now you lie. Whatever would Isabella think?"

*****

That evening Isabella prepared a supper consisting of creamy risotto, a dandelion and onion salad, and fresh bread she'd purchased from a *panetteria* in Pont.

"Can Papa eat with us?" asked Gina.

"Dr. Zucca said he must stay in bed so his leg will heal."

"We could eat with him," Riccardo said.

"No, no. Then he'd have to sleep in a pile of annoying crumbs."

Gina's eyes opened wide. "Papa?"

"Do as your mama says. Besides, I'm not hungry."

"Not hungry for risotto?" Isabella held her hand to his forehead.

"Must I be sick not to be hungry?"

"Perhaps a little wine?"

"No wine, dammit, just leave me alone."

Supper progressed as usual. First Gina spilled her milk, then Riccardo. Twice, Riccardo slid off his chair and helped their mama clean up the puddles. After restoring order, Isabella took them to the stable under their house, where they bounced a rubber ball against the stone foundation while she squeezed milk from Fauna and Vita.

Pietro was left to record market sales into the ledger, a duty he'd taken over from Isabella after the accident. He tried concentrating on the family finances. He tried listening to the music of his children. Their laughter resounded through a hole in the floor, one an ancestor had cut to capture heat generated by the livestock. Not that his bed required any additional warmth. Not after Serina.

"Bed rest becomes you," a voice roared to startle him.

Pietro's leg jerked and he yelled, "Sonofabitch!"

"Whoa, Pietro, it's me, Giovanni." A broad smile raised the older man's cheeks and stretched the peppered stubble across his lower face.

"I must have dozed off," said Pietro, trying to ignore the ricocheting pain.

"I knocked twice. Even went downstairs to visit Isabella. I told her 'Pietro cannot be sleeping. He does nothing all day,' She tells me, 'His leg heals while he sleeps.' Is this true, my friend?"

"Pardone?"

"Never mind, I can see you have other concerns to ponder. Look, if money's a problem, I can lend you some. No interest, of course. What's mine is yours."

Another jerk of his leg forced Pietro to hold his breath until the pain passed. "You're a good man, a good friend."

"More than a friend, Pietro. If I had not found my Serina—"

"But you did."

Giovanni closed his eyes and smiled. "From out of nowhere a bolt of lightning struck. The damn thing pierced my heart, rendering me incapable of her charms. And when our baby survived her early birth, I found God again."

"What more could any man want."

"A second family, Pietro. You are the son I never held. You breathe the air he should've breathed. Now God has made up for my lonely years by blessing me with two families. Someday my Maria and your Riccardo—"

"You and Serina can still have sons.

"Perhaps, but my soldier no longer stands at attention without a helping hand. And that Serina provides. I am the *capitano* she must salute, everyday."

Pietro shifted his weight, kicked the blanket with his good leg. The entire bed bounced as Giovanni slapped the corn shuck mattress with his dry, calloused hand.

"Mi dispiace, Pietro. Here I am, bragging; and there you are, disabled. Patience. Soon, you'll be dipping your stick into life's honey pot again. Unlike this old soldier, you have time on your side."

*****

On Saturday streaks of purple and orange had cast their spell over the mountains when neighbors arrived to encourage Pietro's recovery. After several rounds of wine, Isabella cradled a worn album of faded photographs and escorted their guests to the lower level, away from the livestock. The adults gathered at a long table flanked by wooden benches, consuming more wine and roasted chestnuts while the children played tag on the stone floor and drank tamarind syrup diluted with water.

Upstairs, Leo Arnetti propped his tooled leather boots on Pietro's bed and offered a cigarette from his tin. It would be

Pietro's second that day, his own rationed at Isabella's suggestion to stay within their budget. His words accompanied the exhaled smoke of his first drag. "So, Leo, how long have you been gone?"

"Ever since you gave up your freedom." Leo grinned, his hooked nose hiding a short upper lip. "Ah-h, Pietro, America is not what we dreamed as *rigazzi*, not one street paved with gold. Still, I make good money."

"Farming?"

"Hell no." Leo pushed one hand through the persistent black hair parting on his low forehead. "I mine for copper, out West, in a wild place called Montana."

"Where cowboys and Indians fight, si?"

"Only in the moving pictures." Leo's grin revealed a gold tooth that once housed a wormhole cavity. "Sure, there are mountains, but none as high as the glorious Alps." He stretched his arms to their full span. "And ranches with cattle by the thousands, land almost as pure as the Blessed Virgin."

"Then you're going back."

"Can't afford not to … besides, after six years on my own I feel more American than Italian, more Montanan than *Piemontese*. If only you had come with me way back when."

Pietro shredded the remnants of his cigarette into the ashtray. "That damn influenza nearly destroyed me, and the farm. If it wasn't for Giovanni—"

"That old fart, he sucked the sweet life from you. He even picked Isabella for your wife."

"Everything happened so fast."

"In America everything happens fast. Men no smarter or braver than you and me are not afraid to take chances."

"Why gamble when I got everything here."

"What have you got? Your father's house, your father's life. In America you make your own world, the one you dreamed about."

Pietro shook his head. "Easy words coming from a bachelor."

"Look, I'm not suggesting you desert Isabella and the bambini. Send for them after you get settled." With the finesse of a magician, he produced a picture postcard and wrote on the back. "Here, in case you make it to America, my address and a telephone number."

"You have your own telephone?"

"Where I board, but I'm thinking about buying the place when I go back. Buy now, invest in the future: that's my motto." He glanced at the gold timepiece pulled from the pocket of his leather-fringed vest. "Sorry, Pietro, I promised Licia I'd stop by."

"After all these years, it's still Leo and his vestal virgin."

"More like the lion and his *chiavata*. If not for me, Licia would've died intact."

"Show some respect. Licia will make a good wife."

"Not mine. She'll never leave the mama, the papa, the four *fratelli*. The whole family's got her by the *tette*."

"Come on, what do you expect? Licia is the only daughter."

"For that distinction she owes the family her life? Eternal smothering may be their way but not mine. I had to find my own way, and without the promise of an inheritance. After all, how many times can tired land be divided?" With opened palms Leo balanced two imaginary weights. "My brother or me? Me or my brother?" He shrugged. "Giorgio was firstborn."

"Me, I was fortunate to be an only child."

Leo swung his boots to the floor. "Don't be so sure, my friend. And don't forget what I said about America. Partner with me there and in a few years you'll return a rich man."

After the door closed, Pietro lit a cigarette from the tin Leo left behind. Pietro turned Leo's sepia-toned postcard over and examined a herd of majestic buffalo, another reminder of his curtailed youth, of a time when he and Leo practiced the language of America and planned their great adventure. Beyond the watchful eye of Pietro's mama, they'd lounged in the stable on piles of hay, and rolled loose tobacco into transparent paper. They smoked and talked and passed the jug. Papa knew, but let them dream. Even then, Leo had a knack for embellishing the truth.

At the party below, Pietro's neighbors were calling for more wine and trying to outdo each other with stories heard before. He pictured the scene: *Isabella filling empty glasses, reveling in her guests while the album of sweeter times circles the table. Rounds of spirited laughter swell before the emotional cleansing. After a respectful mourning, Alberto Rossini brings out his concertina. One of the men starts to clap, slow at first, and then to the beat of Alberto's lively invitation for young and old to dance. Most likely, Zia Theresa will surrender to the moment, lifting her skirts to expose the little twigs supporting her elfin frame.*

Pietro left the imagined party when the outer door rattled as it pushed open with the nudge of a familiar hip. "Sh-h-h, little one," Serina cooed, gently rocking to close Maria's eyes while she carried her into the twins' room. For a few blessed hours, Pietro had shoved aside thoughts of Giovanni's wife to accommodate Leo's cacca.

Serina returned, swinging her arms to free them of responsibility. "Your friend from America left?"

He directed his answer to the wall. "You should leave too."

"Poor Pietro—all alone up here with everyone down there celebrating your misery, it isn't fair. You need a party too." She lifted the covers and snuggled beside him.

"Are you crazy?" he whispered, "with Isabella and Giovanni right below us?"

"Sh-h," Serina cautioned with a finger to her pursed lips. Her pink tongue rolled out to the finger, depositing a dollop of saliva she trailed across his scar. "Listen, my darling, Giovanni is telling that pathetic war story, the one where he saves the bumbling lieutenant and two underlings, who in turn reward him by swearing their eternal loyalty. What a pile of cacca. When Giovanni runs out of wind, which won't be for another ten minutes, everyone must hear Bruno's tale: how Bruno, and only Bruno, captured two enemy foot soldiers. After that, Vittorio will drop his pants to show off those scrawny cheeks dotted with shrapnel. Ugh! And they haven't even gotten to the loose photographs—the ones in the box I slipped under the table to buy us more time together."

"But Isabella—"

"Works too hard, and this evening she deserves some pleasure," Serina murmured in his ear while reaching under his nightshirt. "Tsk, tsk, Pietro. Must you be so selfish?"

*****

Three weeks passed before Dr. Zucca made another house call, at which time he declared Pietro ready for crutches.

"I wanted the damn plaster off today," Pietro later told

Isabella. "What the hell does Ernesto Zucca know."

"More than Pietro Rocca … of course, you could always disregard the doctor's wisdom. Get up now and you'll spend the rest of your days straddling the road and the hillside.

"What?"

"You know, to accommodate the permanent limp you will have created. Now quit complaining. Giovanni said he'd make a pair of strong crutches."

"Giovanni, Giovanni. Him with his nose in every piss I take."

"You should thank God for such a friend, and for Serina too."

*****

That afternoon brought Serina carrying the baby, and Giovanni, the crutches. While the twins entertained Maria, Isabella and Serina eased Pietro from the bed, their shoulders supporting his sluggish weight. Pietro stood in a knee-length nightshirt, the leg thick with hair wobbling and the plastered one jutting forward to defy gravity.

"You're as pale as a baby's bottom, my friend," Giovanni said as he maneuvered a smooth chestnut limb under Pietro's arm. "You should sit in the sun, nature's great healer."

Pietro grunted. Talking took more effort than he felt like expending.

"I know," Giovanni said with a wink. "What you need the sun cannot provide. Right, Isabella?"

Pietro felt the pressure of Serina's palm against his back. "Don't be such a tease, Giovanni," she said. "Right now, Isabella has mountains of work and only two hands."

"He's right, Pietro," Isabella said. "I mean about the sun."

*****

During the next month Pietro mastered his crutches and performed simple chores outside. On market days he made coffee while Isabella loaded the wagon. "Leave the twins with me," he said one morning.

"Those little rascals make too much mischief."

"For me they'll behave."

"Si, when you can run on two good legs." She reached over to exchange kisses, her fingertips touching his cheek. At the door she paused, motioning to where he slept alone. "That bed needs to come down. It crowds the room."

Pietro felt crowded too. "Next week," he replied, ignoring Isabella's way of saying she missed their intimacy. He'd not been inside her since the accident. Juggling two women was riskier than juggling two swords. What if Isabella noticed a change? Serina had, crediting herself with improving his lovemaking techniques. He gave himself one more week before letting her go.

After he was alone, Pietro waited another forty minutes before going outside. Gripping the padded supports of his crutches, he swung his weight forward into the dark, avoiding familiar obstacles along a route he'd been navigating alone for several weeks. Giovanni's mule and cart were gone, the door to his house ajar. Pietro steadied himself and with his right crutch pushed on the door.

Wrapped in a blanket, Serina shuddered from the blast of morning air. "What took you so long?" she asked, her bare feet dancing on the stone floor.

"I can't stay."

"Then why did you come?"

"To tell you what's between us must stop."

"Someday, yes, but not this day." She opened the blanket to engulf him. Strands of her hair tickled his nose until he blew them away. If only he could blow Serina away. He closed his eyes and took in her sweetness.

"Ah-h, Pietro, your compassion feeds my heart and soul. And that shriveled up soldier's too. What more can I say? Because of you Giovanni and I have never been happier."

*****

That afternoon Dr. Zucca made an unexpected stop and removed Pietro's cast. He was clearing away the plaster when Isabella walked in with the twins. Gina ran to the bed, put her hand to her mouth, and gasped. "Papa, your leg, it looks like a prune."

Riccardo shoved her aside. He opened his mouth, but only stared.

Pietro sat up, groaned when he saw the atrophied leg. God is punishing me, he thought. "So, Isabella, ask Ernesto Zucca how's he's going to fix this."

"Exercise and daily massages," the doctor replied from over his shoulder. He scribbled some instructions, handed them to Isabella. "Next week throw away the crutches."

"What about riding in the cart?" she asked.

"Of course, if you can tolerate his complaining."

After supper when Isabella was ready to milk the cows, Gina and Riccardo begged to stay upstairs. Pietro sat at the table, his leg propped on a chair and head nodding as he fought to stay awake. He dozed until he heard the teakettle rattle and felt the hot water. His stinging leg jerked to the table, and he yelled a string of profanities that sent the twins scrambling.

"Gina made me," Riccardo told Isabella when she came running.

"We tried to fix Papa's leg," Gina explained with opened palms.

Isabella carted them off, one squealer under each arm. By the time she returned from their bedtime prayers, Pietro had changed into his nightshirt and sat warming the edge of his bed.

"You can't go to sleep yet," she said. "We must exercise your leg."

Merda. He lay back and endured the agonizing routine of Isabella working his leg from hip to knee and ankle while he silently cursed her gifted hands. She massaged olive oil into his muscles, applying pressure to intensify each stroke, her way of punishing him. "Dammit, woman, not so hard."

She responded with unrelenting thumbs.

Pietro screwed up his face and gave in to her. He always did. As her fingertips slowed to a light tread, he brushed a wisp of hair from her forehead. The massage ended.

"I'm tired of sleeping alone, Pietro."

So was he. With Serina, he never fell asleep.

Later, he limped into their bedroom and found Isabella primping at the dressing table, plaiting her hair into a single braid that fell in front of her shoulder. Their eyes met in the mirror, forcing both of them to look away. After he eased into bed, she turned down the kerosene lamp, slipped under the covers, and soon rolled to his side. He was ready for her but didn't want to appear too eager. Or too polished.

"My leg aches from the damn workout."

"You want to sleep?"

"No, I want you to make me feel better."

*****

That night a loud thud disturbed Pietro's sleep. Isabella moved from his arms and lit the lamp. Their room came aglow to shadows and forms and one blank wall with a rectangle of clean plaster. Pietro leaned over the side of the bed and brought up a framed, black and white photograph. Lines of broken glass cut through two somber faces. The bride wearing a proper dress and ankle-high boots, beside her stood the groom, looking smart in the suit his godfather had insisted on buying.

"Don't get excited," Pietro said. "It's only our wedding picture."

She tore the treasure from his hands, blessed it with the sign of the cross. "If I believed those silly tales Zia Theresa weaves, this accidental occurrence would foreshadow a terrible omen."

"But you're not superstitious." Pietro waved his hand to the wall. "See for yourself. The nail came loose." He shifted under the covers and closed his eyes. "Now turn down the light and go back to sleep."

Later he awoke to a stream of daylight and Isabella nudging his ribs. "Get up," she said. "We must talk."

"After I wash and shave."

"Then hurry. The coffee's already done."

They sat down to their usual steaming latté, fresh cheese, and hard bread. Pietro thought the food tasted better, the coffee too.

Perhaps the lingering sweetness of Isabella's touch had softened his edge, improved his disposition, as Ernesto Zucca liked to pontificate. Last night should've put a smile on Isabella's face. Instead she wore a thoughtful frown.

"I've been thinking," she said, stirring sugar into her coffee. "Perhaps we should consider making a new photograph."

"Maybe this fall, after the harvest."

"This Thursday would be better."

"On my first week back to market?"

"Gina and Riccardo haven't sat for a studio portrait since they were infants."

"Only because they can't sit still." When Isabella made up her mind, he usually backed down, more so since the accident. Today he felt like arguing. "Aha, this is about last night, isn't it? You've turned into another Zia Theresa."

"*Assurdità*! I've already put the money aside."

"For this I cut down on cigarettes?"

"What are a few smokes compared to a cherished memory."

"So make the appointment."

"If you insist. Of course, we'll go to Tommaso Mino."

"For him, we will wait a month."

"For me, Maso will do it on Thursday."

"For you?"

"Sì, for him I always save a round of cheese."

Chapter 3

At dawn on Thursday Aldo pulled the Rocca cart into the main piazza in Cuorgnè, and Pietro secured a prime station on farmers' row. The area soon displayed an abundance of dairy products, fruits, vegetables, nuts, and small livestock. Stalls offering house wares, dry goods, and groceries completed the remaining rows to cover the entire square. By seven o'clock customers who crowded the narrow aisles held their money tight and gave their children free reign. Competition was spirited but cordial as vendors held up their products to entice the more discriminating.

Throughout the morning shoppers, and later vendors, stopped at the Rocca cart to welcome Pietro's return with handshakes and shoulder pats or cheek-to-cheek kisses. None left without imparting praise for Isabella's ability to take over in her husband's absence. More than once Pietro closed his eyes and thanked God for the warmth of family and friendship. He gave thanks again after he and Isabella sold all of their dairy products and most of the spring vegetables and bartered for items they didn't produce.

For the twins market day meant weaving through the rows with children no better controlled than they were. But when Isabella issued her final call, Riccardo and Gina obeyed. They stood near the cart, bouncing a red ball across the aisle until an old woman, laden with shopping bags and three caged chickens, hobbled into their game. A flash of red rolled across her path. She stumbled, her belongings scattered. The cage door flew open and amidst a flurry of feathers the squawking hens escaped. Pietro cursed himself for not moving faster than Isabella. She scooped up two hens in quick succession and returned them to their cage. Gina and Riccardo cornered the third.

"Mama, Mama!" Riccardo yelled. "We got it."

"Ouch, the damn thing bit me!"

"Watch your mouth."

"Grab the tail. Ouch, ouch."

"Quit shoving.

"Don't let it get away."

"Watch out."

"Oops."

When the owner grabbed her bird from Gina, it promptly keeled over in her hands. *"Morto, morto,"* the old woman wailed through a smattering of broken teeth.

Isabella remained calm, and with the tip of her middle finger, she revived the hen with a gentle massage to its fluttering breast.

After caging the sedated chicken, the old woman opened her arms to the heavens. "Mother of Jesus, shower your many blessings on this mother of little demons. She heals with the touch of an angel."

"It's only a chicken," Gina whispered to Riccardo.

"Sh-h-h! The *vecchia* might hear you and cast an evil eye."

*****

While church bells pealed the noonday *Angelus*, Pietro piled empty containers into the cart and Isabella carried a round of cheese across the piazza to a shop bearing the bold lettering: *Tommaso Mino, Fotografia.*

"Maso can take us at twelve-thirty, before he sits down to eat," she said on her return. "What's more, he has a room where we can change."

In less than thirty minutes the Rocca family underwent a striking transformation: Pietro in his three-year-old suit, tailor-made but inexpensive; Isabella in pale green georgette with contrasting embroidered collar; Riccardo, a belted jacket with dark socks stretching to his knickers; and Gina, rose taffeta and patent leather buckle shoes. Surrounded by a setting of velvet backdrops and ivy-covered pedestals, they allowed themselves to be readied for posterity as Tommaso Mino tilted heads, positioned hands and pinched cheeks.

At last he stepped back and surveyed the Rocca mannequins. With cupped fingers to his lips, he smacked approval, and then centered his head under the camera cloth. Clutching the shutter bulb in one hand, he spoke with reverence. "*Perfetto*. Nobody move. Nobody move. Nobody—"

Gina giggled.

"All right, everybody, again."

Riccardo turned to chastise his sister.

"Once more."

Pietro delayed another three minutes while he walked off a

debilitating cramp. Then Riccardo put one finger up his nose. Gina giggled again. Pietro coughed. Gina shoved Riccardo. Riccardo shoved Gina.

The fifteen minutes Tommaso had allotted as a favor to Isabella extended to thirty. Then, forty-five. Through the curtained doorway of his living quarters drifted the aroma of garlic and anchovies simmering in olive oil. Twice, his wife called out that dinner was almost ready.

"Everybody, look at the camera."

"Wait," Pietro said, reaching in his pocket. "I almost forgot." He leaned over Isabella and pinned Zia Theresa's brooch to her shoulder. He'd brought the earrings too but decided they could wait for another occasion. The children gave up their poses to ooh and aah over the new treasure. As for Isabella, she snatched a glimpse that produced a smile worthy of the Blessed Virgin.

Using the rumpled camera cloth, Tommaso gathered mounting perspiration from his forehead. "For the last time, p-lease," he implored through a mouth no longer smiling. "I am running out of film."

"And patience," Pietro mumbled.

Isabella, regal and unflinching, raised her voice for the first time. "Nobody move. My stomach's growling louder than Maso's."

Her words restored order. The mannequins froze, and the photographer squeezed his shutter control.

"Bella, bella," he whispered.

Seconds later the Rocca family gathered their possessions and hurried to the anteroom where Tommaso waited, his sweaty hand clasping the doorknob.

"I do not waste time or money developing inferior negatives," he said, motioning the Roccas onto the cobblestone walkway. "Experience tells me that only the last shot will meet the high standards I set." He bowed as Isabella passed by. "Signora Rocca, I will have your order ready next week."

*****

The following Thursday Pietro traveled to Cuorgnè alone; and after the market closed, he walked over to the photography studio. Tommaso brought out the wrapped order: one reframed wedding, one large framed family, six medium-sized in gray folders—one for each twin, Isabella's parents, her two siblings, and the family album.

"I give you Tommaso Mino's best work," he said, presenting the bill. "If my work pleases you, I trust you will pay me next week."

"I'll pay you now." Pietro counted out his lire into the photographer's palm. "If your work doesn't please me, I'll return with my family next week."

A pleasing portrait, was this too much to expect? Pietro had done his part. He'd patched the wall plaster, installed a stronger hook, and tolerated the arrogant Tommaso.

As soon as Pietro walked into the house, Isabella wiped her hands and relieved him of the packages. First, she undid the wedding picture, ran her fingers over the glass, and inspected the wire holder. Her simple nod relieved his initial anxiety. Then she opened the second package, turned the frame face side up. Pietro held his breath. Please God, not another visit to the photographer. No man should have to endure such hell again.

"Maso did not fail me," Isabella said with a smile. "He has accorded us a place in history."

Indeed, Tommaso Mino had captured the pleasing image of a proud father, dignified mother, and adorable cherubs. Pietro Rocca's family had been ensured its place in history, at least on paper.

Chapter 4

The following week Giovanni received a letter from his sister that their mother had taken to her bed with a stomach ailment. He soon wrapped his arms around Serena and Baby Maria, kissed them goodbye, and took the next bus to Ivrea. His long weekend away from home provided Pietro a valid excuse to repay his neighbors by doing some of their chores. Isabella offered to help too, but Pietro insisted she'd already done more than her share. Besides, he needed clean underwear. So when she balanced a basket of laundry on her head and left with the twins for an uphill trek to the clear, spring water and sun-warmed rocks, Pietro trekked over to the Martino house.

After cleaning out Giovanni's stable, he selected a small scythe from a wall of well-honed tools and whacked a few weeds infringing on the grassy area near the house. He worked his way around to the front where Serina invited him in for coffee. He washed up at the kitchen pump, and then made love to her on the table while Baby Maria nibbled on the scattering of breadcrumbs that rained from above. Afterwards, they were still laughing when they brushed away the crumbs sprinkling their hair. Maria's too.

Pietro was buttoning his fly when Serina handed him another

package. "For the metal box Isabella never looks in," she said, "my dowry contrario."

He hesitated before slipping the package inside his vest. "How can you even think about taking Maria away from her papa?"

"Perhaps her papa is not Giovanni."

He grabbed her wrist. "What are you saying?"

"That Maria was already in my belly when I met Giovanni."

"He knew this?"

She cocked her head. "Pietro, any fool can count to nine and Giovanni sees only what he wants to see. Besides, Maria popped out of me like a jack-in-the-box, so tiny even the village crones thought she came early. Remember how she fit in Giovanni's cupped hands, how he paraded her around the room?"

"Your leaving would kill him."

"Si, Pietro, his mother too. Poor woman, Giovanni is her only son."

*****

The next time Giovanni went to Ivrea, Pietro told Isabella he wanted to spend Saturday evening at *Il Sole è la Luna*, The Sun and The Moon. "A chance to recall old times before Leo returns to America," he said, knowing Leo would be around for several more weeks. Isabella didn't object, not even when Riccardo throw up his supper and Gina whined that she'd be next.

A full moon guided Pietro's footsteps on the short mile from his house to Faiallo's only bar and refuge. For a reasonable price Il Sole è la Luna provided wine, espresso, grappe, and liqueur. The village men provided camaraderie and competition. During the day their women and children waited beside the road or perused the attached shop that served as the post office, sold notions and snacks, and shared a common wall with two cows. The proprietor Arturo Gallini lived upstairs with his wife and young son. While Arturo took care of the two businesses, Silvia served as postmistress, tended the house, garden, and cows. She also kept the bar and shop supplied with a mouth-watering array of *panini:* crusty breads filled with soft cheeses, thinly sliced meats, or marinated vegetables.

As Pietro walked into the bar he could hear Leo giving his version of America's Prohibition.

"How can this be?" asked one man. "It's against the law to sell wine?"

"And you want to go back to such a primitive land?" another asked.

Leo flipped his fingertips under his chin. "And why not? America is not so different from Italy. You give a little, you take a little, and nobody pays attention to the greedy government."

His words prompted a wave of discussion, with one table touting socialism and another, the merits of a rising politician named Benito Mussolini. Then Lucca Sasso, a carefree bachelor who couldn't abide either group, put an ocarina to his lips and blew a familiar folk tune. When Leo's companions went outside to wet the ground, he waved Pietro over. Arturo brought out more wine and glasses, which prompted Pietro to dig into his pocket.

"No, no," Leo said. "Tonight, I pay."

Together they raised their glasses. "*Salute!*"

"Come back with me," Leo told Pietro. "If not to stay, then just to see. America was your dream too."

Pietro shook his head. "Even the best of dreams don't always come true. You understand, I have a family now."

He sat through a second bottle of wine before claiming an upset stomach. Something he caught from Riccardo was the story he gave Leo.

"Upset stomach, my ass," Leo said. "No respectable man leaves his friends unless he has a lover waiting."

Everyone laughed, including Pietro.

Outside, Pietro leaned over a ground cover of urine, and brought up the warm wine churning his stomach acids. "For Giovanni," he said aloud, offering up his discomfort as token retribution. He heaved again, this time for Isabella. It was after ten before he arrived at Serina's, and for the first time she invited him into the bed she and Giovanni shared.

"This morning I awoke with a song in my heart," she said, her long hair dangling over his face. "Twice I changed my *mutandine*; I made them damp just thinking about tonight. For you I even changed the bed linens. I want nothing of Giovanni to witness our love."

Love. Inwardly, Pietro cringed when she spoke of love. Love belonged to the memory of his parents, to his children, to his wife. Isabella had not questioned, in fact she seemed to enjoy, the subtle changes in their own intimacies. After Pietro dressed, Serina handed him another package. He told her he wouldn't come back, a statement he repeated after each transgression.

*****

At the end of June Giovanni kissed Serina's turned cheek and promised this trip would be the last since his mama started eating again. After stopping to give Pietro the same news, Giovanni checked his pocket watch—enough time for a stop at Il Sole è la Luna.

"A glass of wine before the bus," he told Arturo, "to hold me until Ivrea."

Nearby, Leo Arnetti sat at a table of young bucks and empty bottles.

"So, Leo, you're really going back on Tuesday," said Lucca Sasso. "Leaving all this, your friends and family."

"I can't afford to stay, not with my big promotion coming up. Better pay for easier work." Leo leaned his head back and tossed a cordial of grappe. "You're a smart man, Lucca. You could make it in America."

"Me, I got my paradise right here."

"So does Pietro. Or so he says."

Lucca winked. "You think perhaps Pietro enjoys the pleasures of more than one paradise?"

"I make no accusations, you understand," Leo said, raising his voice. "But like I said before and more than once: no man leaves his drinking friends, unless he's getting some extra honey. Maybe another man's *patacca*."

"If such an unsuspecting *cornuto* exists," said one man, "he must be blind."

"And have his head up his ass," said another.

Their cuckold remarks generated a round of laughs, from everyone except Giovanni. And when he plopped his cap over a head of throbbing veins before stomping out the door, no one noticed except the amused Leo.

*****

On Saturday Pietro awoke to a blanket of fog and a pounding headache. He let the day pass without Serina and by evening he resolved to no longer be responsible for Giovanni's happiness. And if Serina left, which Pietro hoped she would, he would comfort Giovanni, and later confess his sins. Not to the priest in Faiallo or Pont Canavese or Cuorgnè. In Rivarola, where nobody knew him and the priest supposedly had a lady friend.

By Sunday morning heavy fog hanging over the foothills played havoc with Pietro's head, swelling his sinuses and puffing his eyes and tickling his tonsils. Damp air crept into his bones and made his leg throb, just as Zia had predicted. He finished his morning chores and limped into the house. Isabella and the twins were already dressed in their studio-photograph clothes.

"Hurry, Pietro, or we'll be late for Mass."

"Go without me. This damn leg …" he grumbled, affecting a shuffle that exceeded the intensity of his discomfort.

Isabella wet her thumb with saliva, and cleaned a smudge from Riccardo's face while trying to persuade Pietro that the long walk would do him good.

"I can walk around here and lay down when I get tired," he said. "Go without me or stay home and pray your rosary. Just give me some peace." He did not look up when she passed by, the twins trailing behind. Pietro waited for them to disappear into the fog before he went outside. Isabella was right: the more he walked, the better he felt. And when the fog lifted, so did his limp. By then he had rounded the corner of Serina's house and before he even knocked, her door swung open.

"I knew you would come," she said, showing off her annoying

smile. "If not for me, then for Giovanni."

"No, this time for me—Pietro." He crushed her body to his, dug his face in the hollow of her neck. She let out a soft moan.

"Not here, Pietro." She led him to the bedroom.

"The bambina?"

"Will sleep for an hour if we're quiet."

It took ten minutes to soil the linens. As Pietro rolled off Serina, he glimpsed at the Blessed Virgin sheltered in a wall niche. He lay back and redirected his gaze to the ceiling where little strings of dust webs had multiplied with each romp in Giovanni's bed.

"I gave Giovanni the antipasto," Serina said. "You and I shared the main course. And if Maria cooperates, I'll reward you some dolce."

"After I leave, will you change the sheets?"

"Change the sheets? Tonight, while Giovanni is grunting and puffing, I will roll in the juice you spilled this morning. I want to taste and smell you forever."

"Won't Giovanni suspect?"

"Only a woman would notice such details."

Pietro leaned over his elbow. "What about those times in my bed, do you think Isabella ever suspected?"

"Pietro. If she did, you would not be here now. Nor would I be having so much fun."

She pushed Pietro back and straddled him. He grabbed a handful of hair and pulled her down, burying his face in her luscious breasts.

"Oh-h, Pietro, hold tight for the ride of your life." She giggled and teased and made him hard. "Before I'm through, you'll beg me to stop."

While Pietro released himself to Serina, he did not hear the door open. Nor did he hear the approaching footsteps. But he did hear the snapping of leather, right before it slapped against Serina's back. And then he heard Giovanni.

Stop!" the cuckold yelled, "stop!" Each time Giovanni hurled the word from his mouth, he raised his belt and brought it down on Serina's back. She did not cry out. Nor did she beg his mercy. After the third strike Pietro pushed her under the covers. When the belt swung down again, it drew a crimson line across his left cheek. Instinctively, Pietro shielded his face from the leather crisscrossing his chest and arms. Serina came out from under the sheet and screamed Giovanni's name. Once again, he raised the belt, this time striking her shoulder.

"Filthy pig, I hate you!" She scrambled onto the floor, and with hands protecting her naked belly, she said, "Look, Giovanni, another baby. And like Maria, not yours."

Her words brought Giovanni to his knees. His arm remained poised to strike while his face immobilized into a peculiar outrage bearing the colors of a setting sun. Eyes, wide open and crazed, bulged from their sockets. His mouth of stringing saliva gaped into a silent scream. The wounded bull had run its course; he crumpled to the floor.

"Ma-a-m-ma!" whimpered a voice from the next room.

"Hush, little one," Serina called out in a soothing voice. "Go back to sleep." She made the sign of the cross, and then threw her arms around Pietro's neck. "He's dead. I know he's dead. My poor Giovanni, God rest his soul."

And we killed him. The words stuck in Pietro's throat with no place to go while he fixed his eyes on the Blessed Virgin, hoping for a miracle.

Chapter 5

Pietro was still nestled in Serina's arms when he noticed Isabella kneeling beside Giovanni, her fingers probing his neck for some sign of life. Without looking up, she issued her first order. "Get dressed, both of you."

Pietro cleared his throat. "Isabella, I—"

"Not now," she said, at the same time prying Giovanni's fingers from his belt. She rolled the leather into a tight circle and got up to face Serina, who was fumbling with the buttons on her dress. "Look at me," Isabella said, shaking her by the shoulders. "Your husband needs you. He has suffered a terrible stroke."

Serina squeezed her eyes to release a splash of tears. "You mean he's not dead?"

"For now, God has spared his life." Isabella turned to Pietro. "We need another pair of strong arms to get him into bed."

Glad for a reason to escape, he blurted out the name of Mondo Gotti.

Outside, the twins rolled in a grassy meadow, unaware of their father's deceit and their mother's anger. Pietro moved quickly to put the house behind him when Isabella's voice ripped through the air. "Change those sheets, Serina. Your husband deserves the respect of a clean bed."

"No! No! No!" Serina yelled. "He's dead. He has to be dead." Her short-lived defiance ended with the distinctive sound of slapping. But instead of leather, it came from an open hand.

*****

Getting Giovanni settled into a bed of fresh linens took the combined strength of Mondo, Pietro, and Isabella while Serina stood off to the side, cradling Baby Maria.

"After my poor husband returned from Ivrea, he slumped into the chair, complaining of a headache," Serina said with words one step ahead of her thoughts. "He told me to get Pietro, which I did right away. Poor Giovanni, he stood up to greet Pietro and suffered a terrible seizure. Pietro held on to Giovanni, kept him from hitting his head. That's when Giovanni lashed out in his pain and put that awful scratch on Pietro's cheek."

"It's a good thing Pietro didn't go to Mass this morning," Mondo said, taking a closer look at the swollen wound. "Otherwise, Giovanni might be dead already."

"Giovanni needs Doctor Zucca," Isabella said.

"My mule's already hitched to the cart," Mondo said. "I'll go down to Pont and telephone the dottore."

After Mondo left, Isabella applied a damp cloth to Giovanni's forehead. She sat down to watch him breathe—duties his wife should've assumed. But Serina was now holed up in the bedroom. Pietro stationed himself at a window seat to watch the twins playing outside. Other than the steady tick … tick … tick of the mantle clock, no other sound came from the room. He needed a drink, whisky not wine. Giovanni kept a good stock, but he'd already taken enough from Giovanni. If only Isabella had slapped him too. Or sailed a pot across the room. Or threatened to castrate him while he slept. But like Tobi with the cinghiale, Isabella's punishment would be swift and unyielding.

"Take Riccardo and Gina home," she finally said. "You've done enough here."

Indeed he had. An axe embedded in Giovanni's brain could not have done more damage than Pietro and Serina managed to accomplish.

Outside, the warm afternoon greeted him with a false sense of well-being. "Time to go home," he called out to the twins. They ran ahead, squealing as they challenged each other to a rock-throwing contest. Pietro heard footsteps from behind but he didn't turn around or slow his pace.

"For god's sake, Pietro," Serina called out. "Don't walk away from me. More than ever, I need your help."

He stopped. "You can't leave now," he said when she caught up to him. "If God is merciful, Giovanni will not last the week."

"And what if God is just? Then who will pay—you or me?" She lifted her head and started to leave.

"What you told Giovanni," he said, his voice skirting a whisper. "About another baby, is it true?"

She forced a smile. "Pietro, do you think me stupid? I would not make the same mistake twice."

*****

Isabella spent the next hours organizing the village into round-the-clock shifts. Neighbors brought food and sympathy, mourning Giovanni as though he'd already departed the world they once shared. After Zia Theresa fussed over the back of Serina's dress, stained from weeping wounds, Serina retreated to the baby's room, insisting Maria needed her breast.

"How convenient," someone remarked. "By now she should've weaned the baby."

Meanwhile, Pietro braced himself for Isabella. That evening after milking the cows, he listened to Gina and Riccardo pray for him and Isabella, Tobi and the farm animals. Their bedtime antics capable of lasting an hour ended as soon as Isabella came home and ordered them to sleep. Later, while Pietro leaned against the kitchen counter, puffing on a cigarette, Isabella pulled her chair away from the table and sat down. After flipping his cigarette into the sink, he went to her and dropped to his knees. Unable to look into her angry eyes, he put his head in her lap instead. "Forgive me, Isabella. I behaved like a damn fool."

Isabella expelled an annoyed snort. "This morning when I met Giovanni on the road, he behaved like an idiot. 'The whole village knows I'm a cuckold', he told me. I only came back to prove him wrong."

Isabella's voice gave no hint of emotion; Pietro wanted her to shout.

"You broke my heart, Pietro. I trusted you with my life, gave you all my love."

Isabella expressed her love through work; but until that moment Pietro had never heard her speak the words. He considered taking her in his arms but couldn't risk the rejection. Instead, he pressed his lips to her hand. "On the graves of my parents, I promise never to see Serina again."

"Don't defile their memory with promises you cannot keep.

Not with temptation right across the field." She handed him a fat envelope. "An earlier gift from Giovanni, one he insisted I take when you were bedridden. ' For a rainy day,' he told me. 'Pietro is worried and too proud to ask.'"

Giovanni, the sainted cuckold, may God take him soon. Pietro got off his knees. He shoved the envelope aside. One more burdensome bundle; he still had Serina's stashed in his bureau.

Isabella hadn't moved. He waited for her to cut loose with a barrage of threats about leaving with their children. She'd want to nurse her wounded pride in the home of her benevolent parents. They'd spoil Gina and Riccardo, but only until the twins wore them down. Pietro figured a week at best. He scrambled for the words to change her mind but should've scrambled harder.

"I want you to go away for a while," Isabella said.

Her words stung worse than a fistful of hard cacca. "So I should just disappear, like a puff of wind?" He lifted his arms to invoke spirits of the past. "Papa, Nonno, and all the Roccas who died before I came into the world: did you hear Isabella? This woman I brought into our house now wants me to leave. She wants me to desert our home … our land … our children … my heritage. Mine, not hers, she's worse than a thief in the night."

"Don't be ridiculous, Pietro. You've shamed the Rocca name, you and Serina. Soon, the entire village will buzz behind our backs, snicker to our faces. Already the women are musing over those welts on Serina's back. And we still must deal with Giovanni."

"You think he will come out of this?"

"Only God knows. But if Giovanni does recover and you're still around, it could mean worse trouble. If he decides to kill you, no one will stop him. The law will look the other way. Leave now and come back when some other scandal takes the place of this one. By then, if Giovanni is still alive, he may even forgive you."

While Isabella spoke, Pietro paced. When his turn came, he kept on pacing, his hand rolled into a fist as it punctuated each word. "Time. I need time. Time to think. Time to make a plan."

"Time for Serina to play you the fool," Isabella said. "Time for Serina to destroy what's left of our family." She issued another directive, one posing as a suggestion. "What about your father's cousin, the one who works at the Fiat factory. Maybe he could get you a job in Torino. Think of the money you could save in two years."

"What about you and the children?" He waited for her face to soften, waited for her to bend, just a little.

But her eyes didn't meet his. "We managed when you broke your leg. We'll manage with you in Torino."

Their argument ended when Pietro agreed to Isabella taking the twins to market the next day. He bedded down in the stable, where he tossed all night on a makeshift cot. The next morning it was Pietro who carried his sleeping children to the cart, moved his lips back and forth between their foreheads until Isabella said if he didn't stop, they'd wake up and spend the rest of the day testing her patience. She and Pietro kissed too, lightly to each cheek.

After his family left, Pietro packed the valise that still bore the initials of his papa: RPR for Riccardo Pietro Rocca. The preserved family image on the wall reminded him of those extra photographs Isabella kept in her dresser drawer next to the jewelry box. One gray folder bearing the name Tommaso Mino Fotografia in exchange for the emerald earrings matching Zia's brooch seemed fair enough. He helped himself to a folder and reunited the precious jewelry. Scanning the room one last time, Pietro's eyes stopped at

Family Deceptions

the tall chest. Bottom drawer, metal box—the packages Serina had foisted on him, her dowry *contrario*. He considered taking Serina's earnings to keep her at Giovanni's side: where she belonged in sickness and in health. Instead, he slammed his fist into the chest and turned away. If Serina wanted her money she'd have to go through Isabella.

Pietro belted the valise and left it by the door. His knuckles were stinging as he headed across a series of meadows, walking for an hour to reach a stone building that consisted of four attached residences built over four rundown stables. Testing the strength of his injured leg, he took the worn stairs two at a time, and noticed little difference between the legs. On the outer balcony a knock to the third door brought a round woman with bloodshot eyes and a topknot of gray-streaked hair. She blew her nose into a damp handkerchief and motioned Pietro to enter.

"Buon giorno, Signora Arnetti," he said, removing his cap.

"Ah, Pietro, come in, come in," Leo said, still in his undershirt and drinking his morning latte. "Ma, please, coffee for my friend." After cutting a piece from the round of goat cheese, he passed the plate and knife.

Pietro cut a wedge equal to Leo's, wrapped it into a fold of bread, and chomped down. The cheese couldn't match Isabella's, but what the hell, he was hungry. Signora Arnetti filled his cup, but before he could thank her, she burst into tears and hurried from the room. The woman never could hide her emotions; how else would Leo know what misery he'd wrought on her. Pietro felt obliged to acknowledge her grief. "I'm sorry about your ma."

Leo rolled his eyes. Like his mother, he tended to exaggerate the pitfalls and pinnacles of life. Sometimes he straddled the peak, rubbing his *balli* raw.

Pietro took two swallows of hot coffee before he spoke. "So, you're leaving tomorrow."

"Packed and marking time. Last night all my people came over to wish me well." Cradling the cup to his lips, Leo narrowed his black eyes to Pietro. Slowly, he lowered his cup. "You're not here to say goodbye, are you."

"I'm going to America, Leo, on my own or with you."

"Madonna mia, why not wait 'til I'm already on the boat." He slammed his palm heel into his forehead. "There are forms to fill out, papers to be signed. Getting into America is not like before the war. Quotas, it's all about quotas. And America has a full quota of Italians."

Pietro's shoulders fell. Quotas, papers, forms, before today, going to America sounded easy. He started to speak, but Leo cut him off.

"Listen Pietro, with a little money and a lot of luck—well, just leave everything to me. You do have money, right?"

"Enough to get me there and then some."

"I knew it: that look in your eyes told more than the words you spoke. Not to worry. There's someone in Genoa who can fix your papers."

"Any chance you could leave today?"

"Hm-m-m." Leo rubbed his chin. "The *Conte Biancamano* sails on Friday." He glanced around the room, to where his mother had returned to her corner.

Leo leaned closer to Pietro. "You understand: I need to say my goodbye to her in private."

"I don't want to cause trouble."

"You mean about Ma? Hell, she's been crying ever since I came from America. Today, tomorrow—it makes no difference. As soon as I start loading the cart, she'll throw herself down and latch onto my leg. You go home now and I'll track down Giorgio. With any luck we should come by around one."

"About your brother, can he keep this quiet?"

"For me he will do anything."

Chapter 6

That afternoon Pietro was on his way to Genoa with Leo, and Leo being Leo kept sticking his nose where it didn't belong "What if the old cuckold recovers?" Leo asked. "He could come after you."

"Giovanni? He would never leave the Canavese region, let alone the entire province of Piemonte."

"Maybe not, but what's stopping him from sending an accommodating avenger. Finding Pietro Rocca would be easy."

"Hell, Leo. We are Piemontese, not the *Mezzogiorno*."

"You think only Southern Italians pass vendettas from generation to generation? Remember that one-legged soldier from Lanza who found out about his cheating wife?"

"Never heard of him."

"The cuckold cut off her lover's *balli*. He served those jewels to her on a platter of steaming polenta."

"Give Giovanni some credit. I was like a son to him."

"Si, but that was before you bedded his wife."

*****

Four days later Pietro had all his necessary papers when he boarded the *Conte Biancamano*. As soon as he and Leo were settled in their cabin, Leo hurried off to find a card game which relieved Pietro from listening to his constant blabbering. As the ship moved away from the Genoa harbor, he leaned against the second-class railing and watched those left behind inflict their grief on the excited passengers heading to America. When the waving finally stopped, the tears did too. Pietro shifted his attention to Genoa's terraced spread of red-tiled roofs until the city grew smaller and eventually faded into a blur. The churning water far below soothed his guilt, long enough for a journey that took him back seven years.

*****

It was the year Pietro went with Giovanni to the annual carnival at Castellamonte. Giovanni introduced him to a farmer he knew from the Austrian war. The farmer invited them to his home where they ate a light supper with the family, and then headed back to Faiallo in Giovanni's mule-drawn cart. Giovanni couldn't stop talking about the unmarried daughter.

"You ought to consider her, Pietro. She's healthy as a horse and accustomed to hard work."

"Isabella? She's two years older than my nineteen."

"So much the better, age brings wisdom into a marriage."

"Don't rush me. I don't even know her."

"So get acquainted between the sheets." Giovanni paused, sucking his lower lip between his teeth. "No man should go through life without the love of a good woman."

"What about you?"

"My destiny rests in God's hands." Giovanni made the sign of the cross over his heart.

"This Isabella, she never smiles."

"With you she will."

"But I want to see America before I settle down."

"For what? Listen to me, Pietro. Your house is the house of your father and his father before. You own fertile ground, an envied vineyard, and healthy livestock. What more could any man want?"

"Children," Pietro said, not meaning to remind Giovanni of his dead infant," one day, yes, but not in the near future."

"Isabella will not disappoint you. Already her sister carries one in the arms and one in the belly."

The following week Giovanni fell ill and sent for Isabella to look after him. After his quick recovery, she stayed on to organize his house. Pietro could hardly remember the courtship, but after three months he married her, and with no regrets. Their first anniversary brought Gina and Riccardo, the beginning of joyful chaos.

*****

And now this: *che pasticcio*. What a mess he'd made of the joyful chaos.

The *Conte Biancamano* cut through the rough waters, picking up speed with every knot that pushed him toward his temporary exile—and with an assumed identity. Changing his name had been Leo's idea. Pietro repeated the new one out loud, trying it out like a pair of tight shoes.

"Peter. Peter Montagna. Pete Mon-tan-ya. Pete Mon-tan-ya."

After a while, Pete Montagna began to feel like a comfortable fit. Pietro Rocca, the man he used to be, was left behind, along with Isabella and their twins. God, already he missed them. He gave himself two years. Two years to make good. Two years to atone. Not so long that his children would forget him, but long enough for Isabella to forgive him.

Chapter 7

Six weeks later, Isabella returned with the twins from the market in Pont, a trip requiring an extra hour with Pietro's working somewhere in Torino and her responsible for selling Giovanni's products as well as their own. The fall weather that crept into her bones reminded her there wouldn't be many more market days until spring. Thank God, one less burden to take up her time. But more time to reflect on her humiliation. Not now, later.

Isabella added logs to the stove while Gina and Riccardo hung up their coats and warmed their backsides Instead of brewing a fresh pot of coffee she settled for what she'd made earlier in the morning.

"When is Papa coming home?" Gina asked.

"Not for a long time," Riccardo said. "So quit asking."

"We could visit him. How far is Torino?"

"Basta," Isabella said to the conversation she'd heard before. "Papa will come home when the time is right."

"We could write him a letter," Gina said.

"Not until we receive one from Papa. We don't know his address."

Isabella pushed herself up from the table, squared her tired shoulders, and snuggled them into her shawl. "Put on your coats," she told the twins. "We must see about Giovanni."

Gina stuck out her lower lip. "Do we have to?"

"He needs us," Riccardo said.

"Not as much as Papa does. How much longer must we pray for Giovanni?"

"Until he can walk; right, Mama?"

Isabella opened the door, letting in a rush of cold air before closing it. "Your coats—now."

Gina wiggled into last year's garment, its sleeves an inch above her wrists. "Serina's sick. We should pray for her too."

Riccardo pressed his hand to Gina's mouth. "Sh-h, you weren't supposed to tell. She made us promise."

Isabella reached for the doorknob again, this time to steady herself. "What makes you think Serina is sick?"

"She keeps throwing up," Gina said.

"That's right, Mama. Every day since Papa left."

With head lifted and fists clenched, Isabella marched over to Giovanni's house with Tobi barking and the twins racing to see who'd get there first. *I'll kill her. That lazy no-good slut I'll kill her along with that bastard fouling her belly. First she robs me of my husband. Then she draws my children into her web—does the woman have no shame, always hiding behind her nursing toddler while others do the work. Thank God for Mondo taking over some of the chores, which leaves me with an expanded market stall, two henhouses, two dairies, two households, two children of my own—plus Maria when she's not nursing. No wonder I didn't notice Serina growing another baby—Pietro's, of that I have no doubt. Sweet Jesus, please give me strength to survive this living hell until he comes home.*

Rounding the corner to the house's only entrance, Isabella found Serina waiting at the door opened part way.

"You're late," Serina said, faking a shiver.

"And you're *incinta*," Isabella said, all but spitting the words out. Serina's face lost its color. She dropped on her knees, bent her head.

Isabella felt a tug on her skirt: Gina looking up with pleading eyes.

"She's sick, Mama."

Isabella ruffled her curly head. "Go play with Maria. You too, Riccardo."

They ran to the bouncing toddler, leaving Isabella to deal with the mess on the floor.

"Please don't hate me. If only Pietro—"

"Basta! Your husband needs you. Did you fix his dinner yet?"

Serina got up, patted down her hair. "You know he only eats from your hand."

"What about his bath?"

"But of course, even though he hates me. I see it in his eyes. I hear it in his grunts and moans whenever I touch him. About the razor—"

"Never mind, I'll shave him." Isabella went to the fireplace, held her hands to the glowing embers. "You need more wood."

"As soon as Maria takes her nap, I'll chop some."

"While you're outside, collect all the eggs."

"The hens hate me too, always pecking and squawking." Serina flipped her shawl over her shoulders. After grabbing the wood carrier and egg basket, she almost slipped on a coffee puddle on her way to the door.

One more disabled patient, that's all Isabella needed. She cleaned up the spill and then washed her hands with rubbing alcohol before entering the sickroom. One sniff told her the bed linens needed changing. Giovanni lay there, flat on his back. Serina couldn't prop him without help; she could've asked Mondo but didn't. Giovanni's eyes watered up as he cracked a smile, this time without his usual slobbering. The droop plaguing the left side of his mouth had all but disappeared. Isabella put her hand to his forehead. No fever. She massaged the new warmth of her hands into his, first one and then the other.

"You're growing stronger, Giovanni. One of these days you'll sit in a chair."

He shifted with a grunt, the effort exuding a foul odor. His eyes followed her as she stepped away.

"I know, I know. You want your bath and clean sheets."

Isabella turned on her heels and left the sickroom. The Mother Superior in her cut a path across the cluttered kitchen with determined stride, and flung open the only door that brought her instant relief.

"Serina!"

*****

On a cold, bitter morning in early February Gina stood in the snow, fidgeting on the skis her papa had fashioned from barrel staves the previous year while Isabella secured the leather straps.

"Hurry, Mama, hurry."

"So you can take another tumble? Patience, my daughter."

"But Mama—"

"There, off you go."

With Tobi at her side Gina played catch up to Riccardo as he glided across the snow-packed trail on two lengths of sturdy chestnut. Isabella trudged behind wearing Pietro's boots, every step bringing her closer to another day of aggravation. The thin line of smoke emitting from Giovanni's chimney indicated Serina forgot to feed the fire, again. She never forgot to feed her mouth, which meant feeding the still nursing Maria's too. The woman had ballooned into an elephant—almost the size of Isabella when she carried the twins. Pietro had strutted around like a proud rooster then. And what about now, did he secure the job with Fiat? The least he could've done was write to Gina and Riccardo.

They were racing down a short hill when Isabella reached Giovanni's. Tobi's barking announced their arrival, but the mistress of the house was not in her usual position at the door. Isabella pushed it open to find Serina, barefoot and still wearing her nightgown, pacing the floor with Maria at her breast.

"You'd better wean that baby before the other one gets here," Isabella said as she hung up her shawl.

"Too late, I woke up with labor pains. Already they're coming fast and hard."

"What about Giovanni?"

"Somehow I managed to put him in his chair."

Maria pulled away and slid down her mother's side. She ran to the door calling, "Gee, Gee."

"Gina's coming," Isabella said. She scooped up the toddler, handed her back to Serina, and opened the door. The twins were a few meters away, Riccardo fiddling with Gina's ski straps.

"Don't take off your skis, Riccardo," Isabella said. "I want you to go Mondo's house. Tell him to bring Zia Theresa right away."

Isabella heard Serina's voice calling out from behind. "Stay right where you are, Riccardo. I don't need that old crone."

"What about me, Mama?" Gina asked.

"You'd better go with Riccardo. Make sure he doesn't tell Zia what Serina just said."

Maria wiggled to the floor and ran back to Isabella.

"Not now, Baby. I'll hold you later." With folded arms, she turned to Serina. "In another hour, you'll thank God for Theresa Gotti's gentle hands holding yours."

Serina bit her lower lip until she drew blood. She bent over, and with one hand digging into her lower back, she released an agonizing moan that ended with a whimper. When she finally straightened up, it was with tears in her eyes. "Please, Isabella, just the two of us."

Isabella sighed. She called out to the twins. "Forget about Zia. After you take those skis off, come in and play with Maria—in her room."

"It's too crowded in there," Gina said.

"For how long?" Riccardo asked.

"As long as it took to set Papa's leg—right, Mama?"

While Serina paced the kitchen to relieve her increasing pains, Isabella put on a kettle of water to boil and covered the table with layers of thick padding. Giovanni, who needed a shave and bath, watched from the wheelchair he'd been using for two months. He banged his hand against the arm of the chair. Neither woman bothered with his demand for attention. But when he poked Isabella with his long stick, she turned around to see him level it toward his bedroom.

"In there," he managed to say with garbled words, "where it was conceived."

Serina stopped her pacing. Her face distorted into another pain. She spoke through clenched teeth. "Not in that stinking room or that stinking bed. Right here, on the table. Isabella and I already decided."

He lifted the stick, propelled his chair in her direction. She stomped her foot, hard. Amniotic waters gushed from under her nightgown.

"Now see what you did, old man. I hope you're satisfied."

"You two can fight later." Isabella took Serina's hand, felt it shaking in hers. "Right now, I need you on the table."

"I'm sorry about the mess on the floor."

"Don't worry. I'll clean it up. But first get on the table."

"I don't want that old man watching."

Giovanni banged his stick, garbled more words. "My name. My baby. I'm staying."

"I hate you! A-a-a-h ... A-A-A-H ... A-a-a-h. You dried up—"

"Serina, please, the table ... There, that's better. Now scoot to the end and spread your legs."

After Isabella sterilized her hands with alcohol, she positioned herself on a low stool between Serina's feet. From the bedroom came Gina's whiney voice.

"Mama, Riccardo won't share."

"I found it first."

"Don't come near me," Isabella said. "I mean it. Go back to the bedroom. Go."

Giovanni rolled the chair, banged his stick on the floor. "*Va via!*"

"Push, Serina. I can see the crown."

"Oh-oh, I think Maria's hungry. What should we do?"

"Mama?"

"Give her a *grissini*, Gina."

"She wants her mama."

"I don't care. Give her a grissini."

"But you said not to come in the kitchen."

"Again, Serina, push. Harder, harder."

"AH-H-H-H."

"Again."

"AH-H-H-H."

"Never mind, I think Maria needs the potty chair."

"No, Maria, no. Not there."

"Never mind. Mama, could you come here?"

"Not now, Gina. I'm busy."

"Tobi's barking. Can we let him in?"

"You know better than to ask." Isabella had a good grip on the baby's head. "Push, Serina, push. Keep pushing. Hold it. Hold it. Don't push anymore."

"Easy for you to say. A-a-a-h! What's the matter?"

"Nothing, just the cord."

"The cord—"

"Don't move ... don't move ... one more time."

"Mother of mercy, don't let her strangle my baby."

"Giovanni, please ... old man, get that stick out of my back."

"Mama, what are you doing down there? Riccardo, hurry up. You have to see this."

"Oops. Maria slipped in some water. Yuck!"

"Are you all right, Baby?"

"Mama, what's the matter with Serina?"

"Oh my God. It's a brand new baby. So that's how they get here."

"Wa-a-a-h!"

Chapter 8

One overcast day in early May found Isabella on her knees in the garden, picking lettuce while the dew still clung to its leaves. It was the kind of morning that Pietro often came home with mushrooms, mostly to please her. This spring she hunted her own and still prepared those damn *funghi* that started all her troubles. Now she enjoyed them alone. If only he hadn't broken his leg, if only she hadn't called on Serina's help. If only she hadn't been so trusting. If only ..."

"Oh-oh, Mama, we're getting company."

"Who, Riccardo. I don't have time for games."

"Serina and the bambini."

Serina. She'd not walked over in almost a year, not that Isabella ever invited her. The daily visits to Giovanni were enough for either of them. At least he could now shovel food, even if most of it never reached his mouth. Still there was his bath, his therapy, and the chickens. Not to mention milking the cows, not one tolerated Mondo's clumsy grip. The cheese she didn't mind, especially with her customers asking for more.

Isabella stood up and with her basket of greens, went to meet Serina halfway, a compromise she never thought would happen. The not-yet-weaned Maria ran ahead, excited over Tobi's wagging tail. Isabella couldn't help but love the sweet little redhead. As did Gina and Riccardo, her precious innocents who still laughed but not as much as before their papa left. The infant he didn't know about was secure in her sling on Serina's back. Allegra Gianna Martino. Isabella had chosen the name, only because Serina couldn't think up one on her own.

"Buon giorno, Isabella," she said with that unctuous smile. "A moment of your time, please."

"Right now I'm busy with my own work. I'll get to yours later this morning, just as I always do. But, of course if this can't wait."

"Could we go inside, perhaps sit down for a glass of wine?"

Wine at this hour could only mean Serina wanted another favor. Isabella called out to Riccardo and Gina, told them to play near the house with Maria. The sleeping Allegra didn't stir when Serina followed Isabella into her home. Isabella poured three-year-old wine, now in its prime. Last year's grapes had rotted on the vine. What a pity; there hadn't been time.

No effort was made to click their glasses. Neither woman spoke until after the glasses were empty and Isabella refilled them to three horizontal fingers.

"You wanted to talk," she said.

Serina took a few more sips. "I'd like to take Maria and Allegra to Ivrea for a few days. Giovanni's mother wants to hold the bambini but she's too old to travel here."

"And what if you decide not to come back."

"Where else would I go? I have no family."

"Except for your mother."

"We haven't spoken in years. Isabella, please. I haven't left this damn hill since Giovanni's stroke. If I don't get away, at least for a while, I swear I'll kill that horrible man. With a pillow over his face until he croaks his last foul breath. No one would ever know it wasn't God's will, except you and me. And wouldn't that be a wonderful blessing for both of us?"

"You can't be serious."

"Oh, but I am."

"Basta, I'll look after Giovanni."

"Bless you, Isabella. I'd like to leave before the end of this week but first the bambini and I will need some decent clothes. As you know, I haven't found time to pick up a needle since Giovanni's illness, which brings me to my second request."

Isabella poured two fingers of wine.

"Could you take us to Pont, tomorrow when you go to market? I promise not to get in your way. And the bambini will stay with me while I do my shopping."

"Yes, yes. Just make sure you're ready—"

"I know, by four in the morning. Oh, and there's just one more thing—about the money."

"Giovanni has always been generous," Isabella said. "Since this benefits his mother, he'll agree to pay for everything."

"That's not what I mean. I want to put some money in the bank—for the bambini."

"For that, you don't need my permission."

"But I do need my dowry contrario."

"I don't understand."

"In your bedroom," Serina said, "tall chest, bottom drawer, the metal box that belonged to Pietro's parents."

"You were in our bedroom?"

"It's not what you think, at least not in there. Pietro agreed to hold some money for me."

"If I didn't look before, why should I look now?"

"I only want what's rightfully mine—those six bundles wrapped in brown paper. I earned every lira—on my back, on my knees, and straddling that crusty old goat. He thinks I sent the money to my mother in Courmayeur."

"You told me she lived in Lanza."

"That was before she moved."

Isabella went to her bedroom and returned with the bundles. After wrapping them in a linen towel, she tucked the tight package under the fresh lettuce in her basket, and handed it to Serina.

"Bless you, Isabella. You've saved my life. Giovanni's too." She was about to get down on her knees when Isabella stopped her.

"Please, not that again."

"One more thing, Isabella, about my going to Pont and Ivrea, Giovanni won't listen to a word I say. Will you speak to him on my behalf?"

*****

Thursday morning, six o'clock, Isabella was traveling the gravel road to Pont, again—after Aldo had stopped a fourth time to punish her for the additional weight. She yanked on his reins and continued her trek down the winding route. Snuggled under covers in the back of cart were the twins and Maria, all fast asleep. In the passenger seat Serina slept too, with Allegra sucking greedily at her breast. From a wooded area the red eyes of nocturnal creatures watched. The undergrowth rustled, a snake slithering back to its haven. Chirping birds welcomed Isabella like old friends—except her old friends didn't come around anymore, and not because of Pietro. At the end of the day, she had nothing left to give. Between Giovanni and Serina, they sucked the very life from her.

The moon giving way to the rising sun allowed her to spot a tempting clump of mushrooms. Another time, she might have stopped. But not this morning, she was running late. First Giovanni needed help with the toilet. Then Aldo wouldn't budge after Serina climbed aboard. Coaxing and sugar cubes spurred him some of the way, until Isabella ran out of the cubes.

As the mule rounded the last hairpin curve, Isabella looked down to Pont, already coming alive with her competitors. A line of carts and basket-laden donkeys waited to enter the village, its only access a bridge spanning the swift waters of the Orco that flowed down from the Gran Paradiso and would eventually spill into the River Po east of Torino. There would be no prime market spot for Isabella today, but it would be a good day. After releasing Aldo's rein, she ran her hand along his back, gave a gentle pat to his rump, and climbed back in the wagon. With a single crack of the whip, Aldo took over her burden.

The market came to life as soon as Isabella settled on one of the few remaining sites, an obscure corner near the live poultry. After twins scampered from the cart, they watched Maria slide down with a plop, thank God, with no accompanying tears.

"Can we take Maria for a walk?" Riccardo asked.

"Only if you promise not to let go of her hand," said Serina, still perched on the passenger seat, with Allegra feeding again. "I'll help you as soon as the baby gets her fill," she told Isabella. "Would you mind fixing a place for me out of the sun? Allegra's so fair-skinned. I think we might have another red head."

"Where is her bonnet?"

"On my shopping list, please don't lecture me, not today."

Isabella set her only chair under the shade of a nearby tree. She held her arms out for the baby, cradled her while Serina stepped down and made her throne comfortable with the pillow that cushioned her morning journey. Allegra stretched her fat cheeks into a yawn. Tiny fingers wrapped around one of Isabella's. The infant opened her eyes, not the blue of Serina's but as dark as Pietro's. Not a single hair sprung from her scalp.

"Do you mind if I walk around?" Serina asked. "My legs are so-o stiff from the ride."

"I'm sure Allegra would enjoy the sights from her sling."

Serina slapped the heel of one hand to her forehead. "The sling, oh, no, I forgot it."

"And I must set up my produce. My customers don't like to wait."

"Nor do I," Serina said as she stepped back in the cart. After creating a bassinet from a blanket folded into her shopping basket, she reached down and wiggled her fingers at Allegra. "Naptime, Baby. Come to Mama."

Indeed, the baby slept—in the cart while her mama swished around in her blue dress and the twins roamed the aisles with Maria in tow. Isabella managed to generate new business without inconveniencing her regular customers. Among the first to stop by were Editta Sasso and her son Lucca, who lived down the hill from Faiallo.

"I might as well get my cheese while I'm here," Signora Sasso said. "I don't like to bother you at home."

"For you, Editta, it's never a bother."

"No one makes tomino as good as yours, Isabella. And two dozen of your best eggs, please. You still hold them to a candle, right?"

"I guarantee every one of them." Isabella gathered the eggs, added an extra one for good measure. She wrapped three rings of cheese and placed the order in Signora Sasso's basket.

"When is Pietro coming back from Torino?" Lucca asked. "Everyone at Il Sole è la Luna wants to know."

Signora Sasso whacked Lucca on the shoulder. "Pietro will come home when the time is right." She counted her lire into Isabella's open hand, closed it with an affectionate squeeze. "God be with you, Isabella. 'Til next week, ciao."

For the next two hours Isabella kept busy with her customers. Not once did Allegra cry out, nor did anyone even know what treasure the shopping basket held. Serina returned with a new basket filled with items for Maria and Allegra. She held up a truck and a doll. "For Riccardo and Gina to play with on their way home," she said. "They're so good to Maria. I bought her a cuddly bear, to take the place of my breast. By the way, where is Maria?"

"One aisle away, playing with the twins."

"And the baby?"

"Right where you left her."

"See, I told you they wouldn't be any trouble." She held up two nursing bottles. "For when Allegra gets home, in case she ever needs more than I can give. If you don't mind, I'd like to—"

"Go, while you're baby still sleeps."

"But first I'll bring the chair over here. You look so tired."

As soon as Serina left, the old woman with the caged chickens came from the other direction. "*Zingare, Zingare* everywhere," she yelled. "Hold tight to your children, your pets, and your money." She stopped at Isabella's cart. "Buon giorno, Isabella, did you not hear my warning? Those little demons of yours, where are they?"

"These gypsies, you saw them?"

"Yesterday the lying cheats camped at the edge of our village. Today they moved in closer. Even as I speak they walk among us." She crossed herself. "May I burn in hell if you don't believe me."

"Riccardo, Gina, Maria, now!"

Two curly heads popped out from under an olive vendor's cart.

"We're right here, Mama," said Riccardo. "Maria too."

"We made a new *amico*," said Gina. A dirty face appeared next to hers.

They scrambled out, bringing with them a young boy, about nine years old. His wild hair was black as onyx, his skin as dark as a Mezzogiorno. His pants fell above his ankles; his red shirt was tattered at the cuffs. He bowed from the waist, and when he looked up, it was with one blue eye and one brown.

The vecchia made the sign of the cross again. "Sweet Mother of Jesus, those fiendish eyes have cast a curse on us all." She held out her arm, forefinger and pinkie pointed at the boy. "*Va via. Va via.*"

To Isabella he smiled with even, white teeth, and spoke Piemontese but with a slight accent. "I am Cato. Do not be afraid, Signora Rocca."

"You know my name?"

The vecchia's chickens started fluttering their wings. "He is possessed Isabella, turn your back. You must not talk to the *Cimbri*." She hobbled away, clutching the cage of squawking birds. "Zingare, Zingare."

Riccardo put his arm around the boy's shoulder. "Cato comes from Verona."

"That's a long way from Piemonte," Isabella said.

"But too hot in the summer," Cato replied. "So we travel."

"He knows Serina," Gina said.

"He what?" Isabella plopped in the chair. Maria climbed on her lap.

Cato showed his dirty palms, smiled again. "Only since this morning, Signora, the *bella donna* was admiring my Papa's fine jewelry." With a flourish he swept his arm toward a scattering of trees beyond the marketplace.

Blessed Mother! Isabella couldn't believe her eyes. How could she have been so busy not to notice the row of painted wagons, or the villagers mingling around the wagons.

"Would you like to see? It's not too far. We make our own gold and silver pieces, more beautiful and at better prices than the shops, or even the market."

"Oh, Mama, please can we go?"

"Not today, Gina."

"But I want some earrings."

"Your ears aren't pierced yet."

"Lift up your curls," Cato said and Gina obeyed. Arms folded, he circled around her, viewing her exposed ear lobes from every angle. "Not to worry. My zia can make the holes, with her special needle."

"Mama?"

"Basta, I'll pierce them myself when I get time. You can wear the earrings I wore as a girl."

"We also make pots, all sizes and shapes," Cato said. "Perhaps a new one for your polenta?"

Isabella shook her head.

"Can we take Cato home with us?" Riccardo asked. "He's never slept in a real house."

Before she could refuse, Cato bowed again. "Grazie, Signora. But the polizia have asked us to leave by the midday *Angelus*. And now I must go too. *Arrivederci!*"

The boy disappeared in the crowd of shoppers while Riccardo watched, his arms folded in the manner of Cato. "Cato knows everything, Mama. I hope he comes back some day."

"Should we pray for him, like we pray for Papa?"

"Papa is never coming back."

"Ma-a-m-a."

"Look, I think Maria's hungry."

"Here come some more customers."

"Ma-a-m-a-a."

"W-a-a-a-h!"

"Oh-oh, Maria woke up the baby."

"We'd like some cheese, please," one customer said.

"And I'd like some butter," said another.

"I'll be right with you. Riccardo, find Serina. Gina, you and Maria play with Allegra."

"I think they're both hungry."

"Hurry, Riccardo."

"W-a-a-a-h!"

"Please, Signora, take care of your bambini," the first customer said. "We'll come back later."

By eleven-thirty, Isabella had sold most of her products and was pacing with aisle with Allegra. After a twenty-minute cry for her mama's milk, Maria fell asleep with her new stuffed bear and the twins discovered the toys Serina bought earlier. Then Editta Sasso came strolling down the aisle with her basket overflowing and Lucca carrying three hammered pots.

"I didn't expect to see you again this morning," Isabella said, patting Allegra's bottom.

"We couldn't resist the gypsy carts." Signora Sasso held out her arms. "Ah-h, this must be Serina's little bambino. Let me hold her."

"If you don't mind her rooting on your shoulder," Isabella said while giving up the baby. "She needs her mama."

"Serina's still haggling with the gypsies," Lucca said. He handed two of the pots to Isabella. "She asked me to give these to you."

"But I ... I ... grazie, Lucca." Isabella climbed in the cart, shoved the pots next to Serina's other purchases, and discovered a temporary solution to Allegra's hunger—the baby bottles. She smiled down on Lucca, showed him the bottles. "Would you mind going to livestock area to have these filled."

"Wa-a-a-h."

"Cow's milk or goat's?"

"Either one," Lucca's mother said. "Serina's baby can't hold out much longer."

"Ma-a-m-a-a."

"Oh-oh. Now Maria's awake."

"I think she's hungry, Mama. What should we do?"

"What's keeping that damn woman?" Signora Sasso asked, returning the baby to Isabella.

"Look, Mama. Here comes a parade."

From a side street not far from Isabella's cart the first sturdy wagon appeared—the biggest Isabella had ever seen—painted red and drawn by four large black and white horses, with ribbons woven into their abundant manes and tails. In the front of the wagon sat an older couple, the swarthy man decked out in a yellow shirt and red vest. His plump wife wore a dress of many colors that clashed with those in the long scarf covering her hair. The caravan passed by with younger men driving more wagons, their horses equally magnificent with thick coats in solid colors splashed with white. Their women, some with babies in slings, walked in leather boots and gaudy clothes. Earrings dangled from under their bright headscarves. Necklaces heavy with gold and silver coins hung against their embroidered blouses. Bangles and more bangles jingled and jangled on their wrists. What jewelry they didn't wear, they carried in their hands, and continued to make sales along the route. Their daughters had long braided hair; their swaggering sons needed haircuts. Pots and pans hanging from the sides of the wagons banged and scraped to titillate the barking dogs. One of the men strummed his mandolin; a woman shook her tambourine. The church bells of Santa Maria started their noonday peal.

And Allegra chimed in. "Wa-a-a-a-h."

"Hush, little one."

"Ma-a-m-a-a."

"Thank God, here's Lucca with the milk," Editta said. "I'll just stand here and feed Allegra. Sit, Isabella, you look exhausted."

"Mama, Maria threw her bottle away. What should we do?"

"Lucca, quick. Some music."

He pulled out his ocarina. His blue eyes danced as he played a little tune that enticed Maria to climb onto Isabella's lap and then close her eyes.

"Mama, Mama. I see Cato. I think he's coming over here."

"Look, he's turning a somersault in midair."

"Maybe he'll stay with us."

"Isabella, not that little urchin too, don't you already have enough?"

Cato arrived out of breath and with a letter. "For you, Signora."

She tore open the seal, read the inside with shaking hands.

Dearest Isabella,

The pots Cato delivered to you are my way of saying grazie. Be sure to look in Allegra's basket. I left one bundle for her and one for Maria. Kiss them for me, but don't let them believe that their mama will ever return. As for Giovanni—I leave his fate in your gifted hands.

Serina

Still holding the sleeping Maria, Isabella pushed herself out of the chair. She saw the last painted wagon roll toward Via del Commerico. She saw the blue dress next to the driver before she saw the woman who wore it. There sat Serina—red hair flying loose around her shoulders as she laughed with the cocky young man.

"Sweet Mother of Jesus," someone said. "Do my eyes deceive me, or is that Serina Martino?"

"My god, are the gypsies stealing Giovanni's wife?" came a voice from the next stall.

"I don't think so."

"Mama, is Serina in trouble?"

"Riccardo, don't you dare move. Not one meter, do you hear me."

"It's not too late," said Lucca. "I'll run after the wagon if someone else will tell the polizia."

Signora Sasso was still feeding Allegra, which left one free hand to whack Lucca on the side of his head. "Use some commonsense, my son."

"But that's Giovanni's wife."

"And this time every man, woman, and child in the entire market has witnessed his humiliation. Let her go, Lucca."

To another market in another Piemonte village, Isabella thought, as she watched the caravan move toward the bridge that brought freedom to Giovanni's wife. And maybe peace to those left behind. She felt the grip of Signora Sasso's hand on her arm, heard the quiet words meant for only her ears.

"Rejoice, dear Isabella, now Pietro can come home, whenever you're ready to forgive him."

Book Two—Chapter 9

Butte, Montana—1930

A distinctive blend of musty earth and ripe perspiration inundated the dry room of Anaconda Copper Mining's premier facility as men from The Speculator's first shift stripped off their silicone-laden blue overalls and dank long johns before jockeying for one of the eight shower positions. Pete Montagna stood under the hot water and worked a thick bar of Lava Soap into his ropey frame. With eyes squeezed to the showerhead, he let its unforgiving needles pound dust and grime from his tired muscles, and then turned to brace himself for a final assault before relinquishing the water to an impatient Pole.

"Gave up my real name, just like you probably did, and a lot of others," the man told Pete when they first met. "Good names but too damn hard for these thick Americans to pronounce."

Or, too damn revealing, Pete thought. He preferred the language of America unless he was in the company of Northern Italians. Most of them came to America before The Great War but still remembered Pete's Piemontese dialect, a bastardization of French and Italian. "Speak the common language of the streets," Leo had told him. "That way nobody can make a monkey outta you." Not that Pete still counted on Leo's advice.

While Pete was buttoning up his cropped union suit, Leo sauntered up to the washbasin, swiped one hand across the foggy mirror, and peered at his image, a face on the verge of losing its angular structure. With a snap of his trouser suspenders Leo said, "I got Lady Luck with me today."

"Well I got second thoughts so count me out," Pete replied, knotting a striped tie into his shirt collar.

"Honey, that's what you need."

"Honey can't cure my problems."

"What the hell, Pete. You did good last payday."

"Yeah, but I gave it back on Wednesday."

"So why work if you can't play. We been busting our chops all week."

"No, we been busting our chops three days," Pete said, referring to the job sharing that kept the Butte miners working part time for daily wages of five dollars and forty-one cents.

"I gotta take a piss," Leo said, "so don't leave without me."

Pete dawdled at the mirror, slicking back his hair and grooming a recently acquired mustache that covered the scar on his upper lip. Women still considered him handsome, or so they said.

A stocky man, his face sun-deprived from too many years underground, shuffled up to Pete and placed a gnarled hand on his shoulder. "How 'bout coming home with me," Tony Coronna said, projecting a broad smile under his droopy gray mustache. "My Donatella, she's fixing spidino and there's some real good vino, straight from Meaderville."

Wine from Meaderville sounded almost as good as wine from

Faiallo, but Tony's invitation came with a catch: a daughter twenty-four and ready for marriage. For a brief, delicious moment Pete pictured the Coronna kitchen: tantalizing strings of cheesy pasta simmering in beef broth, the scent of garlic softening in olive oil. Basta! He clutched his mid-section and feigned a painful cramp. "Grazie, Tony, but not today. I'm dealing with this stomach problem."

Tony's smile faded. "Sure, paesano, catch you next time."

Pete grabbed his lunch bucket and tight roll of dungarees but before he could escape out the door, Leo yipped at his heels like some pesky mutt. They walked into a warm summer breeze caressing Butte's summit and while Leo cupped his hand to light a cigarette, Pete surveyed the sprawling town below. Quiet from where they stood on *The Hill*. But down below Boisterous Butte never slept, thanks to revenue from an abundant supply of copper, silver, gold, lead, and manganese. Leo was on his third match when Pete lifted his head to the distant mountains. Their snow-covered peaks made a nice picture but Montana's jewels couldn't compare to his native Alps. A glow finally appeared at the end of Leo's cigarette. He took a few drags and tipped his hat to The Spec's head frame, a gallows supporting cables that raised and lowered men, equipment, dynamite, timbers, and ore cars three thousand feet into the unforgiving earth.

Pete fell into step with Leo and six other co-workers. They started the long downhill trek, passing the Little Minah and other mines intermingled with sooty, frame cottages and two-story flats perched above stonewalled streets. One by one the men drifted off until only Pete and Leo were left to trudge the unpaved portion of Main Street. At the modest white frame church of St. Lawrence O'Toole, Pete made the sign of the cross, a routine he'd begun with his first day on the job.

"You shoulda never started that," Leo said.

"Bullshit, what are the odds?"

"No shit, just playing against the odds. Picture us in The Spec's hellhole, slaving away on the day you forget to bless yourself." He clashed an imaginary set of cymbals. "POW!"

"And what about you: saluting that damn head frame every time we leave."

"It's a habit, and nothing else."

"The same goes for me," Pete said. "One thing's for sure: I ain't superstitious."

"Well, maybe you oughta be."

"As if superstition ever brought you any luck."

"I'm here, ain't I?"

"So'm I, but luck didn't get me here."

"That's right. It was me, Leo Arnetti." He thumped his fingertips to his chest. "And don't you forget it. What's more, I got you this job, showed you how to talk like a real American."

"How to lose like one too. And don't get me started on America's lousy economy."

So far Pete's luck had been nothing but bad, same as Leo's, damn. When they weren't mining copper or listening to old-timers extol the good old days—before The Company rid itself of the union—Leo talked him into panning for gold or taking chances on every conceivable game in Butte. And Pete seldom balked.

After they passed the Lexington, Leo brought up Tony Coronna. "You shoulda gone with him for some of that Meaderville wine, for some of Donatella too."

"That ain't funny Leo."

"Ooh-h that Donatella. She's got … whatchamacallit … the hots for you."

"Basta! I'm a married man."

"Not in America. Not to these people. Better they don't know the real you. And don't forget your godfather. Giovanni ain't about to forgive or forget."

"If God is good, Giovanni's dead. And I'm going back home, just as soon as I get enough money."

"Then what the hell are we waiting for, partner." Leo draped his arm around Pete's shoulder, pushing him where he didn't need to go.

"First things first," Pete said, moving away from Leo's grip.

The two men took a right on Summit and dropped off their dirty clothes at Adie Turner's aging three-story Victorian. Eight dollars a week bought them separate sleeping rooms, one bathroom shared with ten other men, laundry service, and three meals daily, including a full lunch bucket on workdays. Pete had tried rooming with Leo but that didn't last. Not with Leo helping himself to Pete's money and sneaking in floozies after dark.

As they continued down Main Street, commercial buildings outnumbered the houses and concrete replaced the dirt road. When the street traffic picked up, Pete moved onto the sidewalk and wiped dust from his leather high tops.

"Dammit, not now," Leo said, kicking up more dust. "We only got a couple more blocks to go." He stuck his hands in his trouser pockets, jiggled coins to accompany the beat of his footsteps.

Leo the Loser: all talk and no show. And Pete always wound up on the losing end. Getting out of Butte meant first getting rid of Leo.

When they neared Uptown Butte, Prohibition saloons passed as soft drink parlors and billiard parlors stacked hustlers against greenhorns, a lesson Pete had learned the hard way. "My stomach's turning somersaults," he said. "We shoulda grabbed a sandwich back at Adie's."

"As if I need one more glob of navy beans on stale bread," Leo said. "Just you wait, tonight we're gonna feast on thick, juicy steaks."

They eased into the swelling ranks of businessmen, professionals, skilled craftsman, teamsters, laborers, uppity matrons, bored housewives, and all varieties of miners. Vehicles crowding the streets and threatening pedestrians prompted Leo to lift his middle finger to a Model T rolling through the stop sign. "A car, that's what we need. Then we'd show those bastards a thing or two."

Not with my winnings, Pete thought. His getaway money dried up after Leo needed a loan to repay old debts, a loan he had yet to repay. After they turned on Broadway the pace slowed down while Leo lit another cigarette. At Honey's Soft Drink Parlor, Pete hesitated at the beveled glass door.

"Now what?" Leo asked.

"I ain't exactly in a rush to throw my hard-earned money away."

"In that case we drink first." Leo reached around Pete and turned the sticky knob. "And then we play to win."

Inside the long, narrow saloon, large fans hung from an elaborate tin ceiling and whirled and circulated the marriage of tobacco smoke and stale beer with a calliope of tongues—Italian,

Polish, Finnish, German, Czech, and English. Pete recognized thirsty miners from the Stewart, Lexington, Alice, Moonlight, and Parrot. They all crowded around the bar, waiting for Honey, a rotund Irishman moving up and down the stretch of polished oak, filling mugs and ignoring any man demanding service before his fair turn. After he served Pete and Leo, they carried their overflowing mugs away from the bar.

"This beer's lousy," Pete muttered, dumping his into a brass spittoon. "Honey watered it down too much."

"So now you're the expert, you who never drank the stuff before coming to America. Come on, big shot; let's check out the Back Room."

"Not 'til you wipe that foam off your beak."

Honey's Back Room catered to a more universal clientele, namely independent American women who spent ten cents a card on keno, the popular successor to Chinese lottery. They sipped gin fizzes and smoked cigarettes tucked in holders, all the while waiting for the winning numbers to be posted on a large wallboard. Their male counterparts—American and otherwise—played blackjack, faro, or poker. They preferred real beer and their whiskey straight up.

Pete followed Leo through a crush of gamblers, three deep around a roulette table that generated whoops or moans whenever its spinning wheel stopped. After several rounds, the two losers pulled out, with Leo mouthing a string of profanities while he craned his neck to survey the other options. "How 'bout some twenty-one?"

"No way, not after the last time, Pete said. "Them black jack tables gotta be rigged."

Leo rolled his bloodshot eyes. "The trick is to beat 'em at their own game."

"So you said before: pay attention to the dealer and keep a straight face. As for me, I'm checking out the alley."

"Just watch your pockets and don't mess with them Micks," Leo said. "They love a good fight better'n a good lay."

"So tell me something I don't already know."

As Pete headed toward the alley door, he spotted three worthy opponents sitting at a poker table cluttered with beer mugs. He lowered his head and kept walking.

"Well, bust my balls if it ain't Montana Pete," called out Digger Baxter from the Never Sweat, so named because the original owner said he'd never sweat over naming a mine.

"You beat my ass last time we played. Now it's my turn," said Bucky Collins, Digger's mining partner.

Pete stopped.

"Whatsa matter?" asked the third player. "Scared of a little competition?" Josh Stillwater from the Lexington had won The Company's annual field day mucking contest one year by shoveling nine hundred pounds of ore in less than two minutes.

Pete turned around. He opened his hands with a shrug. "Look, fellas, it just ain't right: me taking your money again and again."

"Then give us a chance to take yours," said Digger, patting the empty chair.

Pete cocked his head. If he beat these rummies, the extra bucks could boost his depleted savings. Besides, the late afternoon sun was probably playing hell with the alley crapshooters. "OK, but I ain't staying long."

After the first three hands, Pete noticed Digger rotating his neck and shoulders to stay loose. He'd taken two pots to Pete's one. But the next hand had Pete's name on it, a feeling he held in check so as not to irritate the losers. Josh and Bucky, slouched in their chairs, had quit cracking jokes.

"Your deal," Pete said. He passed the deck to Bucky.

Bucky straightened up. He leaned forward, coughing long and hard to expel black phlegm into his red handkerchief. He cleared his throat and brought up more. "My last hand," he said, "then I'm gonna pounce on my ever-loving sweetie." He shuffled the deck, cards rippling through his fingers faster than snakes through prairie grass. When he finished, Josh tapped the cards. One by one Bucky slapped them down, circling the table until every player had five.

Pete allowed himself no gesture or comment as he picked up each card: the ten of diamonds, king of hearts, king of clubs, queen of spades. Studying his hand, he reached for his last card—the queen of clubs.

Josh tossed two bits in the pot. "Let's get this show on the road."

Digger called.

"I'll see your two bits," Pete said, "and raise it."

"Too rich for my blood." Bucky threw down his cards, and from deep in his throat engaged another gurgle.

Josh discarded three cards; Bucky dealt three more.

Digger discarded two and got two new ones.

Josh opened, saw a raise, and drew three cards. Pete figured the mucker was sitting on a pair, hoping to draw trips. If he guessed right, only three of a kind could better his kings and queens. Inwardly, Pete sighed. If he did nothing, he'd be sitting on two pair, kings over queens: better than the pair of kings but not exactly a blessing. What would he need to win the hand, three of a kind, a full house? The odds pointed to going for the three; but if he didn't get the draw, he'd be stuck with the pair of kings: good enough to win, but no Madonna Mia. Or, he could gamble and draw one for a full house, a real Madonna Mia.

There sat Digger, and trouble. He kept three cards, called a bet, saw a raise. What did Digger have? He could be sitting on three of a kind, stringing Pete and Josh along just to raise the pot. Digger tried that earlier, and had nothing. Was the sonofabitch bluffing again? Screw the rules. Pete decided to go for the full house. He discarded the ten of diamonds, and drew the suicide king of hearts. Sweet Mother of Jesus: a full house. His stomach knotted up just knowing he had to keep a straight face. Digger could keep his three of a kind, or whatever he had. A big part of Pete wanted to throw the cards down and be done with it, but he still had another round of betting, more money to win. He had to break even.

"She-i-it. Didn't get the cards," Josh moaned. "I'm out."

Digger's eyes never left his hand. "Just me and you, Montana Pete. I'll bet two bits."

Digger had to be bluffing, trying to scare Pete out of the game. But not this time. Pete held the cards and soon he'd be raking in the pot. Too bad Digger hadn't thrown more cash on the table.

"See you four bits and kick in another four," Pete said, knowing Digger's pride would keep him in the game. It did.

They laid down their cards. With a full house—kings over queens—Pete didn't even bother to check Digger's hand. Instead, he looked into the faces of the three players, waiting for their eyes to pop when they saw his full house. Goodbye, knot. Hello, pot. But Pete reached for a pot no longer there. Damn! Digger already beat him to it. Jingling coins spilled into the lap of the Never Sweat miner. Only then did Pete look at the winning hand, Digger's. *Queen of hearts high—a straight flush, oh no.*

Pete's stomach knotted tighter than his only case of impacted bowels. He couldn't even manage a faint smile when he nodded defeat. "You got me, Digger." Pushing back his chair, he ignored Digger's invitation to win back his money.

Outside, the setting sun embraced the alley as five sweaty men confronted a wooden fence in need of paint. Leaning over bent knees, they clutched a wad of money in one hand and kept the other free for rolling dice. At one time or another they'd all had a stake in Montana Pete and now they wanted the chance to recoup their losses. Pete rolled up his sleeves, spit on the dice, and made a mental sign of the cross. "*Sette*—seven!" he called, lifting his leg to execute a shot from under the knee. "Halleluiah!" Our Lady of Craps had given Pete her blessing.

By the time moths started buzzing the nightlights Pete had shoved twenty bucks in loose change and singles down his trouser pockets. And certain information he wouldn't be sharing with Leo: one of the shooters had been touting a place back East—south of Chicago, on the Mississippi River. He claimed any man who wanted work could find plenty of it in East St. Louis.

On his return to the Back Room Pete found Leo hunched over the blackjack table, tie hanging loose over his open shirt. Holding the glowing ember of a cigarette stub to a fresh Camel, Leo inhaled greedily and passed smoke through his flared nostrils. He crushed the old butt into an overflowing ashtray, and pushed damp hair from his forehead. If the Loser knew Pete was a winner, he'd hit him up for next week's rent.

"You ready, Leo?"

"Hell no, too much stake," he said without looking up. "You have any luck?"

"Nah. See you tomorrow."

Chapter 10

On Saturday Pete lingered over coffee in Adie Turner's dining room until Leo left with three boarders primed to blow their pay. When the front door closed, Pete carried his dishes into a kitchen so hot it bordered on the fires of hell. Empty plates, bowls, and platters that once held lumpy mashed potatoes, fresh corn off the cob, coleslaw, green beans, cornbread, and egg noodles with slivers of beef lined the maroon linoleum countertops.

"Good dolce—I mean sweets, Mrs. Turner," said Pete, his voice raised above the disconcerting fugue of running water, clattering plates, clanking silverware, and rattling pots.

"Call me Adie. A-D, it's just like the letters in our alphabet. And that's apple cobbler you just ate," his landlady shouted as she took his dishes. At sixty years of age, Adie matched Pete's height and obviously enjoyed the starchy foods her cook prepared for eleven boarders and a handful of outsiders. Adie's hair, the color of yesterday's dishwater, was salon set in rows of tidy finger waves gathered into a sausage roll at the base of her neck. A King Arthur Flour sack apron protected the yellow calico print dress she alternated with two other calicos. "You remind me of my Jimmy," she said with a quivering lip. "A miner he was, same as you. Lost him to The Spec disaster of 1917, along with one hundred sixty-seven other brave souls. Burned up he did. They found his pitiful remains under a pile of soot." Her voice drifted off as she retreated into another time.

Talk of mining disasters gave Pete the jitters. He could've escaped before she opened her eyes but didn't feel right about disrespecting the solemn moment. After a decent pause he cleared his throat. "I'm sorry about your husband. The mines are much safer now."

Her eyes blinked open. "So I hear. Nevertheless, don't ever give advance notice before you quit, or you may not see the light of day before meeting your Maker."

Crossing himself in front of St. Lawrence was another safety measure, as was Leo saluting the head frame. Rather than feed his imagination, Pete changed the subject. "When I go back to the Old Country—"

"If you go back," she said. "Not likely unless you give up gambling. And that bum Leo."

As if on cue, the symphony of kitchen clatter ended its movement; the cook and her helper edged closer to eavesdrop on him and Adie. Pete felt his face heat up, but not from the kitchen temperature. Leo, he dealt with every day, now he had the landlady and her nosy helpers too. None of them were lily white either. Not with that pot of mash on the stove, brewing around the clock and smelling up the entire house—a guaranteed moneymaker with the local bootleggers. Not that Pete cared. For someone weaned on wine, prohibiting alcohol made no sense.

Adie ushered him outside to the back porch steps, all but breaking his eardrum when she lifted her head to bellow, "All right, ladies, back to work!" She took a Lucky Strike from her tin and offered Pete one.

Pete tapped his chest. "Gave 'em up. Too much dust in the mine."

"More power to you. That damn—what do they call it—oh yeah, silicosis," she said, referring to the dreaded lung disease. She exhaled, streaming lazy smoke into the air. "Now, about Leo—"

"Leo my friend," Pete interrupted, more from annoyance than the loyalty he once felt. "Ever since we was kids."

"Well, it's the grown-up Leo I'm talking about. A no-good troublemaker, that one. I almost didn't let him a room when he came back from Italy. But then he paid up his old bill and said you'd be good for any future debts. Not that I believed him, mind you." Adie took another drag and exhaled her words. "Just be careful that Leo don't bring you down."

Pete started to leave but she pulled him back with a firm grip to his forearm. "Not so fast. I could use your help. Of course, I'd make it worth your while."

"You mean work around here?" He was halfway interested. The extra work might keep him away from the parlors, and from Leo.

She lifted her plump, crease-lined neck to belt a laugh. "Hell, no! I'm talking about my daughter. A real looker, mind you, a chip off the old block."

"Mrs. Turner, I can't."

"I told you it's Adie, and yes, you can. I don't care about your past, or for that matter, your future. What I do care about is my daughter's so-ci-al-ity. She's coming home for a few weeks and I need a decent sort to squire her around town."

"Squire?"

"What I mean is, take her places. You know, don't let the riffraff take advantage of her."

"Not me, Mrs. Tur ... Adie. It wouldn't be right."

"Sure it would, for the right price."

*****

The following Saturday Pete turned down Leo's uptown invitation. Personal business, he said, not caring if Leo believed him. That afternoon Pete stood at the window of his third floor turret and patted his vest pocket—a pleasant reminder of the five sawbucks inside it. For expenses, Adie had explained. She also produced two more tens to stash away for his trouble and the promise of another three after her daughter left town. On the street below a taxicab chugged to a halt. The driver scurried around to the passenger side and opened the rear door. A young woman stepped out. She smoothed down the wrinkles of a skirt straining its seams, and shook her hips before sashaying up the stone walk. Behind her trailed the cabby, laden with heavy suitcases. Pete crossed himself. From where he stood, she resembled a younger, blonder, thinner version of Adie Turner.

After Adie's daughter disappeared under the porch roof, Pete flopped down on his horsehair mattress. He laced his hands behind his head and closed his eyes to conjure up the sweet sounds of his children, only to have his mind fail him. After two years he'd lost their voices to history. A lot can change in two years. He'd changed too. Sometimes an entire day passed without thoughts of the twins or Isabella. How could that happen? How could he forget to remember his own family?

Twenty minutes later came the dreaded knock: Adie inviting him downstairs to the front parlor, a room off limits to her ordinary boarders. Pete swung his feet to the floor, got up, and stretched. He ran one hand through his hair and tucked in his shirt. The time had come to earn Adie's fifty dollars.

As he walked into the parlor, the two women sitting on the davenport stopped talking. More like bickering, that much Pete knew, and he didn't want to know any more. "Don't ever step between a mother and her daughter," Zia Theresa once told him.

After an awkward moment, Adie separated her ample hips from the maroon frieze cushion and rushed over to Pete. "Goodness, where are my manners," she said, leading him to the davenport. "Pete Montagna, this here's my daughter, Glory Bea Turner."

"My friends call me Glory. I guess you can too." She extended a flutter of enameled fingernails.

Pete bent over and brushed his lips to her plump hand, a gesture he'd picked up from the dashing actors of moving pictures. Adie's daughter smelled like lilacs, her skin soft as butter. Up close, she looked better than Adie ever could have. Glory Bea patted the indented cushion her mother had vacated, and Pete sat down. The seat felt warm, like a hen's nest.

"Well, I'll just let you two acquaint yourselves," Adie said, pausing for a response that never came before she left.

Pete leaned back, then forward. No point in letting his guard down, even if Adie's daughter was a looker. The tick tock of the mantle clock grew louder as he waited for her to speak. Leo claimed Montana women wanted the first and last words but what did Leo know about women. When this one started thumbing through a tattered copy of The Miner, Anaconda's company magazine, Pete took the lead. "Glory Bea," he rumbled like an invocation to God Almighty. "That's a very nice name."

"Like hell. Whatever was my mother thinking: to curse me with such a ridiculous moniker."

"Maybe she was thanking God for such a bella bambina." More like a miracle, considering the bambina's mother.

Pete spent a long thirty minutes listening to Glory's aimless chatter about her exciting life in Seattle, where she worked as a manicurist in a posh salon. "I just had to get away from Butte. This hick town was just to-o boisterous for someone of my refinement," she said. "You know, rowdy."

Conversation waned when Adie brought in a pitcher of freshly squeezed lemonade. She filled two etched glasses and before leaving, conveyed to Pete a sly wink he pretended not to notice.

"So Pete, how do you propose to keep me happy?"

"Propose?" he asked. "I … uh—"

"Forget about proposing. Just tell me your idea of fun."

"Well, we got movie houses. The Rialto's starring what's-her-name, you know, that Frenchie."

"You mean Claudette Colbert. Nah, I already saw *Manslaughter*. Besides, I'd rather create my own excitement than play make believe."

"We could go to Meaderville." He knew one or two bucks would buy dinner and highballs. "They got some pretty good eating places."

"And plenty of backrooms." Puckering her pillow lips, she raised her penciled eyebrows. "Nah, I'm not in the mood for gambling. Do you dance?"

"Not like they do in America." He pictured men and women in

the Old Country: the graceful way they moved in a slow, sensual manner, hand in hand, their arms held high.

"No matter, I'm a good teacher. Let's go to the Rosemont tonight, that is, if you're not otherwise inclined." She stood and kept talking as she left the room. "No point in getting there before nine o'clock. I don't want us looking like a couple of rubes. And by the way, be sure you call a taxi. I'm saving these tootsies for kicking up a storm."

*****

A good place to pick up a date was all Pete knew about the Rosemont Dance Hall. As soon as they arrived, Glory started raving about the romantic atmosphere, referring to thousands of tiny whites sparkling from a ceiling painted navy blue. Pete didn't think it compared to the nightly display from the copper mines, their lights zigzagging across upper Butte and beyond. Or, the stars on a clear Montana night, better yet, those that shined on Faiallo.

When the orchestra switched from "Muskrat Ramble" to a soft number with wistful strains, Glory grabbed his hand. "Come on Pete, I just lo-o-ve 'Smoke Gets in Your Eyes'."

Out on the polished dance floor he fumbled with first one hand and then the other, trying to figure out where each should land.

"No, not that way, silly … like this." She positioned his hands and nudged his foot with hers before they ventured into a deliberate glide.

"Now see, that's not so hard," Glory said, snuggling her head to his. "Now keep moving and please, please, don't look down at your feet."

She must've closed her eyes because Pete felt her lashes tickle his cheek. If she kept her mouth shut, he could surrender to his imagination. In the other place and other time, he'd never held Isabella like this. Nor listened to such music with her.

They moved through "The Way You Look Tonight" and "My Sweet Embraceable You" before the music shifted to the upbeat "Take Good Care of Yourself." After several missteps, Pete lost his rhythm and treaded on Glory's foot. She let out a yelp, followed by an instinctive backward kick. The heel of her pump caught the silk stocking of another dancer.

"For crying out loud!" snapped the owner of the snagged hosiery. "Watch where you're going or get off the floor."

"Nobody tells me where to get off." Without missing a step, Glory rammed her hip into Snagged.

"Did you see that?" Snagged complained to her partner, a lumbering six-footer concentrating on where to move his feet.

"Maybe we oughta sit down," Pete said, trying to steer Glory in a direction her feet refused to follow.

"Not so fast, dago." Six-footer grabbed Pete's suit coat and separated part of the sleeve from the shoulder before pulling the garment over Pete's head.

While Pete untangled himself, Glory jammed her knee into Six-footer's crotch, leaving him floored in pain. Next, she went nose to nose with Snagged. "You want the floor? So take it!" Curling one foot around her opponent's ankle, Glory brought the woman down. Ignoring two other dancers tumbling over the fallen warriors, Glory wiped her hands together and with an air of triumph, slipped her arm through Pete's. "Come on," she said, "let's get out of here. I need something more palatable than this root beer crowd."

As they walked away from an ensuing melee of toppled dancers happy for an excuse to incite discord, Pete had to speak up. "I ain't no pansy but an apology and a buck for new stockings would've gone a long way."

"Yeah, yeah, then what took you so long? I know all about you foreigners not wanting to make waves. Just remember this: nobody pushes Glory Bea Turner around."

"I thought you didn't like that name?"

She belted out a laugh similar to her mother's. "You're not so bad, Pete Montagna, or whatever your name really is. Maybe a little slow, but before this evening's over, I'll light a fire under you."

After leaving the Rosemont, they followed two arm-in-arm couples down Montana Street until Gloria stopped at a soft drink parlor. The Tin Cup looked no less crowded than the Rosemont; but its main attraction was bootleg liquor. She wasted little time disposing of three watered-down gin fizzes to the single beer Pete nursed.

"It's too quiet around here," she shouted over the din of unruly patrons. "Let's mosey over to Chinatown."

"Chinatown at night is no place for a lady."

"You sound like my mother."

Pete let the insult pass. "There's nothing worth seeing. Most of the Chinese got pushed outta town after the Tong War. Some wound up in prison."

"You've been there?"

"Not me, I've never been in trouble with the law."

"Not prison, silly, Chinatown. Have you ever been to Chinatown?"

"Who hasn't."

"Then you haven't seen the real Chinatown, or you'd want to go back."

It was almost midnight when they left the Tin Cup. They crossed Galena and turned left onto Mercury. Those once lively streets, rarely disturbed by a police force now, were as empty as Glory's pretty head. "Well, I see they still have the noodle parlors," she said.

"You like that food?"

"Silly! My taste runs to the continental."

Near China Alley they stopped to look through the cloudy windows of a remedy shop where the preserved remains of exotic animal parts, colorfully patterned snakes, and other reptiles filled an assorted collection of glass jars. Pete made a face.

"I don't see how they believe such crap will cure their ills."

"No worse than Italians wrapping garlic around their necks."

"That's for colds, and it works."

"Well, the Chinese have their ways too. Come on, I'll show you."

They walked along the shop's narrow passageway to a bleak warehouse where Glory knocked twice on the metal door. When the peephole cover slid open, she said, "Tell Annalee that Glory is here with a gentleman friend."

The door creaked open. A wizened old man with a white beard approaching his waist peered at them through little round spectacles. A black skullcap covered the top of his head, and over loose-fitting black pants he wore a long, black mandarin coat with ornamental loops fastening the buttons. Clasping his hands under the wide sleeves, he bowed. They followed him down the hall and through a doorway decorated with long strands of garish beads.

An intoxicating blend of dried herbs, tea, tobaccos, and poppy seeds infiltrated Pete's senses, along with a weird mishmash of drums and cymbals and string instruments. Even the lighting played tricks on his eyes: a kaleidoscope of red and orange and gray casting shadows onto paper-pleated walls lined with curtained cubbyholes. Circling the gambling tables were animated Chinese men dressed in suits and ties. At their sides, clinging women wore embroidered silk dresses molded to petite figures. They had painted kewpie doll lips and flawless complexions dusted with white powder. No one gave Pete or Glory a second glance, which seemed odd since they were the only outsiders.

"So Glory, you know this Annalee?"

"Better than my own ma," she said. "How do you think we made it past Moon Lin. Come on, I'll introduce you."

The spiral staircase led to a mezzanine enclosed with wrought iron. A thick, somber-faced guard stood with folded arms, prepared to pound the large, upright cymbal if anyone below got out of hand. On the floor bed of gold, fan-shaped ginkgo leaves embroidered on black satin reclined a woman in red silk pajamas. She smiled with a mouth of stained, yellow teeth. Her voice cracked with a singsong quality. "Ah-h, so Glory has returned to Annalee's humble establishment. Does she feel a certain yen-yen?"

"Like a baby craving mother's milk."

Annalee beckoned with ring-laden fingers and long, enameled nails. Glory knelt beside her. "And this time she brings Mister Round Eyes." The old woman leaned forward to study Pete.

"My name is Pete Montagna."

"So you say, but much too quickly. Am I not right, Glory?"

"Don't pay any attention to Pete. He's a foreigner and doesn't understand."

"Oh I understand," Pete said, his eyes drawn to the wall of erotic silk tapestries: men and women woven into drug-induced orgies.

In the shadows near Annalee a scrawny man squatted beside a lamp burning a low flame. After positioning a dollop of opium on the point of a needle, he heated, stretched, stringed, and balled the gooey mass until it formed a paste. He eased the paste into the narrow opening of a bowl mounted on a long ivory pipe, and presented it to his mistress.

Annalee lay down, pillowing her head on a padded contour base. She dragged long and deep from the decorated pipe. Her eyelids dropped as smoke curled from her nose and rouge-caked lips. When the air cleared, she motioned the chef to give his next production to Glory.

The opium ritual had mesmerized Pete but he drew the line at watching Adie Turner's daughter partake. "Come on, Glory," he said in his most appealing voice. "We better go."

"Don't be ridiculous. We just arrived."

He held out his hand. "I ain't leaving without you. I promised your mother."

"Well, whooped-de-do. My mother paid you to make sure I had a good time, and that's what I intend to do. Leave me alone tonight, and tomorrow I might just double whatever she promised you."

Annalee sat up. With pursed lips she clapped her hands. A

young boy appeared, no older than fourteen, the front of his head shaven and a long queue down his back. Mimicking Moon Lin's greeting, he clasped his hands together under the sleeves of traditional garb, and bowed low.

"Glory, you remember Annalee's young grandson," the older woman said.

"He's not so little anymore," Glory said as she leaned over to accept the opium chef's offering.

"Oh no you don't," Pete said.

"Zheng Choi, be so kind as to show Mister Round Eyes some of Annalee's other pleasures."

Pete brushed past the boy and knocked the pipe from Glory's hand. He grabbed her wrist, yanked until she stood up. "I say we're leaving now."

She pulled away. "Let go of me. What's a simpleton like you know about having fun. You're nothing but a money-grubbing wop."

Zheng Choi shifted the weight of his body to one leg. Before Pete could react, the boy leaned sideways, and with the other leg outstretched, hammered him squarely between the eyes. For Pete the irritating music came to an abrupt end. So did any concern for Glory as he felt himself whirling into a black abyss.

*****

The next sound Pete heard came from a horse-drawn milk wagon rolling inches away from his throbbing head. The gutter smelled of stale pee and fresh cacca. The knot between his swollen eyes accounted for their difficulty in focusing to the morning light. He pulled out his wallet. It was empty; so were his pockets. As least they had the decency not to take his papa's watch.

By the time Pete made his way back to Adie's, hungry boarders were scoffing down Sunday breakfast, her best meal of the week: ham, bacon, sausages, scrambled eggs, flaky biscuits, milk gravy, apple pie, peach crumb cobbler, and thick coffee. Pete slipped down the hall. He made it to the third tread on the stairs when Adie caught up with him.

"And just where is Glory Bea?" she whispered.

"Uh-h, she ran into some old friends, said she'd be home later today."

"So that's the way you treat my little girl. God help you if anything happened to her."

Pete climbed two more stairs.

Adie picked up the telephone. "Not another step until I get my seventy dollars."

"But I spent part of it on Glory."

"That I won't know until I see her, which could be a week from now or never." She pointed toward the back door. "We'll resume this conversation in the privacy of my yard."

Pete followed Adie outside. She lit a cigarette and started puffing.

"As long as you're already out here, just keep on walking," she said. "You're no longer welcome to sleep in my house or eat at my table."

Or have Leo on his back when they weren't working. Pete could always find another room, but not another photograph of his family. "I don't want any trouble, just my suitcase."

"And I don't want any trouble, just my money and my daughter. It didn't take the whole seventy to keep Glory happy. So where's the rest?"

"I don't have it."

"Just as I thought, you're no better than that good-for-nothing Leo. I'm evicting him, same as you."

"Look, Adie—"

"That's Mrs. Turner to you."

"I'm sorry, Mrs. Turner. I'll pay you back, every penny. But I need a place to sleep and enough to eat or I can't dig the damn copper. Can't we work something out?"

"How much did you spend last night? And don't you lie to me or I'll burn the damn suitcase."

"Three dollars."

"You let the other sixty-seven dollars slip through your fingers?" Her eyes nearly burned a hole through his while she finished off her cigarette. She dropped the butt, ground it into the dirt with the toe of her shoe. "Consider yourself reinstated, that is, if Glory comes home unharmed, and you pay me an extra five dollars and ninety cents for the next eight weeks."

"But I'm only working part-time. I won't have anything left."

"Consider yourself lucky. After all, I'm not charging you any interest."

*****

That afternoon when facing her mother in the parlor, Glory Bea broke down in tears, claiming she never wanted to see Pete again. Not because he got fresh, which she most certainly would not have allowed, but because he behaved like all the other Butte roughnecks: ignorant, self-centered, and bossy. She tried sidestepping a more detailed account of her whereabouts, but Adie kept hammering away.

"So you stayed with friends last night."

"Uh-huh."

"That nice Miranda Fairchild?"

"Oh Ma, how'd you guess? Sometimes you know me better than I know myself. And Miranda always speaks so highly of you. We just talked the night away."

"You don't say. Well, that must've been some shouting match because Miranda moved to Denver last year."

Glory stomped her foot. "Well, I hope you're satisfied. In case you haven't noticed, I'm not a kid anymore. I come and go as I please. And what's more, I don't need your permission."

"The dago took you to that damn opium den, didn't he?"

"Nobody takes Glory Bea Turner where she doesn't want to go."

"Well Annalee's taking you with her, straight to hell."

While Adie honked into a crumpled handkerchief, Glory headed for the doorway.

"Don't you turn your back on me, missy. Oh lordy, lordy. Your father would be so ashamed."

"Daddy always loved me, no matter what I did."

"Your father doesn't even know you exist."

"Doesn't know I exist?" Glory was already in the hallway when she turned around. She came back to the parlor and closed the pocket doors. "You mean I'm adopted?"

"Don't you wish. But I have witnesses to my twenty-eight hours of intense labor preceding your grand entrance. Even then you needed an audience."

Glory stuck her face in Adie's. "Was my father there?"

Adie stepped back. "Jimmy Turner was."

"Give it to me straight, Ma. Otherwise, I swear I'll burn down this house. You bet, some night when you're asleep in it."

"In that case, you'd better sit down." Adie patted the cushion. She lit a cigarette, took a few drags.

Glory checked her watch. "I don't have all day, Ma."

"Well, it all started with the summer of 1907." Adie picked a tobacco shred from her tongue, wiped it on her apron. "Jimmy and me, we'd been childless for twenty-three long years. He thought it was God's way of telling us something."

"What? That you weren't fit."

"If you don't mind, I'll tell the story. Anyway, that 'Praise the Lord Traveling Revival' came to Butte, set up an impressive tent in the Flat."

"Near Silver Bow."

"Right. On telephone poles and in the windows of Protestant-owned businesses, posters advertising a two-week revival showed the renowned Brother David Spencer, his arms outstretched to heaven as he proclaimed, 'Yes, miracles can happen—but only to those who believe.'"

"Don't tell me you fell for that hogwash."

"I just had to see for myself. I begged Jim to go with me. He refused, citing his Catholic beliefs, which didn't recognize itinerant preachers of lesser faiths. I reminded him he'd not set foot in St. Lawrence's since leaving the sixth grade."

"Once a Catholic, always a Catholic," Glory said. "And Butte's a Catholic town."

"Renowned—that's what the poster said about Brother David. That means he's famous."

"Did you ever hear of him before?"

"Well, no. Neither did Jimmy. He pulled The Spec's second shift for the next month so I went alone to the revival's opening. I arrived early, along with fifty others, and squeezed into the last space on the front row bench. I pushed the dry August air around my face with a hand fan promoting Jorgenson's Mortuary."

"I know about the heat, Ma."

"Some bossy woman ran the show. Her puckered face showed the restrains of a too-tight corset."

Glory rolled her eyes. "Evidently, she wasn't from these parts. Even then Montana women had better sense than to lace themselves into distorted versions of God's gift to man."

"One by one, members of the Protestant church choirs filled four tiers of the raised platform. At seven-fifteen the pianist played a spirited rendition of 'Onward Christian Soldiers' to hasten the socially inclined audience of the old, young, crippled, robust, skeptical, and mostly curious to their seats."

"I can see it now."

"There were two choral presentations, one with a soprano soloist squeaking like an abused violin, before I got my first glimpse of Brother David. Even in the shadows of the stage his shoulder-length blond hair gave off a halo glow."

"Oh, Ma, don't tell me you fell for that."

"He bent one knee to the platform, and with forehead to fingertips, he prayed. Twenty feet away a local preacher beseeched him to appear and save souls in the name of Jesus Christ."

"Get to the point, Ma."

"Brother David walked into the spotlight. No more than twenty-five and slight of build, he wore a pinstriped suit and carried himself tall, bible in one hand and cross in the other. When he talked about salvation, I knew he directed every word to me. When his eyes wandered the room to touch the souls of every sinner, they always returned to mine. My simple nod indicated I accepted his wisdom."

"Ma!"

"Coin and paper money filled the collection baskets. The choir rendered an extended version of "What a Friend We Have in Jesus" while Brother David raised his arms and called all sinners to come forward. I pushed ahead to be first, to feel his soothing touch on my head. He asked, 'Do you accept Jesus Christ as your Lord and Savior?'"

"And you said yes."

Adie nodded. "But before I could ask for my miracle, the whale-boned woman ushered me away to make room for the long line of repentant sinners. Some, like me, wanted a miracle. Others cried for forgiveness. One elderly woman, most likely suffering from severe rheumatism, shuffled down the sawdust aisle. Brother

David touched her. She threw down her cane, did a jig, and more people lined up."

"That must've been some show."

"During the final prayer, Brother David slipped out without any fanfare. Hoping for a personal consultation, I waited around for everyone to leave. When the last light flickered out, I gave up and went home too.

The next night I arrived early and took the same seat. I riveted my eyes on Brother David and again accepted Jesus as my savior. But I left disappointed. On the third evening I skipped the revival and waited behind the tent.

"'I missed you tonight,' Brother David said when he came out. He touched his fingers to my cheek. I put my hand over his. When I told him I came for my miracle, he performed it right there, while the choir sang inside. It was the most glorious night of my life. And that, Glory Bea, is how you got your name nine months later."

Glory sniffed as she patted her eyes. She stood up and hugged her mother. "Oh, Ma, without a doubt, that is the most beautiful love story I ever heard in my entire life."

Chapter 11

Eight weeks of paying back Adie gave Pete one benefit. It kept him away from the gambling houses, which irritated Leo and for a time relieved Pete from having to finance any further losses, his or Leo's.

"Hell, you was a fool for letting that bitch squeeze you," Leo said after Pete cleared the debt. "You shoulda waited 'til the middle of some moonless night and just skipped out. If you ask me, the whole thing was a setup."

"So who's asking."

"At this rate you're never going home. Maybe going home ain't in your cards. Maybe you oughta start thinking about a new life."

Pete grabbed Leo's collar. He spoke through gritted teeth. "Maybe you oughta keep your mouth shut. If it wasn't for the money I lent you and never got back—"

"If it wasn't for your *pisello* and Giovanni's wife, there'd be no money and you'd be in Faiallo instead of Butte."

*****

Several weeks later Pete hurried from The Spec's dry house

with a four-day pay tucked in his vest pocket and a firm decision to avoid the gambling parlors. The sweltering heat of August discouraged all but the most necessary exertion but he moved like a man on a mission, in this case getting a head start on Leo. The Loser had spent the entire day boasting about his luck changing, and Pete wasn't about to touch the secret crapshoot reserve.

"Hey, paesano," a voice called out. "Wait up."

Paesano could've applied to almost half of the day shift so Pete kept walking until he heard his own name shouted. He turned to see the only other miner he'd been avoiding. Forcing a smile, he clasped Tony Coronna's outstretched hand. "*Ciao*, paesano, good to see you."

"I been trying to catch up with you for weeks," Tony said. "You know, there's this Italian Club in Meaderville. How 'bout meeting me there tomorrow."

"Ah-h, I don't know, Tony. I promised Leo—"

"So bring him too."

Pete hesitated, wishing he'd not brought up Leo.

"Whatsa matter?" Tony asked. "You already got plans?"

"Leo might."

"Hells fire, you can't take a shit without Leo wiping your *culo*?" Tony slapped him on the back. "Come on, paesano. Us dagos, we gotta stick together. You know, mix with our own kind so as not to forget where we came from. What better way than to play a little bocce ball, drink a little wine."

That evening Leo returned from Honey's with a few extra bucks in his pocket. At the mention of Meaderville, he invited himself before Pete could extend Tony's invitation. "Me and you'll team up for bocce and show them know-it-alls how to beat the pallino," Leo said.

"Speak for yourself. I ain't played bocce in years."

"Don't be such a weenie." He wrapped his hand around Pete's chin and squeezed. "With Leo Arnetti you ain't got a thing to worry about 'cause after this evening I'm feeling damn lucky."

*****

The next day found Pete stretched out on a grassy patch with Leo, both of them eating crusty bread and aged salami while waiting for the streetcar to Meaderville.

"Beats the hell out of Adie's chicken and dumplings floating in that damn yellow broth," Pete said, smacking his lips.

"Yeah, Adie's last hen was so old she keeled over without a fight," Leo said. "So, what's keeping our bullshitting rooster?"

"If you mean Tony, he's meeting us there."

"And Donatella?"

"At home where she belongs. What the hell, I ain't her keeper. Besides, this club's for men only."

"Too bad, I keep thinking about her for myself." Leo tilted his head back and drained the bottle. "Damn, we could use more wine."

"Wait 'til Meaderville."

"Yeah, already I can taste the grappa. Anyway, here comes the streetcar."

They took the vertical front seats across the aisle from a young mother who reminded Pete of Isabella at her best: proud with a certain dignity. And like his twins, the woman's two little boys couldn't sit still or keep quiet. About seven or eight years old, Pete figured. He watched their every move, hoping for some reminder of Gina or Riccardo. Finding none, he winked and tossed a few coins to the boys, giving them another excuse to wrestle. The mother admonished her sons in a tongue he didn't understand. Not that it mattered. A mother's scolding tone translates into any language.

Leo's elbow brought him back to the moment. "Hey, wake up, Valentino."

"I ain't sleeping."

"No, but you was dreaming. This here's our stop."

Pete tipped his fedora to the young mother. He and Leo hopped off the streetcar, watched it glide down the track.

"Why torture yourself," Leo said, "That worn-out mama ain't the mama for you. I know, I know: you miss the wife; you miss the bambini. But they're in Faiallo and you're not."

As if Pete needed a reminder. He tolerated Leo's rambling bullshit as they strolled down streets lined with log and frame houses built low to the ground and covered with flat or hip roofs. The business district boasted a variety of shops offering groceries, dry goods, hardware, and medicinal aids—all closed to honor the Sabbath, a tradition that evidently didn't apply to Meaderville's saloons flourishing on every corner, and behind every saloon a bocce court.

Leo rubbed his hands together. "Forget Tony's club. We could make us a killing out here."

"Your chance will come soon enough," Pete said as they approached the porch of a narrow, white clapboard building.

The aroma of garlic and aging grapes met them at the door to the Italian Club. Short, rectangular screens held windows open to admit a stingy breeze that large oscillating fans mixed with stale air. On one wall a framed print of Pope Pius XI hung beside a hand-written sign advertising the forty-cent Wednesday special: ravioli or spaghetti plus beverage, which meant wine. From another wall the majestic head of a six-point elk stared from glass eyes. The flags of America and Italy shared the platform with a rickety podium. The bartender and only occupant guarded his mirrored shelves lined with grappa, wines, and digestive liquors that reminded Pete of Faiallo's Il Sole è la Luna. He bought two chances on *Polizza*—Italy's weekly lottery that no Montana Italian had ever won—and Leo blew a quarter on the five-cent punchboard. Both passed on the number games and other lotteries.

"Bocce?" Pete asked.

The bartender motioned toward the rear door.

Outside, a yard full of bunchgrass and Douglas firs and cottonwoods pushed through dry, rocky soil, but the only trees that caught Pete's attention were the two supporting a stretch of white canvas. *ANNUALE FAMIGLIA GIORNO*, the sign read. Just what Pete needed: the Club's Annual Family Day. Ignoring Leo's pent-up snickers, he surveyed a distant spread of wicker baskets on tables covered with red and white checkered oilcloths. Under the bordering cottonwoods, women in their Sunday best were hand gesturing to accentuate non-stop chatter while children shimmied up tree trunks, swung from inner tubes, or played hide and seek. Near the essential kegs of wine, men with jauntily cocked caps and cheap panamas had rolled up their shirtsleeves and loosened their ties to play card games—*scopa, briscola,* and *tresette,* or *morra* and bocce. The common language was Italian, formal or a provincial dialect.

"Ain't that Tony's daughter?" Leo licked his lips. "Over there, by the outhouse. See the plump one falling outta her frilly yellow dress. Um, um, um."

"Don't get started on Donatella."

"Dammit, Pete, if you don't want her, maybe I—"

"Leave her alone, Leo. She ain't your type."

"That's what makes her special. And if you was any kind of friend, you'd put in a good word for me."

"Stick to the whores on Galena Street, where you won't make enemies or embarrass me. Now come on. Let's find Tony."

Following the choppy sounds of intermittent laughter and cheers, they spotted him sitting across the table from a fierce competitor. With right arms bent, each man shouted a prediction of the total number of fingers about to project from his opponent's side fist as it pounded the table.

"*Sette!*"

"*Uno!*"

"*Zero!*"

"*Due!*"

"*Cinque!*"

The game went on and on until Tony let out a victory yell. After swooping up a four-bit ante, he introduced Pete and Leo to the man he defeated at morra.

Freddo Ponte stood up, his arms resembling two hams molded into a barrel chest. He grinned from a lumpy potato face and had a thick nose wedged between eyes the color of a trout's. After pumping hands, he narrowed those lackluster eyes and spoke in English, asking the usual question. "So, Pete, where you from?"

"Butte, up near Walkerville. We just came out for the day."

"Yeah, we work The Spec with Tony," Leo chimed in.

Freddo shook his head. "No, no. I mean where you from in the Old Country."

"Piemonte, near Pont Canavese."

"Is that so; maybe we knew the same people. Ever been to the market in Castellamonte?"

"Once or twice," Pete said, ignoring Leo's nudge. One more reminder Pete didn't need; Castellamonte was Isabella's village. He turned to Tony. "So paesano, how long before we get the court?"

"We're up next, me and Freddo against you and Leo. But first you gotta try our vino."

Sitting around a sawhorse table, the four men filled their glasses from an earthenware pitcher as a new game of bocce began. A wiry man, at least seventy-five, threw the wooden *pallino* onto a dirt-packed court. He followed up with a red bocce ball, aiming it as close as possible to the pallino. One of his elderly opponents edged out the first red ball by a good fifteen inches. Red team's first toss didn't stand a chance; but when its second player nudged the fifteen-incher, an animated uproar ensued over who came closer to the pallino. Out came the stick: to measure a distance so close the kneeling men went nose to nose before agreeing that blue had the edge.

After the game resumed, Tony reminisced with Freddo about the Old Country and to Pete he extolled his daughter's homemaking skills. Left-out Leo soon announced the need to piss.

Then Tony left with the empty pitcher.

Freddo started drumming his fingers. "So, Pete, you got anybody special?"

"I'm alone. How 'bout you?"

"Alone and lonely. My mama—God rest her soul—she died six months ago. Things ain't been the same since. The woman lived the life of a saint. She took care of me—good as any wife, except for—well, you know. And that I get once a week on Galena Street."

So did Pete, if money allowed. When he first came to Butte, he wanted no part of the Galena Street whores; but Leo said a healthy man could go mad without some form of release other than his own, so Pete strung along to test the theory and for a change he had to agree with Leo. As for Freddo, Pete had never run into him on Galena Street. A man like Freddo, he would've remembered.

"So Pete, you ever met Tony's daughter?"

"Once, when Tony invited me to dinner."

"Lucky you. I'd like a shot at her but I think Tony has somebody else in mind." Freddo cracked a smile sadder than any sorry clown's. "Like maybe you, Pete."

"That ain't gonna happen, but don't tell Tony I said so. He's a good paesano and I don't want hard feelings."

"You think maybe I got a chance?"

"I'd lay odds, two to one."

Tony came back and they killed a second pitcher of wine. By the time their turn on the court came up, Pete had to track down Leo.

"Damn!" Leo grumbled as he left a game of morra. "You shoulda come sooner, or a helluva lot later. I already dumped two bucks on them bastards. We better win big at bocce."

"Easy, Leo. We came here for some fun."

"You bet, at two bucks a game."

"Two bucks, are you *matto*? That's way too steep."

"So we put 'em outta their misery real quick."

"Like hell, these guys play all the time. What's more, they belong here and you and me are the strangers. Trouble, I don't want."

"Trouble? Come on, Pete. You know me better'n that."

Pete and Leo took the blue balls, their opponents, red. Tony flipped a nickel and Pete called tails.

"Sorry, Pete, it looks like me and Freddo go first." Tony showed the Indian head stuck between the bulging veins of his hand.

"Yeah, yeah," Leo grumbled. "So quit fooling around and let's play."

Freddo tossed the pallino down the court and the game soon evolved into a string of as-close-as-you-can-get combined with what-the-hell-I-don't-believe-it. As the sun got hotter, so did the tempers. It was typical bocce.

"Atta way!"

"Shit!"

"You call that close?"

"You don't believe me? Get the stick and we measure."

"Oh, no!"

"Madonna mia!"

"Easy ... easy ... easy."

"SH-I-I-T!"

"Anybody waiting for the court? No? OK, two out three."

"Damn!"

"Damn, damn, damn!"

"Get the stick!"

"Three outta five."

"Holy mother of—"

"Get the stick!"

"For chrissake!"

"That's it. Let's get the hell outta here."

The losers each gave up five dollars. They were about to leave when Tony pulled Pete aside. "Look, paesano, I don't need your money."

"No, no, Tony. I'm okay with this. Your team won fair and square."

Wrapping one arm around Pete's shoulder, Tony folded five bills into his hand. "Stay and eat with us, Leo too. My daughter brought some real good food."

"Mi dispiace, paesano," Pete apologized. "But me and Leo

already got other plans."

"Then how 'bout coming for supper on Tuesday? Donatella's got these garden tomatoes—firm and ripe and oh so sweet."

Games, Pete had taken chances on more than his share but this one had touched a different nerve. His hand was still entrenched in Tony's when he returned the money. "You honor me by such an invitation, but I gotta tell you, Tony. This paesano ain't the right paesano for your table. Now you take somebody like …" Pete looked at Leo, ten feet away and looking back at him. With a few well-chosen words, Pete figured he could get The Loser off his back and onto Tony's—but this was one game not worth playing, especially with the stakes so high. "As I was saying, you take somebody like my new friend, Freddo Ponte." Pete put his other hand over Tony's. "Now, there's a good paesano, one who's ready to settle down and make a loving woman the queen of his heart."

Chapter 12

Faiallo, Italy—May, 1930

Rabbit stew and polenta, Giovanni's favorite dish. No one could prepare it better than Isabella, a task requiring everyone to stay out of her way. From his chair near the window Giovanni watched her stir the corn meal and water over a low heat, a production that took a good forty minutes before the mixture grew creamy and pulled away from the sides of the heavy pot. The same pot Isabella brought home from Pont the previous year. The same day Isabella took his wife to the market, but failed to bring back the worthless slut. But she did bring back his precious children—Baby Allegra, asleep in his lap, and Maria playing outdoors with the twins. Pietro's Riccardo and Gina were part of Giovanni's family now, along with Pietro's wife Isabella. Giovanni lived for those hours when she tended to his needs, when the entire family sat around his table and ate the food she cooked. It was Isabella who ran his home and his farm. She still ran Pietro's farm too, which was where Giovanni's family spent most of the day, without him. And where Isabella insisted they sleep each night, without him.

After giving one final stir with her wooden spoon, Isabella poured the polenta onto a platter and cut it into sections with a string held taut between her hands. Those same loving hands brushed against Giovanni's when she took Allegra from him. While she carried the sleeping baby to her bed, he banged his stick against the open window casement and managed to call out, "*Mangiamo*!"

The rest of his family came running—the boy first, as it should be.

"Wash your hands," Isabella said. Like good little soldiers, the trio obeyed.

Giovanni banged his stick on the floor and the twins reported for duty. He held out his arms for the boy. Riccardo yanked forward; Gina pushed from behind. With one practiced motion, the little troopers pulled him upright. While he swayed like a tree threatening to topple, they positioned themselves under his armpits, held tight to the elbows, and waited for his next command. "Va, va, my little crutches. To the table, I'm hungry."

He eased into the only chair equipped with arms; the children took their usual places. He tucked his napkin under his chin; they followed his example. A square of polenta already sat on each plate as Isabella circled from behind, applying generous helpings of rabbit and sauce.

"*Formaggio?*" she asked on the second go-around.

Giovanni tapped his fingers to the wood and received a grating of cheese.

She came around again, this time with wine. Everyone received an appropriate amount, including a half finger for Maria. Isabella sat down, adjacent to him in case he needed her help. He blessed the food, and the meal began. With fingers gripped around the spoon, he filled its shell with a tasty morsel. To his relief the food found its way to his mouth on the first try. Thank god, his first prayer of the day had been answered.

Giovanni and the family ate for several minutes in quiet bliss before Isabella spoke. "Zia Theresa paid me a visit this morning, after she finished cleaning your house."

Giovanni formed the words in his mind before he allowed them to leave his mouth. "What does she want now, more money for less work?"

"Be grateful for the help she gives. I only have two hands."

Two gifted hands. Those patient hands had brought his damaged limbs back to life. "Mi dispiace, Isabella. What news did the … our neighbor bring this time?"

"Yesterday at the market Zia met an old friend—Anna Arnetti. You know, the mother of Pietro's good friend, Leo Arnetti. You remember Leo, don't you?"

Leo, ah yes, the bastardo had called him a cuckold, given him his first public humiliation. Giovanni sent a row of fingers to the side of his head. "Maybe I knew him but not anymore."

She patted his hand. "Well, Signora Arnetti told Zia that Pietro came to her house on the day Leo left for America. Perhaps Pietro went with him."

"Papa went across the ocean?" Gina asked.

"Perhaps, I only know he's not in Torino."

"Maybe he went to heaven," Riccardo said.

Or maybe to hell, Giovanni thought. Maybe Serina met up with him there. Wherever they were, he didn't want them in Faiallo or anywhere near Piemonte.

"Don't you have a friend in America," he heard Isabella ask.

He answered with a shrug.

"I mean the one who sent you a Christmas postcard two years ago from ... from ..." She got up, went to his cabinet drawer, flipped through the preserved mail. "Here it is, from Colorado."

Giovanni tapped his glass.

She poured more wine for both of them, and sent the children out to play before she sat down with the postcard. "Look, a picture of some mountains. Leo talked about the mountains too. This Nunzio Drago, do you remember him?"

Giovanni remembered but he shook his head. The bumbling idiot served under him during ... what war?

"Nunzio writes that he owes you his eternal gratitude."

Si, for saving his life in the ... Austrian War. Giovanni tapped his glass.

"According to this note, Nunzio works as an enforcer. I suppose that means the police."

He tapped his glass again. She moved her hand, but only to cover his.

"Call my little crutches," he said. "I'm tired."

"Giovanni, look at me."

He never tired of looking at her.

"I need my husband. Riccardo and Gina need their papa. Maybe Nunzio Drago can help us locate Pietro."

Nunzio? The idiot couldn't find the buttons on his shirt. "You write the letter, Isabella. I'll sign it."

Chapter 13

Denver, Colorado—June 1930

Nunzio Drago had read Giovanni Martino's letter a dozen times, maybe more. He sensed the urgency of his request to locate a wayward paesano. Look for Pietro Rocca in Montana, Giovanni wrote. Tell him to come home. His family needs him and all is forgiven. Giovanni even wired money, enough to cover six weeks of work and expenses, and this Pietro's return passage to Italy. To refuse such a request from his old army comrade was unthinkable. After all, the man had saved his life during the war against Austria.

During Nunzio's ten years in America he'd traveled the country and held a variety of jobs—from street cleaner and window cleaner to garbage collector and bill collector—but the last five years in Denver's Little Italy had been his most satisfying. He slept on a cot in a rented room behind a produce store. He cooked his landlord's vegetables on a hot plate, usually with some salsiccia. His vino came from across the street. He worked on call, and this evening he had one more job to perform before beginning his obligation to Giovanni. Tomorrow morning, he planned to be on the train to Billings, and if he liked Montana better than Denver, he might decide not come back. He already told the landlord not to hold his room. The bastardo wanted him to pay rent on the damn thing while it sat empty.

Before he left for his final Denver job, Nunzio gathered the tools of his trade—a pair of brass knuckles and a pearl handled switchblade. He wasn't sure which one he'd need tonight. The knuckles packed a surprise blow that made any tough guy see stars. For the sissies who pretended they were big shots, he preferred the knife. It worked best with women too, if they made him go that far.

He took the trolley across town, walked two blocks to a run-down section of little houses and scrubby yards. He checked the address Whitey gave him, and this time made sure to knock on the right door. It opened a crack, to the lower half of an unshaven face.

"Russell Harper?"

"Whatever you're selling, I ain't buying."

Nunzio slipped the knuckles over his hand. He kicked his way in, and busted Harper in the nose before going for the mouth. "I came for the thirty bucks you owe Whitey Blake."

Harper spoke through a mouthful of blood. "Thirty? I only borrowed twenty-five last week."

"Next week it'll be thirty-five. Whitey runs a business, not a mission."

"Have a heart, please. I ain't worked in a month."

Deadbeats, they all had a story. A little girl peaked around the kitchen door. He heard a baby cry. If it wasn't for leaving in the morning, he might've considered a payment plan. Still, there was tonight. "Your wife, tell her to come here."

"She's sick, really sick."

She came out of the kitchen, baby in her arms and girl hanging on one leg.

"Sick, hell, the woman's too skinny."

Nunzio reached in his pocket, pulled out a twenty, and threw it at Harper before he left.

When he stopped by Whitey's, it was to clear the deadbeat's debt, again with Giovanni's money.

*****

As soon as Nunzio arrived in Billings, he put himself in the shoes of a man without his family, which meant undertaking a thorough study of the city's brothels. The close up and personal research resulted in little enjoyment, considerable expense, and no clues to Pietro Rocca's whereabouts. From Billings to Helena Nunzio employed the same tactics, each time without success until one whore bent over backwards to please him.

"This man you asked about," she later asked, fingering the extra dollar he tipped her. "What's he look like?"

Nunzio shrugged. "Like any Italian—dark hair, dark eyes."

"Like any Mexican too. You need to be more specific."

Nunzio thought a minute. "The nose could go either way—straight or hooked, but always big. About Pietro Rocca's, I ain't for sure."

"Forget Pietro Rocca. Any man can change his name, especially a foreigner. What you need is a picture."

Chapter 14

A series of four-day workweeks garnered Pete some extra cash so he agreed to accompany Leo uptown, on the condition of bottoming out their losses at five dollars each. As it turned out, they both did well and after three hours left Honey's with more cash than they had brought. Pete checked his pocket watch. Eleven fifteen and Main Street hadn't even yawned. High on The Hill lights from dozens of mines flickered like candles in the night. Soon, miners from all the three-to-eleven shifts would descend with fresh money.

Butte at night rivaled Butte in the afternoon. Horns tooted. Brakes squealed. People laughed, shouted, cursed, argued, and engaged in spirited discussions about the sad state of the economy or the absence of a mining union and the prolific growth of other unions. In doorways and under streetlights young couples openly smooched, their amorous fondling encouraged by the raunchy night crowd. Such behavior wouldn't have been tolerated in Faiallo. But Butte played by different rules and after two years in this wild, outlandish town Pete had begun to feel at home.

"Damn, I almost forgot," Leo said, snapping his fingers. "Opal asked about you, said to tell you hello."

Pete furrowed his brow. "Opal? I don't know any Opal."

"Sure, you do." Leo bounced imaginary breasts. "Space between her front teeth and great big milkers."

"That sounds like Alberta from The Copper Club."

"Si, the same, she moved up to The Galleria," Leo said, referring to the brothel whose whores took their names from the area's elements: Goldie, Silvia, Zinnia, and Maggie. Or local gemstones like Sapphire, Garnet, and Opal. And precious stones from far away: Ruby, Emerald, and Diamond.

"Which explains the new name," Pete said. "So what'd she say about me?"

"That not one of her last two hundred johns could match the likes of Montana Pete."

Pete grinned. "Only two hundred, I been away from her longer than that."

"Si, but Opal has a lot of repeaters. She said to stop by real soon."

Pete pulled out his timepiece again and contemplated its roman numerals. At one time the watch had been his father's prized possession. And Pete had honored his father's memory by naming his own son Riccardo. Would Riccardo ever have reason to honor Pete? Not if he didn't make up for lost time. Eight hours and thousands of miles away meant Sunday morning in Faiallo, his family preparing for Mass. Did they still remember to pray for him?

"Wake up," Leo said, snapping his fingers.

"I was just thinking."

"Well, don't 'cause no amount of thinking is gonna put you back where you think you oughta be. Nooky, that's what you need right now."

Pete felt the weight of Leo's arm on his shoulder. Sometimes The Loser wasn't so bad, those times when he had his own money to spend. "What the hell, Leo. If we hurry, there's just enough time to beat the second shift. *Andiamo!*"

*****

In the alley between Galena and Mercury Streets a chorus line of determined women with skirts hiked over their thighs vied for the attention of men hanging on to their money. For a miner, the price of a quick lay amounted to a third of his daily wages. For a whore, plying her trade amounted to a monthly fine of ten dollars, payable at the police station. Failure to comply doubled the fine, and gratis sex to the law enforcers.

Pete and Leo strolled past the rear entrances of Spanky's, The Copper Club, Sweet Rhapsody, and The Continental Divide. All the ladies knew Leo, a weekly john who sometimes came more often. They knew Pete too, but not as well. And when neither man gave them the courtesy of an appreciative glance, the skirts went a little higher to flash manicured mounds of tempting fluff.

Halfway down the alley a neon sign marked The Galleria. Red lights blinked above the door guarded by a bull-necked man with full lips and a fold of skin pressed between heavy-lidded eyes. The Lithuanian called Stanley held out his hand for an obligatory fifty-cent gratuity and then opened the door to Butte's most revered arcade.

Ragtime music from the front parlor's player piano filtered through the carpeted main floor and up the open stairwell to the second level. All doors to the cribs were temporarily closed, which accounted for the handful of men in the hallway checking their watches. But Pete and Leo had other ideas; they took the back stairs down to where the air changed from warm and stifling to dank and musty, like that of The Spec.

And like specialty shops of a retail gallery, eight-foot square rooms with big windows displayed the local merchandise. Behind glass bordered with blue lights, women leaned against the window frames, or spread their legs in easy chairs or rockers. They read or crocheted or embroidered, and wore flimsy peignoirs, or see-through chemises and crotchless panties, or Sunday-go-to-meeting clothes for johns who liked to pretend they were undressing virgins.

Pete and Leo passed several windows with drawn curtains before stopping to view a scantily clad Eurasian with short black hair shingled to curve into her pretty face. The eighteen-year-old grew up on Mercury Street, a second-generation Gallarian whose mother once reigned as number one whore. Scarlet lips puckered into a Cupid's bow, and from delicate fingers she blew a kiss meant for either taker. Leo pointed to the crib door. She opened it, and assumed a hands-to-hips stance.

"Hey, *Leonardo di Canavese*. You wanna be treated like a great master?"

Leo lifted an eyebrow. "Does that mean I get more than ten minutes?"

"Only if you pay me twice." Barely five feet tall, she stood on tiptoe to peer over his shoulder and winked at Pete. "We won't be long, Mr. Mountain. Then I show you my mountains."

"Next time," he called out as the curtain closed over her window. Zinnia had a beautiful body and knew how to please Pete, but this night belonged to Opal.

He strolled down to the last crib on the right where a chenille spread covered the tarnished brass bed, but not the chamber pot underneath. The washstand crackled with green paint held a pitcher and bowl, bar of Lifebuoy Soap, and stack of washcloths. In one corner a wood-burning stove waited for cold weather. Gray paper with pink cabbage roses splashed across the walls and from the ceiling dangled a single naked bulb, the crib's only light source.

Slumped in an easy chair, Opal had nodded off with *The Police Gazette* in her lap. She awoke with a start, and seeing Pete, flashed her toothy smile. She whipped off her reading glasses, extracted her hips from the chair, and bounced in a flimsy red gown and tattered mules to the door.

"Come in, and be quick about it," she said, grabbing his arm. She gave the door a kick, closed the curtain, and planted a long, wet kiss over his mouth.

"Leo said you asked—"

"Later. But first you have to pay, just like everybody else."

He counted out two dollars into her hand, and with a grin said, "Keep the change."

The money went into the washstand drawer. She set the ten-minute alarm on her Baby Ben, and wound the key tight; and when the clock started ticking, she plopped a crochet-covered pillow over it. "I missed you, Petey," she said, circling her arms around his neck. "Where have you been?"

"Around, just not on Galena Street." He glanced over to the little pillow, knowing the time he couldn't see still ticked away. "Leo said—"

"Forget Leo, will you. At least until we tickle each other's fancy."

What Pete liked best about Opal was she did all the work and made no demands. Not like Serina used to do. Serina … what made him think of Giovanni's wife now? Since leaving Italy, he'd hardly given her a second thought. Still, he knew better than to imagine

Opal or any other woman as a fill-in for what he once had with Isabella. To do so would have been a sacrilege.

The next six minutes passed too quickly, but when he erupted like an oilrig, Pete knew he got his money's worth. After a back rub from Opal, he pulled up his pants and straightened his shirt while she crawled around the bed, fluffing pillows and smoothing chenille. When she uncovered the clock, less than a minute remained.

"Okay. I'll make this quick or else you'll need to fork over more money. Last week some rough-looking guy came around asking about an immigrant by the name of Pietro Rocca. No one except yours truly was smart enough to figure out who he might've been talking about."

"Pietro Rocca?" Pete chewed on his lower lip while pondering the name and shaking his head. "Never heard of him. This guy doing the asking, what'd he look like?"

The alarm clock went off, and Opal held out her hand. "Sorry, Pete." She took his two dollars and continued. "No taller than you, but heavier. Walked like he had a cob up his you-know-what. Beady eyes set close together and kind of weasely. For sure a dago—uh, I mean an Eye-talian. That I know from the way he talked—just like you."

"How old?"

"M-m-m, maybe fifty, and tighter than a drum."

"Whadaya mean?"

"If the skinflint had opened his billfold a little wider, I might've remembered things differently."

"Like what?"

"Like maybe a guy fitting your description came through here last year on his way to California. Ain't seen him since."

He patted her rear with the intimacy of an old friend. "Grazie, Opal."

She put a forefinger to her temple. "Oh yeah, there's just one more thing. About this guy, he's still in town, and you just never know. He could come back."

Pete pressed another two dollars in her palm. "In case he does, be sure to tell him the California story."

*****

It was after one before Pete and Leo left the Red Light District. The cool mountain air sent a shiver down Pete's spine, prompting him to turn up his collar and hunch his shoulders as he walked uphill. With hands shoved in pockets, he quickened his pace while observing every man on Main Street. Perhaps Opal's stranger was doing the same. After a stretch of silence, they crossed Broadway and Leo said, "So, what'd she tell you?"

"Who?"

"You know who—Opal."

"Not much."

"Come on, Pete. Quit shitting me."

"What's to shit? So what if some stranger came around The Galleria asking about Pietro Rocca."

Leo stopped. He struck a match against the stone wall, cupped one hand to the flame, and lit his cigarette. "This stranger, what does he look like?"

"Half the miners in Butte," Pete answered from over his shoulder. "Tall as me but heavier and twenty years older."

"I knew it! The old cuckold did survive. He's sent some *stronzo* to get you."

"Hell, you don't know that."

"Think about it, Pietro …."

"Don't ever call me that again. My name is Pete. Pete Montagna."

"I say we find the shit before he finds you."

"Look, I ain't worried. If he sees Opal again, she'll tell him Pietro Rocca went to California last year."

"This *stronzo* is no dummy. If he traced you to Butte, he'll be in no hurry to make California."

"Just drop it, Leo."

"Hell, we ain't making money here in Butte. Maybe we should just take off."

Pete stopped. "Look, get this straight. Right now, I ain't going nowhere."

Leo dropped his cigarette butt into a ribbon of water trickling down the gutter. "The hell you ain't. Stay in Butte and the only place you're headed is six feet under."

Chapter 15

When Nunzio Drago asked the clerk at Butte's Main Post Office if he had any mail, the bastardo slid an official receipt pad over the counter without so much as a grunt. He continued the disrespect, cleaning gunk from under his nails while Nunzio printed his name and scrawled an illegible signature on the pad before returning it.

"Next!" the bastardo called out as he handed Nunzio an envelope stamped Air Mail Delivery from Pont Canavese, Italy.

Nunzio stuck the envelope in his pocket. Shuffling across the lobby, he tightened his asshole to calm an angry knot of hemorrhoids threatening greater discomfort than what they'd already inflicted. The large clock towering over the heavy doors showed four o'clock—too early for eating supper, too late for opening more wine in his room. But just enough time to inspect the package and to take a nap before his nightly rounds.

He forced his heavy legs to move toward the Thornton Hotel where ten days before he'd negotiated the cheapest accommodations, a converted utility room for six bits a night. His next stop that first day had been the Golden Horseshoe where he passed through those swinging doors with hopes of increasing his purse. Giovanni's too, in case Nunzio needed to extend his pursuit.

Two hours later he left with his pockets fifty bucks lighter.

Two doors short of the Thornton, Nunzio paid ten cents to a pushcart peddler for two apples. He entered the hotel, and encountered no one while climbing the three flights of stairs that brought him to his room. Shedding the coat was like shedding his armor, especially with Giovanni's money sewn in the lining. Nunzio sat on the creaky bed, and slit open his Pont package before using the switchblade to peel and core both apples. He ate with relish, plucking fruit particles from between his teeth with the blade while he studied the picture of Pietro Rocca and his family. Nunzio tried imagining how the course of several years could change a man's face. And what demon possessed this man to leave such a proud *donna è due bella bambini.*

Along with the photograph came the reminder of a second paesano who might know Pietro's whereabouts, Leo Arnetti. Nunzio felt certain that one of Butte's many miners or maybe a Galena Street whore would know this Leo Arnetti or recognize the face of Pietro Rocca. If not in Butte, then Missoula. And if not in Missoula, he would backtrack to Helena and Billings, even if it meant spending some of his own money. This he owed to Giovanni Martino.

*****

Over the next few days Nunzio concentrated on the more distant mines, waiting for the changing shifts to merge from the Berkeley, Moonlight, St. Lawrence, and Rarus. Not one man he stopped knew the face of Pietro Rocca or the name Leo Arnetti. At least the miners didn't expect money for zero information. The street whores were a different story, demanding four bits up front before they agreed to even look at the picture. None of them would admit to knowing Pietro. At night Nunzio succumbed to the brothels, doling out an additional two dollars for a carefully selected lay that provided more frustration than satisfaction. The pricey whores claimed they didn't recognize Pietro either. Nunzio had his doubts.

Then he overheard someone talking about a know-it-all at the Galleria. On his way to see this Opal, he passed an exotic beauty leaning against the window. Zinnia, the sign read. She stuck her tongue out, snaking the pink flesh in and out, just for him. Such a tantalizing *bocchinara*.

"Another time," he promised her and himself.

Chapter 16

On Wednesday Pete clocked out of The Spec, intending to catch a quick nap before supper. Instead it was Leo who caught up with him. Both of them soon became willing participants in a game of craps with three Granite Mountain miners. Several hours later and several dollars richer found them back at Adie Turner's. Aromas of supper permeated the hallway, the unmistakable scent of ham hocks and northern beans, a hardy dish Pete had resisted at first, then found almost as comforting as polenta. Taking the stairs two at a time in a race to the bathroom, both men stopped when Adie called out Pete's name.

"Somebody named Opal telephoned. Said to tell you hello."

"That's all?" Pete asked.

"Oh, yeah, excepting that she mentioned Leo too."

Pete thanked Adie and continued up to the stairs, ignoring Leo's audible sighing from behind.

"Wait a minute, Pete. You got nothing to say about Opal calling?"

"Not 'til I see her after supper."

"Supper, hell! How can you think about eating?"

"I think better on a full stomach." Pete stepped up to the toilet, unbuttoned his fly. "And an empty bladder."

"You heard what Opal said. Giovanni's Dog must be hunting me too, just 'cause I helped you. Listen, either we get out of town or we get to him first. Whadaya say?"

"I say, first we eat."

*****

After putting away two helpings of the ham and beans, sky-high lemon meringue pie, and honey-laced coffee, Pete and Leo carried their dirty dishes into the kitchen. They kept right on walking, out the back door to avoid any tagalongs. The sun disappearing into the horizon reminded Pete of sunsets spilling over the Alps. In Faiallo his children would be sleeping, Isabella stirring from her bed—her bed, not theirs. And on Main Street Leo was suggesting they visit Opal together.

"No way," Pete said. "Remember, she charges more'n double for what she considers a trio."

"Hell, we're just gonna talk."

"Talk … fuck, with Opal, it's all the same. It's about time. And time's about money."

"OK, OK. While you talk to Opal, I'll fuck Zinnia. Or Diamond. Or Garnet, who knows, maybe all three."

Pete grinned. "So Leo Arnetti thinks he can turn a hat trick, does he. That's a lot of fucking, even for a paesano."

"Shit, you just never know."

"Know what?"

"When I'll get another chance," Leo said. "You know, in case we leave town in a hurry."

Pete stopped. He put his hand on Leo's shoulder. "Hells bells, this ain't your fight. If I go, I go alone."

One more block brought Pete and Leo to the Galleria entrance. As usual they paid Stanley before heading downstairs. First stop: Zinnia, in a see-through number and leaning against her crib window. When Leo tapped the glass, she snapped to attention and opened the door. Blowing Pete a kiss from one hand, she grabbed Leo with the other.

"Leo the Lion," she said, pulling him inside. "Oh, baby. Do I have a special tail for you."

Pete moved quickly to Opal's window, only to find the curtain closed. Dammit, a wait of more than ten minutes could mean a big spender, or a down-on-his-luck gambler going for broke. Or some dago buying information. Pete paced the hall, folding two one-dollar bills into little squares while wishing he still smoked the cigarettes he'd denied himself for well over a year. He needed to steady his nerves, especially with Leo on the verge of losing his.

During Pete's first winter in Butte, a hacking cough had kept him down for a week. Time away from The Spec meant lost wages that depleted his meager savings. After the cough improved, Pete decided tobacco smoke and silicone dust could rob a man of his youth, so he gave up the cigarettes but stuck with mining, figuring a few more years underground couldn't do that much damage. Besides, when times were good, so was the money. Too bad the good times didn't last longer. Still, money that once went for smokes should've made a difference in his savings, but somehow the difference never made it to the hole in his mattress. Pissed away, just like his life.

This stranger that Leo referred to as Giovanni's Dog was chasing a man whose bones were already licked clean. As for Pete Montagna, whatever had been between Pietro Rocca and Giovanni Martino no longer mattered. For chrissake, he could hardly remember the woman's face or body, or why he'd been so taken by her. Better he should forget about ever going back. Maybe he could send for his family, as soon as he had enough money.

The door to Opal's crib swung open. It closed, leaving in the hallway a well-heeled businessman, chin dug into his pinstriped chest and a tightly woven panama pulled over his upper face. He exited through a metal door into The Underground, a labyrinth of tunnels connecting the basements of Butte's lowliest to its most prestigious. When the crib door opened again, Opal appeared, wearing a satin slip trimmed with lace.

"Well Petey, don't just stand there," she said, yanking on the strap sliding down her plump arm. "Come in and warm your cockle-doodle-do." She held his crumpled bills up to the light and clucked her tongue. "Mm, mm. These bucks look as though they been through hell."

"My landlady said you called."

"Not so fast, Petey," she said, putting the money in her bed stand drawer. She set the Baby Ben, didn't bother covering it, and reached for Pete's belt buckle.

Pete stepped back.

"Don't you want to play?" she asked.

"First we talk. Then we play if there's still time."

Opal pursed her lips into short, little kisses. She sat on the bed, patted the chenille, and Pete joined her. "Serious stuff first," she said. "I called because he came back last night, this time with a picture of Pietro Rocca and his family."

"Oh yeah, this Pietro Rocca, what'd he look like?"

"Without the mustache, somewhat like you," she said, "or for that matter, any number of other clean-shaven Eye-talians."

"You told him the California story?"

"Just like I said I would."

"He asked about Leo?"

"Only in passing. He thought The Lion might know something."

Leo the Lion, Leo the Loser—which Leo would back the California bit?

Opal put her hand on Pete's buckle again. "So what's it gonna be, Petey: chew the fat some more or have us some monkey business?"

His eyes trailed over to the clock. Seven minutes left. "Let's go for the monkey."

*****

Damn, the bocchinara's curtain was closed. Nunzio Drago squelched an impulse to kick his foot through the door. Instead, he sprayed pee against the wall and then pressed his ear to her window. From inside the crib came the throaty roar of a jungle cat, followed by a vibration of gentle purring. Nunzio put his hand in his pocket to calm his own restless critter while the feline noises grew faint and then subsided. Soon the door opened. Out came *Il Brute*, a homely *stronzo* with floppy dark hair and a *naso grande* looping down to cover his upper lip. Nunzio's competition glanced to the right before turning left toward the exit while the bocchinara rubbed her body against the crib door and purred.

She winked at him. And licked her lips, so red and moist he could almost taste them when she asked, "You come for Zinnia?"

Si, Zinnia, like the flower. Nunzio allowed himself to be led into her crib. After handing over two dollars, he took off his shirt and shoes and stepped out of his trousers. When he undid the last button on his union suit, Zinnia's eyes opened into saucers. She put one hand to her mouth and let out a gasp.

"Never have I seen such manliness," she said. "My only desire is to please you."

"Just give me what you gave the ugly one."

"Hm-m, the ugly one?" She pondered a moment.

"The one before me."

"Oh, you mean that Leo fellow."

Leo, could he be the same Leo who Giovanni said might know Pietro's whereabouts? No point in trying to catch up with Il Brute now, especially with Zinnia about to perform her magic. Nunzio had wait until after the final act to find out if the Leo who made her purr was his Leo Arnetti. Better yet, maybe this bocchinara knew Pietro Rocca.

The next ten minutes passed too fast and before they ended, Zinnia made Nunzio howl. Whether he still impressed her Nunzio could not determine. His limited experience had taught him that good whores make great actresses. Although he'd shot his wad, no fuck was good enough to deter his true mission. He handed over another two dollars to watch Zinnia bend over and wiggle into her see-through slip. After that, she straddled his ass and tickled her fingers over his back, her touch so deft, he closed his eyes and shut out the world.

No more than three minutes passed before he stirred. One eye cracked open as he spoke from the corner of his mouth. "What about the ugly one—you called him Leo."

"I did?" She leaned over and nuzzled his ear. "Oh Honey, I call lots of men Leo."

"Even those who go by other names?"

"Why sure. You know how it is. With some men I just can't help bringing out their uh, um-m ... beast."

She must like it rough. Nunzio could play rough too. Lifting his chest on powerful forearms, he let her rock against his back. He enjoyed the feeling, but not enough to forego his mission. "Get off, little flower. I have something to show you."

Zinnia slid onto the bed and propped her body on one elbow. The timer buzzed. She held out her hand. "Sorry, another two dollars, please."

He handed her the money, along with the photograph. "This man, he has family back in Italy. You ever seen him?"

Tucking the money between her thighs, she lay back to examine the picture. "Well, it's kind of hard to tell. I entertain so many handsome men."

She traced her finger over Pietro's image while Nunzio climbed into his trousers. He pulled another dollar from his pocket and added it to her nest. "Maybe you saw him with the ugly one you called Leo."

"Not so fast." She closed her eyes. "I need more time."

"How much time you need?"

"Um-m-m, about ten dollars worth."

He did some quick arithmetic in his head. "That's a lot of time. Lemme think about it."

"Sure, Honey, you have about three minutes left on the clock." With hands overhead to the brass headboard, she stretched herself into a cat preparing to snooze.

Nunzio didn't take his eyes off her while he thought about Giovanni's money and all the whores he'd paid and how many more dollars it would take to buy information that might go nowhere. Still, he had this feeling in his gut. He considered another method, one that always gave him results.

The buzzer went off and Zinnia held out her hand.

"What the hell!" he grumbled. "That was no three minutes."

"Time flies when you're having fun."

She laughed, but not Nunzio.

"The clock's rigged, you little cheat."

She stopped laughing when Nunzio snapped open his switchblade. He was on her in a flash, clamping one hand over her mouth while he held the blade tip high on her cheek and pressed down to draw a trace of crimson red. "Scream and I slice your face like Sunday's roast beef," he whispered. "*Capice?*"

Her eyelids blinked in rapid succession.

He took his hand away from her mouth, but kept the blade pressed to a face still beautiful but frozen in fear.

"For now, we forget about money, capice?"

She blinked.

"But not about time, 'cause this is the last time I'm asking. The ugly man before me, he was Leo Arnetti?"

She didn't answer.

He drew a line of blood further down her cheek, letting his blade stop at her throat.

Zinnia mouthed a silent 'yes'.

"The man in the picture, you know him?"

She gulped, forcing out another droplet of blood. "He sort of resembles Montana Pete."

"And the last time you saw this Montana Pete?"

"Tonight."

She whimpered when he cut the straps away from her slip and took back his three dollars. He put the knife and the money in his pocket and finished getting dressed. He used a washcloth to wipe the blood from her cheek and throat. "Say one word to the guy at the door, and I cut him bad. Then, I come back and do worse things to you. Capice?"

Zinnia rolled to the wall, drew her legs into her chest, and sobbed.

Propping one leg on her bed, Nunzio bent over and tied his shoe. He turned her face to his. "I can't stand to see no woman cry, not even a whore. So you better stop on your own before I make you."

She stopped, and bit her lip until it bled while he fumbled with the lace on his other shoe. He straightened up and tipped his cap to her. "For what it's worth, you're the best tail I ever had. I'm never gonna forget you or this night, and I hope you never forget me."

Back on the street Nunzio felt like a new man, strong and young and ready to complete his quest. Even the knots in his asshole had taken a break. As for Zinnia, those little nicks he gave her were nothing more than love bites that demanded respect. Before leaving Butte, he would call on her again and make her purr like she'd purred for Leo.

What follows a fuck so good it makes a man's head go dizzy? Good vino of course. Nunzio remembered an Italian place he'd tried once or twice, and decided to drop by. Who knows, a little vino, a chance to pass around the picture. He was closing in on Pietro Rocca. And when Nunzio found him, Pietro would be so grateful he'd hurry back to the family that needed him.

*****

Zinnia waited until she was certain the pervert had left the Galleria before she hurried to Opal and described her terrifying experience. The older woman listened with her tongue clucking and head shaking.

"Let me tell you, Zinnia, I grew up on a ranch near Helena. When an animal foamed at the mouth, my pappy said the only cure was putting it down, which he did with the help of my brother. And if Pappy wasn't around, it was me who helped my brother. You know what I'm saying?"

Zinnia nodded. "I sure hope somebody cures this beast before he attacks Montana Pete."

"Not to worry. I expect to see Pete within the hour." She held up his watch. "He forgot this."

From Opal's crib Zinnia hurried to the brothel's steamy laundry room where clean bed linens and towels were stacked on the tables. Wall shelves held neatly wrapped packages, waiting for fussy bachelors willing to pay top money to the Chinese woman hunched over the ironing board.

When the laundress saw Zinnia, she moved to the only chair, sat down, and patted her lap. Zinnia dropped to her knees, put her head in the woman's lap, and sobbed until her body shook. Silver stroked Zinnia's fashionable hair, so different from her own, paintbrush bristles worn in a blunt cut.

"Ma, I've been violated!" Zinnia wailed.

"The hazards of a noble profession, my daughter."

During her Galleria heyday Zinnia's mother had chosen the name Silver. By the time she turned forty, her older johns had lost their stamina and the younger ones didn't appreciate her wisdom. Silver saw the light. She exchanged her trademark silk kimonos for loose, cotton pants and a wraparound top that did little to conceal a body growing round with age. The only reminder of the life she once led—a pair of red and black cloissone earrings dangling from her stretched lobes.

"Perhaps it's time for me to consider another occupation," Zinnia said, "maybe a first marriage."

"And waste the best years of your life, nonsense."

"Then I want ... no, I deserve retribution."

First tell me what happened."

They drank ginseng tea from tiny porcelain cups and smoked cigarettes filtered through the end of ivory holders. After listening to every detail of Zinnia's story, Silver examined the wounds with a magnifying glass. "The one at your throat should disappear without a trace."

"But what about my face?"

"Perhaps with the aid of special potions," Silver said.

Tears welled in Zinnia's eyes. "And the money he took back?"

"The money is a more serious offense, one that cannot be dismissed. The perpetrator, this cowardly beast, what did he look like?"

"Sloppy for a dago, and fat. Baggy gray suit, blue work shirt, and cap. Shuffles like he has piles."

"May they multiply faster than maggots on rotting flesh." Silver made a face and spit on the floor. "And Montana Pete, you think he'll return this evening?"

"I talked to Opal before I came here. She said Montana Pete forgot the watch that once belonged to his father."

Silver checked her own timepiece, an enameled locket hanging from a neck chain. "We haven't much time, my daughter. I want you to call your Great Auntie. Right away, before the yen-yen takes over to cloud her mind. Tell her what happened. Auntie Annalee will know what to do."

"About my face, or the beast?"

"Both, but we must defer to the wisdom of age and let Auntie decide which will come first."

*****

After leaving Opal's crib, Pete caught the unmistakable odor of fresh urine in the hallway—some *caccata* behaving like a damn dog marking his territory. Outside in the foggy alley he spotted Leo, a cigarette hanging from his mouth while he warmed both hands over a barrel of burning trash.

"So what'd Opal say?" asked Leo as he squinted through eyes watering from the refuse smoke.

"Not here. I need some vino."

They walked back through the alley and had turned onto Main Street before Pete spoke. "Giovanni's Dog came back, this time with a picture of Pietro Rocca and his family."

"Shit, what about me?"

"Like I said before, this ain't your fight. It never was. The Dog thought you might know where to find Pietro."

Leo shrugged. "Hell, last I heard Pietro went to California."

At Park Street they went into an Italian bar called Uno and laid claim to the only empty table. After sharing a bottle of wine and playing a few games of Keno, Pete loosened up. So did Leo, more like his old self only quieter. No doubt Zinnia's magic had not yet worn off. Halfway through their second bottle, Pete reached into his watch pocket. "Damn! I must've left my watch at Opal's. You wanna go back with me?"

"Nah, you go on. Better we split up for a while, until that damn dog grows tired of sniffing." Leo called for another bottle of wine, sat back, and closed his eyes.

Outside, the temperature felt twenty degrees cooler. As usual, Pete pulled his hat down, his collar up, and hunched his shoulders against the mountain chill. With eyes downcast he observed each step hitting the pavement and tried not to think about his father's timepiece. Had he been watching the street instead of his feet, he would've seen the stocky man in a rumpled suit, crossing Park and heading toward Uno.

*****

Nunzio Drago stepped into the smoke belching, rambunctious Uno. Anointing such a dump with the title One insulted every decent bar throughout Northern Italy. Still, Nunzio remembered his place and behaved. He checked out the crowded counter, hoping for an empty stool where a man could sit alone, but not feel alone, where he could take a few chances on the punch cards. Penny-ante stuff yet to bring him any luck, but he never gave up. Damn, no vacancies. One look around the room changed his luck, this time for the better. Over there, alone in a corner: the homely one with dark floppy hair, and a nose looping down to his lip.

Toting two glasses and a choice bottle from California's finest grapes, Nunzio made his way to the table where Zinnia's john sat with his coat unbuttoned and tie hanging loose. "*Buona sera*, paesano. This chair, is it taken?"

Il Brute looked up through lidded eyes and with a limp gesture, invited him to sit. Nunzio poured a glass for his table companion and one for himself. They sipped slow and easy, savoring each drop.

"Good," Nunzio said, "but not so good as the vino from Piemonte."

Il Brute straightened up. "You're Piemontese?"

"Si, and you?"

"The same."

Nunzio moved his chair closer. "So, Leo Arnetti, I hear you're an honest man. Smart too."

Leo laughed. "Says you and my mama."

"Then I'm in good company." Nunzio cleared his throat and refilled their glasses. "You're looking at a paesano in need of help.

Of course, help comes with a price."

"How much?"

Keeping his bundle of tens under the table, Nunzio counted out a small stack as he watched Leo's eyes grow wider. "Uno, due, tre, quattro, cinque."

"That's a lot of help," Leo said.

Nunzio pushed the money toward Leo. "Take it."

Leo reached, hesitated, and pulled back empty-handed. "What's your game?"

"No game."

"No shit. In Butte everything's a game."

Nunzio shrugged. "You could say I'm on a mission."

"Like a priest?"

"More like a messenger." He leaned over to Leo's ear. "Giovanni Martino sent me." Leo started to get up but Nunzio stopped him with the point of his blade between two ribs. "Don't move, paesano. I can kill you now, and no one will know. 'Too much wine,' they'll say. 'Let him sleep it off'. Your blood will run like spilled wine until some poor fool takes a nosedive in it. Or, maybe a pretty bocchinara, maybe the one who pleasured you this evening.

Leo's hair stuck to his sweaty forehead. He croaked out a few whispered words. "I don't want no trouble."

"Good, then you capice. There's this friend of yours I need to find—Pietro Rocca."

"Pietro? Hell, he went to California last year."

Nunzio applied more pressure to the blade. "Look, paesano. Your shirt, it's bleeding."

"Sweet Jesus," Leo whispered.

Nunzio shoved the fifty dollars back in his pocket. "So far, me and your mama's half wrong: you ain't smart, but you still got a chance at being honest. Now, for the last time, where do I find Pietro?"

Chapter 17

While Pete walked down the Galleria hallway, he noticed a handwritten sign on Zinnia's door: *Closed for Repairs*, it said. Odd, since Zinnia never shut down during her busiest hours. Before he could consider her motives, a shrill whistle penetrated his ears: Opal at the far end, two fingers between her lips. He narrowed the distance between Opal and him with long, determined strides. She planted her usual wet kiss and he slipped her a dollar bill. "For the watch I forgot."

Opal smiled and returned the money along with his treasure. "This one's on me, Petey."

He bussed her cheek. "Thanks, Opal. I'll catch you sometime next week."

"Not so fast. I have some news—good or bad, depending on how you handle it. Leo telephoned in a state of high anxiety. He said to tell you Giovanni's dog tracked him down. According to Leo—need I say more—he fought clean and hard but still took a knife in the ribs."

"Leo's hurt bad?"

"Oh, hell, it takes more'n that to put Leo down. Anyway, he

must've been scared shitless 'cause he wasted no time telling The Dog where to find you."

Pete looked up to a ceiling of peeling paint and opened his palms. "Holy Mother of Jesus—"

"Settling this is gonna take more'n invoking help from the Blessed Virgin."

"Maybe I should stick around, explain to The Dog how this whole thing with Giovanni happened."

"You don't understand, Petey. This Dog's gone mad. He cut Zinnia too, right after you left this evening. That's how he made her finger you and Leo."

"Shit! Just because of something that happened back in Italy."

"You need to vamoose, now."

No sooner had Opal's warning left her mouth than The Underground door opened. Pete stepped back and clenched his hands into tight fists. "You!"

The Chinese youth clasped his hands together and bowed. "I am honored you remember me, Mister Round Eyes. Be assured, this encounter takes place under more favorable circumstances than our last. I am Zinnia's cousin, and at her request our Imperial Grandmother Annalee has sent me to assist you."

"You mean like the last time? Me in the gutter, with black eyes and empty pockets."

The hint of a smile crossed Zheng Choi's lips. "Do you prefer having me with you, or against you?"

"Hell, I don't know."

"Well, if you don't know, let me help you decide," Opal said, shoving Pete through the door. "In about two shakes, that damn dog will be yipping at your heels. Now go!"

Pete followed Zheng Choi through the shadowy passageway, its layout patterned after the streets overhead but with countless detours into darkness. From the low ceiling an excretion of continuous moisture made the walkway slippery and slowed their pace. Pete took shallow breaths of pungent air, similar to the pee stink hanging over The Galleria's basement, only stronger. Not so different from The Spec walkways except this hellhole wasn't nearly as deep. Still, a man could die down there; and with a sprinkle of lime, his remains would dissolve into dust.

Minutes later Nunzio passed Zinnia's crib. He didn't notice the closed curtain or the sign on her door. His eyes and mind were focused to the far end of the hall where the fat whore stood, flaunting her tits and wearing a smile he might have to wipe off her face. He moved quickly, intending to cut her down to size for giving him the runaround about Pietro, but by the time they were nose to nose, she spoke the first words.

"Well, I didn't expect to see you so soon." She leaned closer, as if to share a secret, and her voice dropped to a whisper. "Say, about that picture you showed me, the one of the Eye-talian and his family. Well, wouldn't you know, this very evening he came back. In fact, he just left a few minutes ago."

"You're lying. I woulda seen him."

"Not necessarily. Of course, if you're not interested, what do I care."

Nunzio pulled out a dollar. "So, where'd he go?"

"Keep going."

He gave her another two.

The fat one's hand didn't move until he added two more, bringing the total to five. She opened her robe, exposing the start of a bulging belly, and tucked the bills into her garter belt. "Through this door," she said, her hand encircling the knob. "And don't look so squeamish. It's nothing but a shortcut to Chinatown."

"What's a dago like him doing in Chinatown?"

"Same as any other man, I guess. They say the Annalee women have special techniques that drive men crazy. Little metal balls they stick up their you-know-what and, well—need I say more? 'Course, that's only hearsay."

"I ain't no fucking patsy," said Nunzio, his concern centered on Giovanni's money hidden in his coat lining. He started to reclaim the dollars it took for the fat one to open up, but she stepped back, out of his reach.

"Oh no you don't," she said. "You asked where the dago went. I told you, and that's the plain truth."

"OK, quit your bitching. This Annalee, how far?"

"From what my johns tell me, only a few blocks. Go through the door and turn right. Stay on the main drag 'til you see a turnoff with a flashing red light. That's China Alley. Go to the end. You can't miss Annalee's."

Nunzio cocked his head. "Shit, I ain't no fool. Why stay underground when I can go back upstairs and find my way on the street."

"Sure, if you ain't in a hurry and you don't mind paying another somebody or two, for directions. Annalee runs a private club, you know. Or, you could wait 'til tomorrow and start searching all over again. By then, the Eye-talian could be long gone." The fat one sidestepped him and started back down the hall. "Now if you'll excuse me, I have some pressing business."

Nunzio let her go because he wanted to believe Pietro was only minutes away. He listened to the heels of her backless slippers clicking against cheap linoleum patterned to resemble fancy carpet. When the clicking sound faded, he opened the metal door and ventured into near darkness. He paused to accustom himself to the rank odor and dim lights before taking a satisfying leak. He had not gone far when the sight of two men heading in his direction proved as reassuring as soldiers on night patrol passing their comrades. It reminded him of the real battle he'd fought in the Alps years before. Nunzio Drago and Giovanni Martino, side by side against the Austrians. God, he owed his life to that man.

If the fat whore told the truth, Annalee's place shouldn't be hard to find. He'd resolve this Pietro thing tonight and tomorrow he could relax. Maybe try the gambling again. Or, a Chinese whore with those little balls. Or, buy a trinket for Zinnia and tell her he was sorry. Maybe she'd let him back in.

Nunzio passed a number of cryptic turnoffs, relieved he'd not have to test his courage any sooner than necessary. At last he came to the flashing light. Looking down the passageway, he narrowed his eyes to the only visible doorway and made out the silhouette of a small man in oriental clothing. As Nunzio moved closer, he could see the Asian: old and weak and one step away from departing this world. A second man came out from the shadows. Wait, could it be His Man?

Nunzio ran toward him. "Pietro Rocca!" he called out. A clear view of the man's face told Nunzio his search had ended. "I bring a message from Giovanni Martino!" he yelled, the words choking out in a jumble as he ran faster. He fumbled in his pocket, through a mishmash of paper slips and crumpled money. When Giovanni's note eluded his grasp, he settled for what he knew best. Out came the switchblade. By now he stood four feet from the paesano. "Pietro Rocca?"

With a show of palms, this Pietro backed off, shook his head. Like the biblical Pietro who had denied Christ, this one blurted out his first lie. "You got this all wrong."

"Like hell," Nunzio said through a spew of spit. "I know you're the man in the picture, the one who deserted his family."

"My name is Pete Montagna."

"Sonofabitch! Maybe that's what you go by now, but in Italy you was Pietro Rocca."

As if by magic another person appeared, more boy than man. Nunzio would have to set him straight. He flipped open his switchblade. "Stay away 'cause I bring an important message from—"

Before Nunzio could say what he came to say, the young Chink stepped forward. He leaned over, shifting his weight on one leg while lifting the other. Nunzio started to duck but caught the blow to his left ear. He went down, his fingers still wrapped around the knife. He had to get up and cut the little bastard. That would make Pietro Rocca listen with respect. Nunzio rolled onto his knees. To his left Pietro was shouting something to the kicker that Nunzio couldn't hear due to the buzzing in his ear. To his right closed in the one so frail he looked like death—a cord stretched between his skinny hands.

Damn! Not now. Not like this. Not before he delivered the message.

"Pi-e-tro! Gi-o-van—"

Chapter 18

Zheng Choi resumed his attack stance, waiting to Pete to make the wrong move while the kneeling man struggled to hold onto the last breath Moon Lin was squeezing from his throat. Pete only wanted Giovanni's Dog to quit hounding him. But then the knife came out. And the two Chinese reacted. And even though Pete had yelled for them to stop, they seemed compelled to go on, to play out a predestined ritual.

As soon as Moon Lin loosened his stranglehold, Zheng Choi backed off. He peeled the dead man's fingers from his knife, slit the lining of his coat, and pulled out four bundles of money. The boy stood up, bowed to the old man with fingers of steel, and handed over the loot. Three bundles disappeared into the sleeves of Moon Lin's long coat. With a slight bow and extended hands, he offered Pete the fourth bundle.

Repeating his earlier gestures to the dead man, Pete shook his head and showed his palms. "No blood money for me."

"Weigh your words with care, Mister Round Eyes," Zheng Choi said. "A wise man knows when to take his leave. Yours is now or never."

Do you prefer me with you, or against you, the boy had asked before leading Pete into the tunnel. Pete knew his place. He returned a bow similar to Moon Lin's and accepted the money.

"Now if you please, Mister Round Eyes," Zheng Choi said. "Through this door, you will find stairs leading to China Alley."

Pete glanced over to the body. "But what about—"

"Do not be concerned with that which no longer concerns you. It is for my uncle and me to restore order to The Underground."

As Pete walked away, he heard a match strike. He turned to see Zheng Choi and Moon Lin burning the dead man's personal effects. What they planned for the body he didn't want to contemplate.

*****

If one good thing came from Pete's leaving Butte in a hurry, it was leaving Leo behind: a feat accomplished by stopping at Adie Turner's long enough to pack his suitcase and vamoosing before either Leo or the sun was up.

While the Northern Pacific rolled eastward, Pete stared out the coach window, seeing but not seeing the landscape that gradually transformed from mountainous high desert to lush rolling foothills, and later to flat prairie land shimmering with tall grass reflecting the sun's rays. In his private hell Pete relived the events leading up to an execution he never expected. Embedded in his brain forever would be the sight of the condemned man on his knees, crying out the last words he would ever speak: *Pietro and Giovanni.*

Book Three—Chapter 19

East St. Louis, Illinois

After a long stopover in St. Louis Pete's train chugged out of Union Station and past the sprawling French-style city hall where a gigantic thermometer registered ninety-five degrees, the hottest temperature he'd ever seen recorded. Crossing the Mississippi River on the elevated bridge, the train left a skyline of old brick and teeming commerce, of stateliness mixed with destitution as it approached Illinois. The east side of the river resembled a passed-over stepchild, one deprived of interesting architecture or character. As with Butte, both small cities bustled under a layer of industrial smoke; but in Butte, on most days he could see mountains of evergreens from all four directions and on a clear day, blue skies that seemed to embrace the entire planet. From where Pete sat, East St. Louis didn't seem capable of showing off anything majestic. But, what the hell, at least he was still breathing.

Damn, if it hadn't been for Leo and the gambling, he could've been cruising on the *Conte Biancamano* instead of the Northern Pacific. This time, nobody would hang onto Pete Montagna; nobody would keep him from getting what he wanted. He had money again, blood money. Two hundred dollars, thanks to the poor bastard dogging him until the Chinese put him down. Forget him, forget them. That's what he had to do, erase that scene like chalk from a blackboard. This time he'd be smarter. So what if he was lonely. He'd get over it. At least he wouldn't have to answer to anyone but himself. No more sharing bottles of wine or invitations for risotto and chicken. No single daughters of well-meaning friends, or nosy landladies or bitchy females. No more Leo, thank God. Only Isabella and the twins, and they'd have to wait a little longer.

*****

Pete stepped off the train, walked ten paces, and smacked headfirst into an invisible wall—the combination of heat and humidity so unforgiving it sucked the breath from deep within his lungs. His temples started throbbing. He trudged to the closest bench, loosened his tie, removed his suit coat, and sat down. While cursing the events that brought him to this inferno, a blast from the train's whistle assaulted his ears. Wait a minute—forget Illinois. He needed to chase down the lazy caboose wobbling over the track, and keep on traveling until the weather got friendlier. He jumped up, flung the coat onto his shoulder, and grabbed his suitcase. The damn thing slipped from his fingers and sent up a cloud of dust. Shit! He couldn't muster enough energy to pick it up and still run like hell. He slammed his coat to the ground, and was wiping sweat from his forehead when a fellow passenger came strolling by.

"Welcome to the Mississippi Valley and East St. Louis," the man said. He pointed to a flyer posted on the utility pole. "If you're looking for work, check that out."

National City, home of the nation's second largest stockyards, the poster read. It listed the meatpacking houses of Hunter, Armour, Swift, and Circle Packing along with convenient and inexpensive housing for working men. Pete rented the only available room on Whiskey Chute, a seedy street leading to National

City. Fourteen dollars, paid in advance, secured him a dingy second floor flophouse and shared bath with fourteen men he knew better than to trust.

"We don't serve meals and we don't allow no cooking on the premises," warned desk clerk Wilbert Hayes.

That night after sliding a beat-up chair under the doorknob, Pete opened his window wide and fell asleep to the rhythmic sounds of trains and trucks delivering cattle to the unloading sheds. In the morning he hid half the blood money under a loose floorboard and the other hundred into his work shoes before wedging his feet into the cushioned bottoms.

Downstairs, the desk clerk had his nose buried in a racing form while he swiveled on a stool. Pete waited a long minute before clearing his throat.

"So, what'll it be?" Wilbert mumbled from behind the form.

"Where can I get some coffee?"

Wilbert lowered the form to give Pete the once-over. "Outside and around the corner," he drawled, a thread of spit trickling from the side of his mouth into a three-day growth of whiskers. After rolling a wad of tobacco around his teeth, he ejected a brown stream into the tin can underneath the counter. "And if ya'll be needing a bank, try four blocks east, three blocks north."

"Shit, he don't need to go that far," said a lanky fellow holding up the wall. "Stockyard Bank's a helluva lot closer. If'n you have a mind to lighten your load, I kin show you the way."

They spoke in accents unfamiliar to Pete's ears, drawing out each syllable as if letting go required too much effort. "No mind to and no load," Pete said, unconsciously mimicking their speech patterns. "I need a job before I need a bank."

"Try Armour's. One of their guys got his head busted in."

"On the job?"

"Hell no, on the riverfront."

Digging his hands in his pockets, Pete stepped outside into a morning as stifling as the previous afternoon and headed down Whiskey Chute toward the stockyards. Contrary to what he'd admitted to minutes before, banking was his immediate concern and a constant reminder as he wiggled his cramped toes into the insulation protecting his feet from the gravel road. At nine o'clock the street blight of spilled garbage cans and cats chasing rats seemed short on human life, which added to his discomfort but only temporarily. Legitimate pain came from a board across his back and behind both knees. The attack lacked Zen Choi's graceful speed and required two bastards. The one missing part of his right forefinger held Pete down while the other cleaned out his pockets and emptied his shoes. After they ran away, Pete ached from the sting of the board but not from the loss of the money. In fact, its absence put a greater distance between him and Chinatown, which suited Pete just fine. But the shits had taken his father's timepiece, and that he could not abide. Pete rolled to his feet. He slapped his hands against his clothing, ridding himself of Whiskey Chute dust.

Before the day had ended, he found work at Armour's.

*****

Unlike mining, stuffing sausages was neither hazardous nor backbreaking. But like any job this one had certain drawbacks. In Pete's Faiallo, inflating the empty intestines of pigs with their own ground-up tissue and organs was an annual event involving family and friends and jugs of wine. As an everyday chore without socializing the same activity produced unrelenting boredom that created too much time for mulling over the life Pete should've been leading. Like the Butte crapshooter said: any man willing to work could find a job in East St. Louis. But he didn't say how dismal the place could be without friends or family. The meatpacking house employed Hungarians, Poles, Slavs, Lithuanians, and Germans—but only a few Italians and those Pete avoided. As for the other workers, he managed a friendly demeanor without making a single friend.

When Pete received his first paycheck, he strolled downtown and opened a savings account at the First National Bank on Collinsville Avenue. With his second paycheck he splurged on a Philco radio found in the window of Sam's Pawnshop. Phil, he christened the dome-shaped, wooden box. Played low each evening so as not to attract the attention of sticky-fingered neighbors, Pete's steady companion introduced him to the St. Louis Baseball Cardinals, which he followed with one ear while boning up on English by reading pages from the East St. Louis Journal. And during the day while Pete stuffed his Armour sausages, Phil kept silent under a rug-covered trapdoor made by a previous tenant.

The third paycheck sent him back to the pawnshop. This time Sam Friedman almost cracked a smile as he pulled out every small weapon from the glass case. Pete settled on a hand-carved switchblade, basing his decision on how the knife took to his palm and the speed of the blade when it snapped open. Imported from Italy, the broker said, not that Pete cared. Nor did he dwell on the last switchblade he encountered in Chinatown's Underground. Every morning and every evening he acquainted himself with his new partner: opening and closing the knife, flipping it into the worn floorboards and pitted door until its grip felt as natural as second skin.

The following Friday Pete let two meat wrappers talk him into a night on the riverfront. Freight houses and warehouses intermingled with betting parlors, saloons, and brothels along Front

Street created an atmosphere rivaling that of Butte, down to the wayward husbands cheating on their housebound wives, and payroll-flushed miners—coal instead of copper—from the outlying communities of Troy, Collinsville, and Glen Carbon. But most of the carousers primed to drop some bucks along with their pants were stockyard cattlemen: Missouri and Illinois farmers who came in trucks and wore rubber boots, swaggering cowboys who came by train and wore leather boots. Either way, their footwear came embedded with stinking manure.

Pete lost his co-workers to the gambling and pool halls while he opted instead for the nearest brothel, a place called Sweet Dreams. One glance at the pathetic stable convinced Pete he wouldn't be missing much if he never went back. No chummy whores with clever names here, only tough sluts who'd sell him out if Giovanni ever sent another dog snooping. He forked over five dollars for fifteen minutes in the company of a nameless woman with orange hair and pencil lines for eyebrows arching into question marks. During their perfunctory quickie, he caught the odor of her previous johns, something he'd never noticed on Opal and the other Galleria jewels. When Orange Hair finished on a lick and a promise, she called Pete the Eighth Wonder of the World and told him to hurry back. He replied with a half-hearted wave, and on his way out nodded out to an embarrassed German, a family man he knew from Armour's.

Across the street in the window of a brick building blue neon lights flashed the name *Mooch's*. Pete entered the dive and cut his way through dense smoke to reach the crowded bar. Unsure of the wine, he ordered beer but expected near beer, a kicked-up version of the government-approved, less than one percent alcohol swill. Instead, he got the real thing, drawn from a spigot and so cold it demanded slow enjoyment.

From the far end a voice called out, "Hey, barkeep, the hands on your wall clock ain't moved since I sat down."

"That's 'cause time stands still when you're having fun."

"Anybody got the real time?"

To his left Pete felt a slight jostle. His porky neighbor pulled out a watch, held it up to the light, and yelled, "Half past ten."

Pete's gaze followed the watch until it disappeared into Porky's vest pocket. He gave its keeper the once over: a broad-shouldered man, thirty pounds heavier and two inches taller than Pete's five feet eight inches. "Another beer," Pete told the barkeep, "and one for my friend here."

Grabbing the first of two frothy beers sliding down the polished wood, Porky lifted his glass in Pete's direction and squinted through bloodshot eyes. "Do I know you?"

"Maybe we met, but I ain't for sure," Pete said, extending his right hand for a quick shake. No missing joint. Still, this fellow could've been the one who emptied his shoes. "About that pocket watch you just pulled out—"

"What about it?"

"If RPR is engraved on the back, it belongs to me."

"Not any more. I bought this prize from a pawnshop on Collinsville Avenue. Sam's, I think."

"And I say two bastards stole the watch from me."

"Well, I have a receipt that says I ain't no thief. And another piece of paper called a birth certificate that proves John J. Gibson ain't no bastard."

"In that case, I take back what I said—about your birth."

Porky became Gibson. He emptied his glass and patted his vest pocket. "Tells real good time."

"Si, it did for me too."

"'Course, for the right price I might consider parting with the little gem."

"How much?"

"The thirty I paid, plus ten more."

"Too much."

"Too bad."

"So, you say I must buy back what was stolen from me."

"Depends on how bad you want it."

"OK, but only out of respect for my father's memory. Not here, the money's in my truck."

"You want I should step outside?" Gibson stuck his doughy face in Pete's. "Whadaya take me for. Stupid, I ain't."

"We'd both be stupid to flash money in this dump. Outside we at least have some privacy."

"Don't be fooling with me, dago, 'cause in this town I have more connections than the B & O." He sat back to suck air through his teeth.

Pete almost felt sorry for Gibson when he cracked half a smile and caved.

"Yeah, I guess a fella such as yourself might be on the up and up. Let's mosey on."

As they walked through Mooch's parking lot, Pete's hands shook until he pocketed them and rattled his room key against loose change. He stopped at the tailgate of a beat-up truck, dropped a handful of coins. "Dammit, there went my keys." He knelt down and inhaled the familiar scent of barnyard manure. "Shit, they're here someplace."

"Lemme see," Gibson said, easing down to teeter on a wobbly knee.

Pete turned sideways to execute three quick punches to Gibson's gut before Gibson clipped him over the eye. Pete grabbed the man's balls, squeezed until Gibson let out a moan and crumbled to one side. Holding his switchblade to Gibson's throat, Pete kept his voice low and tight so as not to give away his own fear. "Don't move. I only want what's rightfully mine." With one knee jammed into Gibson's back, he reached around the vest for his father's watch. "Now, how much did you pay?"

"It coulda been twenty. I ain't for sure."

Pete stood up and tossed two sawbucks on the ground. "Twenty sounds about right."

After two well-placed kicks, he left Gibson hugging his knees—a sight that gave Pete no pleasure. Before Chinatown and before Whiskey Chute, he'd not considered such violence part of his makeup. Still, he owed himself the protection of his life, his possessions, and his honor. In this case retrieving his father's watch had met two of the three conditions. When he returned to his room, he found the door unlocked, rag rug shoved aside and trapdoor wide open. He plopped down on the bed and buried his face in his hands. Losing Phil hurt almost as much as losing a close friend.

Pete slept until mid-morning. While shaving, he leaned into the mirror and for the first time noticed a two-inch cut over his eye, a souvenir from Gibson that eased Pete's guilt. After packing his belongings, he went downstairs and sliced his knife down the crease of Wilbert's racing form.

"What the ..." Wilbert said, spewing tobacco fluid over the separated reports of yesterday's results.

"Somebody broke into my room last night. My radio's gone."

"How should I know where the damn thing went?" Eyeing the knife, Wilbert attempted a weak sneer. "Besides, any fool knows radios ain't allowed here. The damn things use too much juice."

"Don't call me a fool."

"You're lucky I don't charge you extra."

"You'll be lucky if I let you live." Pete grabbed Wilbert's tie and twisted the knot against his leathery neck. "Whoever stole my radio had a key to my room."

Another crank of the knot into Wilbert's throbbing Adam's apple induced bulging eyes and a puffy face. Wilbert bleated out a denial. "Well, it weren't me."

"Well, you're in charge, ain't you?" Pete kept his voice in the same menacing pitch he used on Gibson, all the while holding the switchblade to Wilbert's startled expression. "Which means you gotta pay."

Pete left with thirty dollars, the price of a new radio. He relocated four blocks east to the St. Clair Avenue Rooming House, still a convenient walk to his meatpacking job and closer to the shopping and entertainment district on Collinsville Avenue. Compared to his Whiskey Chute residence, this humble two-story frame resembled a palace. The door to his room had a deadbolt, and the landlady promised to change the sheets every Monday. That first night the street traffic lulled him to sleep but he preferred the sound of music or baseball.

On Wednesday he set out to buy another radio, and checked out the window of Sam's Pawnshop for a good deal. He went inside where the owner greeted him with a handshake.

"You I didn't expect to see so soon," Sam said. "What can I show you?"

"That radio in the window."

"Ah-h, yes, the Philco, it came in several days ago." Sam retrieved the radio, set it on the counter. "For you, I make a special deal—twenty dollars, cash."

"I bought this radio from you last month. Somebody stole it from me on Friday."

The pawnbroker shrugged. "The merchandise comes in; it goes out. I can't remember from yesterday."

Pete showed his switchblade, snapped it open. "Do you remember this, old man?" He threw ten dollars on the counter and walked out with Phil under his arm.

*****

Pete waited until his next payday before returning to the pawnshop. This time Sam showed some respect. He even helped Pete decide on the import from Belgium: an old .380 caliber semi-automatic Bayard. Less than six inches overall and weighing a mere seventeen ounces, the handgun made a comfortable fit in his waistband. Having hunted pheasants and rabbits since his youth, Pete knew all about shotguns, but he'd never held a small pistol before. Sam had mentioned an indoor target range located in the old City Library's basement on Seventh and Broadway so that's where Pete spent his Sunday afternoons. Holding his right arm taut and steady, he would adjust his aim to the bull's eye and then pull the trigger. For hours Pete repeated the routine with the same dedication he'd employed when learning to handle his knife. After several months, he maintained a shooting accuracy of ninety percent, a feat that earned him the respect of the other sharpshooters, mostly local cops honing their own marksmanship.

*****

When January's weather plummeted to ten degrees, one of the outside sorters caught pneumonia and Pete volunteered for the job no one else wanted. The bitter cold cut through his wool-lined leather gloves and two sets of woolen union suits, but Pete didn't mind. Moving animals around outside sure beat stretching pig gut inside, or tunneling into the earth like a desperate mole.

During his first Illinois winter most of Pete's free time revolved around his immediate neighborhood. He tried putting aside his Butte years, but Adie Turner's home-cooked meals kept creeping back to water his mouth, especially after suffering the blue-plate specials Theo's Diner served, along with burning indigestion, steamy windows, and sticky countertops. After some brazen cockroach commandeered a slice of meatloaf Pete suspected of whinnying instead of mooing in a previous life, he bought a hotplate and started cooking in his room. Not cooking in the real sense, more like warming up cans of beans and pale, over-processed vegetables. Soon, rejuvenated chipped beef over greasy fried potatoes gained his acceptance, as did the salty Spam he mixed into scrambled eggs. Washed down with a decent homemade wine, most of his concoctions provided ample nourishment. After supper he read the newspaper and often fell asleep while listening to Phil play baseball or comedy or music ranging from Italian opera to jazz and piano, with George Gershwin a particular favorite.

When spring came, the pleasant weather made sorting cattle and hogs more tolerable but Pete had already set his sights higher. His savings account hadn't produced the kind of money he needed for a return to Italy in style—enough to make his family forget how long he'd been gone, and why he left. So he centered his immediate goal on Armour's best paying but not the most desirable job. He went to Marty Burke, shop foreman and controller of every union job in the plant.

"Pete Montagna, Pete Montagna." Marty repeated the name several times. Stretching out his lips to their full extension, the foreman chewed and puckered while considering the foreign sound. "You know the butchers?"

"Most of them."

"Then you know they either came from Germany or their fathers did."

"This I don't hold against them."

"That ain't what I meant. These Deutsch are damned good at what they do. In fact, the best and why they prefer keeping it all in the family. You know, a skill handed down from father to son."

"I can hold my own."

"But if they don't like you ..."

"Like I said, I can hold my own."

"All right, your name goes on the list, but you wait your turn."

"How many ahead of me?"

Marty flipped through the sheets on his clipboard. "As of now two, Alphonse Haas and Norm Schmitt."

"How long before my name comes up?"

"Who can say, six months, two years."

"Maybe never."

"It's all about attrition, in itself a lengthy process. You know, a desirable job opens up when a good man gets too old or too sick, or just plain ups and dies." Marty winked. "Or maybe, he gets caught in bed with another man's wife and has to make a quick getaway."

Pete felt a rush of blood circling the rims of his ears. He leaned over the cluttered desk, and spoke with determination. "For a shorter wait, I could pay."

"And I could lose my job. So could you. And then we'd both be outta luck. This here's a union shop, Pete. Just be patient, and learn to play the game."

Pete knew the art of playing games. On Friday evening he hitched a ride to Front Street, an area he avoided since recovering his father's watch. One thing was certain: there'd be no going back to Mooch's. Instead, he strolled over to Sweet Dreams and from the shadows he watched every man who entered the brothel. When he finally saw the right man, Pete took another five minutes before going inside. He joined three cattlemen leaning against a wall, and faked interest in the five parading whores—the youngest, maybe sixteen. The cattlemen paired off with their choices, which left the last two waiting for Pete's decision. One fussed with her hair; the other popped chewing gum.

"So, take you pick, mister. My girls ain't got all night."

Pete followed the coarse voice with his eyes. Perched on a high stool was a nearly bald woman, with smeared lip rouge and sagging breasts. She pointed to her wristwatch.

"Whatever happened to the girl with orange hair?" he asked.

"She's with a regular. For the right price, you can be her regular too."

"No thanks. I'll take my chances elsewhere." He headed toward the exit.

"Cheapskate!" the madam yelled to his back.

Within minutes, Alphonse Haas walked out of Sweet Dreams and directly into Pete's path.

"You oughta be ashamed," Pete said. "Patronizing a dump such as this is an insult to your wife. At least the Arlington Hotel women keep themselves clean."

Early Monday morning Alphonse went to Marty Burke and requested his name be withdrawn from the butcher list, at least temporarily. Something about a family matter, Alphonse said. What he did not tell Marty was the special arrangement he'd worked out with Pete Montagna. In exchange for Alphonse going to the bottom of the list, Pete promised not to tell the wife about his weekly visits to a certain carrot top.

*****

Norm Schmitt presented a more difficult challenge. The penny-pinching fart held his money tight, and, like Pete, rarely mixed with co-workers. Pete got to know Norm, but only from a distance, while learning to operate a Kodak camera he'd picked up for a song at Sam's. He also learned that the confirmed bachelor lived with his mother, and that they attended services together at Bethany Lutheran where Norm passed the offertory basket. One Sunday Pete walked two miles to the yellow brick church. He stood behind the last pew and observed the crowd of worshippers spill into the side aisles, which forced Norm to carry the collection basket out one door and to re-enter from another. The next Sunday, Pete made a second visit; but instead of joining the congregation, he wandered around the church grounds with his Kodak. He was behind a shrub when Norm came out the side door, carrying the heavy collection—a load he lightened by depositing a handful of loose change into his pocket. Snap, snap. Pete's Kodak caught him in the act. On the third Sunday, Pete stepped out from behind the bush and photographed Norm a second time. This time he approached the red-faced butcher.

The basket rattled between Norm's hands. His pocked face lost its color. Still, he went nose-to-nose with Pete, and sneered. "What's a greaser like you doing here?"

"Trying to save your soul." Pete held out the photos he'd taken the week before.

While the voices of Bethany's choir sang praises to God Almighty, Pete accepted Norm's generous offer for his top spot on the butcher list.

"Oh, and one more thing, Norm, put the change back in the collection and promise me you won't pass the basket anymore."

Chapter 20

September 1932

It was an early autumn day meant for July, a hot, sticky Friday that prompted East St. Louisans to keep their windows closed and their children indoors—whatever it took to escape air foul enough to induce spontaneous reactions from the hardiest of stomachs. Emanating from the stockyards, the lower atmosphere carried an unmistakable odor: the decaying flesh of butchered cattle deemed unworthy for human consumption. Those rejected carcasses stored in tanks waited for alkali and chemicals to speed their dissolution. For the slaughtered, the failure to render a proper decomposition epitomized their final revenge.

As with every Friday seven thousand hogs arrived by truck or by train at National City stockyards, its size surpassed only by the Chicago yards. Manure-splattered sorters grouped fifty hogs at a time into pens to grunt and squeal and wait their turn with the butchers. The wet heat reached one hundred-degree temperatures in the killing room where Pete wore nothing but a long apron over summer underwear and knee-high rubber boots, the same room where he dispatched hogs by sticking his knife into their jugular veins to bleed out the bad blood. The carcasses were then hoisted up on chains, their heads dispatched and bodies sawed in half. Pete longed for the *fare il maiale* in Faiallo, a major event each fall when they "did the pig," letting it slowly bleed to death so the meat would taste better.

For him, butchering had become as boring as sausage stuffing. But this job allowed no room for his mind to wander, not with the ever-present danger of slipping in ankle-deep blood or getting kicked by half-crazed animals. Hogs proved less predictable than simple-minded cattle. At least bovines had the decency to go down with a stun gun, or sometimes a baseball bat instead of the knife. In any case, Pete couldn't complain about the pay: enough to grow a decent bank account that still included the remaining Butte money he couldn't bring himself to spend.

His co-workers considered Pete a loner. He considered himself a man of habit. Both descriptions fit, thoroughly nurtured and well deserved. After two years dedicated to self-improvement and justifiable gratification, he still spent Sunday afternoons honing his shooting skills. Tuesday and Wednesday evenings he patronized Century Cigar Store, not for the tobacco but for the gin rummy and ticker tape results of horse races from Arlington, Pimlico, and Saratoga Springs. His betting was controlled, his winnings steady but not significant. On Thursday evenings he rode the trolley to St. Louis for the symphony or a vaudeville show, sometimes burlesque if Sally Rand and her feathers were in town. Saturday afternoons found him at the East Side's new City Library at Ninth and State Streets, returning a week's worth of books and checking out new ones, most often the classics or novels by Sinclair Lewis or Ernest Hemingway. Saturday night belonged to The Valley, the strip around Broadway and Missouri Avenue where a never-ending supply of eager prostitutes hung out. Pete usually took one of them to the Arlington, but never the same one twice.

When not pursuing pleasures, he still found time for Phil, preferring to follow the St. Louis Cardinals from the airways instead of the bleachers. One visit to the ballpark had convinced him the sport was better enjoyed in the company of friends, which he still managed to do without. Trying to understand American humor, he listened to, but never understood like Jack Benny, Fred Allen, and Eddie Cantor.

On Friday evening the Collinsville Avenue business district stayed open late and attracted shoppers from East St. Louis and the adjacent communities east of the Mississippi, all eager to spend their paychecks. Even the occasional foul air from the stockyards did not deter their patronizing the five and dime stores, upscale clothing shops, furniture stores, bars, cafes, and movie theaters air cooled with ice.

When it came to theaters, Pete preferred the Orpheum or the Majestic because they carried first-run films. He'd developed into a movie buff, escaping into a ninety-minute fantasy while surrounded by strangers he didn't have to acknowledge. On this Friday of the foul air he stopped at the Majestic, his choice based on an enticing poster of Jean Harlow, the Blonde Bombshell. Taking an end seat halfway down the center aisle, he slid down into the plush, red velvet cushion and reflected on the Majestic's elaborate walls of frescoes designed after those in Italy. The theater lights dimmed, the curtain opened, and while the previews for upcoming attractions filled the black and white screen, Pete gave way to thoughts he'd practiced avoiding.

Pete Montagna, a man on the run but going nowhere. He knew where he should be going, but for some reason the longer he stayed away, the less inclined he was to reach his destination. He'd been away from his family for over four years, two years longer than he had promised himself. If he went back now, it would not be empty-handed, but no amount of money could erase the shame of not returning sooner. The twins were nine years old, no longer babies. Did they still need him, or had they toughed it out and learned to get along on their own like he had? Riccardo and Gina had every right not to forgive him; he'd not been there to watch them grow bigger and stronger. As for Isabella, she'd always made her way better than any other woman, and most men.

The film music swelled to introduce the main attraction as Pete prepared to watch another fantasy promising humor that usually escaped his wit but made everyone else laugh. No matter, he would sit back and imagine himself romancing the celluloid blonde. Directly behind him chirped the voices of three females—too old to be girls too young for women—whispering and giggling over little secrets. Had there been another end seat, he would have moved. Instead, he slouched into the cushion. He must've fallen asleep because a light poke to his shoulder made him bolt upright. More giggles.

After the movie ended, Pete followed a line of movie patrons next door to Schroeder's Drug and Candy Emporium. Made-from-scratch candies such as caramel pralines, heavenly hash, fluffy pecan divinity, and chocolate peanut clusters perched on paper doilies in display cases tended by a plump woman dressed in white uniform, stockings, shoes, and cap. Miss Nadine, her badge said, but Pete thought of the fussbudget as an inflated marshmallow.

He took a stool at the gray marble soda fountain and ordered coffee while trying to ignore the Majestic girls giggling from a nearby booth. Rich spoiled brats, Pete determined without having seen them. Go home little girls and play with your dolls he wanted to say. Through the mirrored wall behind the counter, he observed their reflections: pretty teenagers sucking ice cream sodas through double straws and wearing the latest fashions, probably from Seidel's Apparel across the street or one of the pricey St. Louis stores. Two brunettes flanked a blonde with hair as pale as Harlow's, but not because of any bottled peroxide. This girl's features were as delicate as a budding flower, and she wore a rose-colored dress. Their eyes met in the mirror, just as his and Isabella's had often done. Embarrassed, he pulled away and ordered another coffee. The girls were laughing again, light and melodious and innocent. But now they no longer annoyed him, especially the blonde.

Pete had already ordered his third coffee when the druggist closed the pharmacy section and called it a night. Most of the customers had left too, but not the Majestic girls who switched to cherry fountain cokes. Or the two grubs lingering at the news rack, their caps pulled low over whiskered faces. The one Pete dubbed Tall Shit kept looking around while the stockier fellow flipped through magazines—with an index finger missing its first joint.

Pete walked over to the blonde and her friends. Blondie smiled as if the movie encounter had made them friends. "Well hello there, Mr. Sleepy. Won't you sit down?"

He shook his head. "You ladies should go home now, before trouble starts." His warning came too late.

Tall Shit had bolted the front door and was pulling down the shade. "Nobody move!" he yelled, prancing around with a 45-caliber revolver while Stub made a dash for the cash register.

Holding out a brown lunch bag, he snarled, "OK, candy nurse. Put the money in here,"

As she took the bag between the tips of shaking fingers, Miss Nadine screwed up her face over a smear of dried boogers clinging to the side. "Oh dear," she said, letting the bag tumble to the floor.

"What the hell!" Stubs looked to Tall Shit for direction.

"Tell her to pick the damn thing up."

"I can't, I won't," wailed Miss Nadine. "The horrid thing is contaminated."

"Contaminated?"

"Filthy, disgusting!"

"Best do like my friend says, candy nurse. He ain't one to tolerate female stupidity."

While the grubs argued with Miss Nadine, Pete moved away from the booth, dropped to the floor, and fired two shots. The first relieved Tall Shit of his weapon; the second to his leg brought him down.

Stub had already raised his hands to the ceiling. "Don't shoot, Mister. I ain't armed."

Pete walked over and smacked the butt of his gun across Stub's face. "Neither was I when you robbed me on Whiskey Chute."

"Oh-h-h, my jaw," Stub groaned while spilling tears.

Pete dug his foot in Tall Shit's ribs as he stepped over him to retrieve the stray gun. The injured man was still moaning while Pete unlocked the door and Miss Nadine clicked the telephone receiver.

Outside on the street a black Packard sedan screeched to a stop. The driver kept the motor running while his scrawny sidekick scrambled into the Emporium. "Sorry about the delay," he said to Blondie. "Me and Jackie G had a slight emergency."

"We did too," she said with a sweep of her hand to the injured men.

The tardy fellow clutched his sunken belly and took a big gulp. "You all right, Miss Fallon?"

"That man over there, he saved our lives."

"The whole ordeal was just ghastly," said one brunette.

"That's right," confirmed the other. "Ask Miss Nadine."

Miss Nadine took a deep breath that lifted her ample bosom. "Why, yes, that is correct. And I, of course, used my wits to distract the thugs, thus enabling him to disarm the gunman."

"Nevertheless, this man is an honest-to-gosh hero," the blonde said, smiling at Pete, "and everyone should know it."

"Indeed they shall," said Miss Nadine. "After calling the police, I alerted the Journal. Those street reporters relish an exciting story, especially one involving unexpected heroics."

"Come on, Miss Fallon," her scrawny protector said as he opened the door. "We better remove you and your friends from here immediately if not sooner. Connie ain't gonna like this one bit."

"Don't worry, Beans," Fallon whispered as they were leaving. "I'll cover for you and Jackie G."

Pete hurried out too. He didn't turn around when Miss Nadine called out. "Oh, Mister, aren't you going to wait for the police? Who knows, you might see your name in the newspaper. And, if you're really lucky, maybe they'll print your picture on the front page."

Chapter 21

Weeks later after Pete finished target practice he was ready to cross Ninth Street when the Packard from Schroeder's forced him back onto the sidewalk. Out hopped the ferret man who had done the piss-poor job looking after his blonde charge.

"You Pete Montagna?"

"So what if I am?"

"Mr. Latimer wants to see you."

"I don't know any Mr. Latimer."

"Ever heard of Premier Lumber?"

Pete jutted his lower lip. "Si, who hasn't."

"Well, Conrad P. Latimer owns the place," the ferret said, gulping air before crooking his face to Pete's. "Most everybody calls him Connie but that don't mean you're his friend, or that he even likes you. So don't get any ideas. By the way, I'm Beans Taggert, and don't ask how I acquired my name. Me, Connie likes." He inhaled with a snort, sucking his upper dentures to the roof of his mouth. "Anyways, that was you in Schroeder's the night it almost got robbed, right?"

"So what if I was."

"Connie's daughter happened to be there too, likewise, two of her many girlfriends."

"If you say so; I never noticed."

"Sure, you did. Everybody notices Fallon Latimer. Just don't get any ideas about her either. Anyways, Connie wants to meet you, and he don't like being disappointed." Beans opened the rear door.

Connie Latimer, a big shot with big bucks. He might fork over a few to show his thanks for Pete doing what his own men should have done. "OK, but make it quick. I don't have all afternoon." Pete climbed into the back seat. Beans slid in beside him and reached over to poke the man half-asleep at the wheel. The driver yawned and reached for the ignition switch.

"Hold your horses," Beans said. "Jackie G., meet Pete Montagna. Pete, this here's John Gibbons, otherwise known as Jackie G."

The driver shifted his body around to Pete. As the two men studied each other, their faces registered mirrored images of narrowed eyes and twitching nostrils.

"What, you two know each other?" Beans asked.

"We met before," Pete said.

"Yeah, two years ago at Mooch's." Jackie G glued his eyes to Pete's. "You even bought me a beer. And then we went outside to take care of some business."

"I changed my mind," Pete said, the muscles in his neck tightening into a vise grip. He went for the door handle just as Jackie G started the engine.

Beans moved fast as a ferret to relieve Pete of his pistol. He snorted again, gathering air for his words. "Like I said, Connie don't like being disappointed."

Turning onto Missouri Avenue, Jackie G headed east and soon left the city burdened with industrial smoke. When the houses grew sparse and open spaces turned into fields of fall crops waiting to be harvested, he let the Packard cruise at forty miles an hour. With Jackie G at the wheel and Beans with the pistol, Pete needed to resolve some issues. He tapped the driver's shoulder. "About my father's watch—"

"What the hell, Jackie G ain't one to hold a grudge. If you're OK with Connie, you're OK with me."

In that case Pete had to make damn sure he'd be OK with Connie. "So how much further—"

"Don't bother Jackie G when he's driving," Beans said. "Just relax and enjoy the ride. We get there when we get there."

If Pete got there—wherever *there* was—and no guarantee he'd ever get back

Outside, the sky had reverted to God's blue, clearer than any he'd seen since the outskirts of St. Louis two years before and the black soil of rich bottomland better than the rocky terrain he used to farm. Had the crop in Faiallo been good this year? And did Isabella ever think of him? She ought to relegate him to the past, like a widow who sheds her black and returns to the living.

Looking east, Pete caught his first glimpse of towering green, river bluffs that once held the banks of the Mississippi. The range spanning as far as the eye could see told Pete how small his world had been without access to an automobile. And how little he knew of the area beyond East St. Louis and the entertainment St. Louis offered. He needed to expand his boundaries or else move on. But first he'd see where this road led.

Jackie G slowed down at a sign hanging between two posts: *Latimer Farm*. He pulled into the long driveway, passing well-tended fields before continuing under a canopy of American Elms.

"See that hill." Beans pointed to the grassy mound elevating a two-story Dutch colonial house. "They, as in super-smart archeologists, say it's burial ground for the Cahokia Indians who lived here eons ago. Who knows, maybe their spirits still roam about."

"Yeah, well I wouldn't remind Connie of such rumors," Jackie G said. "He ain't one for superstition. Or sharing what's currently his, irregardless of who had first dibs on it. You savvy, Pete?"

"Uh-huh," Pete said, his attention centered on the impressive manor with well-designed additions jutting from either side. The lumber business must be booming.

Jackie G slowed down for two Mexican boys who hopped on the running board and rode into the loop. When the car stopped, they hopped off and Pete followed Beans up the broad porch stairs. Before they reached the front door, it opened from inside. The striking woman who guarded the entrance reminded Pete of a Russian wolfhound.

Bella Bianca! He couldn't help but stare. A closer look revealed an uncertain age betrayed by her coiffured abundance of hair turned white before its time.

Beans handled the introductions again. "Billie Creznic, meet Pete Montagna."

They gave each other the once over, neither backing down. She looked too old for Pete and judging from her noble manner, way too snooty. Maybe she belonged to somebody else. Maybe the Old Man, this Connie Latimer everybody worshipped.

"Yes, of course. Come this way, Mr. Montagna." She spoke in a flat Midwestern voice, enunciating his name from a mouth not smiling. "Connie is expecting you."

Already Pete knew she didn't like him. Maybe she considered him an intruder, wished he would go away. In that case maybe he should stay. From down the hall came the recorded words of Al Jolson singing about his Mammy, a silly contradiction since Pete had seen Jolson in St. Louis and Jolson could never pass for a Negro, even with his face blackened. The prissy bitch stopped, made a tender fist, and rapped twice on the walnut door before opening it. Jolson stopped singing, and she walked away, leaving Pete on his own.

Behind a grand desk the grand mucky-muck warmed the seat of a high back swivel chair while puffing on his grand cigar. Smoke curled up to a full head of coarse gray hair restrained with Brill Crème. He stood up to tower over Pete and extended his hand. "Connie Latimer," he said, as if there could be any doubt. He motioned Pete to the leather sofa and offered a drink from his impressive liquor supply. Wanting a clear head, Pete declined.

"So be it," Connie said. "According to my sources, several weeks ago you prevented a robbery at Schroeder's."

"How'd they know it was me?"

A slight smile crept over Connie's mouth, ending at his cigar. "Do you always carry a gun?"

"Ever since I got robbed—by the same two men at the candy shop."

"Hm-m-m. Beans said one of the crybabies had a stub finger.

Getting robbed must've been quite a hardship on your family."

"I live alone."

"So I'm told, at a boarding house on St. Clair Avenue. And for a living you butcher livestock." Connie sent up a trickle of smoke rings. "Knee deep in all that bloodletting, a nasty but necessary occupation I for one appreciate. Of course, my own start wasn't much better. I suppose that's why I sometimes lend a hand to the less fortunate."

Condescending bastard, Pete wanted to say but held his tongue and poker face while Connie nursed his drink and watched from over the glass rim, a pose similar to Leo's the day they left Faiallo. But Pete had come a long way since then.

"How old are you, twenty-five or so?"

"Thirty."

"And still a bachelor." Connie paused for a confirmation that didn't come. "So, how would you like to work for me?"

"I know a little farming."

"I already have a farmer, a damned good one. Sebastian Diaz provides an endless supply of Mexican relatives to work the fields. Did I mention the furnished cottage? Just big enough for one, you understand, no more. And, of course a car comes with the job."

Connie paused again.

For chrissake, the man said a car. Pete made a slight shift in his chair, hoping not to give away his sudden interest. Too late, Connie's eyes telegraphed an upper hand.

"I'm a busy man, Mr. Mont-Monteg-na." Connie stumbled over the name—too obvious for one who seemed otherwise smart.

"Er, do you mind if I call you Pete. That is your name, isn't it?"

"Si, Pete Mon-tan-ya."

"Then Pete, it is. And you can call me Connie."

"Si … Connie."

"I'll come right to the point. You've met Beans and Jackie G, both good men, loyal, and true; but not right for this new position. What I have in mind is a promising individual to serve as my right hand, an outsider with no obligations. Twenty-four hours a day, doing whatever I determine needs to be done."

And maybe drive the blonde around. A young girl like that needed someone to keep her out of trouble. "About the car—"

"Not to worry. There's only Billie and me. My daughter's away at school."

Pete felt his eyes glaze over. Twenty-four hours a day sounded more like marriage without the sex.

"You can start on Monday," Connie said. "I'll square things with Armour. They should have no trouble moving another ambitious man into your job. Well?"

Pete didn't answer. Giving up the butchering didn't concern him, but what about the rest: those after work pleasures that filled his waking hours and for which he answered to no one but himself, the bank account steadily growing to someday take him home.

"I'm offering you a way out, Pete, a chance to make something of yourself, to work with clean hands."

About the clean hands, Pete had his doubts. Two years in East St. Louis and the two in Butte had taught him when to spot an offer too good. He shook his head. "Maybe this isn't the job for me."

"Did I mention money? No, I thought you understood what working for Conrad Latimer meant. Double whatever you now make."

"It's not just the money. Some things I like doing on my own."

"And rightly so." Connie chomped down on his cigar. "I suppose I could give you some time off. That is, after you learn the job."

"Besides, I don't drive."

"You can learn; you learned to shoot."

"You know about that?"

"I know you could have killed that grubby thief instead of splintering his shin. I make it my business to know what goes on around here. Happenings beyond Southern Illinois may take longer but eventually I find out anything I set my mind to. So, what do you say?"

"Let me think about it."

Connie stood up. "Of course, just don't think too long, or too hard."

Chapter 22

After meeting with Connie Latimer, Pete spent the rest of the weekend considering his offer. The money sounded good. So did learning how to drive a rich man's car. But working for this rich man and dealing with the hoity-toity Billie didn't seem reason enough for Pete to give up his freedom. Not that the blond daughter stashed away like precious jewels mattered one way or the other. He could hardly remember her delicate features and the way she laughed, or how the dress she wore at Schroeder's slid over her youthful curves.

On Monday Pete was heading to the locker room when he met up with Marty Burke, a pained look on his face. "Sorry, Pete, but I'm moving you back to sorting. There's been a cutback."

"Since when? I never heard about any cutback."

"I just found out myself."

"Ah, shit! You know I'm a good worker, Marty, as good as any Deutschman."

"That you are, but this ain't about your work. You know the way it goes: last one hired, first one … well, you're not fired, just moving back to the pens 'til things pick up."

"What about Alphonse and Norm? They came after me."

"Yeah, I always wondered how that happened, them pulling back and you moving to the head of the wait list. Anyways, looks like I'll be finding something else for them too."

Pete went back to sorting animals, a job he didn't mind until his next paycheck reflected the lower salary. Giving up life's pleasures or saving less money: neither choice appealed to him. And when Alphonse and Norm were still butchering because Marty couldn't find time to transfer them, Pete knew he'd wait a long time before returning to his old job. All because of Connie Latimer, Pete's head told him to kiss Latimer off. But his gut said to take a chance. At this point what did he have to lose?

Another week passed before Pete went to the lumber company. The place buzzed with activity: stacks of fresh cut planks, trucks moving in and out, and clean sawdust underfoot instead of fresh blood. Connie kept him waiting for an hour before inviting him into his office. He kept going through a stack of work orders while Pete sat across the desk, cooling his heels. Finally, Pete made the first move. "That job, it's still open?"

"For Pete Montagna, of course, provided you can start right away."

"After I give notice to Armour's, it's only right."

"Don't bother with Armour's. I have a few connections there."

*****

The next morning Pete packed up his belongings and turned in his boarding room key. At eight o'clock he was waiting on the stoop outside when Jackie G pulled up. The back seat of the Packard made an easy adjustment to the weight of his few possessions: Phil, a carton of well-read books, and the valise he'd carried from Italy.

"Consider yourself one damn lucky stiff," Jackie G said as they drove away. "Nine years I been working for Connie—we're distant cousins, thrice removed even though kinship don't count for shit—and not once did he offer me a place to live."

"Look, I didn't ask …"

"Hell, no need to explain. Connie's a generous man, and he takes care of me in other ways. Anyhow, I got the wife and three kids, so for me that little cracker box on the farm woulda never worked. Besides, Ethelmae, she likes our Pennsylvania Avenue bungalow. Close to the Sunken Gardens, bus line and shopping, and just far enough away from the stockyards—if you get my drift." He laughed hard, easing up on the accelerator until he secured his bearings. "I'll say this: there's not a place in the whole country that holds a candle to East St. Louis."

That's for sure, Pete thought.

"But," Jackie G continued, "make no mistake about where the power behind this city lies. Not with the mayor or the commissioners or all them union bosses, but with men like Connie Latimer and a few others you probably never heard of. Two things the real bosses got in common. One is making money. The other is keeping their name outta the papers. Which is where you'll come in, leastways that's my thinking."

"How am I supposed to that?"

"It's for the boss to decide. He's tougher'n he looks so don't let those fancy French cuffs fool you." Jackie G rolled through his stop sign and around a Dodge already in the intersection. "They say Connie killed three men before his thirtieth birthday, one for each decade. But I never told you that."

"You think it's so?"

"What I think don't matter one iota. I'm not paid to think. I do my job and don't ask questions."

"Anything else I should know?"

"Yeah, for sure don't ever lie to Connie. No matter how bad the truth is. Somehow he always finds out, and then there's real hell to pay."

*****

Hester Dempsey introduced herself to Pete by way of a little curtsy and told him she'd just finished with her cleaning. "I do hope everything's to your satisfaction."

Embarrassed for her demeaning manner, Pete turned away and muttered, "Grazie."

She waited, mop and bucket in hand while he surveyed his new place.

Neither Connie nor Jackie G had underrated its size or simplicity. The pot-bellied stove provided winter warmth and two cooking burners. A single bed pushed against the wall made room for other castoffs: an oak table and two straight backs, soapstone sink, icebox, club chair, floor lamp, and chifforobe. Velvet drapery from another decade, maybe another century, separated the lean-to containing a wood-fed water heater, pedestal basin, flush toilet, and open shower with wooden slats over the dirt floor. Not the Ritz or the Latimer house, but the private bath made it better than any place he had lived in since coming to America. Even his house in Faiallo had no indoor plumbing, which he planned to correct on his return, that is, if Isabella agreed.

"I reside in the big house," Hester said, "in a room every bit as nice as this and with me own water closet, thanks to Willajenka, that's Billie's given name but don't let on I told you. She was named for her ma, otherwise known as Big Willajenka."

"Willajenka? What kind of name is that?"

"Croation, maybe, I'm not for sure; I could be wrong. Anyways, it was Billie who hired me; Billie who insisted on nothing but the best for me. I was, still am, a friend of her mother, you know ... no, I guess you wouldn't know. Big Willajenka's a saint, if ever there was. Seven o'clock Mass every Sunday, the rest of the week on her knees cleaning the tile floors at City Hall." Hester paused to catch her breath. "So, if you'll not be needing anything else ..."

"Grazie," Pete repeated, "nothing."

"In that case, I'll resume my regular duties." Backing out of the doorway, she stopped and tapped her mouth. "Well forever more, I almost forgot the most important thing. As soon as you settle in, you're supposed to come up to the big house. Billie said so."

"I thought I worked for Mr. Latimer?"

"Oh, lordy, make no mistake, you most certainly do, but didn't nobody tell you about Billie? She runs the Latimer Farm and household. And, just about everything else, 'cepting maybe the lumber company. About the supper club, I ain't for sure."

"There's a daughter?"

"That would be Fallon, Connie's girl. Billie's too, but not hers from birth. The real ma came from money. Premier Lumber belonged to Alma Crenshaw's pa until he died, passing it on to Alma's husband, Connie Latimer. Then Alma died from a bleeding of the brain, leaving Connie a broken man until Billie picked up the pieces. Another saint, I tell you, caring for that child since she was a toddler. Almost grown up now and studying at a Sacred Heart convent in Indiana, Fallon is, bless her heart. She made such a fuss about leaving in her senior year, what with all her friends here and nobody worth knowing there." Hester looked around to make sure no one was within earshot. "Them two might be running Fallon's life now, but in a couple more years she'll be flapping her wings. She's a de-e-light, that one, with a mind of her own."

*****

As soon as Pete walked into the Latimer breakfast room, Billie ordered him to sit across the table from her. He couldn't tell if Hester had her ear bent to the closed door but she did appear with two pilsners of beer, cold and refreshing even though the balmy weather didn't warrant a lady such as Billie drinking before noon. He expected a tea drinker but La Bianca handled her beer with grace. She still had an air about her but didn't seem as snooty as his first impression. Maybe he'd also mistaken her face, pretty and unlined, with years to go before catching up with the remarkable hair. She wore an expensive dress made to look simple with its lace collar, puffed sleeves, and buttons down the front. Listening to her speak for Connie, mouthing orders as to what Pete could do and could not do, wore on his nerves like fingernails over blackboard.

"Breakfast with Connie at eight. Plan each day and evening around Connie's. Do whatever Connie asks. Don't question Connie's authority. Supper with Connie at seven—unless he disinvites you, in which case do not be offended."

To offset what he couldn't afford to let fester, he tried imaging her naked. Ah-h-h. Somewhere under that hard veneer was the flesh and blood of a real woman. Carry on, *Venus de Est Santo Luigi*.

"Dress at all times like the gentleman Connie expects you to pass yourself as. Avoid using hackneyed slang and foreign phrases. Don't ever discuss Connie's business affairs with anyone, except me, of course.

All Pete heard was, *"Blah-blah-blah-blah-blah."*

"Do I make myself clear?" she asked after the litany ended.

"Si," he said, putting her clothes back on.

"Not 'si.' Discipline yourself to say 'yes.' After all, you've been in America long enough."

"Long enough for what?" he asked, tired of her harping.

"Long enough to have been elsewhere before you came to East St. Louis. I know very little about you, Pete Montagna, and not enough to pass a fair judgment, at least not yet. It's up to you to prove yourself." With shoulders squared, she fixed her eyes on him. "Now tell me your morning schedule."

Don't make an enemy of her. Pete left her clothes on and returned her gaze, hoping to locate some degree of softness behind those violet eyes. Finding none, he forced a pleasant voice. "The first thing I gotta do is practice driving."

"I *have* to do," she corrected him. "Jackie G will get you started. Let him suggest where to eat lunch, but you are to pay for his and yours. The same applies whenever you're with Beans."

"I don't understand."

"Had you been listening to my earlier instructions, you would have. As Connie's right hand man, you're expected to pay since you'll be earning more money. Don't worry. Connie will make it up to you. This afternoon Jackie G will take you to Seidel's. Get three new suits, six dress shirts—white and pinstriped. Five ties—nothing garish. And two pairs of black leather shoes, one patent, of course. Charge everything to Conrad Latimer's account." She stood up, just as Connie had done when he ran out of steam. "We dine promptly at seven. Don't be late."

*****

Pete's first driving lesson began on a deserted country road in St. Clair County and came easy to him. He sat behind the wheel of one of two Packards Jackie G was responsible for maintaining along with the rest of Connie's garage: a Ford roadster Billie tooled around in and two Studebaker pickups for Sebastian Diaz and his farm crew.

"Doing good," Jackie G said from his shotgun position, "but you got a ways to go before you're good enough to drive for Connie 'cause he's always in a hurry."

"I'm gonna be a driver?"

"That's what Billie said, leastways at the beginning. You'll switch off with Beans."

"What about you?"

"What the hell, I don't mind giving up some work hours. The wife, she's on her high horse again, making threats about throwing me out if I don't spend more time at home. For her it ain't enough that I warm her toes by three every morning and then breakfast with the kids. Now she expects one or two evenings and Sunday morning Mass."

Pete let him rattle on. Had Jackie G asked for advice instead of giving it, he might've told him to enjoy his family today because tomorrow could change everything.

"Now you take Beans. With him it's different," Jackie G said. "He lives with his ma. Like all good mothers, Ma Taggert does his laundry and fixes what few meals he eats at home. What's more, there's no demanding family tying him down, keeping him from doing a decent job."

"Except for driving Connie around, just what does Beans do?"

"Cleans up mostly, like a sweeper. Not that he dirties his hands all that often, you understand. But he knows who to tap for the messy assignments."

After Pete had practiced for an hour on the back roads, Jackie G took over the wheel and picked up a highway. "You need to see Connie's roadhouse, Club One Eleven," he said. "A mere fifteen miles from Connie's manor, and conveniently located outside the jurisdiction of East St. Louis, you know what I mean? Good."

Nestled in a clump of weeping willows between Illinois State Routes 40 and 111, Connie's One Eleven overlooked the eastern leg of Horseshoe Lake. From a distance the building with its wrap-around screened porch, stone chimney, and cedar shake siding resembled a sprawling lake house designed for easy living.

"Nice," Pete said. "How's the fishing?"

Jackie G laughed. "Depends on what you wanna catch. You name it; we got it—gambling, whores and booze—first class all the way. Just wait 'til you get a load of this little gold mine at night." He pointed toward a clump of trees. "Behind them, there's another treasure, a warehouse full of liquor brought in from Canada."

He glanced at a watch pricier than the one Pete had reclaimed, and said, "We better hit the city. I'm starving."

*****

At Blue's Chili Parlor on Broadway Pete didn't object to Jackie G picking a table near the entrance. Nor did he object to Jackie G ordering for both of them: bowls of thick, meaty chili with plenty of saltine crackers. Between slurps, Jackie G managed a wave or nod at every man glancing in his direction.

"Cops and union bosses make Blue's every Tuesday," Jackie G said. "Myself, I don't come that often, especially if me and Beans are working together. In case you didn't notice, he's afflicted with a stomach problem: too many chili beans and bingo, he's whistling 'Dixie'."

"Whistling what?"

"You know: tooting, passing gas, or whatever guys like you call it."

"What do you mean: guys like me?"

"You know, Eye-talians. Your kind generally keeps to the coal mining towns northeast of here. Not that I figure you as the mining type." Jackie G scraped the bottom of his double-order bowl and smacked his lips. "Blue makes the best chili on either side of the river, irregardless of what they say."

"I don't know, what do they say?"

Jackie G leaned across the table and lowered his voice. "That Blue uses dog food in place of beef. That he's got cases of canned horse meat locked away in his kitchen. Every so often he replenishes his stock."

The horse meat Pete could understand, having eaten it in Italy which is not to say he liked it. But dog food, no way. He pushed aside the remaining half of his chili. "I ain't so hungry anymore."

The laugh Jackie G snorted expelled chili through his nose. "Hell, Pete, don't pay no never mind to what I just said. The stuff's good eating, and that's what counts."

Pete picked up the tab, and when they walked outside, he spoke from over his shoulder. "I'm going to Seidel's and don't need to see you before five."

"You want I should drive you?"

"Nah, I need to work off that chili," he said, pleased with Jackie G's quick acceptance of his first directive.

As soon as Pete walked into Seidel's men's department, a spit and polished salesman welcomed him with a broad smile. "Ah, Mr. Montagna," he said, surveying Pete's frame. "I've been expecting you. May I make a few suggestions from our better line?"

"I like picking my own clothes."

"Yes, of course, but Miss Creznic called. She asked that I offer my expertise. Of course, if you'd rather not—"

"Yeah, OK. Let's see what you have."

Miss Creznic, Pete preferred La Bianca. She wouldn't be satisfied until she stuck her nose in his underwear. Dress like the gentleman Connie expects you to be, *humph!* To Pete's surprise he agreed to everything the salesman brought out, all of which surpassed anything he would've selected for himself. In the fitting area, he fastened his eyes to the full-length mirror while a slender man in rolled up sleeves wielded his chalk, nipping and tucking the blue serge double-breasted to fit Pete's frame. When the tailor started repeating his movements on the gray gabardine, Pete checked his watch, plenty of time for an Arlington quickie.

"That does it," the tailor said as he got off his knees. "If all goes well, your suits should be ready by the end of the week."

"How about one suit before five o'clock today?"

"Impossible. I have a stack of alterations ahead of your

"That's too bad 'cause I'm having dinner with Connie Latimer."

"But of course, Mr. Montagna" he said with an ingratiating smile. "We mustn't disappoint Connie Latimer."

*****

On their way back to the farm Pete listened with one ear to Jackie G's patter without absorbing the words or offering any commentary. He had digested enough for one day: La Bianco and her directives, learning to drive and learning to boss, new sleeping digs and new clothes. Sticking animals had been hard work but not as tiring as transforming into another new man. When Pete arrived at the cottage, he shaved his five o'clock shadow and took a cold shower. Wrapped in a thick towel, he fell across the bed for some shuteye. Later, he awoke to Hester pounding on the door and a room gone shadowy with the approaching sunset.

"Pete! You in there?" she called out. "It's ten to seven, and Connie don't like to be kept waiting."

Already he felt the tight squeeze of giving up his evening. He used six minutes to slip into a new shirt and the gabardine suit, comb his hair and hurry out the door. He lost another minute going back for his just-in-case arsenal before running across the field.

When he arrived at the back door, Hester yelled for him to enter. She was leaning over a multi-tiered cake, swirling mounds of creamy white icing. "Hurry, Pete. God forbid, you don't want to make him mad, not on your first day."

The grandfather clock started bonging from the hallway. Pete straightened his tie and walked into the dining room just as Connie and Billie were about to sit down. The Kingpin wore a tailored business suit and diamond studded onyx cufflinks. Cranberry crepe accented his lady's pale skin.

"Ah, a man of promptness," Connie said of Pete but not directly to him, "however, an arrival earlier than the appointed time does signify respect and a certain commitment."

"Mia … I'm sorry," said Pete, altering his language to accommodate earlier instructions from La Bianca. "I did not want to impose myself."

"Should you ever do so, I'll be the first to let you know. Now please." He motioned Pete to his right and held the chair to his left for their female companion. "So tell us, Billie, what's on tonight's menu?"

"We start with fois gras," she said with a smile meant for Connie and the first Pete had observed from her lips. "Followed by a clear beef broth garnished with chives. Then roasted chicken and from the garden: new potatoes, tomatoes, and green beans. For dessert the Waldorf's very own recipe for devil's food cake."

"Billie has the touch of a gourmet." Connie patted her slender hand. "She works wonders in the kitchen."

And elsewhere, no doubt, Jackie G had hinted to a shady past. While nodding and smiling on cue, Pete endured the evening with thoughts of cool bed sheets and a soft pillow until Hester brought out slices of cake as red as Billie's dress. About the Latimer food, he could find no fault. Old-fashioned American to the core—in spite of the crackers and goose liver disguised as fancy French. And not a trace of the Old World reminded him of his former life.

The end of dinner came with a swift brush of white linen across Connie's mouth. He stood up with a look that told Pete he should do the same. "I'm ready for the club. Unfortunately, I gave Beans a special assignment right before Jackie G came down with some intestinal disorder."

Billie smiled. "He must've talked Pete into chili at Blues."

"So, Pete, are you up to taking over the wheel yet?"

"I, er …" Pete stammered as he tried avoiding Billie's glare.

"Wel-l, according to Jackie G, Pete did quite well," she said. "But perhaps it is a little too soon. Now Connie, if you don't feel up to driving yourself, I suppose I could do the honors."

"Wouldn't hear of it," Connie said. "As busy as your days are, you need time to relax."

The room went silent. And Pete abandoned his plans for an early night. Those two were playing him like cats pawing a worn-out mouse. Thank God Jackie G had explained how to switch on the Packard's headlights.

"Well, Pete, can I count on you?"

"No problem. I can do it."

*****

With The Kingpin enthroned in the back seat like carriage royalty, Pete slid onto the driver's seat, adjusted the mirrors, and turned the ignition key. He shifted into first and let the wheel glide through his palms to follow the driveway curve.

Who were they trying to kid? One short lesson and already the driving job belonged to him. Pete needed to play it smart, smarter than either Connie or Billie if he didn't want them pushing him around. He'd make time his best ally. Hang on for a year or so and earn enough money to hold his head high when he finally went home.

Night driving, at first the approaching headlights seemed more like the gaping eyes of nocturnal creatures. Relieved for the light traffic, Pete let the speedometer hover around thirty-five. From behind came the sound of Connie's fingers drumming on the armrest.

"How about injecting some extra oomph," Connie said. "A

higher speed would cushion the bumps and ruts fouling this damn county road."

"Sure thing, Connie."

"At night a smooth ride sets my mood for One Eleven. And in the morning I need a level field to plan my lumber day. It's all about time, Pete, and time is money." Connie slumped down and tipped his fedora.

Pete pushed the needle to forty-five, and hoped he wouldn't have to deal with passing any cars. Connie didn't move so much as a muscle when he called out again, his voice bordering between edgy and groggy. "Dammit Pete, if I have to do your job, I can't do mine. For now it's only a cat nap I need."

Pete held his foot to the accelerator; the speedometer registered an easy climb to sixty miles per hour. At that rate it didn't take long to catch the taillights of a slowpoke up ahead. Gripping the steering wheel, Pete hunched his shoulders, eased into the left lane, and made an effortless pass. As soon as he cleared the vehicle, a red light spun from its top and a siren went off. Pete slowed down and edged over to the side of the road, as did the other car. A uniformed cop got out and sauntered over with his right hand poised on the revolver butt jutting from his holster.

"You in a hurry, Buddy?"

"Yes sir, but not for myself," Pete said, "for Connie Latimer in the back seat."

"Evening, Duncan," Connie said from behind the glow of his cigar.

Duncan tipped his hat. "Evening, Connie. New driver, I see."

"That he is, and from now on you'll see him on a regular basis.

Orville Duncan, meet Pete Montagna."

After a token exchange of nods, the cop mumbled something about driving with care before he turned away. Pete followed him through the rearview mirror, waiting for the patrol car to pull out first. Before that happened Connie leaned forward, his hot breath all but singeing the back of Pete's neck. "Dammit, just take off and resume whatever speed you were going. We're running late."

"What about—"

"Duncan? The deputy did what I pay him to do. He pulled us over because he knew my car, but not you. Now he does, so move on."

At ten o'clock Pete made his final approach to One Eleven. How different the setting looked from when he first saw it. Same house, same porch, but now the lights inside were low and the music blared, and no doubt money flowed like water over rocks. In the crowded parking lot late model cars occupied the prime spaces, all except for one near the front marked 'private' that Connie told him to take.

Pete got out, hurried around the car, and opened Connie's door, not because he wanted to but because Jackie G had said certain duties came with the job. After four years in America Pete wanted to believe he'd moved beyond kowtowing, but money still talked louder than pride. Through a symphony of croaking bullfrogs and stridulating katydids and crunching gravel, they circled around to the lakefront while Connie batted at a squadron of mosquitoes the size of grasshoppers, buzzing like ace pilots fighting for control of the still air.

"I'm sure you know that in nature, every creature has its place," Connie said, "even these damn pests. More important than serving as tasty morsels for the birds, they keep my customers at bay, inside and spending money."

Pete caught the faint odor of expelled stomach gas before he saw Beans huddled on the porch steps, amidst a little pile of crimped Tums wrappers.

"Been waiting long?" Connie asked Beans.

"What the hell, I don't mind. Out here the world's kinda peaceful."

Pete followed them inside to an unmarked door and office unworthy of Connie's stature. The small yet functional space contained a large roll top desk, green banker's lamp, filing cabinets, swivel chair, and several oak chairs. An enlarged aerial photograph taking up most of one wall caught Pete's attention.

"That's St. Clair and Madison Counties," Connie said, "a broad perspective of my extended home."

More like his little kingdom.

Connie played host: scotch for himself, beer for Pete, and nothing for Beans, who declined without an explanation. Before sampling his scotch, Connie sat down and swiveled to the rusty tune of a pin needing oil. "So, Beans, about that personnel problem?"

"No more sticky fingers, no more shorted registers." Beans unrolled a length of butcher's paper soaked with blood.

Pete steeled himself to look at the first joint of a severed finger. *Christo!* For this Connie hired him, to be his butcher? A bastard like this must have his share of enemies. No wonder he sent the daughter away.

"A most unpleasant reprimand," Connie said, "but sometimes the only way to maintain honesty and integrity within the ranks.

Wouldn't you agree, Pete?"

"I'm not so sure the guy missing his fingertip would."

Connie laughed. "Well said, and without the blubbering of a yes man."

"More to the point, Connie, I didn't give up animal butchering for this. What's more, I don't have the makings for a patsy."

"Patsy? I should hope not. Any man working for Connie Latimer sets his own boundaries on morality. Right, Beans?"

"Right, Connie. And just so you know, Pete, I don't butcher either. But I ain't above giving the job to somebody who can use the money. See, I got certain connections—"

"So keep them to yourself."

"Gentlemen, please. Agree to disagree on your time, not mine. Beans, you show Pete around. I have some work to do."

For the next two hours Pete let Beans introduce him as Connie's personal assistant, a title that carried some respect judging from the way employees accepted him. The men offered crooked smiles as they looked up from their duties: mostly dealing cards or tending bar or grilling meat; and those with free hands, shook his. He met the women too. Some he recognized from the Arlington.

"Connie don't want you fraternizing with any pussy on his payroll," Beans said. "That goes for the whores or the waitresses. What you do on your own time is your business, just not with his girls."

"About my own time …"

"Hell, you just started." Beans clicked his dentures. "Don't worry, you'll get time off. But first you learn the job."

The setup in One Eleven's back room reminded Pete of Honey's: blackjack, poker, and roulette tables. But instead of Keno, Connie supplied horseracing tickertapes. Compared to the Montana crowd the Illinois patrons looked snappier, all gussied up for a special night out. Highballs and other mixed drinks were favored over beer. The only wine, a chilled syrupy Mogendavid, assaulted Pete's senses after one sip so he stuck with a single beer.

When Beans made his second dash to the restroom, Pete wandered back into the supper club area, which featured Dixieland jazz from across the river. The quintet of black musicians played non-stop and avoided direct contact with the patrons, although every so often they took turns slipping outside for a leak and more fortifying booze. The waitresses looked young and, considering their short skirts and high heels, like they belonged in a chorus line. With the energy of early-stage marathon dancers, they hustled back and forth, supplying a continual run of alcoholic beverages along with thick steaks and pork chops—direct from the stockyards and served with potato croquettes, creamed peas, baby onions, and spicy applesauce. Desserts were popular but limited to warm fruit pies with flaky crusts made from lard and topped with vanilla ice cream.

A perky brunette hurried by, balancing a shoulder-high tray of dirty dishes on her palm. She winked and with a show of perfect teeth, asked, "Later?"

"Never," Pete said. No point in rocking Connie's tight little ship. Women he could get anywhere.

By midnight Beans had developed a full-blown case of diarrhea so he went home as soon as Connie emerged from his office. The Kingpin pandered to his customers, starting in the backroom and working around to the supper club as he nodded and exchanged first names. Clearly, Connie at One Eleven was Connie at his best, the benevolent host allowing his subjects the chance to rub shoulders with the sweetness of success by default.

Another hour passed before Pete caught a look from The Kingpin, one that said his show had run out of steam. Two beefy bouncers guarding the entrance all but genuflected when their boss went out the door. To Pete they gave an OK nod. And a queasy feeling as he recalled an adage from Zia Theresa: always leave by the same door you entered.

Outside a bevy of moths danced around the porch lights, unaware the yellow glass bulbs were supposed to deter them, while further out fireflies blinked their tails above the flat roofs of cars. Pete was bushed. He didn't want to think about breakfast with Connie, less than seven hours away. Damn! When did the man find time to sleep, or make love to La Bianca?

As Pete approached the Packard with Connie, two men in their early forties stepped out from behind a parked car. One carried a hatchet and a ragged two by four. The other had his right arm supported by a sling and his index finger wrapped in blood-soaked gauze, swinging a tire chain in his left hand as he yelled, "Connie Latimer, you no-good slimy sonofabitch!"

Connie made a fluid transition, shedding his respectable facade to adapt the stance of a street fighter. "Thief! Count yourself lucky to lose no more than a fingertip. Now go home to mama, crybaby."

"Not before I take a piece of you with me."

The hatchet man moved forward, and yelled, "Open wide for a taste of your own medicine."

Pete couldn't wait any longer for the guards who did a disappearing act. With one swift movement he clicked open his knife, sending it through the air and directly into the arm of hatchet man who dissolved into a whimper. Pete had his pistol drawn and ready to fire when Connie grabbed the one-armed bandit's injured finger and began twisting. Agonizing screams brought Connie's two bouncers in a flash, too late for the rescue but just in time for the cleanup.

"Get them out of here—now," Connie growled as he brushed off his clothes. "And boys, make sure I don't read about this little scuffle in tomorrow's Journal."

On the return trip Pete felt more at home behind the wheel. He opened the car up to sixty miles, taking charge of the road with no coaxing from the backseat. Connie must've liked the feeling too because the only sound Pete heard besides the humming motor was that of gentle z-z-s. Like Jackie G said earlier, there's more to Connie than French cuffs. Still, Pete didn't know if he liked the dirty fighter, or how long he'd want to put up with the phony shit.

When they pulled into the mansion's driveway, Connie came back to life with a snort. "So, Pete, about the parking lot incident …"

"You're asking me?"

"Just for an opinion," Connie said, "not an infallible proclamation."

"In that case, I'd get new bouncers or some outside men, maybe both."

"My sentiments, exactly, I knew I made the right choice when I hired you."

*****

Pete's stint as chauffeur lasted three months before Connie

relinquished the duties to Jackie G, who claimed he needed extra money and more time away from Edna. "It was the wife's idea," he told Pete with a wink. "She said twice-a-day whoopee cramped her bridge games."

"She told the truth?"

"Hell, yes. With the kids in school and me at work, she'd been playing cards almost every afternoon."

"That's not what I meant."

"Lemme tell you how things work, Pete. The only way I was ever gonna regain some of my freedom was to nibble away at hers. Women, you gotta know the score to beat them at their own game. Those ever-lovin' broads would wanna rule the world if we gave 'em half a chance."

Chapter 23

July 1935

Moving up fit Pete with as much comfort as the tailored suits he could now afford, and he liked the feeling both provided. He'd been managing One Eleven for eighteen months, a promotion that coincided with the Repeal of Prohibition. Not that he had complete control of the show; Connie still ran the overall operation, and Billie still ran Connie. But from two in the afternoon until Connie showed up around ten, Pete ran the club and its subsidiaries with no help from The Kingpin or La Bianca.

"Remember, Pete, with power comes responsibility," Connie had said when he first offered him the position. "Are you up to the task?"

Pete welcomed legitimate responsibilities that beat the hell out of tagalong errand boy. As club manager he stayed at One Eleven until it closed at three in the morning, and he rarely got up before nine, which ruled out the breakfast routine with The Kingpin. Working for Connie took up most of his life, and sometimes the only escape was to his new bed, the only piece of furniture he'd replaced since moving into the cottage, and with good reason. The four walls and lean-to offered little more than a place to sleep, shit, shower, and shave. And, change into clean clothes. But then he had changed too—into a polished, hardnosed businessman.

Overall, he liked the new man he'd become, a man who could go back to Italy with his head held high, whenever he felt the time was right and if Connie could spare him. And when he did go, he knew he'd have to come back—with or without Pietro's family. Life in America offered too many opportunities. Granted, he'd not developed any new enterprises, but he did manage to hold on to what Connie had started and to keep it flourishing, in spite of the repeal that took away the pleasure of flaunting unpopular laws. Still, local law enforcement and politicians demanded their dues for the numbers games, parlor betting, prostitution, and fixing races. Managing Connie's money had become Pete's number one priority, and with good reason. In less than two years his salary had doubled, along with his savings.

At the club Pete called all the customers and employees by their given names, the personal touch a crowd pleaser he'd picked up from Connie, and further exploited by expressing interest in their lives without getting suckered into their problems. What the workers thought of Pete gave him little concern, as long as they treated him with respect and kept their hands out of the till. He kept his hands clean too, by leaving retribution in the hands of Beans, who still struggled with ailments he called colitis.

*****

Pete waited for Connie's new Packard to exit onto the main road before he strolled over to the big house where Hester kept the coffee hot in the kitchen. She'd left a note about going shopping and that Billie wanted to see him. After two cups and dry wheat toast, he wandered down the hall to indulge his reading habit. The fiction section of Connie's library represented a balanced mix of the classics and newly published, including a few autographed first editions. But to Pete's knowledge, The Kingpin seldom cracked a book for the sheer joy of reading. Newspapers and financial reports remained his forte.

Pete stopped short of the entrance when he saw La Bianca inside, her back turned to him as she played librarian, running her fingers over leather-bound spines, pretending to search for a particular book. He allowed himself a prolonged view of Billie's backside, an unapproachable pose he figured she engineered at his expense. After a long minute he cleared his throat to break the silence. "Buon giorno, Billie."

Instead of turning around, she raised and lowered her shoulders in cadence with an impatient sigh. "Now Pete, after nearly three years must you still use that damn Italian greeting."

"I don't always."

"So I've noticed, only when Connie's not around."

"Don't be so sure," he said, anything to stir up some jealousy, to remind her of the bond that had developed between him and The Kingpin.

"You wanted to see me?" he asked.

"Just checking on the cottage's leaky roof."

"Sebastian had one of the field hands repair it last week."

"Of course, I must have forgotten. By the way, Connie called to say he's giving you the night off. He plans on going to the club early to entertain the mayor."

"Connie gave you the night off too?"

"I do whatever I please, with or without Connie's permission."

Their eyes locked, which gave Pete enough confidence to make the first move. Putting one finger to her lips, he felt them quiver, just a little. Perhaps the ice queen could be made to melt, just a little. "We have the place to ourselves. Jackie G took Hester shopping."

"And why should I care what Hester thinks? Without me, she'd be peddling apples on the corner of Collinsville and Missouri Avenues."

"Ah-h, and in return you have her everlasting loyalty."

"Are you mocking me?"

"My apologies, Billie. You've been good to Hester. And to me." Anything to soften her up. "How can I thank you?"

"Like a gentleman."

"I would be gentle." He kissed the inside of her wrist where her pulse throbbed.

She returned the kiss with one to his forehead, in a way that further expanded the ten or so years between their ages. "Your offer flatters me, but not enough to allow even one isolated moment of intimacy."

"Perhaps another time?"

"Highly unlikely." She turned around to search the shelves again.

"Can I help you find something?" he asked.

"You help me? Please, it was I who selected and personally catalogued almost every book on these shelves."

Pete wanted to add 'with Connie's money.' Instead, he picked up a Sinclair Lewis novel and flipped to his marker. Her face softened, obliging him to make peace. "So what's your favorite?" he asked.

"Is this some kind of test?"

"Just friendly conversation, I like to read and thought maybe you did too."

"Not today. Fallon's coming home this afternoon and I have lots to do before then." Turning on her heels, Billie left empty-handed.

Thanks to an endless supply of scuttlebutt, Pete knew her and Connie better than they knew him. What a team, married in every way except on paper. Connie, the oldest of five, never made it past eighth grade. He started out on the loading docks and the rail yards before working his way up Premier Lumber's ladder. Billie, an only child raised in poverty, worked her way up from vaudeville and burlesque to bawdy houses specializing in knickered boys on the verge of leaving puberty. Even now she passed herself off as a former tutor to the wealthy.

Enough with Billie and Connie, Pete let his thoughts drift to Fallon. He'd only seen her twice since Connie hired him. She was her father's daughter, all right, that same self-effacing manner when she first introduced herself to him as 'the invisible Fallon,' as if anyone could ever overlook her presence. On her next visit home, Fallon suggested they get better acquainted. Pete wasn't about to start something he couldn't stop, especially when she accused him of being afraid of her. She reminded him of Billie, sending out just enough tease to keep him interested. But with Fallon he didn't know how far she'd go, or let him go. No point in rocking another boat, especially The Kingpin's. Besides, Pete knew his place. He just didn't know how long he'd be able to keep it.

When Pete first suggested closing One Eleven on Sundays,

Connie balked. Six months of monitoring the Sunday revenue changed Connie's mind. For Pete, a whole day off meant a matinee and dinner across the river where he could lose himself in the crowd. But now with Fallon at home, he decided to change his routine.

On Sunday morning he staged his exit from the library to coincide with Connie's passing in the hallway.

"What? I didn't expect to see you on the Sabbath," Connie said. "More often than not you disappear quicker than Houdini slips through handcuffed chains."

Pete held up the Mark Twain novel he'd just started. "Not today. I'm holing up in the cottage to finish this."

"Nonsense. That Connecticut Yankee can sit tight in King Arthur's Court. You're having dinner with us, one o'clock sharp. By the way, my daughter came home. Have you met her?"

"Once or twice, but only briefly. She probably doesn't remember me."

"Fallon? She has the memory of an elephant but don't ask where her allowance goes, or what she did last night."

*****

Later that morning Pete added another ten minutes to his grooming routine, not that the extra effort made much of a difference. When it came to looking like a big spender, seventy-dollar summer suits on his reedy frame and two-bit weekly haircuts from the city's best barber went a long way. He arrived at the manor early and found Connie and Fallon sitting on the front porch glider. Her face had lost its baby fat, making her cheekbones more pronounced. She crossed her long, slender legs and dangled white sandals from her feet. Although the temperature bordered on eighty-five degrees, not one drop of perspiration beaded the skin her skimpy sundress exposed.

"Pete wasn't sure you'd remember him," Connie told his daughter.

"Oh, Connie, you're such a tease. How could I ever forget the man who saved me and my friends."

"Any man worth his salt would've done the same," Pete said.

"You're too modest," Fallon said. "We were simply scared to death. H-m-m, I wonder whatever happened to those inept bumpkins."

From the doorway came Billie's soothing voice. "God only knows. By now they may have sought redemption and gone to their heavenly reward."

How true, if Connie got to them first and played god. Or maybe the grubs got lucky and skipped out after finding out whose daughter they accidentally scared. If they did get dispatched and if La Bianca stuck around to witness the deed, she wouldn't have flinched—ever the actress pretending to be above reproach with her mightier-than-thou attitude. All decked out in lilac and purple. Not Pete's favorite colors but combined with La Bianca's white hair they sure made her look good. Stately best described her. The siren floated over to her aging lover, and held out her hand.

"Please, Connie, let's dispense with unpleasant talk. Could we just go into the dining room and sit down to a lovely meal."

"Whatever you say, my lovely Willajenka."

Willajenka, oh yeah, Pete contained his amusement. Willajenka the Conqueror, no wonder she preferred a man's name.

With Connie lording over the head of the table and his two

women flanked on either side, Pete was directed to take the chair beside Fallon. As soon as she moved her arm, he caught the scent of perfume and quelled an instinct to close his eyes and draw her into his senses.

Conversation centered on Fallon and the two months she'd recently spent abroad. Having little knowledge of Europe beyond Northern Italy, Pete reverted to the role of good listener, one he'd mastered since working for Connie.

"Before going on to France, we enjoyed two glorious weeks in Italy," Fallon said. "Such amazing cities: Rome, Venice, Milan, and Florence. Do you know them, Pete?"

"Only from what I've read."

"And from whereabouts do you hail?"

"North of Torino, in the mountains."

"Oh, shoot. We didn't travel that far."

"You enjoyed Paris?"

"Like a kitten rolling in catnip."

Billie put her finger to her lips. "Now Fallon, let's not be common."

Fallon common? How about Pete Montagna the commoner in a field of catnip with the princess—what a common, vulgar, tempting, sensual, forbidden roll.

Fallon laughed as if she'd read his mind. "Oh Billie, I just can't help myself when I reminisce about Paris. The Left Bank where we stayed was so-o divine, all those artists and writers and intellects and Bohemians."

"I hope you took some time to peruse the city's architecture," Connie said.

His daughter blew a kiss from her fingertips. "Spoken like a man whose life revolves around construction."

"I'll have you know the construction business paid for your trip."

"And for that I am truly grateful, but Paris offers so much more than old buildings."

"Such as?"

"Sophistication, creativity, a certain panache."

"Arrogance you mean."

"Um-m-m, suppose I meet you half way and settle on pride. In any case, I'm glad to have experienced Europe now, before this situation with the Jewish population gets any worse. There's talk of that pompous Hitler everywhere, on the streets, in little cafes."

"At your age you shouldn't be concerned about foreign politics," Connie said.

"There's more to this uprising than politics. The man's a monster." She took a sip of iced tea and continued. "And another thing, I'm twenty years old and no longer a child."

"You won't be twenty for another two weeks."

"Fallon, please, remember your father's gastritis. Shall we talk about something else?"

"That's not fair. What's the point of sending me to a college sympathetic to social issues if I'm not free to express concerns for the downtrodden?"

"Now Fallon, of course we want you to be a caring person. I'm sorry if—"

"No need to apologize, Billie," Connie interrupted. "I can handle this."

"This? Now I'm a *'this'*, please."

"No, you're a Latimer. And I expect you to conduct yourself like one."

This, she called herself a 'this?' For this Pete gave up a Sunday matinee at the Ambassador? No wonder Connie sent her away to school. Pete wanted to quiet that brazen mouth, cover those raspberry lips with his straight shooters, except his didn't always tell the truth.

"Cat got your tongue, Pete?" Fallon asked.

Pete felt his face heat up while he searched for a clever retort.

"Now, Fallon, don't be fresh," Billie chimed in.

"Good god," Connie bellowed. "I hope we're not boring you, Pete."

"Not at all. I just don't mix politics or squabbles with my meat and potatoes."

"Ah-h, Pete. You do have a way with words." Connie shoved his remaining cucumber and watercress salad aside and stifled a stomach-rumbling burp. "Billie, tell Hester to bring in that overpriced pot roast."

Even Hester had an occasional off day. Pete attacked the leathery beef with his table knife. Had he been alone, he would've snapped open his blade and shredded the damn meat. Next to the meat wobbled a gelatin mold of chopped carrots, walnuts, and celery. Judging from past experiences with this particular menu, he could've made book on prune whip for dessert, one of Connie's favorites. But for now the main course continued, along with table talk that switched to polite conversation about people Pete didn't know or care about. Given a choice, he would've returned to the main event: mouthy Fallon bucking The Kingpin and La Bianca.

While chomping long and hard on the resilient beef, Pete felt a tickling sensation from under the table, then a slight tug. Before he could dispatch the ever-expanding glob from his mouth, Fallon's bare foot had wiggled under his trouser cuff. When her foot inched up his leg, he reacted with an impulsive gulp. The beef locked in his throat. He tried forcing it down, coughing it up. Nothing worked. Gripping the table with one hand, he reached for his napkin with the other. At that point all conversation stopped. Three pair of eyes focused on him. Had he been able to speak, Pete might've asked for help, much as he hated admitting to a situation he couldn't handle on his own.

"Is there a problem Pete?"

He nodded.

"Here, try some water."

He shook his head.

"Pete?"

He pointed to his throat.

"Oh my god!"

"Connie, do something!"

Pete saw a blur of slow motion, right before his eyes rolled back. How common, cashing in his chips right before their royal eyes—just like Giovanni's Dog had done before his common eyes.

Only this time there'd be no help from the Chinamen.

WHAM! A single well-placed wallop across Pete's back dislodged the glob and catapulted it through the air. He resurfaced and gasped for a precious breath. Gaining control of his senses, he surveyed the war zone across the table: the offensive missile from his mouth jiggling in the middle of La Bianca's gelatin mousse. He scrambled to his feet and leaned over to make a quick recovery with his napkin. He had to admire Billie's polite restraint, the way she used her own napkin to cover one of those stingy smiles reserved for Connie.

"My apologies," Pete said, more embarrassed than sorry. "Please forgive me."

"Nonsense," roared Connie. "I had a similar experience last year. Right, Billie?"

"If you say so."

"In any case, thanks for the helping hand, Connie."

"Don't thank me. It was Florence Nightingale who came to your rescue. Good work, Fallon."

She patted her patient's arm. "My pleasure, Pete. After Schroeder's this makes us even. Better yet, now you owe me."

Chapter 24

Pete was in the library on Saturday when the annoying sound of a throat being cleared interrupted his reading. Expecting to do battle with La Bianca, he looked up and received the pleasant alternative of Fallon leaning against the doorframe, her arms folded over a soft blouse. She wore lightweight jodhpurs and the flush of an early morning ride.

"Good morning, Pete. I can see you're busy so I'll make this quick. I expect you at my birthday party next week."

Oh, yes. La Bianca had taught her well. But Pete had his own agenda. "I might have to work," he said.

"On a Sunday, I hardly think so, unless Connie's planning further expansion of his naughty empire."

"With him you never know. Sometimes he comes up with special assignments."

"Not on my birthday. He promised me no business. I want you there, Pete. More than anyone else so don't you disappoint me." She raised her chin and spun on the heels of leather riding boots before making a royal exit.

She wants! What the hell did he care what Miss Spoiled Brat wanted, that high-priced lure trolling deep waters in search of the elusive catch. Too old for jailbait, but with a name like Fallon Latimer she might as well be, since Pete's touching her would amount to nothing less than a crime in Connie's eyes. Why Pete, when she could have her pick of any man? Maybe she wanted to show Papa Bear that he couldn't run her life like he ran everything else. Well, Pete Montagna was no dummy. He'd come too far to risk losing what he'd given up so much to get.

Later that morning Connie summoned Pete to his den. Beans was already there, fidgeting to contain a gaseous condition Pete hoped wouldn't explode before the meeting ended. He contemplated wormholes in the wood-paneled walls while The Kingpin chomped his cigar with half-closed eyes, a posture Pete had witnessed before and usually preceded some problem involving discretionary control. When the cigar lost its appeal, Connie cleared his lips of tobacco shreds, and said, "We have a rather sensitive issue. One I want handled with the utmost care before it gets out of hand."

Pete assumed his role of listener, and Beans uttered his usual question. "Who?"

"Orville Duncan."

"Why that two-bit double crosser. What's his price?"

"None, so he says.

"What about his family?"

"He's an orphan with no wife or kids. Not even a mutt."

Beans winced while massaging his growling stomach. "I don't get it. Duncan was one of the best cops on our payroll. Not once did the cocksucker demand more than his fair take, not even after that run-in we had with the temperance league. Why he's as honest as—"

"That's the problem," Connie said. "Duncan has reached a fork in the road of life. The man's loyalties are so conflicted he came directly to me."

Pete pushed his shoulders into the chair. Damn, one of his pay-offs had gone over his head, straight to Connie.

"No disrespect against your management, Pete," Connie reassured him. "Duncan says he wants out, that he can no longer turn his back on One Eleven's irregularities and whatever else goes on under his watch. It seems he got religion and has taken up with some bible-thumping female touring with that revival show camped on the riverfront."

"Holy Beelzebub, this could be serious," Beans said. "Ain't nobody more righteous than a first-time repentant sinner."

Pete shrugged. "So the revival troupe moves on in a couple weeks. Duncan will soon forget the woman, and when that happens, he'll come to his senses."

"Life should be so easy," Connie said. "Duncan wants to talk the do-gooder into staying behind. Worse yet, he wants to marry her. When he's not using his law enforcement credentials to crusade against the likes of businessmen such as myself, he wants to pastor a little church in some abandoned storefront. One with a soup kitchen he says."

Beans shook his head. "What a terrible waste. You want I should take care of this?"

"Too risky, we can't afford trouble over a cop gone soft." Connie turned to Pete. "Make this your top priority. I want it resolved on the q.t., and, if possible with no violence."

Connie always wanted something, just like his daughter. "This woman, what's her name?"

"Damned if I know. Duncan calls her his angel. According to him, she's capable of converting the worst of the worst."

What the hell got into Duncan, taking up with some 'holier-than-thou' broad passing through on her way to god only knows where. Duncan seemed smarter, or maybe tougher. Of course when it came to the allure of women, Pete was in no position to pass judgment on the stupidity of men.

*****

On Sunday Connie yielded to Billie's suggestion to alter their usual routine and took her to St. Louis for dinner and a matinee. Pete wound up in the kitchen with Hester, eating yesterday's leftovers disguised in a catch-all she called hash: beef, carrots, potatoes, and onions passed through a food grinder, dumped into a cast iron skillet, and cooked in sizzling bacon fat until the flavors melded and a brown crust formed around the edge.

"Goodness gracious, of all Sundays for you to hang around the farm," Hester said. "Even Fallon took off."

Pete tried not to let his shoulders slump. He would've bet a week's wages on Fallon's staying behind. "She went with Connie and Billie?"

"They offered, she refused, said she wanted to spend time with chums from her days at East Side High."

"Good for her," Pete said, but not for him. "I guess she'll be gone all day."

"With Fallon, it's anybody's guess."

After picking through the second helping of hash Hester forced on him, Pete topped his meal off with a bicarb and soda water. Two explosive belches in the privacy of the library delivered instant comfort. He spent the next five minutes stifling an overwhelming urge to bang his fist against the wall.

Another day lost, a day he could've showed her how little she meant to him. His only day off, and she went chasing off with silly friends. 'Come to my birthday party next week,' she'd ordered. As if he cared about some flashy party, watching higher-ups fawn over her as if she was common royalty. If only she wasn't so damn special to everyone else.

Pete waded through ninety pages of a book that didn't hold his attention, all the while listening to the grandfather clock tick and chime away the afternoon. He lingered into early evening, longer than he should have, considering the impending situation he needed to resolve, as much for Connie as for himself. It was almost seven o'clock before he climbed into his roadster, the four-year old Model A inherited from Billie when Connie gifted her with a new car. Pete rolled down the driveway, gathering momentum until he ripped onto the main road and left behind a trail of dust. His destination was the East Side riverfront, site of the revival that had corrupted one of their most reliable allies.

After parking on cobblestone pavement bordering the Mississippi, Pete followed the voice from a distant loudspeaker issuing an invitation for sinners to gather at the river. As he got closer, a blaring trumpeted version of 'Amazing Grace' welcomed him, along with a handful of other latecomers. Inside the grand tent, a patchwork of mended canvas accommodated ordinary folks struggling with the heat as they jammed benches and stood along the pegged perimeter. Pete pushed his way through and found a convenient pole to lean against. He adjusted his vision to the drooping strings of yellow lights, all leading to the stage where a young woman enticed the audience into a fevered reverence.

She raised her arms, the sleeves of a long white robe cascading from her wrists. Looking up to the canvas pinnacle, she shouted, "Praise the Lord!"

"Amen!" chorused the all-white young and old, male and female.

With the grace of a dancer, she moved back and forth across the stage. A loose plait of long, blonde hair intertwined with daisy streamers rippled down her back. Duncan's angel gripped the sinners, mesmerizing their souls with all the fervor of a mythical bird preparing to swoop down on its submissive prey.

"Jesus loves you, one and all!"

"And you too, Glory Bea!"

Squinting for a better look, Pete did a double take. Sure enough, Orville Duncan's angel was none other than Butte's Glory Bea Turner. She smacked two rows of fingers to her pale lips before disappearing offstage, her departure coinciding with the quartet of trumpeters heralding the main attraction. Every man, woman, and child who was seated joined those standing. At the choir director's prompting, they undertook a rhythmic clapping that swelled each time they pounded their hands together.

"Brother David! Brother David!" they chanted over and over.

Pete got shuffled to the edge of the aisle just as three solemn men paved the way for Brother David's entry. A slight man, the preacher appeared to be in his early fifties. He wore a white robe similar to Glory Bea's, and the open-toed sandals of a Franciscan. His biblical hair had made a natural transition from blonde to white and a radiated a soft, spotlight-induced halo around his head.

As the preacher walked by, he stopped long enough to place his fingertips on Pete's shoulder, an unexpected gesture that made Pete flinch. After looking into eyes so intense they seemed capable of penetrating his soul, Pete turned away, resentful of the intrusion.

"God forgives you, but first you must forgive yourself," Brother David said. He continued up the aisle, reaching out to followers who wept as he touched their outstretched hands.

Pete wanted no part of Brother David's sermon, no finger-pointing reminders of past transgressions he wanted to forget. He stepped outside and took a deep breath, grateful for the air as impure as his soul. After walking the length of the tent, he turned the corner, and almost stumbled over his dropped chin. There, twenty feet away on a stack of concrete blocks sat Duncan's angel, chin to palm and elbow to crossed knee.

Seeing Glory Bea away from the limelight brought back memories of Chinatown and The Underground where he left Giovanni's Dog. Maybe she knew about the execution—information garnered from Butte's Red Light rumor mill, or from Annalee's closeted network. Pete's involvement would give Glory Bea the upper hand, an advantage that could send him packing. Back to Italy, where he belonged. As he strolled toward Glory Bea, she stood up. Pete tipped the brim of his straw hat and cracked a skeptical smile. "Been to Annalee's lately?"

Glory Bea returned his smile with one that turned into sweet laughter. "I don't believe what my sorry eyes tell me."

She grabbed his face between her warm hands and planted a soothing kiss, the nicest he'd experienced in a long time. Her soft skin still exuded the same lilac perfume he remembered from Butte. After an affectionate squeeze, Glory Bea released her grip and stepped back. "Is that really you … uh, uh?" A flutter of fingers demanded his silence. "Now, wait. Don't tell me. Your name is right here. See." She rolled out the tip of her tongue for Pete's inspection.

"Nice," he said.

"I'm just teasing. You went by Pete ... Pete ... Pete Montagna, right?"

"Then, you do remember."

"Darling Pete, how could I ever forget? First Ma's god almighty meddling, and then yours." She laughed, this time bussing his cheek. "You darling man, you saved my soul."

"You've mixed me up with somebody else."

"Silly. If it hadn't been for you and that little brouhaha over Annalee and the yen-yen, Ma and I would never have had words. And such a colossal row it was. Dear Ma just h-a-d to resurrect a cache of buried secrets." She sat back down, and patted a second concrete stack for Pete.

"As I was saying: it turns out that many moons ago a certain young man came to Butte, of all places, and planted his seed in the dried up womb of a certain older woman. Lo and behold, God deemed that tiny particle worthy to sprout a miracle baby. Voila! Twenty-eight years later, Yours Truly."

"And this preacher, he makes you happy?"

"You bet." Shielding her mouth with her hand, Glory Bea spoke in a whisper. "He's my Sugar Daddy, and my real Daddy. But we don't openly acknowledge any kinship. Some folks, you know the less sophisticated variety, might not understand."

"Are you telling me what I—"

"Don't look so shocked. It's not like I confessed to something as awful as witnessing a murder, Chinese style." She put her finger to his lips. "Secrets, the best kept ones are such a hoot, don't you agree?"

Pete swallowed hard.

"Come on, Pete, don't be so stuffy. Did you get a gander at those tent people? They come from miles around to see me—and, of course, Brother David. We give them drama and music and laughter and tears. What's more, nobody goes away feeling the least bit cheated. Where else can folks enjoy live theater in exchange for a few coins in the collection plate? By tugging at the heartstrings of sorry sinners, we help them mend their wicked ways. And when we run out of souls, or steam—whichever comes first—we carry our message elsewhere. Since parting company with Butte first and later Seattle, I've crisscrossed this great country four times."

Raising her arms to the sky, she threw her head back. "Thank you, Jesus." When her eyes came back down to earth, they settled on Pete. "So, what brings you here?"

"Got room for one more?"

"Why, Pete, you silly devil. Who would've thought: after all this time you still have a thing for me."

Chapter 25

The following evening Pete returned to the riverfront tent and commandeered an end seat two rows from the front. He crossed one leg over the other, endured the singing, and contributed a sawbuck to the first collection—for the local needy. He expected another Glory Bea appearance before Brother David's; instead the preacher made an early grand entrance—a carbon copy of what Pete had witnessed the evening before. As soon as Brother David hit the stage, he spread his arms into a wingspan that hushed his jubilant audience.

"Brothers and Sisters—all you sinners just like me. And you innocent children—the saints I can never hope to be again." *Applause, applause.* "I come to you this evening with my heart filled with the bittersweet mix of joy and sadness." Restless murmurs passed through the audience. "Last night as I lay in bed after my prayers, a dove flew to the open window and perched on its sill. The bird stayed motionless, as if waiting for sleep to overtake me, which it eventually did. And that's when God came to me, in the most wondrous of dreams."

"Hallelujah!" someone shouted.

"Praise the Lord!"

Brother David motioned for silence; the audience obliged. "He told me I'd completed my work here in East St. Louis—"

"No!"

"Never!"

"We love you, Brother."

Seven hundred pairs of feet stomped in place. The preacher raised his hand again.

"But I'm not leaving without taking part of East St. Louis with me. The man I refer to is sitting among you."

Shoulders twisted, necks lifted, heads turned as Brother David held out his inviting hand. His magnetic eyes held Pete's as a hush came over the crowd. "Like the disciples who followed Jesus, this man has sacrificed his worldly possessions and financial security for the chance to spread the word of Almighty God. Many of you already know him, if not from personal experience, then by reputation."

The pianist began to play, "Stand Up, Stand Up for Jesus." The congregation obeyed.

"Brothers and Sisters, may I present my new evangelist-in-training—former St. Clair County deputy sheriff, Orville Percy Duncan."

The applause started at the back of the tent and followed Orville's every step as Glory Bea escorted him down the aisle toward Brother David. Her apprentice was decked out in a white suit, and so enthralled by all the attention he didn't even realize the anonymous benefactor who made all this possible stood but a few feet away. But Duncan's angel took notice of Pete, and managed a quick wink on the way to her next performance.

*****

The next day as Brother David and his humble motor caravan rumbled south on Illinois Route 3, it passed by a black Packard parked a discreet ninety feet away. Pete sat in the back seat with Connie.

"You say they're heading for Little Egypt?" Jackie G. asked from over his shoulder.

"All the way to Cairo," Pete said.

"Ah, the tip of the state and every bit as corrupt as Chicago," Connie said. "Brother David's newest protégé will have an abundance of transgressions in which to sink his teeth." He leaned his head back to send up a trail of smoke. "I have to hand it to you, Pete. Resolving this dilemma in less than forty-eight hours surpassed my greatest expectations. So how much did it cost you to accommodate Duncan's calling?"

Pete made a wavy motion with his hand.

"What the hell, Pete. You know I don't understand Italian."

Nor did he need to know every time Pete took a piss. The two thousand dollar contribution to Brother David's ministry represented an investment in Pete's future.

With a forward motion of his forefinger Connie signaled Jackie G to start the engine. While the Packard bolted and the driver cursed an unsuspecting pedestrian, Connie lowered his voice to Pete's ears. "By the way, don't be looking for a handsome bonus."

"None expected."

"Spoken like a loyal employee. Still, I want to show my appreciation. What would you say to ten percent interest in One Eleven?"

"I'd say 'thanks,' and then some. You won't be sorry, Connie. This I promise you." Pete contained the excitement Jackie G was not privy to sharing, and started doing some mental arithmetic.

"We'll work out the details later," Connie said. "Oh yes, one more thing. About this weekend—Sunday, in particular—I'd like you to stick around for my daughter's birthday. Between Fallon and Billie, my lovely ladies got carried away with the guest list. The prospect of several hundred people poking around the farm makes me more than a little uneasy."

"No problem," said Pete, still reeling from The Kingpin's generosity. "You can count on me, whatever it takes."

"In that case, check with Billie. She might need your help with some advance preparations."

*****

The next morning Pete waited for Connie to leave before he tracked La Bianca down in the small sunroom that served as her office. She almost smiled when Pete offered his services.

"How sweet," she purred from the cherry wood desk that overlooked her cottage garden. "Of course, such generosity must've originated with Connie. He's always so concerned about my working too hard."

"I guess he doesn't want you soiling those lily-whites."

"Really, Pete, by now you should know I work with my head not my hands."

"My apologies." He started to walk away. "I'll be in the library if you need me."

"Now don't go sulking off to lick your wounded pride. I'm sure I can come up with some worthwhile task for you. Let me think ... h-m-m." Resting her chin on her knuckles, she gazed through the window, to a hummingbird drinking from the feeder. "Jackie G is committed to Hester for grocery shopping and decorations. And Sebastian put a fresh crew of relatives to work assembling tables and benches and that blasted dance floor." Billie pursed her lips; she perused the ceiling molding. "H-m-m ... maybe you could—"

"I could use some help," said Fallon, a flowered dress flowing from her hips and a broad-brimmed hat concealing half her face.

Pete didn't know how long Fallon been standing in the hallway, or if she'd caught the cat and mouse banter between La Bianca and him, but he welcomed her intrusion.

"Drive me to St. Louis, will you, Pete?" she asked. "I promise to finish my business in time for yours at One Eleven."

"Really, Fallon, why didn't you speak up sooner," Billie said, craning her sleek neck to check out the front driveway. "If you hurry, maybe you can catch Jackie G."

"Sebastian said he left ten minutes ago with Hester. And Beans is tied up with Connie." She walked away, and then turned around with her hand on her hip. "Well, Pete, can I count on you, or must I drive myself?"

"You'd better go," Billie said with a sigh. "Connie doesn't like her crossing the river alone."

Pete left before La Bianca could change her mind. He pulled the car around to the front of the house where Fallon stood, fanning herself with a hankie. He leaned over the passenger side, opened the door, and she slid onto the seat.

"I usually don't close the car door," she said, looking straight ahead.

Just then Sebastian happened by. *"Buenos dias*, Senorita Fallon," he said, tipping his hat as he closed her door.

Pete took off.

"Sorry if you find my impromptu request demeaning," Fallon said as they pulled onto the highway.

"I gave up chauffeuring a long time ago."

"You could've said no."

"I should have. Connie expects me to help Billie with your grand party."

"P-lease, you know as well as I that Billie doesn't need you. Not like I do."

He concentrated on his driving while Fallon fiddled with the radio. Settling on Bing Crosby crooning "Prisoner of Love," she leaned back and closed her eyes. "How romantic: to love someone so much you'd give up everything else, just to be with that person. Don't you agree?"

Pete didn't take the bite. Having moved up a few notches since the roast beef encounter, he wasn't about to encourage another flirtatious distraction. They crossed Eades Bridge into St. Louis and turned onto the grand thoroughfare of Washington Avenue. "So, where do you need to conduct this business?" he asked.

"Not around here, further west. I'll let you know when to stop."

He battled the hectic downtown traffic and then the wholesale garment area that soon tapered off into light industry.

"Not yet," Fallon said as they approached the mid-town theater district Pete used to frequent before One Eleven consumed his evenings.

They continued west, passing block after block of stately mansions built before the turn of the century to imitate grand European styles. Gigantic urns filled with lush ferns enjoyed the protection of covered porches and northern exposures while annual displays of phlox, daylilies, and zinnias thrived across the street. After crossing the broad expanse of Kingshighway Boulevard, he pulled over and turned to Fallon.

"You did say St. Louis, didn't you? This is the end of the line."

"Not quite." She pointed to the wooded area bordering Kingshighway. "The city limits include Forest Park." She giggled like the schoolgirl who first caught his attention. "Come on, Pete, don't be such an old poop. You looked miserable waiting for Billie to dream up some asinine assignment so I offered you a plausible escape."

As with God's first man, Pete had taken a bite from the apple. After winding through the park's maze of woods and ponds and natural landscapes, he parked the car because Fallon wanted to stretch her legs. Their short stroll turned into an hour excursion around the zoo and the longest uninterrupted time he'd spent with a female since that crazy night on the town in Butte. Again, he relegated Glory Bea to his past and hoped she had given him the same courtesy.

"Kind of scrumptious, don't you think?" Fallon asked.

"Uh … yeah."

"You have no idea what I'm talking about, do you?"

"I guess I drifted into my private world."

"And where is that, someplace in Italy?"

"Nah, someplace up ahead," he said. "How about a nice, juicy hotdog smeared with mustard?"

"Yum, yum," she said and moved her tongue over those lips. "Oh, Pete, isn't it simply wonderful—the way we think alike?"

He ate hotdogs with her and drank lemonade while seated on a bench. It overlooked a pond of sea lions and walruses. A prairie dog scurried over from its barren village of little mounds and craters, only to make the fatal mistake of tempting the water mammals. The ensuing ruckus of barking and squealing brought Fallon to tears so they continued their walk. She slipped her arm through his, which made Pete uneasy when they passed similar couples who smiled and nodded as if they shared a mutual society reserved for young lovers. But after a while he relaxed and let Fallon pull him into her dreams of making the world a better place.

"If the poor were better educated, they could fend for themselves," she said, as if no one had considered such a solution before. "That's why I want to teach."

"Little kids?"

"Why not, I love children."

"Somehow I can't picture you wiping dirty noses."

"Connie said the same thing when he gave me his blessing. He may not always be on the up and up but when it comes to helping the downtrodden, he's not the least bit miserly. Money, money, money—the damn stuff carries so many burdens. Squeezing, allocating, justifying, guarding, and scheming, there's no end to making more."

"You seem to be doing okay."

"Mostly because of Billie, but sometimes she can be

smothering. Going away to school turned out better than I expected. Deep in the woodlands of Indiana I don't have to uphold the Latimer name. Or more appropriately, defend it."

After a while Fallon ran out of words and Pete found comfort in the silence, which only lasted until they came to a boathouse and lagoon.

"Oh, Pete, the sign says this place dates all the way back to the 1904 World's Fair. What a perfect way to end the perfect day. Let's rent a boat and sail to never-never land."

"Some other time, I need to look after One Eleven."

"But it's not even one o'clock yet. Please don't disappoint me."

"OK, but only for half an hour."

After paying the twenty-five cent rental, Pete helped her into a snug boat designed for two. He shed his jacket and rowed through calm water meandering under bridges and into secluded coves. Fallon shed her shoes, hiked her skirt, and stretched her bare legs to the sun. "Just like the good old days of the World's Fair," she said. "Except I don't have a parasol and you don't have a handlebar mustache. And neither of us has to be good, unless you insist."

"I shouldn't have let you talk me into this," he said, not wanting to let on how much he enjoyed her company.

"What better way to get acquainted? Besides, I just had to escape from the farm, if only for a few hours. Out here there's no Billie monitoring my bathroom habits. No Connie squashing my every thought and treating me as if I were a prized possession."

"Come on, they care about you."

"Like zookeepers care for precious animals. I guess you haven't heard the latest. No, of course, you wouldn't have. There's a certain fellow Connie thinks would be perfect for me—Hamilton Steele. He just finished law school and is ready to join his father's practice in Belleville."

Pete's neck muscles tightened up. "Connie's right. The man sounds perfect."

"Billie hasn't said much, which makes me wonder."

"You need Billie's approval?"

"I trust her judgment, even though we don't always see eye to eye."

"Then maybe you should follow your own mind instead of complaining about Connie and Billie interfering."

"How perceptive of you: to say just what I wanted to hear."

Fallon leaned over and before Pete could react, she wrapped her arms around his neck. Her lips locked on his, sending a surge through his every vein and artery. Was this the bolt of lightning Giovanni had described when he first saw … what's her name—Serina. Serina the beguiler, Serina the troublemaker, enough! Calling on every ounce of willpower he could muster, Pete forced Fallon back to the seat.

"Don't do that," he said. "I'm not the perfect man for you, not like this Hamilton Steele."

"I know, that's what makes you so wonderful. I can't help myself, really I can't. What's more, I know you feel the same way. I see it in your eyes when you watch my every move." She started to get up again.

He stopped her with his outstretched palm. "You know nothing about me. You're still a kid, a spoiled brat used to the best, and I have nothing to offer. Now stay in your seat before you dump us over."

"A spoiled brat, that's how you see me? You led me on; let me make a fool of myself." Fallon lurched forward, her hand poised for a smack across his face. "I hate you, Pete Montagna. You're nothing but a pretentious phony."

"Watch out!" Pete yelled as Fallon started to lose her balance.

He stood up, prepared to steady her. Too late, the boat tipped over, sending both of them into the pond. They emerged through a tangle of white lilies and tall grass. Pete prepared to tread water, but then he felt the bottom sludge oozing through his toes. The lagoon's depth couldn't have exceeded four feet, judging from the way Fallon's breasts were bobbling on the surface. Her hair had taken on a hue of chocolate mud splashed with green algae and coiled from her scalp like a nest of young sea serpents. But it was the expression on her face that moved Pete, that same imperial look Connie wore when plans went haywire. Opening her mouth, she spit out a dragonfly along with a single word. "Bastard!"

"Bitch!"

"How dare you! You're nothing but a two-bit peon."

"You can't say I didn't warn you." He grabbed onto the boat. "Now shut up and help me turn this damn matchbox over."

They saved the rest of their energy for righting the boat, which took thirty minutes and the help of two high school boys who happened by in another rental. Not a word passed between Fallon and Pete as he rowed back to the dock. On their way to the car Pete sloshed ahead in his shrinking suit while barefoot Fallon cursed the pathway strewn with pebbles and her dress that clung like second skin.

"Dammit, Pete, wait up. I will not be treated like some squaw walking in her warrior's footprints."

"Well this Indian works for a living and doesn't take orders from any squaw."

"I hate you!"

"So you said. Just don't forget it."

They brought the remaining sludge into the car and headed back to Illinois. When the familiar river bluffs came into view, Fallon slumped against the door. Tears rolled down her cheeks.

"Every bit of this is your fault," she said, smearing her face with the muddy handkerchief Pete had offered.

"I told you not to stand up."

"Connie will have a fit."

"Not if you don't tell him, sure as hell I won't."

"You forget Billie. How will I ever get to my room without her seeing me?"

"Quit whining and use your head. Go where Billie never sets foot—in the kitchen. From there take the backstairs. And don't worry about Hester. She's not due back 'til late afternoon. Now shake the weeds out of your hair and behave like the princess you think you are."

*****

For the rest of the week Pete stayed clear of the big house. When Connie asked about the birthday plans, Pete assured him Billie had everything under control.

"What an extraordinary woman," Connie said. "I don't know how I'd get along without her. Nevertheless, I need your help on Sunday, mostly to keep an eye on Fallon. She's been moping around all week. God only know what's bothering her now."

At least Fallon hadn't run to Connie or La Bianca with some wild story about the dago taking advantage of her. That day in the drink—the way she looked, like a goddess rising from the sea—Pete could've taken her right there, but then she opened her mouth and out popped the flying insect. He didn't know whether to laugh or to smack her. Not that he would ever smack a woman, but this one kept worming her way into his head.

*****

On Sunday evening the East Side prominent and wealthy spilled onto Connie Latimer's sweeping front lawn. They sipped straight whiskey or champagne punch or draft beer and sampled finger foods from trays carried by Mexican girls who didn't speak English. The young waitresses twisted their hair into chignons and wore embroidered blouses with red, tiered skirts and comfortable huaraches. A quartet of musicians who sometimes appeared at One Eleven played Cole Porter and Irving Berlin tunes as couples danced on the portable floor under Chinese lanterns. Large oscillating fans kept the mosquitoes at bay, no small feat considering the proximity of the horse stables. And if the bloodsuckers found a few delectable morsels, the guests suffered in silence out of respect for their host.

At Pete's suggestion bouncers from the club volunteered their night off in exchange for bringing their wives and girlfriends to the party, a money-saving decision Connie thought brilliant. The burly men moved through the crowd, more for show than protection since these guests were not inclined toward rowdy behavior. Most of them belonged to Connie's circle instead of Fallon's, although she did have a select clique. Pete recognized the two from Schroeder's and from the way they giggled at him, he figured they remembered him too.

When the band played the opening bars of "I Only Have Eyes for You," Fallon accepted the outstretched hand of a tall, young man with sandy hair and Anglican features. He held her close and she nestled her head to his shoulder. Pete circled around the perimeter, observing any questionable outsiders while keeping vigilance over Fallon and her dance partner. The fellow, this Hamilton Steele, must've had a great sense of humor because Fallon laughed at everything he said while they twirled around like the Top Hat team of Astaire and Rogers. Fallon wore the same rose color as the night he first saw her. And Steele wore a look newly acquired money couldn't buy: the confidence of ancestors who had come over generations before and already made their mark.

"They make a lovely couple, wouldn't you agree?" Billie meowed. She caught Pete off guard, not by her comment but because he'd not been aware of her standing next to him. "If you say so," he said, mimicking her standard reply to questions she evaded.

"Hamilton Steele can give Fallon what most men around here cannot: prestige, respect, and money."

"You forget love."

"Why Pete, I didn't figure you as a romanticist."

"I wasn't speaking for myself."

"Of course not, you're way out of Fallon's league."

La Bianca, fishing again for Pete's soft spot and he had no intentions of taking the bait. "I thought Fallon planned on going back to that Indiana school."

"Perhaps, only time will tell, and, of course, Connie. But if she stays home, St. Louis has some excellent colleges for women."

The music stopped, positioning the Top Hat dancers in front of Pete and Billie.

"Oh, Billie, what perfect timing," Fallon said, placing the older woman's hand in Steele's. "Ham was just telling me that he wanted the next dance with you."

Steele's perfunctory bow masked the surprised look on his face. "Would you do me the honor?" he asked Billie, and then whisked her away.

"Whew!" Fallon said. "After that performance I could use a drink."

"Punch or lemonade?" Pete asked in the dry tone of a waiter.

"What I meant to say was, 'Let's get a drink'." Fallon walked a good ten feet before turning around. "Well, don't just stand there. I thought you were here to look after me."

But not to play her lackey. Had they been elsewhere, Pete would've told her so. He took a flute of champagne from a passing tray for her and a pilsner for himself, expecting the cold beer to cool his steaming temper. He followed her through the crowd, beyond the bright lights defining the party boundaries, to the stable area. Fallon sat down on a bench and motioned Pete to join her.

"Well, what do you think?" she asked. "I mean about Hamilton Steele."

"Connie made a good choice."

"This isn't about Connie."

"Nor about me, so why are you asking?"

"It's important for me to know how you feel."

"What I feel doesn't matter. Like Billie said, I'm out of your league."

"Billie said that?" Fallon giggled behind her hand. "She has such a way with words."

"She spoke the truth."

"For a guy who's been around, you're such a lunkhead." Before Pete could defend himself, Fallon stood up, lifted her skirt, and straddled his lap—just like a pro.

"What the—" It was all Pete got out before she covered his mouth with those raspberry lips that had haunted him since the lagoon. She was yanking his shirt out of his pants and he didn't want her to stop.

"You want me. Dammit, I know you do," she whispered. "Say it, Pete. I want to hear you say it."

"Yo, Pete! You around here somewhere?" The voice belonged to Beans. "If you hear me, you better get your sweet ass back to the party."

Pete stood up, dumping Fallon from his lap. "Yeah, be right with you." He leaned over to pull her up.

"Say it," she whispered, her lips tickling his ear. "Or I'm not leaving."

"Yeah, I want what I can't have. Now get the hell out of here."

After tucking his shirt in, Pete walked out to the moonlit area and found Beans lighting one cigarette with the butt of another.

"Damn, I didn't know you was with some dame," Beans said. "Sorry for the nooky interruptus."

"No apology needed. I was checking out the stable and stopped for a leak. Now, what's the problem?"

"Billie's in a snit. She thinks the birthday girl took a powder."

"Not a chance. Ten minutes ago I saw Fallon drinking champagne. If she's powdering anything right now, it's her nose."

By the time Pete returned to the party, Hester and Sebastian were rolling a gigantic cake ablaze with candles onto the patio. Hamilton Steele had latched onto Fallon as if he'd already laid claim to her feelings, which both galled and amused Pete. When she bent over the multi-tiered confection, her eyes skirted past Steele and over to Pete's direction. She smiled, and then swooped across the cake to blow out all the candles.

"Looks like you'll get your birthday wish," Connie bellowed. "And, young lady, it better be a good one. Now how about a dance for the old man."

He took Fallon's hand, and like Moses parting the Red Sea opened a path through the guests. With the floor to themselves, they danced to "Daddy's Little Girl." Had Connie asked, Pete's advice would've been 'enjoy it while you can. She won't be your little girl much longer'. But Connie must've known, especially with Steele waiting on the sidelines. Without even trying, Pete was giving Steele a run for his old money. And Pete could've won, hands down, if he didn't already have a wife and children.

The evening culminated with an extravaganza of fireworks. Pete figured the show set Connie back a couple thousand bucks but that was before Jackie G said the materials came from the city's Fourth of July stockpile.

"The mayor owed Connie a favor," Jackie G went on. "So did some other guys. Most of what you see here tonight came by way of donations. You gotta hand it to Connie: he's a giver who never quits getting."

A Buick sedan transporting the final load of guests pulled away as Pete stood on the porch with Connie, watching Sebastian's relatives start the dismantling production.

"What a night," said Connie, his face flushed from the effects of non-stop alcohol and cigars. "I consummated more deals in the past six hours than the Arlington's most prolific hooker does in six days."

"Enough to cover this shindig?"

"And then some," Connie said with a laugh. "You've been a godsend, Pete—loyal and trustworthy to the core." He draped his arm across Pete's shoulder. "You know something? I'd like to show my appreciation."

"You already did, with ten percent of One Eleven."

"I mean beyond One Eleven. But you tell me what you want. After all, a mind reader I'm not."

How well Pete knew. He took advantage of The Kingpin's generosity by reaching for a realistic star. "How about some time off? I'd like to go back home to Italy." The words tumbled from his mouth like stray dogs escaping the city pound.

Connie all but aspirated. Sliding his hand from Pete's shoulder, he reached for a handkerchief to muffle a sudden hacking cough—such theatrics for a man of his stature. But the Kingpin's word was as reliable as twenty-four-carat gold. "I can think of no better way to celebrate your success," Connie managed after regaining his composure. "What's more, I'll even reimburse you the cost of travel expenses—upon your return, of course. How much time will you need to prepare someone to manage One Eleven?"

"With the right man, I figure six weeks. How about Tom Baker?"

"Good choice. He's dependable and not afraid to keep people in line. Now how long did you say you'd be gone?"

*****

On the walk back to his cottage, Pete felt light-headed after throwing off the burden he'd been carrying around. Five years wasted. In seven weeks he'd be back where he belonged, spending his waking hours getting reacquainted with Gina and Riccardo. At night he'd make Isabella forget why she ever forced him to leave. After a few months, he'd bring his family to America. That is, if Isabella agreed.

Pete slipped his key in the lock but the door pushed open on its own. He went inside, already knowing what to expect. Fallon had positioned herself in his easy chair, her skirt hiked above crossed legs. "It's past your bedtime," he said.

"Billie tucked me in an hour ago."

He pulled off his tie and tossed it aside. "Look, Fallon, I don't want to hurt your feelings but the sun will be up in a couple hours and I'm too tired for silly games."

"Then let's not waste any time. I came to collect my birthday wish." She stood up and wrapped her arms around his neck. "You said you wanted me. Was that a silly game you played to get rid of me?"

"Not exactly, but you and me were never meant to be playmates." He started to pull away, but Fallon held tight, even when she lifted herself to encircle him with those long, slender legs. "Whoa!" Pete lost his balance and they both toppled to the floor. He didn't know whether to laugh or to apologize; she didn't give him the chance to do either.

"Now look what you made me do. How humiliating: me, Fallon Latimer, on my knees begging for a kiss."

"That does it. One kiss and you're out of here, OK?"

"Uh-huh."

"Say 'one kiss,' I want to hear you say the words."

"One kiss, dammit, but you better make it good."

What is the measure of a single kiss? Pete started with Fallon's lips, and then explored her mouth. Had she pulled back, he might have stopped there and called it a night. Instead, she invited more. Not once did his lips leave her skin as they covered both eyes and one ear before trailing down her neck, across her shoulder, and resting at her fingertips. The cool touch of her skin had warmed considerably on the back track and detour. His journey ended in the crease of her breasts when Fallon released a soft moan.

"That's it?" she asked. "You really want me to leave now?"

"I wish to God you'd never come. Stay or go. You make the choice. Either way, this is one night I'm going to regret."

"Oh, Pete, I promise to be good and you're never, ever going to regret this night."

They moved onto the bed where Pete introduced Fallon to lovemaking at its best: the unhurried kind between a man and woman wanting nothing more than to please each other. And Fallon responded with the eagerness of passion awakened.

"The first time may not be the greatest," he murmured in her ear afterwards, "but it's the one you never forget."

"Oh, Pete, you mean this actually gets better? Show me right now."

He checked his watch. "One more round like the last one and you'll be meeting Connie on his early morning walk. This time you really do have to leave."

"Not before you say it."

"What's left to say?"

"That you love me."

"I already showed you. You're everything a man—"

"I'm not a thing. I want to hear you say that you love me more than anyone else in the whole world—because that's how I feel about you. I love you, Pete. I love you more than Connie or Billie or even myself."

"OK, I love you."

"More than anyone else in the whole world?"

"More than anyone else."

"You swear?"

"On my mother's grave."

Chapter 26

After Fallon left, Pete lay awake trying to justify his last words to her. A promise extracted in the aftermath of first sex could not be compared to the vows of marriage. He'd crossed his fingers when he swore on his mother's grave, and asked for God's forgiveness as soon as Fallon closed the door. But what really bothered him more than his conflicted profession of love was how she got under his skin in ways Isabella never had. The feeling provided little comfort, considering his earlier commitment to go home, a decision that nothing or no one—not Fallon or One Eleven or Connie—would ever change.

That afternoon Pete promoted Tom Baker to One Eleven's assistant manager. The advancement came with a ten-dollar raise on Tom's weekly paycheck and the promise of another ten when Pete left for Italy. "How long you gonna be away?" asked the gaunt man with thinning hair and a pencil mustache.

"A month, maybe two, I haven't decided."

"Damn, I ain't been back to Tennessee since I left twenty years ago. You have family across the ocean?"

"Mostly friends," Pete said.

"Well don't be staying too long, or maybe you won't wanna come back."

"No chance of that."

"Spoken like a true American."

Not exactly, although obtaining American citizenship ranked high on Pete's priorities, one he promised to resolve on his return. But for now, his main concern was leaving before he dug himself a deeper hole.

*****

During the next four days Pete had no contact with Fallon. The choice to stay away had been as much his as hers since Fallon had also made herself scarce. Her royal response to first sex—pretending it never happened—got Pete off the hook, but he still couldn't get her out of his mind.

On Friday he walked out to the Latimer porch just as Fallon scampered down the steps. She was dressed in tennis whites and tossed her racket in the rumble seat of Steele's roadster before snuggling next to him. They took off with a blast and although Steele had not been introduced to Pete, he waved along with Fallon and zoomed away. As Pete watched the roadster's trail of dust, he caught a familiar scent of perfume from behind.

"Connie expects an engagement before the end of summer," La Bianca said.

"Don't you have some books to catalogue?"

"My, my, aren't you testy this morning. Not getting enough sleep?"

"Sorry, I have things on my mind."

"Connie tells me you're going back to Italy."

"Just for a visit."

"Fallon seemed surprised when I told her."

"I only decided a couple days ago. Besides, what difference should it make to her?"

"None whatsoever, she's having too much fun to concern herself with the help."

"That leaves me out, not that it matters. You're looking at the part owner of Club Eleven."

"And you're not telling me anything I don't already know. Ten percent seems extraordinarily generous of Connie but token ownership doesn't buy your way into the Latimer household."

La Bianca and the spoiled brat, enough alike to be cut from the same cloth—one with the balls to equal any man's, the other flaunting herself to get a rise from Pete's. As if he cared. Like hell he cared. He couldn't get Fallon out of his mind. She made him crazy, soaring through his every thought like some witch on her night run.

"Now whereabouts in Italy do you hail from?" La Bianca asked.

Pete prepared for another cat and mouse game. "The mountains."

"Just the mountains, no village?"

"None you ever heard of."

"No doubt your family will be happy to see you."

"I'm going back because there's business to settle."

"You must've left in a hurry."

"In Italy nothing is hurried. Not like America, where time is money. Now if you'll excuse me, I'll put my own time to good use—making money for Connie. And for me."

*****

When Pete wasn't working or showing Tom the ropes, he kept busy with his travel arrangements, a journey that would take him back to Pietro Rocca's life and all the changes since he left. But in America he still had to deal with Pete Montagna's life, and with Fallon. He shouldn't have allowed her inside his head or his heart. Avoiding her kept him from brooding over Steele's accelerating courtship, which the little witch seemed to enjoy. Pete should've shown her the door instead of his bed. Fallon's one night with him had not fazed her but it haunted him with sweet pain. Stupid for a man his age with a wife he hadn't acknowledged in years and a bevy of whores whose names he couldn't remember.

On Sunday Pete returned to his St. Louis routine, a pleasure he didn't enjoy as much in the summer since no amount of air-cooling in the theaters could temper Mississippi Valley heat. After the Myrna Loy matinee and a lonely dinner, Pete went to a waterfront dive. He pissed the hours away under a whirling fan while nursing cheap wine and listening to the local Cardinal fans extol the escapades of Dizzy and Daffy Dean. He was ready to leave when a firm thigh brushed against his. A pair of silk stockings caught his attention as their owner slid onto the next stool.

"You look like a man who could use some company," the woman said in a voice gravelly from booze and smokes. Her black lacquered helmet of rigid hair surrounded an almost pretty face.

"Arlington Hotel?" he asked.

"Home sweet home, who knows, maybe we once played house together."

"Business must be slow with you working this side of the river."

"Nah, this Mary Magdalene takes Sundays off, same as my johns. They're mostly family men. You know, morning church followed by chicken dinner. At night respectable jazz with the little woman, after they play nasty with me."

Pete nodded. "The American way."

She laughed, louder than the comment warranted. "For a man with a sense of humor, I could make an exception."

"Thanks, but Sunday's my day off too." He tossed two dollars her way, and walked out alone.

As Pete crossed Eades Bridge, he looked through the rear view mirror. The western sky showed off a setting sun that reminded him of an orange-red bocce ball—one game he hadn't played since Butte. Not since he and Leo got in over their heads, scrambling like hell for a few bucks destined to elude them. Leo would shit if he could see Pete now. Thank God he couldn't.

Back at the farm Pete bypassed the Latimer house. Although dusk had drifted into night and a breeze stirred the trees, the cottage still cooked like a hotbox. He stripped down and took a cold shower, his third that day, and stepped into a new style of drawers called Jockey boxers. With a cold beer in hand and the damp towel around his shoulders, he plopped into his easy chair and tackled the Fitzgerald novel he'd started weeks earlier, before Fallon started bothering him. He'd managed the first four pages of Chapter Fifteen when the door flew open.

There stood Fallon, a blouse tied at her midriff and shorts

swinging like the Forty-second Street dancers. She assumed her bossiest posture—feet spread apart, hands on hips—and demanded to know where he'd been.

Pete stood up, one hand covering the fly of his boxers. "Connie's been looking for me?"

"Not Connie, me."

"You shouldn't have come. The lawyer might not like his girl being alone with some other man. Neither would Connie."

"When you're with me, forget Hamilton Steele. Forget Billie. Forget Connie. Dammit, I don't want you thinking about anybody but me—Fallon Latimer."

*****

During the next month Steele's presumed monopoly on Fallon entailed early morning horseback riding, tennis or picnic weekends, and party rounds with people Billie referred to as 'the smart set'. But at two in the morning when Pete came home from the club, he always found Fallon waiting in his bed and for the next two hours, she belonged to him. After listening to the humorous details of Steele's conservative wooing, which had progressed to the kissing stage, Pete would cut loose and make love to her in ways he wanted her never to forget.

"How can you do this to me," she said one night after they had finished what he considered his best performance.

"I didn't please you?"

"Oh yes, most definitely. What I meant was: how can you think about leaving me in two weeks."

"Tom Baker is as good as he's ever going to get. I've booked passage on the—"

"And you'll be gone how long?"

"A month, maybe two, I haven't decided."

"Haven't decided! Well, you just never know. I might decide to marry my lawyer friend before you return."

He rolled on top of her, pinning her wrists against the rumpled sheet. "Go ahead, if you think that namby-pamby has the balls to make you happy."

"Billie said—"

"Who cares what Billie said." He rolled over, wishing he still smoked so he could reach for a cigarette. "I thought you had a mind of your own."

"Oh, Pete, I do. And I've all but worn it out over you. I can't stand the idea of your being away for two days, let alone two months. Take me with you. I want to see where you came from and meet all your childhood friends."

"We're not talking your kind of life. My Old World has bedrooms no bigger than Hester's pantry, and lumpy, straw mattresses."

"If the bed creaks, we'll try some new positions."

"And the toilets are glorified holes in the floor."

"No worse than camping. Did I tell you about my summer in the Rockies?"

"This is no vacation, Fallon. I have important business to settle."

"When you're busy, I can go off on my own. My Italian's good enough—"

"Not where I'm going. My people speak a dialect."

"I'm a quick study. But if I can't learn the language, I'll use my hands or put my feet up and read. And when you come back to our tiny room with its glorified hole in the floor, we'll make passionate whoopee until the neighbors bang on the walls. In the morning we'll drink cappuccino and—"

"Connie would never give his permission."

"Not unless we get married first. If you can't wait, we'll elope and honeymoon in the Alps—what more could any girl want."

"You don't understand."

"I won't give you any trouble. You'll hardly know I'm around, except at night. And then you better take care of me, just like you do now. I'll take care of you too, like any good wife would. Dearest Pete, I love you so much!"

Before Fallon left his bed that night, Pete extracted a promise from her not to say or do anything until he resolved some issues.

In the morning, he told Connie the trip had been postponed until September.

"No problem with Tom, I hope," Connie said.

"Tom's ready. But between the locals and all those rich college kids from across the river, business is booming. I better wait one more month."

"A wise decision, I taught you well, Pete. And the more I know you, the more I trust your judgment."

Connie's words stang like hot tar on tender skin — a most unpleasant predicament when accompanied by feathers, the least violent scene Pete could envision if Connie ever found out about him and Fallon. Postponing his trip had been Pete's way of buying time until he could leave without giving Fallon any warning. Part of him wanted her engaged to Steele, even married before he returned. Then he'd have to get her out of his system. He owed his allegiance to Pietro's family. Bringing them over would upset Fallon, but she'd still have Steele. And Steele would have Fallon, to hold and to love.

*****

On a full-moon night in late August Pete and Fallon lay in bed listening to the sounds of hooting owls trickling through the open window when she said, "I've decided not to return to Indiana."

"So Billie talked you into a St. Louis school."

"Not exactly. I need some time off."

"What about your teaching certificate?"

"A dream I haven't given up, just postponed."

"Ah, the dutiful Fallon doing Connie's bidding. So when's the wedding."

"As soon as the groom and I agree on a date."

"Let's see." Pete held up his hand, willing it not to shake as he counted on his fingers. "One week for the newspaper announcement, two weeks for parties, and three weeks for St. Anthony's to publish the wedding bans. That means Fallon Latimer could be Mrs. Hamilton Steele by the end of September."

"Highly unlikely. I'm not marrying Ham unless you want him to stand in as the father of our baby."

"Our what!"

"You heard me, our baby."

Pete felt the blood drain from his face. The lump clutching his throat reminded him of the one Fallon had dislodged a few months earlier. Better he should've choked then instead of now.

"This cannot be. I was always careful."

"Not the first time. How prophetic, remember when you said it would be one I'd never forget."

Pete saw his return to Italy dissolve into another pipedream. He made no effort to mask his feelings. "Oh no ... not me, not now."

"What are you suggesting, Pete? That I gave myself to another man?" Tears spilled down her cheeks. "Poor Ham, he hasn't even touched me, except for a few kisses and to hold hands. Oh god, you think I'm a tramp."

"You know me better than that. It's just—well, I can't marry you now." He wanted to add: not tomorrow, not ever. "Give me some time. I'll work things out."

"You better make it quick. Billie already suspects."

"She saw us together?"

"Not unless she followed me at two in the morning, which I doubt since she always waits up for Connie. But she does keep track of my monthly visitor. Remember last month, those four days I stayed in bed with terrible cramps? Hester even brought me tea and toast. Well, I faked the whole thing. Then I mixed up my make-believe schedule and Billie started counting off days on the calendar. She keeps eyeing me, waiting for me to pray to the porcelain goddess."

"Porcelain goddess?"

"You know: the toilet. Poor Darling, how would a confirmed

bachelor know about the nastiness of morning sickness? If Billie and Connie insist on a hurry-up wedding, trust me—you won't be the groom. Don't look it me that way, Pete. I can't take much more. After tonight, I'll take to my bed again, only this time for real. I'm so wrung out I could sleep for a week."

Pete couldn't stop his head from spinning at the thought of a new baby on the way after deserting the two who were no longer babies. Logic told him to stick to the plan. Take his savings and get the hell out. And if he ever came back to America, avoid the Midwest, or any other place within reach of Connie Latimer's tentacles.

*****

Several days passed without Pete seeing Fallon, time he used to withdraw his savings and finalize plans for catching the Sunday train to New York. On Saturday he waited until Connie had finished breakfast before requesting an immediate meeting. The Kingpin seemed preoccupied, but agreed to accommodate him. They assumed their usual positions across the desk, and Pete waited while Connie struck a match to his fresh cigar.

"So you've decided not to postpone your trip after all," Connie said, beating Pete to the punch.

"An emergency came up, but how did you know?"

"You might say intuition; Billie's not mine."

La Bianca, always with her nose in Pete's business. In this case, he couldn't blame her. She loved Fallon as much as he did, or thought he did, maybe more. He should've left two months ago, before this mess with Fallon started. He would've given anything to be someplace else right now.

"Too bad about the wedding," Connie said. "Oh, I guess you

haven't heard, but then why should you. You've been so busy. My daughter's getting married, within the month."

Pete was off the hook, or maybe impaled. Another man raising his baby might provide a better life. Better than he gave Gina and Riccardo. He squared his jaw before he spoke. "Hamilton Steele is a very lucky man."

"Or very stupid, I haven't decided which. You, on the other hand, appear very relieved. Is there something you want to tell me?"

Whatever the problem, don't ever let Connie catch you in a lie, Jackie G once said. Pete met Connie's cold gaze when he answered the question. "Nothing you haven't already guessed."

"But not confirmed until I saw the look on your face. I should be surprised, but somehow I'm not. This whole business with Steele was so unlike Fallon. I should've known she wanted to throw suspicion away from a less desirable suitor. But you of all people! God help me, I would never have figured the man I trusted with my life taking advantage of Fallon, until Billie wised me up."

Pete shifted uncomfortably but offered no excuses. Connie's scowl showed nothing but contempt as he fired another round.

"You dago bastard! Fallon was a virgin until your damn itch needed scratching. You took away her innocence. Now she's upstairs, crying her eyes out. My lovely daughter never had a care in the world, except to make me proud. Yesterday she nearly lost the baby—your baby. God bless Billie for her quick action in calling Doc Murdock."

"Look, Connie I didn't know all this. What I mean to say is, I just found out several days ago, but until now I didn't know Fallon was sick."

"Stop your blubbering! She made herself sick. Do you

understand what I'm saying? Fallon tried to rid herself of the baby. My grandchild, a Latimer almost flushed down the toilet like a bowl of shit."

"My God, she's all right now?"

"No thanks to you. And the baby's still tucked inside, where it damn well better stay for the next seven months. Dammit, Pete, I could kill you myself, inch by inch, starting with that damn weenie which had no business inside my daughter. Now she's in a state of hysteria, worrying you might disappear from the face of the earth. That I could make happen, and every commonsense bone in my body tells me I should, but that would make my grandchild illegitimate, and no Latimer will ever be a bastard."

"About Steele—"

"Shut up! The audacity of your bringing up his name turns my stomach. Hamilton can seed his own babies so why should he raise yours. The fellow's a twit but not a fool, and neither is his father. A trumped-up wedding followed by a seven-month baby would make me beholden to the Steele family forever after, not that I didn't consider such a union. But Fallon absolutely refused to go along with the charade." Connie snuffed out his cigar and leaned forward, curling his upper lip. "Now about the wedding—"

"Look, Connie. I can't marry Fallon. If I could, I would."

"You can and you will!" Connie jumped up, bolted across the den, and yanked the door open. "Billie! Get in here!" His voice reverberated from the walls like a wayward boomerang.

Connie kept his back turned and shoulders squared as he waited for Billie, which gave Pete a breather. Between his perennial bickering with La Bianca and her contempt for him, Pete thought she might welcome an excuse to see him go—feet first or at least on his knees. Maybe he still had a chance, slim at best, of returning to Pietro's family.

The clicking of Billie's high heels announced her imminent arrival. She hurried in, wearing her usual air of superiority as she took the chair next to Pete's. Having returned to the comfort of his swivel, Connie cracked his first smile, more ironic than pleasant. "Well, Billie my Love, once again you've proven your wisdom. I only regret not heeding your words sooner."

"Now, now, Connie, we'll just have to make the best of an embarrassing situation. Of course, Pete—"

"Has agreed to accept responsibility for his actions, right, Pete?"

"Of course, I'll pay. The baby will have—"

"A father married to its mother. And you will pay, believe me, you will pay. Tell him, Billie."

"For starters, you will forego any trip to Italy. You won't have time, what with wedding plans and a few parties. And there's—"

"Basta! Before you go any further, let me explain my situation. I can't marry Fallon. Not now, not ever. I already have a wife."

Connie slammed his fist on the desk, splintering its veneered edge. "I knew it! I knew you had a skeleton rattling in some far-off closet. A man like you, ambitious and hard-nosed, not wanting to marry the best catch in all of Southern Illinois."

Billie put a finger to her lips. "Connie, please. Remember your ulcer." She turned back to Pete. "This woman, I suppose she was your reason for returning to Italy?"

"This woman is my wife. We have two children, twelve-year old twins—a boy and a girl. I haven't seen them in seven years."

Connie leaned forward. "Seven years, you say? H-m-m, then legally you are dead in the eyes of the law."

"But not in the eyes of God."

"You dare to blaspheme God. You desert one family and try to run out on another. If you can't abide the sacrament of marriage, perhaps you should consider the only alternative sacrament—final rites."

The flush of Connie's anger had progressed to the crimson stage, a color Pete had witnessed only one other time, on Giovanni Martino. Causing a second man's stroke seemed extreme, and one Pete did not relish. Then, La Bianca interceded.

"Now Connie, we mustn't make Fallon a widow before she's a bride." She moved behind his chair, and massaged his neck with long, defining strokes. "Shall we return to our current business? Pete, I suppose you've been providing for these people?"

"Not exactly—"

"Means, no."

"That's why I was going back. To make up for wasted years."

"I've heard enough." Connie slid a pencil and paper pad across the desk. "Write down the woman's name and address. I'll see to it that she receives a monthly stipend—out of your One Eleven profits, of course."

Pete hesitated. He'd not written Isabella's name since coming to America. His secrecy had sheltered her from further disgrace.

Connie's face softened. "For god's sake, Pete, what kind of monster do you take me for? Write the damn name."

"She's not to know where the money comes from."

"On that you can be sure," said Connie. "I expect your lack of communication to continue as before." He patted Billie's hand. She responded with extra pressure to her last stroke before sitting down again. "Billie, I want you to contact Monsignor Duggan right off. See if the rectory needs a new roof, or if he has a worthwhile project in need of funding. Do whatever it takes to push this wedding through without a hitch."

*****

Billie with a mission had transformed into La Bianca at her best. While initiating the preliminary wedding plans, she also handled arrangements for Pietro Rocca's family, or as she referred to them—those people. Two hundred ten dollars, half of the ten percent profit Pete had yet to see, passed from Billie's hands to Connie's lawyer, from East St. Louis to Pont Canavese where a second lawyer received a stipend to administer the funds.

Pete didn't want to consider Isabella's reaction to the financial windfall. Nor the act of bigamy he was about to commit. After living his lie for so long, Pietro Rocca had evolved into Pete Montagna, moderately successful and about to marry a beautiful young woman who loved him above all else. And privately admitting how much he loved Fallon had elevated the forced marriage to an exhilarating level.

Another week passed before Fallon gained enough strength to participate in the wedding plans. When she learned the extent of Billie's elaborate preparations, she went to Connie and demanded a simple ceremony and no reception. "We could use the money for our baby," she explained. "After all, Pete doesn't make a whole lot. At least not yet, although I hope time will change your attitude toward him."

"Nonsense," Connie said. "Since when has money ever been an issue where this family is concerned. You and Pete will live here and raise the baby in the manner befitting a Latimer. Now be a sport and let Billie plan the wedding she's always dreamed of for you."

When the betrothed couple met with Monsignor Duggan, Pete submitted the same forged papers he'd secured before leaving Italy. And when the monsignor asked for proof of his baptism, Pete used his most sincere expression to explain his little parish church had been destroyed in the Italian/Austrian war, along with all its pertinent documents.

"Not to worry," the monsignor said. "We'll do another baptism, a conditional one just to keep the records straight."

Chapter 27

Summer, 1938

Whenever Pete looked into the face of his two-year old son, he saw the children he left behind: those same black eyes, round and full of mischief, the sweet innocence of youth. But now Gina and Riccardo were on the cusp—no longer children, not quite adults. And he had lost them forever, their mother too. Sending money helped, even under the charade of anonymity. Still, Isabella would know its source. She was always clever, except when it counted most—the summer of Giovanni's wife. Even then, Isabella had all the answers. In that respect she reminded him of La Bianca—a grand matriarch, tough and unyielding. Not like the trusting Fallon who adored him and in return, demanded every fiber of his being.

Even now, after nearly three years as Mrs. Pete Montagna, Fallon didn't know she was married to a bigamist. Nor, did he know if his crime affected the legality of their son. Still with a name like Daniel Latimer Montagna, and The Kingpin's money backing him, the boy would never lack for anything. As for Pete, he had resolved not to worry. Rewards in this life meant giving a little in order to receive a lot more in return. And comprising his mortal soul meant having to share his son and his secret with Connie and Billie.

Pete had been staring at the strips of paisley wallpaper for so long the patterns were merging into a kaleidoscope of colors. He slouched down into the club chair and stretched his legs over the ottoman, furniture Fallon had selected for their upstairs wing of Connie's house. Besides Danny Boy's room, the suite consisted of a sitting room and two bathrooms. Both Pete and Fallon enjoyed the living arrangements that freed them from mundane household duties, allowing him to concentrate on One Eleven and her to care for Danny Boy and to volunteer at their parish and Catholic Charities in East St. Louis.

Hearing the door push open, Pete closed his eyes and waited. Fallon slid onto his lap, brushed the stray hair from his forehead, and kissed his eyelids.

"OK, most high potentate and daddy of all daddies, time to return to Earth." After a long, wet kiss, she put her head on his shoulder. "If you must have your head in the clouds, just make sure I'm the only one up there with you."

"I wouldn't have it any other way," Pete said, feeling the effects of her kiss. He wanted to roll onto the floor with her. Copulate like savages, as Fallon often described their lovemaking. But habit overruled desire. He glanced at his watch, holding back the inevitable sigh he felt.

"Make time," she said. "After all, you are the boss."

"If you don't count Connie."

"Who's counting? Except for weekends, he leaves the place in your hands."

"And my job is making sure everybody else does theirs."

"I should come first."

"You already had your turn."

"But that was hours ago. I'm still hungry."

Pete slid his hand under her dress and found the flare of her silk tap panties. "This should tide you over 'til I come home tonight."

She giggled. "That's not fair, but don't stop yet."

He removed his hand and stood up, taking Fallon with him.

"You're such a tease," she said. "All talk and delayed action. Which reminds me, I'm still waiting for our trip to Italy."

"Later," Pete said, already moving toward the door.

"By the way, speaking of Italy I almost forgot. Yesterday at Catholic House, I received a telephone call—some oily fellow with an accent like yours, only not so polished. I guess he saw my picture in the Journal, you know, the one where I'm presenting our check to Sister Mary Joseph. She was so—"

"This man, what did he say?"

"That he was an old friend of yours from The Galleria. I asked if he meant that magnificent structure in Milan, which he found quite amusing judging from his snickering. And then I remembered you've never been to Milan."

The muscles in Pete's jaw tightened up to project his controlled voice. "He left his name?"

"Of course I asked, but all he said was, 'I'll catch up with him later.' Any idea who ... Pete? Dammit, you know how I feel about talking to your back." She followed him into the hallway. "I swear, you're as bad as Connie."

Too late, he was already racing down the stairs.

"Pete! You forgot to kiss me goodbye."

*****

By eleven that evening Pete had weaved through the club twice, a practice he limited to the evenings Connie stayed away. Since Danny Boy's birth, the Kingpin had mellowed, preferring to spend his evenings at home with Billie to monitor the child's progress. Naming him after Connie's father had been Pete's suggestion, a coup that eliminated any ill will Connie harbored over the shotgun marriage. He remained firmly entrenched in The Kingpin's good graces, and intended to stay there.

Pete walked out to the back porch and loosened his tie. He took in a deep breath of night air and slowly exhaled to expel the foul air permeating One Eleven.

"Hey, paesano, long time no see," said a voice from the shadows. "Can you believe it's been eight long years?"

Leo the Loser, the last person he wanted to see. Still, the man's presence came as no surprise. Pete accepted the outstretched hand into his and allowed it to be pumped. They studied each other in the moonlight. Leo wore his thirty-eight years like the shabby suit Pete recognized as one he'd left behind in Butte.

"I gotta hand it to you, Pete, ditching me like yesterday's newspaper. Me, your best friend and benefactor."

"My leaving had nothing to do with you."

"Why, if it wasn't for Adie Turner telling me about her holier-than-thou-Glory Bea running into you, I woulda never thought about stopping in this hellhole. See, I'm working my way back to Italy. For Ma, she ain't doing so good."

"I'm sorry." Pete envisioned the distraught woman clinging to her son's leg when Leo had talked of leaving Faiallo. At the time Regina Arnetti seemed ancient; she must've been all of fifty-five.

Leo opened his arms as if to encompass the breadth of One Eleven's structure and then smacked the cupped fingers and thumb of his right hand. Pete dismissed the unctuous demonstration with a wave of his hand. "Don't get any ideas, Leo. I just manage the place."

"So I hear, for your father-in-law."

Pete sat down on the nearest step and Leo joined him. Leaning their elbows back to the porch floor, they stretched out their legs like the two young bucks. Leo spoke first.

"This reminds me of those nights when we was kids, me and you and the stars. Not that I'm the sentimental type. Still, a lot's gone down since Faiallo, Butte too. I never woulda thought you had such *balli*, giving up one family to start another. What was that all about?"

"About the here and now, and not the past."

"Your new wife, I saw her picture in the newspaper—bella, bella." Leo bent his arm and gestured another approval. "She told you I called?"

"You could've found another way to let me know you were in town."

"But my way got faster results. Damn, I swear every highbrow and lowbrow in East St. Louis knows the name Pete Montagna. And to think, if it wasn't for me, you'd still be Pietro Rocca—on the lam and looking over his shoulder."

"You always could stretch a story."

"Remember Giovanni's Dog? How could you forget, me

either. My ribs still carry the scars from his knife. Damn, I fought like hell protecting your whereabouts. He cut me good before I gave in and told him you might be at The Galleria. I thought for sure he set out to make you a soprano, and then changed his mind and decided not to let you sing 'cause the next thing I knew, both you and him had dropped off the face of the earth." Leo nudged Pete. "So now I think maybe you got to him first."

"Never laid a hand on the man, maybe he got sidetracked."

"Or, got stopped in his tracks." Leo shook his head. "It just ain't fair, the way Lady Luck shines on some more than others. You take on a second wife, a rich one at that, while I'm still single and scratching for a buck. I hate going back to Italy with empty pockets. Maybe I oughta stick around here for a while and look for work. Say, you got any pull?"

"Maybe the stockyards."

"Take a good look, Pete. I ain't got that kind of stamina anymore. Not with these lungs." He coughed and patted his chest. "Forget mining, or any other hard labor. Hell, I paid my dues and then some. I had inside work in mind, maybe an opening in this fancy club."

"No chance. I let two men go last week."

"Ouch, with all those cars jammed in the parking lot? Well, enough about work, leastways for now. There's plenty of time to discuss my options."

Time. Pete glanced at his wristwatch, any excuse to end what had become tedious. "I need to get back."

"Look, I ain't some bum asking for a handout. If there's one thing I hate, it's mooching—except when it comes from a paesano. You know, like the way you came to me and I gave you a helping hand."

"As I recall, you still owe me three hundred dollars."

"Hells fire, Pete, how can you bring up such a *merdosa* amount? Take a gander at the life you got, even one more son. Yeah, I know about the boy, Connie Latimer's grandson. Damn, what a sweet deal. I hear you're in tight with the old man."

"Only if I keep producing," Pete said, "same as mining, only above ground."

"And no sweat to spoil all the niceties, like that car parked out front and a fancy farm you don't have to work but your son will someday inherit. Yeah, I heard about the mother lode too."

"Theirs, not mine."

"So, Pete, these two women—your new wife and the old one—what do they think of each other?"

While Pete struggled inwardly for a plausible answer, Bean's voice cut through the darkness. "Hey, Pete, excuse me for interrupting but there's a problem in the backroom needing your immediate attention."

How long Beans had been standing there, Pete didn't know; but he welcomed the excuse to leave.

"Don't let me keep you," Leo said. "You got a business to run and I gotta check on my room. You wouldn't believe the mice and cockroaches."

Pete pulled out a roll of bills and peeled off four twenties. "Try the Arlington on Broadway. But don't tell anybody I sent you."

Pressing the handout to his lips, Leo gave a loud smack. "Grazie, paesano, I knew I could count on you."

"Just don't spend those bucks here. I don't ever want to see you around One Eleven again, capice?"

*****

The next day Billie eavesdropped on Beans telling Connie about the conversation between Pete and an outsider named Leo. At least the part Beans overheard, which covered the people in Italy and a murder in Butte. The murder was news to Billie, but nothing about Pete really surprised her. Not even his obvious love for Fallon, and the little boy they all adored. The immigrant had proven his worthiness, but thus far had managed to keep his hands reasonably clean. And off of her, although had he persisted long enough, she might've considered giving in, maybe once. But she couldn't take a chance on what Connie would do if he ever found out. Not to her but to Pete. And all this was, of course, before Fallon had stolen his heart.

"So whadaya think, Connie?" she heard Beans ask. "You want me to arrange for this Leo's immediate exit? Maybe an accident at the Arlington."

"It's Pete's problem to resolve."

"Yeah, but it involves Fallon too."

That was Billie's cue to walk in, and ask, "What involves Fallon?"

Connie motioned his head toward the door, Beans' cue to leave. He stifled a belch as he passed by her. Still, she lifted her brow and he excused himself.

"You're late for breakfast," he said. "Hester already poured my coffee."

"That's what you get for waking me in the middle of the night." She poured him another cup and sat down. "What's this about Fallon?"

"Nothing Pete can't handle."

"Pete handle Fallon, please. It's all he can do to manage the club."

"While she manages her volunteer crap and you look after Danny Boy. You give her too much leeway, Billie."

"You're evading my question."

"And you're evading my answer. Now if you'll excuse me I have a business to run." He leaned across the table, brushed her cheek.

"You can do better than that," she said. He kissed her again, this time with the authority she loved to challenge.

Chapter 28

After eleven o'clock Mass on Sunday Pete left St. Anthony's with Danny Boy in his arms and Fallon at his side, the start of a good day until Leo Arnetti showed up.

"Buon giorno, Pietro," The Loser said. He pumped Pete's hand, chucked Danny Boy's chin, and tipped his hat to Fallon. "Bella donna, this must be Signora Montagna." With a slight bow he took Fallon's hand and held it to his lips until she pulled free, more amused than repulsed.

"I recognize your voice," she said. "You called several weeks ago, didn't you?"

"Si, me and your husband are the best of friends. We go back a long way."

"You knew each other in Italy?"

"Like brothers we were."

"How wonderful, Mr.—"

"Leo Arnetti."

"Well, Mr. Arnetti, you must—"

"Be on your way," Pete interrupted. "Sorry, Leo, my day's jam-packed with business, maybe some other time."

"How 'bout Tuesday, some bread and wine, a little cheese. Just like old times."

Fallon tugged on Pete's arm. "Perhaps Mr. Arnetti could—"

"Leo, please call me Leo."

"I'm sure Leo wouldn't want to impose," Pete said as he slipped him two twenties. "I'll catch up with you later." Without waiting for another show of Leo's gratitude, Pete steered Fallon down toward the parking lot.

"It's not like you to be so rude, Pete. After all, Mr. Arnetti … uh, Leo is your only tie to Italy."

"Ties I don't need. My home is here in America, with you and our son."

"Oh, Pete, sometimes you say the sweetest words. Is it any wonder I love you so much."

Ten feet away and dressed in a splash of red poppies against a white background stood Billie, who'd observed the Leo scene with eyes and ears as sharp as an insect's antennae.

Her words were directed at Fallon but she meant them for Pete. "Really, Fallon, for the life of me, I can't imagine why you'd want to associate with that dreadful man. Or expose our Danny Boy to him."

"You're such a darling," Fallon said, giving Billie a hug. "But you don't have to worry about me. That's Pete's job and he's simply marvelous at it."

*****

The next morning after Connie went to work, Billie drove her roadster to East St. Louis. She parked on Broadway and walked the two blocks to Sam's Pawn Shop. Instead of going inside, she window shopped next door for another five minutes. When she finally entered Sam's establishment, the owner came out from behind the counter to greet her.

"Willajenka, it's been too long."

"Now, Sam, you know I prefer Billie."

"That I do. It's just that we go back a long way and sometimes I forget." He rubbed his hands together. "So, what do you need this fine day? A brooch, earrings, perhaps a string of pearls?"

She shook her head.

"Surely you don't have something for me?"

"As a matter of fact, I do." She opened her purse, just enough for him to see the fifty dollar bill inside."

"We'll talk, away from the window." With a snap of his fingers Sam's young wife stopped her sweeping and took over the counter duty.

"You have other customers in the shop?" Billie asked.

"No, but it looks good to have a Friedman near the cash register should anyone walk in."

Billie followed him into the backroom where he kept his private stock—antiques and estate jewelry from across the river. The furs too—mink and sable, with their labels removed. Not that any of his stolen merchandise interested her.

"Sit, sit," he said, clearing boxes from a sagging chair.

"Another time, I need a favor. Of course I'll pay." She handed him the fifty. "Understand what I say, Sam: no one must connect my name with this favor."

He backed off. "As in Connie?"

"Of course Connie knows. But, you are never to mention our conversation to him, or Beans, or Jackie G, and especially not to Pete. Not a soul, do you understand?" She handed him another fifty.

"For god's sake, Willajenka, we go all the way back to—"

She handed him a ten.

"You know I run a legitimate business, most of the time."

"And you know so many people that I don't know. And some of those people know other people." This time she handed him a slip of paper, not the perfumed variety she favored but from a five and ten tablet. "This name belongs to an individual so despicable that—"

"What's he done?"

"A terrible crime."

"The one against children? He needs to be run out of town."

"No, Sam. He needs to be carried out, feet first. And soon."

"Then how about—"

"Don't tell me who or how, just when I can expect results."

*****

That evening at the lakeside of One Eleven, Pete greeted Leo with a surprise right hook.

"Merda," Leo said, rubbing his cheekbone. "What the hell was that for?"

"*Leccone!* For sucking up to me in front of my wife."

"Not like the first wife, huh, when you needed me to make your getaway."

Pete hit Leo again, this time cutting his lip. "That's for bringing up the past. Think about the here and now; what I want is you out of my life—forever."

"Hell, that's all I ever wanted too, besides enough money to visit Ma again."

A left to the jaw sent Leo to the ground. Pete pulled him up by the belt, and stuck his face in Leo's. "Your ma died three years ago."

"God rest her soul. So I want to put flowers on her grave, visit my brother and his family. Is that a crime?"

"Listen up, Leo. If you go back to Italy, you'll get no help from me. Go anywhere else, so long as it's a thousand miles from here, and I'll give you a fresh—and final—start. But don't ever come back here."

Leo spit out a mouthful of blood. "Don't go back to Italy, don't come back here. Who the hell made you my keeper?"

"Stupido, I'm trying to save your hide. With me you have nothing to worry about. Not so with Connie Latimer. The man has connections all the way to Italy, and if you ever pull a stunt to upset his daughter's life—"

"Basta, I get the picture. I hear Arizona's got some decent mountains. 'Course I don't know if I can take the damn heat."

"Look, I don't want to know where you land, just don't ever bother me again."

"And to think I once saved your hide." Leo stepped back, showed his palms. "OK, two thousand bucks and I'm out of here."

"One thousand, that's all I can afford."

"Kind of chintzy for a big shot such as yourself," Leo said.

"I just manage the money. Connie holds the purse strings and he doesn't tolerate fools. If he knew what you were up to, we wouldn't be having this little talk. But me, I have a soft spot for losers."

"So when do I get my thousand?"

"Wednesday noon, at the train depot."

*****

The next morning Fallon found Hester in the kitchen talking on the telephone.

"For you, dear," she said, handing Fallon the phone. "It must be one of the new nuns. A Sister Mary Magdalene she said."

Fallon sat down, prepared to field another request for her time or money, or both. "Hello, Sister. How can I help you?"

"One moment, please." The response came from a telephone booth at the Arlington, where the whore with a lacquered helmet of hair collected two dollars for the acting assignment. Her nervous john grabbed the earpiece, pushed her from the stall, and closed the door.

"Leo Arnetti here," he said. "You remember, Pete's old friend from Italy."

"Of course, Sunday at St. Anthony's."

"Don't repeat my name, Mrs. Montagna. I fear for my life—your husband's too. I did him certain favors, and he owes me big time. We share a secret about his past life. God only knows what would happen if the police or the newspapers got hold of the information. Worse yet, I worry about the reaction of your father—Connie Latimer, ain't that his name?"

"Perhaps I could help."

"I knew I could count on your generosity—you being a giver in a world full of takers."

"How much?"

"Two thousand dollars would put me on the next train out of here. Forever, along with your husband's secret."

"Tomorrow morning, ten o'clock. Do you know Schroeder's Drugstore, next to the Majestic Theater?"

"God bless. Pete is one lucky man to have you at his side."

Fallon hung up. She sighed, drumming her fingers on the table.

"Problem with the new sister?" Hester asked.

"Nothing a little sugar can't cure," Fallon said. "In case Billie has plans, could you be a dear and watch Danny Boy tomorrow morning? A troublesome charity case needs my personal attention."

Chapter 29

Breakfast at the Latimer house catered to the individual appetite and this Wednesday was no exception. Connie dipped buttered toast into the yolks of two sunny-side-up eggs while packing away six slices of bacon. Beans slurped through a bowl of oatmeal and sliced peaches fresh from the orchard. Billie partook of her usual hot herbal tea, no sugar, and six stewed prunes Hester had already pitted. And when Connie pushed aside his plate of egg whites, she filled his cup with coffee and cream skimmed from the top of the milk.

"Fallon's gone riding?" he asked.

"Hm-m-m, not today, Hester mentioned an early meeting with a new nun."

"I thought you kept better track of my daughter."

"The day has hardly begun, my darling." She leaned over and wiped his mouth before kissing him. "Have I ever let you down?"

"I don't know how I'd manage without you." Connie stood up. He tapped Beans on the shoulder. "Enough with the mush, we have to resolve a numbers problem today. It seems another collector has shortchanged the take."

"Oh, Connie," Billie said with a tsk-tsk. "Will these people never learn."

Five minutes later, the telephone phone rang. Hester was busy with Danny Boy so Billie answered it with her most refined hello.

"Willajenka, is that you?"

"Yes, but—"

"Sh-h, don't say my name. Just listen. About that special order, expect delivery by eleven this morning."

Billie hung up the phone and checked her watch. Hm-m, enough time to change into her city clothes, and check on Fallon before settling her business with Sam. Hester said Fallon would be meeting some nun at ten o'clock—Schroeder's, of all places. And since when did a nun indulge her sweet tooth in public?

Upstairs in the Montagna wing Pete stirred from his deep sleep. He stretched out to Fallon and instead found a note she'd left on her pillow.

Darling,

I went into town early to settle an old debt and will be back in time for lunch. Give Danny Boy a kiss and save one for me.

Love,

Fallon

Pete rolled the card stock between his fingers, and wondered why Fallon would acquire any debt since she kept a bank account for her personal use. He quickly showered, dressed, and hurried down the main stairs. He checked out the dining room. Empty. He went to the kitchen for a morning ritual that began with, "Hey, where's my big boy?"

Danny Boy scooted off his chair. He ran to Pete and jumped into his waiting arms. Pete lifted him into the air, wiggling the boy until he squealed.

"You'd best stop that before he upchucks on your nice suit," Hester said.

Pete sat down, with Danny Boy in his lap. "Looks like the whole gang has deserted us."

"Ain't that the truth," Hester said, pouring his coffee. "First Fallon drives off, then Connie and Beans. Even Billie had business needing her attention."

He snapped his fingers. "Oh yeah, now I remember. Fallon said something about going downtown."

"That's right, a meeting with Sister Mary Magdalene."

"That name sounds familiar."

"Ought to, you met her Sunday at St. Anthony's."

He cocked his head. "I don't think so."

"Well, Fallon did. Leastways, that's what I overheard. You might be thinking of Mary Magdalene from the bible—you know, the woman with a questionable past. Anyway, Fallon's meeting this modern day sister at Schroeder's of all places, at ten this morning. She said something about a sugar cure."

While Hester rambled on about the evils of ingesting sugar before noon and Danny Boy scrambled down to play with his Tootsie trucks, Pete turned his thoughts elsewhere. Another nun wanting money? Not so unusual, considering Fallon's dedication to charitable work. Her way of making up for Connie, she told Pete. She told Connie too, not that he cared. But, on Sunday she met only one person. And that was Leo. Leo! Pete checked his watch, nine-thirty. If he hurried, maybe he could make Schroeder's by ten.

*****

By the time Fallon had withdrawn two thousand dollars from her personal banking account, the clock looming from the building at Missouri and Collinsville Avenues began pealing ten chimes. As she crossed the busy street, Fallon could see Leo through the window at Schroeder's, waiting at the candy counter while Miss Nadine arranged his sweets in a fancy box suitable for traveling. He paid for his purchase just as Fallon walked through the door. She sought out a booth at the far end, away from customers lolling over their coffee and Danish pastries. Leo strolled down the aisle and slid onto the bench facing her.

"I knew I could count on you, Mrs. Montagna. But you oughta know this ain't just about the money."

"Of course it's about the money, Mr. Arnetti."

"Leo, call me Leo."

"I prefer keeping our transaction on a business level, Mr. Arnetti. Now, about this information you have."

"If you don't mind, first the money."

She handed him an envelope and he gave her a rumpled sheet from his suit pocket. "It's all written down, names and dates, near as I can remember."

While Leo flipped through the bills, Fallon pulled a lighter from her purse. She ignited the lighter with her thumb, held the flame to Leo's paper, and watched his secrets burn.

"Hey, every word I wrote was true," Leo said. "Things you should know about Pete and his life back in Italy."

"You should leave now, Mr. Arnetti, before this meeting gets back to my father. I wouldn't want you to miss your train."

Leo stood up. "You're right. I'm headed for New York and from there, to Genoa. I've been away from home too long."

"Bon voyage, Mr. Arnetti."

He tipped his hat. "*Arrivederci*, Mrs. Montagna."

"I think not."

As Fallon watched the burning paper crumble into a brittle heap, Leo left in the wake of Schroeder's jiggling bell. At that same time Billie was driving her roadster down Collinsville Avenue, searching for a suitable parking space. Not one of them was aware of Pete standing in front of the Majestic, feigning interest in a Clark Gable movie poster. And of those three he only saw Leo pushing through the door of Schroeder's. Inside, Fallon noticed the box of sweets that dreadful man left behind. She picked it up and hurried toward the door.

While Billie continued looking for a parking space on Collinsville Avenue, Leo started across the street with both hands shoved in his pockets. He puckered his mouth into a whistle and approached the centerline with the assurance of a man who'd been dealt a good hand

Then Pete saw Fallon run out of Schroeder's. She stood at the curb, waving a package.

"Mr. Arnetti!" she called out. "Mr. Arnetti, you forgot your candy."

Leo turned and acknowledged her wave. He started to retrace his steps when the sound of a single gunshot cut through the traffic noise.

Pete heard the crunch of shattering glass and the squeal of careening tires, but he couldn't take his eyes off Leo who was too scared to run for cover. The Loser's luck ran out with the second shot, which found its mark between his eyes. With feet buckling, Leo Arnetti cashed in his last chips before he hit the pavement.

The cinematic sequence had mesmerized Pete into that of a gawking spectator. The incessant blasting from the horn of a nearby car pulled him back to reality. He turned to his right and what he saw brought the contentious lump back to his throat. He ran toward the drugstore, pushed through the curious bystanders.

On the sidewalk in front of Schroeder's a shower of radiator fluid sprouted from the disabled roadster, its lifeless driver slumped over the wheel. Blood spilled through the snow-white hair of a perfect coiffure. From the vacant expression on Billie Creznic's face and the size of the crater exposing her brain, Pete knew she had issued her last directive. He pushed her off the steering wheel, his only way to silence the damn horn proclaiming La Bianca's ill-timed departure.

In the deafening quiet that followed, Pete remembered Fallon. He backed away from the car, knowing he had to spare her from seeing Billie. He yelled out Fallon's name. She didn't answer so he yelled again. When she still didn't answer, he scanned the gathering crowd, and then moved his eyes to the pavement. His search ended with a scream, piercing the air with the force of a disaster whistle before it tapered into a mournful wail. Pete didn't realize the pathetic sounds he heard originated from the depths of his own throat, not Fallon's. He found her pinned under the front wheel of the roadster.

Dead; just like Billie.

Book Four—Chapter 30

Faiallo, Italy—1939

"But the money, Mama, there's so much and we have so little," said the pretty girl with eyes competing with every word she spoke. "Why can't we spend some of it on necessities?" Gina stuck out her lower lip. She stretched out a handful of faded material from her skirt. "I could use some new clothes. These make me look like a pathetic peasant."

Riccardo gave his sister an exasperated look. "But you are a pathetic peasant so don't be a testa dura too. How many times does Mama have to explain? She's saving the money for emergencies."

While the twins engaged in their usual banter, Isabella flipped through a stack of lire, the regular monthly stipend she received through an attorney in Pont Canavese. Anonymous benefactor, humph, did Pietro think her an idiot? What good was the money without a single word of affection or concern for his family's well being? He'd missed out on so much: the joy of watching his beautiful children transform into young adults, the love of a woman who regretted her foolish pride that sent him away. Wagging tongues be damned; after Pietro left, the village tongues were soon occupied with other scandals: first Serina and the gypsies, then a priest from Rivarola who ran off with the baker's wife.

Eleven years without Pietro. Eleven years without the strength of his arms, the warmth of his lean body against hers, the smell of shaving soap when he lathered his beard. The first time they met, he captured her heart without even know it. But Papa knew, and when Giovanni took him aside to ask for her hand that same day, Papa said the young friend he brought would make a better match.

"Mama, pay attention please," she heard Riccardo say. "Where should I store this month's bundle?"

Isabella turned to her son. She searched his face and found Pietro's. That handsome face, it stayed with her every day and haunted her dreams at night. At least Pietro was still alive, and evidently doing quite well. So why had he not come home?

"I'm waiting, Mama. Where do you want the money: in the well, the loft, or the stable?"

Isabella left her private world for the practical one, drumming the table as she mused aloud. "Well, let's see. We've run out of metal boxes, so that eliminates the rafters or the stable—those damn rats. Remind me to inquire about another cat when we go to market."

"About the money, please don't suggest the *gabinetto* again," said Gina. "I absolutely refuse to look for another hiding place in that smelly outhouse. I just don't understand your thinking. After all, everybody knows that money in the bank draws interest."

"Si, the curious interest of our Fascist government," Isabella countered. "The money at our fingertips will be secure and I will decide when and how we use it. Besides, I expect these stipends will soon dry up, what with *Il Duce* declaring war on Albania. It won't be long before he tries to gobble up some other countries, just to impress that arrogant Hitler."

Riccardo ejected an imaginary wad of spit, the only kind acceptable in her kitchen. "Il Duce, Il Duce—that damn *leccacula*, as if my friends or I cared about the politics of Italy and its neighboring countries."

"Let the Fascists take their fight to foreign soil," Gina said. "Italy must protect its priceless treasures."

Humph! What good are priceless treasures without the freedom to enjoy them? Isabella closed her eyes to the naiveté of sixteen-year-olds and prayed for the wisdom to help her family survive a war destined to affect all of Italy. No prayer would be complete without Maria and Allegra, as much her children as the twins. The girls called her Mama, and adored her as much as she adored them. To see Giovanni's withered face light up when the combined families sat around the table made her sacrifices almost worthwhile. The old goat would never be the man he once claimed to be, but by the grace of God, she'd managed to resurrect him from near death. When the two families took their meals together, it was Giovanni who sat at the head of the table. Pietro had been such a fool. But so had she.

*****

Within months Isabella's prediction came true. The stipends from Pietro disappeared as the threat of war against America loomed. Italy ordered its sons in foreign countries to come home, at least those the government could locate. Some returned to fight with their paesani, but not Pietro Rocca. In every village and city the dreaded government notices were posted: all able-bodied men must join the military or face a firing squad. Riccardo weighed his decisions: fight for the fascist cause he didn't support or die labeled a cowardly traitor. He signed up in Pont, and soon became a foot soldier in a military poorly trained and saddled with out-dated equipment, which further fueled his hatred for Mussolini. Still, he fought for Italy in Albania, and later in Greece when Il Duce became entangled in Hitler's web. He had to show the world his power by declaring war on France and Russia.

Shrapnel in the back and a bullet in his side earned Riccardo a trip to Sicily to recuperate in a palazzo that had been converted into a makeshift military hospital. On the day before his scheduled return to active duty, Riccardo leaned back in a recliner on the hospital's sun-drenched terrace. He was one of fourteen patients, all clad in blue pajamas, striped robes, and gray slippers. He'd survived too many battles to spend these final hours of peace reliving the war in his head. If he were home, Mama would've dismissed his demons by sending him up the hill to check on their animals. Gina—dear God, how he missed his twin—would've given him some ridiculous reason to tease her. Allegra, who he'd determined was his half-sister, would be too shy to ever bother him. Not so with the lively Maria. Somehow she managed to bring sunshine into his life on the cloudiest of days. Old Giovanni made a decent godfather, but he couldn't take the place of Pietro Rocca. Riccardo had given up on him long ago.

Pressing one hand to his flat stomach, he expelled the revenge of his noonday meal. "*Scusi*," he said to the man reading beside him, a Genoese whose fair skin and sandy-colored hair made him appear more German than Italian.

"It's that damn Siciliano spaghetti with tomatoes," Flavio Bonelli said from behind his newspaper. "I prefer my pasta as tortellini with pesto."

"For me, it's ravioli with cheese," Riccardo said. "Not that I expect to return home anytime soon."

"Yesterday we were in our underwear, playing futbol with the hospital staff." Flavio lowered his voice for only Riccardo's ears. He kept the newspaper up to his face. "Tomorrow we will change into our gray uniforms and once again fight for Hitler's lapdog. Where do you think they'll send us?"

"Who can say," Riccardo whispered. "Maybe back to Greece."

"Anywhere but there, it's not their uniformed soldiers I fear, but those radical civilians hiding in the mountains."

"Ah, they possess the tenacity and courage of their ancestors. I share that passion, that desire for freedom above all else."

"Just be careful of those who hear you express such admiration." Flavio lowered his newspaper. He glanced around to the other patients, followed twelve pairs of eyes turned upwards to the sky. He nudged Riccardo, and pointed to a formation of planes bearing the familiar swastikas. "Look, more of Hitler's damn *Tedeschi*."

"This time the Brits are chasing them." Riccardo swung his feet to the terrazzo and got up. "Why can't they conduct these damn air battles over their own soil instead of ours, dammit."

When two planes swooped down and two more followed, a crippled patient shook his fist at the deafening noise. "Blessed Mother of Jesus!"

"They wouldn't bomb a hospital," yelled another.

Flavio pointed to a nearby hangar. "But what about that damn shed filled with explosives!"

Every mobile patient started running, walking, or limping away from the storage shed. Riccardo lowered his head and took a zigzag course of seventy meters, the rat-a-tat-tat of gunfire at his heels. He tumbled into a ditch, and was soon buried under the pile of men following him. Dirt filled his mouth and nose as the ground shook from an explosion, so powerful it produced maddening echoes in his head that couldn't drown out screams of the injured. Smoke assaulting his lungs made him cough until he gagged. The Siciliano spaghetti traveled up his throat; he swallowed it again. He tried to pray but the words wouldn't come, his fear so great he couldn't release the tears crowding his eyes. He conjured up a movable collage of Mama, of Gina and the girls, even Giovanni. But the face of Pietro Rocca remained frozen in a framed photograph, the recorded history of their broken family.

During a brief respite from the popping explosives, he heard a muffled voice from above, Flavio Bonelli's. "Riccardo, are you alive?"

"Only by the grace of God."

"Anybody else?"

Silence.

Riccardo welcomed the powerful hand that yanked him away from those poor bastards God had not graced, at least not in this life. He brushed the dirt from his eyes and saw Flavio covered in powdery dust, the sandy hair streaked with blood. One man in the pile had lost his face, another his head, and the third was scattered in pieces. Riccardo looked around to a scene of more death and devastating injuries. The terrace where patients had lounged minutes before was now twisted rumble. Flames poured from shattered hospital windows. While three burning ambulances threatened to explode, their spilled fuel igniting more fires.

"Have you seen enough?" Flavio asked. "Tell me you still feel that passion for freedom."

"More than ever."

"Good, then exchange your identification tag with one of the dead. I'll do the same."

Two planes collided in midair while Riccardo and Flavio pulled the bloody chains over their heads.

"We need some quick transportation," Flavio said as he rolled the remains of two bodies into the burning rubble.

Riccardo scurried around until he located a motorcycle that still worked. As it carried the pajamaed duo into the dense forest, Riccardo leaned into the vehicle's handlebars, his hands molded to the grips and Flavio's strong arms circling his waist from behind. The ground wobbled and shook from repeated blasts, but the one Riccardo didn't feel hurled him high in the air. Where it sent Flavio and the motorcycle, he didn't know.

Chapter 31

"This cannot be," Isabella said months later on a June day in 1941. She clutched the official government document to her breast, rocked back and forth as she sat in her chair. "I refuse to believe my Riccardo is dead until I see his body."

"Impossible, Mama." Gina choked back tears with her next words. "The letter said Riccardo burned up in a fire."

"Don't talk that way. Your brother was ... is ... too clever, too brave. God would not do this to us."

"Oh yes God would. He picks the best, to intensify the agony of those left behind. Yesterday two more soldiers were reported dead, one from Pont and the other from Locano. That brings the number in our district to twenty."

"Nineteen. I told you not to count Riccardo."

"Did you hear about Arturo Gallini's son, the one who loved to play futbol? He lost one leg above the knee. Now he can stay home and tend bar at Il Sole è la Luna. Or help his mama sort the post office mail."

"Basta," Isabella said. She went to her bedroom, knelt below the sagging Christ that hung from the wall, and made the sign of the cross.

"How can you pray now?" Gina asked from the doorway.

"What better time to ask for Riccardo's safe return and for the rest of us to persevere while we wait. Now go fetch your sisters and leave me to confer with God."

"Should I bring Giovanni too?"

"Not if you have to wake him from his nap. I'll tell him later, in my own way."

*****

For Riccardo's life, Isabella prayed her rosary. For his safe return, she implored the Blessed Virgin's intercession. She called on St. Michael the Archangel to deliver a message to Pietro Rocca, address unknown but somewhere in America, probably not Montana. Although the war prohibited Pietro from coming home—unless he wanted to fight in it—she wanted to believe he'd somehow find a way, if not for her, then for Riccardo. Gina too, she needed her own papa, not that Giovanni ever slighted her. Nor did Gina need Giovanni's money. Pietro obviously had money. But money didn't make him a rich man.

Isabella was still on her knees when she heard Gina return with Maria and Allegra. The young girls were growing into beauties, one going on thirteen and the other eleven years old. Both liked to play with their long red hair, just as Serina once did with hers. At least the silly woman had sense enough to play dead these past ten years. For all Isabella knew, she might be dead, especially if she'd stayed with the gypsies whose very presence provoked Hitler's Nazis into shipping them off to camps not of their own making.

Isabella moved her lips for the final prayer, a silent one she said each day but not always with reverence, nor on her knees. "Please dear God, wherever Serina is, keep her safe and away from here."

As soon as Isabella walked into the kitchen, Maria rushed to her and burst into tears. "Mama, Mama, Gina told us about Riccardo. My heart is breaking—I loved him so much."

"And you still love him because he is not dead. We must pray every day for his return."

"But Gina said …"

Isabella steadied Maria's quivering chin in the web of her hand. "Listen to me, and only me. Riccardo will come back to us. This I promise you."

Maria sniffed. "I want to believe you."

"And I do believe you," Allegra chimed in. "Papa will to, no matter what the letter said."

Giovanni, the only papa Allegra knew. It pained Isabella to remember a time long ago when she'd wished Serina's unborn would never take its first breath. But that was before Isabella eased its tiny body into the world. Before she gave the infant girl a first name and Giovanni gave her his family name.

Isabella hugged both girls as one. To Gina, she said, "Fetch me a stack of lire."

"Now, after all this time? As if I care about shopping, with my poor brother … missing. Besides, the local villages have sold all their decent merchandise and God only knows when new shipments will get through from Torino."

"Gina, please. Just bring me the money. Right now the concerns God and I have do not involve the latest fashions."

*****

That evening Isabella walked Maria and Allegra back to

Giovanni's where the girls slept at night and spent part of their days, a routine now in its fourth year, and one Isabella established after determining Giovanni could manage without her constant oversight. When the girls were in school, he even made occasional trips to the markets with her, not that she encouraged his company because it slowed down her busy schedule. He was waiting outside in his usual stooped position as they turned the corner of his house.

"I already know," he said, his eyes brimming with tears. "Mondo stopped by this afternoon. His ma heard the news from Sylvia Gallini."

The postmistress of Faiallo could read the contents of a sealed envelope just by pressing it to her brow. Or so she often said. Isabella stifled a sigh. "And what did Mondo tell you?"

"That our Riccardo is dead."

Isabella bit her lower lip from the inside. Maria started crying again, and Allegra comforted her. "There, there, Maria. Riccardo can't be dead until Mama says he is."

"Then we'll take your mama's word instead of the government's," Giovanni said. "Now let's get ready for bed. I'm tired." He opened the door for the girls but kept his eyes focused on Isabella. "Will you come inside and drink with me?"

She shook her head. This evening Riccardo's twin needed her more that Giovanni did. Giovanni always needed her. After Isabella returned home, she and Gina sat around the table. They drank cordials of *limoncello* and developed a plan for using the first stack of money.

*****

On Monday morning Isabella and her daughters went to the market in Pont. She left them to handle the produce and dairy sales while she visited the various stalls, taking notes in her little black book as she spoke with the farmers and venders. After canvassing the market, she stopped back at her wagon.

"Did you take extra care with the basket?" she asked Gina.

"With the same attention you would give," her daughter replied.

Isabella held her head in a manner befitting royalty as she carried the covered basket across the piazza to Pont's premier hotel, which now housed the local conscription center on its ground floor. In the smoke-filled anteroom solemn young males—more like boys than men—and their sobbing mothers waited to hear their name called. Voices fell to hushed whispers as Isabella made her way through the crowd.

"My son is missing, not dead," she told those who gathered around to press her hand or kiss her cheek.

"But someone said Riccardo—"

"Pray for him and I will pray for you and yours. I'm only here to beg the comandante's indulgence. Riccardo might be suffering from amnesia. Or perhaps the *Inglesi* have captured him." She crossed herself.

At the reception desk, Isabella waited for the uniformed clerk spotted with adolescent acne to acknowledge her presence. When he didn't, she cleared her throat and said, "I wish to speak to the comandante."

"Comandante Avino is a busy man, with important quotas that must be filled," the soldier replied without looking up. "You may wait with the others but I cannot guarantee he'll find time to see you today."

Isabella bent over the desk and pressed two lire notes in his hand. "Five thousand for you, five thousand for the comandante, perhaps you could persuade him."

He pulled out a chair, told her to sit. She prayed a dozen rosaries before the anteroom emptied out. Only then did the clerk usher her into the office of Comandante Avino. There sat the stocky peacock, bristling over a mound of papers covering his desk. With one hand he waved her to a chair and with the other, concealed a satisfying belch.

"Buon giorno, Signora …"

"Rocca, Isabella Rocca."

"Be seated and state your case, please with a minimum of emotion."

Isabella handed him a page from her notebook. "I'm here on behalf of these young men from the Canavese district, brave soldiers fighting on the frontlines for—"

"Rest assured they will bring victory to Il Duce and to all of Italy."

"Perhaps they could serve in other vital positions, like that of the young man guarding your door."

"Ah-h, you noticed my dedicated clerk—an exemplary individual who has the good fortune to meet a strict criteria."

"As do the four men listed on my paper." She stood, lifted the napkin covering her basket to reveal a round of cheese and bottle of wine.

He leaned back, showed her the palms protecting his face, as if to ward off the evil eye. "Signora, please. In time of war the offering of gifts—however practical—is highly improper. And one my immediate superior and his immediate superiors would most likely misinterpret. Unfortunately, certain perpetrators who once acted with the best of intentions now languish in the cruelest of prisons." He closed his eyes and shuddered. "As for myself: to be caught accepting such favors would be unthinkable."

Isabella pressed her knees together to keep them from shaking as she projected a smile worthy of the Blessed Virgin. She slid a fat envelope across his desk. "Exchanging favors is akin to the lubrication a delicate machine. To work in harmony each unit must receive its proper share of the oil."

*****

By the time Isabella returned to the market place, every wagon was gone except hers. Maria and Allegra ran to greet her, showered her hugs and kisses.

"Such a welcome," she said. "Didn't Gina tell you not to worry, that I might be late?"

"But she wouldn't tell us where you went," Allegra said.

"That's because she didn't know," Isabella said, for now a simple but necessary lie. "Now get in the wagon before this lazy Guido decides not to pull us back home."

"Not Guido, Mama. Guido came after Sam."

"You two, in the back of the wagon—now." This time they obeyed. "*Avanti*, Belva."

The mule turned on to Via del Commerico.

"You're right, Mama. This one is Belva."

"And Sam came after Aldo."

Aldo, the mule pulled Pietro first, Isabella thought. Then he pulled her too and later the twins. He pulled the Rocca four, then he pulled but three. And now he pulled five.

"Gina, what about our dog, *Due*?"

"His true name is Tobi Number Two, after the first Tobi."

"God rest Tobi *Uno's* soul."

"Dogs don't have souls, silly."

"Mama said Tobi went to heaven, as did our first mama."

On the windy road to Faiallo the girls named every cow and goat they'd ever milked while Gina whispered in Isabella's ear.

"So Mama, tell me about the fascist pig you visited today."

"He is a vulgar man who understands the value of harmonious relationships. Fortunately, we speak the same language—*tangenti*. And soon reached what I expect will continue to be a profitable arrangement for him and our young men of Canavese."

Chapter 32

By mid-summer of 1941 every report filtering through Cuorgnè and Pont Canavese indicated Mussolini would soon extend his official enemy list to include the United States. Italy against America gave Isabella one more burden to carry in her thoughts. What about Pietro? What if this Roosevelt forced him to fight against his own paesani? Pietro never liked to fight, but the one battle Isabella should've let him win was when he wanted to stay and she made him leave.

Her arrangement with Comandante Avino continued to thrive, but now with increased discretion since she couldn't save every Canavese soldier on the front—from the very beginning she'd promised her prayers and nothing more. But when a worried mother complained about her poor son's feet, Isabella extended her mission to include useful items for any Canavese soldier. She collected thick socks, foot powder, skin lotions, reading glasses—whatever gave a weary soldier comfort and Isabella a reason to carry her covered basket to the comandante.

One morning in Cuorgnè while Isabella was conducting her usual canvass of the market, a farmer three stalls across the aisle caught her attention with the slight lift of his forefinger. She stopped at his wagon, inspected his array of vegetables. Not bad, but they couldn't rival hers.

"Open your book," he said while arranging a stack of onions. "Pretend you're taking some notes."

Two more farmers strolled over and Isabella scribbled imaginary names as they spoke in low voices and tried to appear nonchalant.

"Il Duce has gone mad. He's digging our graves."

"The bastardo will destroy our entire country."

"The Nazis keep moving north. Soon they'll eat our food, drink our vino."

"We need your help, Isabella."

"I'm already doing what little I can."

"But not for our *partigiani*."

"You mean the Resistance?"

"Sh-h-h, no one must know. Expect a visitor tonight."

*****

No one must know, not even Gina. That evening after the girls went to Giovanni's, Isabella sat with Gina on a cushioned bench under the clear sky of twinkling stars and a sliver of the moon. She rubbed the arch of one foot against Due's back as he lay on the ground, and listened to her daughter's dreams, of which there were many.

Gina finally yawned. "Someday, I will study art restoration in Torino."

"After the fighting ends."

"By then I could be dead."

"You're only eighteen. Don't talk that way."

"Torino has an excellent university."

"The Nazis keep moving north. Soon they'll be eating our food."

Gina yawned again. "Buona notte, Mama, am too tired to argue." She leaned over, kissed Isabella's cheek. "What about you?"

Isabella hugged her shawl. She held up her rosary. "First, my prayers."

"What, not on your knees in front of the crucifix?"

"My knees need a rest. I'll pray out here."

After Isabella finished her prayers, of which there were many, she waited another ten minutes. Due moved away from her foot. He lifted his tail and rumbled out a low growl.

"Steady, Due ... steady."

A few clucks erupting from the henhouse prompted Isabella to leave the bench and strike a match to her lantern. Holding it up, she looked directly into a bearded face, the man's blue eyes peering into hers.

"My God, you startled me." She moved in closer. "Is that you—?"

He held two fingers against her mouth. "Don't say my name. Can we talk somewhere?"

"In the stable, follow me."

Although Isabella's animals stayed outside all summer, the

smell of hay lingered under the house. She opened a bottle of wine, filled two glasses, and slid one across the table before sitting down.

"Does your mama know you're alive?"

"If she did, I wouldn't be here." Lucca Sasso sniffed the wine, took a sip, and smacked his lips. "*Eccellente*. From what year?"

"Nineteen thirty-five, one of our best."

"Mine too, before the conscription and Albania, then Greece. That's when I ... left. Do you know what the Fascists do with deserters, Isabella? They shoot them—in the back or against a wall."

"Please, Lucca—"

"Sometimes they confiscate the family property. That's why I stay away from Mama. The less she knows, the safer we both are."

"She's a good woman."

"Who cannot keep a secret. Do you know what the partigiani do with people who talk too much? They shoot them—in the mouth or against a wall."

"It's getting late." She pulled a bundle of money from her apron pocket, handed it to him.

He kissed her hand. "Grazie, Isabella. Your generosity is legendary, but we also need your help in other ways." The flickering lantern caught the edginess of Lucca's face. "Perhaps to deliver a few messages."

Perhaps to make her children orphans. "Give me a few minutes, Lucca. I must think this through."

"I don't have all night. Nor anyone else I dare trust. When it comes to Il Duce, his friends are as fierce as his enemies."

She poured more wine, sipped as she stared into space. *Riccardo, where are you? Pietro come home. Dear God, what should I do?* Her pondering ceased as the stable door slowly creaked open. The fear she felt reflected in Lucca's face. He tossed her monetary contribution in a corner. They both stood up, Lucca with a gun hugging his side.

"It's only me," Gina said, one hand clutching the robe over her nightgown. She pointed up to the ceiling hole that warmed her room. "I couldn't help but hear every word."

Isabella gripped the table's edge. "Go back to bed. We'll talk in the morning."

"We'll talk now, Mama. Do you know what the Nazis do with the partigiani? They shoot them—in the stomach or against a wall."

*****

The next morning Isabella's head was crammed so full it felt like Pandora's Box about to burst. Her eyes smarted from lack of sleep when she walked over to Giovanni's. He came out of the henhouse, a basket of eggs in one hand and his cane under the other. His scruffy face broke into a wide grin and she noticed another loose tooth. Other than a mouthful of ugly teeth growing uglier and a lazy left side from head to toe—despite all her rigorous therapy—Giovanni enjoyed decent health for a man of sixty-nine. Although he thrived on complaining, his mother in Ivrea had moved into her ninth decade with barely a whimper.

"Giorno, Isabella. Already you're here to make cheese?"

"Later this morning, after I finish with mine. Right now I just need time away from Gina."

"What now?"

"She's pouting because I won't let her play today."

"Gina deserves a rest. No one can keep up with Isabella Rocca, not even me in my prime. Did I ever tell you about the—"

"Can you believe, Gina wants to ride her bicycle to Ceresole?"

"My God, all the way up there."

"Way too far for a young girl to travel alone."

"Maria should go with her."

"And leave Allegra and me with all the work?"

"Isabella, Isabella." He squeezed her chin with his coarse hand. "Don't be so hard on Gina. She's only asking for one day. We'll have Mondo work a few more hours."

"He moves slower than a turtle."

"But he always comes back the next morning."

"And always to eat, ever since his ma died. God rest Zia Theresa's soul."

Isabella's mind still raced as she made the return walk to her house, this time with Maria at her side. The girl looked too mature for her fourteen years. She'd inherited her mother's full breasts, slender waist, and lyrical manner of speaking. Her stride outpaced Isabella's, but only when she was excited.

"My bicycle might need air in the tires. In fact, we should take the pump, just in case."

"Si, just in case."

"I've never ridden so far, not that I'm complaining, you understand."

"*Bene, bene.*"

"How long has it been since we were last in Ceresole? It's the nicest resort I've ever seen."

"And the only."

"I know, I know—at first, no time and now the war. Do you think when we get to … Mama, are you listening to me?"

"Of course, what did you say?"

"About Ceresole … never mind … look, over by the shed, there's Gina. I hope she's in a good mood."

"She's worried about Riccardo."

"I love him too—but not as a brother."

Gina was bent over her bicycle, applying oil to the sprocket. She stood up, wiped her hands on a rag.

"I hope you don't mind my tagging along," Maria said with a nervous laugh. "Papa insisted and I just couldn't refuse him."

"Neither can I." Gina hugged her. "You're an angel."

"Did you hear that, Mama? She thinks I'm an angel."

And so you are, Isabella thought.

"I'll get my bicycle," Maria said. "It might need air in the tires, maybe some oil."

"I already took care of all that," Gina said. "Your bicycle is over there, by the tree."

"But how did you know—"

"You packed the panini, Gina?" Isabella asked.

"Si, the cheese and wine too. Get the basket, Maria. I left it in the kitchen."

Maria all but ran. The blue skirt against her pale legs reminded Isabella of Serina's translucent skin and the blue dress she wore that day in Pont—the day of the gypsy parade.

"Pick out some nice apples while you're in there," Isabella called out. "But don't take forever."

"How much does she know?" Gina asked.

"Only what we agreed to tell her, *niente*."

"Mama, please. I can't stand that look on your face."

"Don't tell me not to worry. I must've been out of my mind, letting you talk me into this."

"But every farmer or shopkeeper who ever heard of Isabella Rocca knows she never stops working until Sunday. Who would suspect two carefree girls bicycling up to Ceresole Reale?"

"Basta." Isabella showed her palm. "Now, one more time: those Canavese farmers sympathetic to the Resistance."

"Not again. We stayed up half the night going over the list. Trust me, I've seared every name and location in my brain."

"And the paper with the names Lucca wrote?"

"I burned it, just like he told me."

"When you arrive in Ceresole—"

"Sh-h-h, here comes Maria."

After Gina strapped the basket to her handlebars, Isabella hugged and kissed her and Maria with an extra measure of love. Her daughters mounted their bicycles and pedaled away, with sweaters wrapped around their shoulders, skirts hiked to the knees, and hair hanging loose under headscarves. She waved her arm in a sweeping motion in response to Maria's arrivederci and Gina's kiss from the fingertips.

My beloved Gina, do you know what the Nazis and the Fascists do with people who aid the Resistance? They shoot them—in the heart or against a wall.

Isabella waited for the bicyclists to glide into their first hairpin curve before she turned and went to her kitchen. The gray crock she'd filled with milk the day before had curdled from rennet of a nursing calf Giovanni had sacrificed. She ladled the contents into layers of cotton gauze, twisted the cloth into a tight sack, and hung it over her sink. While the whey drained from the cloth, she gathered four apples and two leftover panini into a napkin and carried it down to the stable. She pushed the door open, expecting to face Lucca with his gun. Instead she found him curled into a ball behind the hay, so sound asleep he didn't even stir when she left the food nearby.

When Isabella finished with her cheese, she allowed herself a glimpse at the clock. She figured Gina and Maria would be resting in Pont. As she headed back to Giovanni's, her legs stretched into long, purposeful strides without any concern the number of steps they'd journeyed over the past fourteen years since Pietro left. For now, she put her bicycling daughters in God's hands and allowed a few moments for the child she had not hugged or kissed or sent up the hill in almost two years. She clung to the belief that Riccardo was still alive, even though the Italian government had declared him dead, and honored her for sacrificing her only son. But if he wasn't dead, where was he? Hiding, imprisoned, or perhaps with the partigiani—she couldn't refuse their request for help. Nor could she refuse Lucca, the once carefree bachelor-turned-deserter who chose to fight in his own way for Italy. God help them all if he should get caught in her stable. He promised to leave tonight after dark.

This time when she reached Giovanni's, it was Allegra who came out to meet her. The petite girl's dark eyes danced with every word she spoke, just as Gina's did, the only physical resemblance to the Rocca side that Isabella could detect. Nor did Allegra take after her birth mother, other than the red hair attracting attention wherever she went, as did Maria's.

Allegra led the way into the house and spoke from over her shoulder. "Papa's helping Mondo in the garden."

"And what have you done so far?"

"I squeezed every drop of whey from the cloth and scrubbed the table as clean as I could, just like you showed me."

"Bene, bene, with the two of us working together, it shouldn't take too long."

After Isabella dumped the curd into a bowl, she waited for Allegra to add salt and pepper before she mixed in the seasonings with her hands.

"Is it true your hands are gifted?" Allegra asked. "Papa said you heal the sick."

"With the help of God I try, and only because Dottore Zucca is tending to our wounded soldiers in far away Sicily." She picked up a handful of thick curd, pressed it gently between her palms. Allegra did the same. They worked in harmony, facing each other across the table as they laid out the molded patties in precise rows.

"Do you think Maria and Gina have arrived in Ceresole yet?" Allegra asked. "It's almost eleven o'clock."

Three long hours, Isabella didn't need the reminder. "Not yet, but they're riding along the Orco and should've passed by Locano." She saturated two cloths with vinegar, handed one to Allegra. "Make sure you wipe enough on each tomino."

"Next time can I go too?"

Dear God, don't let there be a next time. Just bring them home safe.

"Mama, next time—"

"You missed those two in the corner. Where are the leaves?"

"Cleaned and piled on the counter behind you."

They wrapped each tomino in grape leaves, and one by one arranged them in a large blue crock. When the crock was filled, they tipped the bottom rim and rolled it close to the door. Isabella called for Mondo. The burly man came limping from the garden.

"More cheese for the cave?" he said. "I'll get the little wagon."

"Can I go with him, Mama?"

"We're running behind schedule. You peel the potatoes, make the salad, and set the table. I'll help Mondo."

As he pulled the wagon, Isabella walked alongside it, her hand steadying the crock until they stopped at her house for the other crock. She told Mondo to wait with the wagon; instead he followed her into the kitchen. He lifted his lumpy nose, sniffed the air as if he expected the inviting fragrance of simmering stew.

"What's that I smell: Pietro's tobacco?"

More like Lucca's; he must be downstairs smoking. Isabella managed a smile. "Sometimes I light a cigarette, just to relax."

He shamed her with his forefinger. "Giovanni wouldn't approve."

"You know I don't answer to Giovanni."

"I was only teasing, Isabella. I think maybe you still miss Pietro."

She nodded. "But you must never tell anyone about the cigarettes, especially Giovanni. I don't want to upset him. Do you capice?"

"Si, don't upset Giovanni or he might have another stroke."

"Andiamo, Mondo. Get the cheese crock."

Tucked in a hillside near the Rocca house was every farmer's ideal storage, a natural cave. Its year-round cool temperatures preserved an abundance of dairy and garden produce that extended the market supply into the fall and early winter months. Stone-carved shelves from earlier centuries lined the walls of an area as big as Isabella's kitchen, but she preferred keeping the freshest products deeper into the cave, away from the entrance.

"Did you ever follow those tunnels to see where they end?" Mondo asked as he handed her the last of the tomino.

"No and neither should you because if you lost your way, we wouldn't know where to find you. Now let's go back to the house and have something to eat."

*****

"I'm starving," Maria said as she and Gina approached the village of Noasca. "How much further is it to Ceresole?"

"Keep pedaling," Gina said from behind. "We'll eat when we get there."

To their left, the rushing blue Orco that ran parallel to the Locano Valley created miniature white caps over its waterway of boulders and stones. To their right, the foothills grew higher as they merged into the approaching mountains.

"Oh-oh, Gina. There's a roadblock up ahead. I see some soldiers."

"Keep pedaling. We'll stop when they tell us to."

"But why would they stop us?"

"Because we're young and pretty, silly."

"Oh, Gina, I'm not as pretty as you are."

"Quit fishing for compliments."

"Look, that soldier is waving his arms. What should we do?"

"Slow down and put on your brakes, Maria."

"*Alt!*"

"Dammit, Maria, your brakes!"

"*Alt! Alt!*"

Maria skidded to the side of the road. She tumbled off her bicycle. Gina swerved to avoid her and almost hit a tree before she flipped over the handlebars. The basket came loose from its straps, and four young soldiers in gray uniforms came running. One pulled Maria to her feet, another helped Gina, and the other two took charge of the bicycles.

Soldier uno returned Maria's headscarf. "Are you all right,

Signorina?"

Maria shook the wavy hair from her forehead. "I think so. My sister and I are going to Ceresole, just for the day." She turned to Gina. "What about the wine and panini?"

Gina was still reeling from the fall when Soldier due returned her basket. "Do I smell cheese and salami?" he asked.

"I made a few extra. Would you like some?"

"Uno momento," said the voice of authority, their *capitano*. Sergio Davito stood tall and lean, his pencil thin mustache riding high over a stern mouth. "Both of you follow me, please. And bring your basket."

Gina and Maria walked behind the strutting officer. "Have you ever been to Ceresole?" Maria asked his back.

He didn't answer but soon stopped at his outdoor office, which consisted of a wobbly table and chair under the shade of a tree. "Show me the contents of your basket, please."

Gina's hand shook as she pulled back two checkered napkins. One by one, she placed the items on the table: four large panini wrapped in newspaper, two rounds of tomino, four apples, one bottle of vino rosa, and a container of water.

"My men are hungry," he said. "Our rations are meager."

"Please, capitano. Take everything but our water."

"But Gina, we—"

"Grazie, Signorina. Enjoy your day in Ceresole."

*****

The final thirty minutes of silent, uphill pedaling brought Gina and Maria to Ceresole Reale, the last village leading into the snow-capped mountains of Italy's Gran Paradiso. Gina and Maria stopped at the side of the road for the first person who greeted them. The white-bearded farmer tipped his broad-brimmed hat while herding a flock of sheep down the sun-filled corridor of the alpine resort. When his barking dog brought up the rear with a few stragglers, Maria licked her lips and asked Gina if she could have some water.

"You emptied our container the last time you asked," Gina said. "There's a spring up the way where you can get more water."

"Look, I'm truly sorry for what happened with the soldiers. It's my fault."

"If you tell your papa, he'll never allow you to make another bicycle trip."

"I swear I won't say a word." Maria crossed her heart. "What about Mama?"

"I'll tell her—when the time is right and in my own way." Gina kissed her cheek. "Come on. Let's look around before we eat."

"You mean we have money?"

Gina produced a smile comparable to Isabella's. "Enough for a nice meal, and your favorite gelato."

In time of war people still need time to play, as evidenced by the large number of vacationers wandering through the village or photographing the hovering mountains, their deep white crevices turning into waterfalls that fed unseen pools of deep blue water. Gina dragged Maria around the few busy shops—ever looking, never spending—until the tired girl finally collapsed on the nearest bench.

"It's one o'clock, Gina. I cannot walk another step until I put some food into my mouth."

They went to a popular trattoria and sat under the umbrella of a round table, one among many on a terrace overlooking a deep ravine of evergreens, and munched on long, thin grissini until an elderly waiter brought two bowls of ravioli floating in clear broth. He followed up with soft cheese and spinach layered between thin slices of bread.

"I feel much better," Maria said as she dipped her spoon into a bowl of fruity gelato. "Do you think we could go back to the shops? Allegra will be disappointed if we don't bring her a souvenir."

Before Gina could answer, a middle-aged woman at the next table leaned over to say, "You look so familiar. Do I know you from the market in Cuorgnè?"

"We're there every Thursday with our mother."

"Then please, sit with me and my friend for a while."

"But Gina—"

"Here," Gina said, handing Maria a few thousand lire. "Look around in the shops while I visit with the signori."

As soon as Maria left, Gina moved her chair to the other table. The woman patted Gina's hand, and said with a smile, "Perhaps we know the same Canavese farmers."

*****

That evening outside the Rocca house an orange sun had cast red and purple streaks across the sky as it prepared to set behind the mountains. Giovanni shifted his weight on a stone bench across from the one holding Isabella and Allegra. "What time is it?" he asked.

"Ten minutes later than the last time you asked." Isabella replied, fingering the rosary beads in her pocket. She positioned herself for an optimal view of the road and rubbed her foot over Due's back.

"Maybe they stopped in Pont," Allegra said.

"I don't like them wandering around the village," Giovanni said.

"But Pappa, it's not like any—"

"They're too young for romance. So are you."

"I'm never getting married."

"Stop it, both of you," Isabella said.

Due lifted his head, his ears shot up. He shook off Isabella's foot, and got up. His trot toward the road turned into a race with Allegra.

"I see them, Mama," she called out. "You can quit worrying."

Five minutes later, after a round of hugs and kisses, Giovanni hugged Maria again. "Your day, it was good?" he asked.

"Ceresole is so-o beautiful. Someday we must all go."

"Any problems along the way?"

"Oh, Papa, you worry too much." She turned to Allegra. "Here, from Gina and me—we managed to scrape together a few lire."

Allegra tore open the package, and waved a pretty scarf. "Bella, bella. Grazie, Maria and Gina. This is better than having to bicycle all day, although next time—"

"Buona notte, Isabella" Giovanni said from over his shoulder.

"Buona notte, Gina. Andiamo, my daughters, this old man is tired."

When the Martinos were out of earshot, Isabella patted the bench and Gina sat down. They stretched their legs out and leaned their heads back to the darkening sky.

"Tell me about your day," Isabella said. "Did you make the connection?"

"Right on time."

"And Maria, did she cause any trouble?"

"Maria was perfect, Mama. In fact, she exceeded our expectations."

Chapter 33

During the summer of 1941 Gina delivered two more verbal messages from night visitors other than Lucca Sasso—the first on a Thursday after the market in Cuorgnè ended. She and the unsuspecting Maria pedaled ten miles south to Rivarola, and while Maria bought *cioccolata* from a sweetshop, Gina sat on a bench, relaying information to a one-legged man. Two weeks later she and Maria pleaded for another day trip to Ceresole. On the way they stopped at the roadblock outside Noasca, and minutes later pedaled away, leaving Capitano Davito with enough food to feed ten men for two days. Gina's contact that day was the sheepherder who had tipped his hat to her on the last Ceresole visit.

For centuries life in Italy had revolved around the enjoyment of food, but now it revolved around the lack of food. So few resources and so many to feed: the Italian soldiers defending the roads; the Nazi soldiers marching over those roads; the partigiani hiding in the hills above those same roads. And the Brits hiding with the partigiani—that ever-growing band of brothers they called the Resistance. As the weather turned colder with the approaching fall, Isabella continued to add cheese and butter and eggs in her cave, but there always seemed to be empty spaces on the shelves. She tolerated those thieves in the night feeding from her treasury, hoping some other mother would extend the same compassion to

Riccardo if he were hungry.

One Saturday evening in early October while Gina played cards at Giovanni's, Isabella made a second visit to the cave, this time for cream she'd forgotten hours before when Mondo was helping her.

"Buona sera, Signora Rocca," said a voice from the dark tunnel. Not Lucca's, his Isabella would've recognized, also those of the two men who came after him. This voice had a distinct accent. She struck a match against the wall, held it to the hanging lamp. A soft glow illuminated the room. From the shadows appeared a young man with hair black as onyx and the complexion of a Mezzogiorno. He carried a cap in his hand, and wore dark trousers and a plain vest over his gray shirt. With a sweep of one arm, he bowed from the waist, and when he looked up, it was with one blue eye and one brown.

Isabella stepped back, one hand clutching the breast of her pounding heart.

"Do not be afraid, Signora. It is I, your old friend Cato." He smiled with those still perfect teeth.

"Si … from long ago in Pont," she said. His face was baby smooth then; a three-day growth of whiskers sprouted from it now. "I did not expect to see you again."

"I never say 'arrivederci' unless I mean it."

She allowed him to take her hand and lead her to the bench where she occasionally lingered on a hot afternoon.

"Sit down, Signora. You look so pale."

"And you must be tired and hungry."

He sat beside her. "Your cheese is quite good, but I could use some bread and wine. Perhaps a warm place to sleep."

"Where's your wagon?"

"Far from here, in a safe place, God willing ... the Nazis—"

"I know, those filthy *maiale*." She asked the question that begged for an answer. "About that day we first met in Pont."

"Si, I remember it like yesterday."

"Whatever happened to the young woman who left with your caravan?"

Cato crossed himself. "Alas, she died five years ago, at the hand of a jealous suitor."

"You saw this with your own eyes?"

"Signora, please, my heart still aches from the terrible incident. She was my ... friend."

Isabella leaned her forehead into her palms and attempted a prayer for Serina's soul, not sure she was truly dead. But wait. She looked up, tried to read that intriguing face she wanted to believe. "Then how did you know the way to my house?"

He hesitated. "I followed you on foot, all the way from—"

"You're lying." She cocked her head, narrowed her eyes to his. "Gypsy men don't walk when they can ride."

"But first they must have a proper horse and wagon."

"Perhaps you'd better leave. I don't want any trouble."

"Please don't be angry, Mama." Another voice came from the shadows. "I told him how to get here."

And not Gina's, Sweet Mother of God.

Maria stepped out, wringing her hands. "It's not what you think, Mama. He needs your help."

Cato hurried to her side. "She's right, Signora. I do need your help."

"Move away from her, gypsy. Maria, are you out of your mind? Go home before your papa has another stroke."

"Papa knows I came here, to tell you Gina will spend the night with us."

"You told me, now go home."

"But Mama—"

"Do not speak of this to anyone—not Gina or Allegra or your papa."

"I only did what I thought was right."

"Now, Maria, before I send you into that tunnel with the back of my hand."

As soon as she left, Isabella pushed herself to stand. She stuck her face in Cato's "The girl is only fourteen. How could you?"

He stepped back and showed his palms. "I swear on my beloved *madre's* grave, I didn't so much as lay a hand on your daughter." He crossed himself again. "Although in our culture a girl of fourteen makes an ideal bride. Better yet, a bride of twelve or thirteen comes to the marriage before she's been corrupted by—"

"Basta! I've heard enough." She walked to doorway, hesitated before turning to face him. "One night to eat and sleep that's all you get. Come to my stable when the sky is so dark you can't see your next footstep."

"Grazie, Signora … but wait, aren't you forgetting something?"

Please, not Serina, she wanted to say. Instead, Cato handed her the container of cream she'd forgotten earlier.

"But how did you know?"

"Perhaps I read it in your face."

"Perhaps you took it from my basket this afternoon."

He smiled. "What better way to assure you'd return, this time alone."

*****

As soon as Isabella returned to the house, she stuffed paper into those holes in the floor that telegraphed every sound or smell from the stable, just in case Gina changed her mind about sleeping at Giovanni's. This visitor Isabella would handle on her own. She figured him to be around twenty-two or so—three years older than the twins, and too much a temptation for Gina, especially with no young men around to court her.

Sure enough, Gina did come home around ten, and went straight to bed complaining that Giovanni had cheated at cards again. Isabella listened for her soft, steady breathing before she filled a basket with bread, salami, hard-cooked eggs, spinach, and biscotti. She put on her shawl and carried the food down to the stable. Due was at her side when she oiled the door hinges. She kept him with her when she sat down, waiting for the door to open without creaking. Instead, Cato's shadowy figure emerged from the corner. Isabella jumped up, knocked the bench over.

"Mi dispiace, Signorà, I did not mean to startle you again." Cato straightened the bench. He knelt, extended his hand to Due, who licked it as though they were the best of friends.

Isabella's hands went to her hips. "You've been here before."

"Only to sleep."

"Well, sit down and eat now. You must be hungry." She laid out the food, watched him devour it. She poured wine; they both drank. She dropped her eyelids for only a moment and when she lifted them, Cato was pouring more wine. "Start talking," she said. "This time you are to speak nothing but the truth, or by God—"

He stood up, started walking back and forth. "For weeks I've roamed these foothills, trying to make contact with the partigiani." He held up his palm. "I know what you think, that gypsies don't involve themselves in politics or war. But this gypsy has witnessed the evil Nazis perpetrated. Most of my family now makes their music in an enemy camp far from Italy." He grabbed his shirtsleeve. "This is not the shirt of a gypsy, nor the pants or the vest." He reached inside his vest, brought out a pair of gold earrings, and laid them before her. "For Gina, did you ever pierce her ears?"

"Don't speak my daughter's name."

"She's saving herself for the right man, right? Pray for her, Signora." He brought out two more sets of earrings. "For your other daughters, so they won't be envious." He leaned over, showed her his unadorned earlobes. "These holes dare not display the gold of my heritage." He took off his vest, lifted one foot to the bench, and showed her his boot, the finest leather in need of a good polishing. "These are all I brought with me, besides my horse. I ask you, what good is any gypsy without his horse?"

"Or a young girl to—"

"Signora, please let me finish. I couldn't risk exposure so I put a patch over one eye and limped around the market in Cuorgnè. That's when I noticed Maria. Such red hair could only belong to the daughter of Serina. The other girl too—Allegra she called her." He swung his foot to the ground, sat down beside her, and leaned in even closer. His breath carried the scent of her wine. "All morning I listened to the whispered conversations about the saintly Isabella Rocca and how she helps those in need. That's when I approached Maria to help me."

"There was no school that day ... some problem, I can't remember what. But you, you seduced a child with your words."

"Gypsies don't kidnap innocent young girls—or older women in need of love. Those outsiders who join our caravan do so under their own free will."

"Like Serina. She's not dead, is she?"

"She might as well be. I saw her board a Nazi train to that faraway camp."

This time Isabella crossed herself. Somehow that same hand wound up in Cato's. He pressed his lips to her palm and then the inside of her wrist, moved those warm lips up the tender part of her arm.

"My tribe has wandered this land for centuries, Signora. Suffered the persecution of those who misinterpret our god-given right to travel and enjoy the freedom of everyday life." His other hand unbuttoned her blouse. "And the occasional love of a lonely woman." His lips found hers. Before she had the chance to protest, he undid her skirt. She watched it fall away as his tongue traveled to her ear. "I want to join with the partigiani to help defend those rights. Please, will you help me?" Once again, he took her hand, led her to the soft hay. He pulled off his shirt, rolled it into a ball, and used the ball to pillow her head.

"But I don't even know any partigiani," Isabella said as he

kissed her eyelids. She welcomed the weight of his body on hers.

"What about your son?"

Her eyes opened wide. "You know for sure Riccardo is alive?"

"I only know what I hear from others."

That's when she invited him to enter her private domain.

*****

The next morning after preparing a stew of cinghiale, potatoes, carrots, onions and green beans, Isabella left it to simmer on a low fire. The bright sun shone on her and the daughters as they walked down the road wearing lace mantillas and clothes reserved for Sunday Mass. Usually Maria chattered non-stop while Allegra agreed with whatever she said, and Isabella listened to Gina's dreams about her someday life in the city. This morning the quartet walked in the silence of their thoughts. Along the way they passed Il Sole è la Luna where the men of Faiallo still gathered, at least those who were too crippled or too old to serve Il Duce. The ringing bells of Santa Caterina welcomed their arrival at its roadside chapel, constructed in the seventeenth century out of stones dug from the hill. Women and children and filled the pews, along with a few elderly men.

"Let's sit in the back," Gina whispered.

Isabella kept walking until she stopped at the right front pew, facing the stature of St. Joseph, the loyal husband who never deserted his virgin wife. She knelt for a quick Hail Mary, sat back, and waited for the tinkling bell. It soon announced the beginning of Mass. The enticing fragrance of burning candles and heady incense filled her senses as Padre Picco conducted the ancient ritual that never failed to provide her comfort. She stood and knelt and sat, responded in Latin just as she did every Sunday and holy day. But when her daughters went the altar to receive Holy Communion, Isabella continued kneeling in the pew.

"What's the matter, Mama," Allegra whispered on her return.

"I forgot it was Sunday and broke my fast with a sip of water after midnight."

"But you never—"

"Sh-h-h, no talking in church."

After Mass Isabella told her daughters to wait outside while she lit a candle for Riccardo.

"We should all light candles," Maria said. "Maybe God will pay more attention to our prayers then."

"Not today," Isabella whispered before kissing her daughter's cheek. "I need time alone with God. Now go—"

"Si, Mama, right away."

Isabella genuflected at the hanging crucifix as she moved over to the left of the altar. After depositing three coins in a small, metal box, she lit Riccardo's candle and two more—one for Pietro, and one for the partigiani. She knelt before the Blessed Virgin's statue, shifted on the hard wood surface, and bowed her head. Her lips moved with without speaking.

"Dear God, I beg your forgiveness for the adulterous sin I committed last night, and also for enjoying the immense pleasure it gave me. Had Pietro been where he belonged, I never would've submitted to such temptation, especially with a gypsy almost young enough to be my son. Please don't hold this against Cato since he lives by standards lower than the rest of us. Just take him far away from here—but not to heaven yet, nor to the fires of hell where Hitler should burn for all eternity along with that traitorous Mussolini. As always, I pray for Riccardo's safe return. Amen."

Isabella kept her eyes closed until the kneeler groaned under the weight of a second pair of knees, as did their owner, a woman shrouded in widows black. She crossed herself, put her palms together, and whispered, "Did you remember to pray for our cause?"

"A certain young man wants to help."

"You mean a deserter?"

"No, a gypsy."

The woman sucked in her breath, crossed herself twice. "Can he be trusted?"

"What can I say? He hates the Fascists; he hates the Nazis. He loves his freedom."

"Wherever he is, don't let him leave. You'll get your answer tomorrow in Pont."

Meanwhile outside, Isabella's daughters grew restless while waiting for Isabella to open the chapel door. Gina walked across the road to chat with a friend, leaving Maria and Allegra perched on a large boulder.

"Mama seems in good spirits," Allegra said. "Other than not taking communion."

"Never have I seen her as angry as yesterday in the cave. She wouldn't listen to me."

"Do you think Papa knows about the gypsy? We didn't realize he was standing in the doorway when you told me."

"Well, Gina did catch him cheating at cards later."

"Sometimes she forgets that we're supposed to let him win."

"Sh-h. Here she comes, and Mama too."

*****

When Isabella and her daughters returned to the Rocca house, they found Giovanni waiting outside on the bench.

"What took you so long?" he asked, a question guaranteed to grate on Isabella's nerves.

"Mama lit a candle for Riccardo," Maria said as she helped him get up.

"And said a dozen prayers for his safe return," said Allegra, holding the door open for him and Isabella.

"What's for dinner?" he asked, lifting his beak. "Wait, don't tell me—cinghiale. Bene, bene, it brings back a host of memories."

Isabella refused to acknowledge his longing eyes but she remembered too—how Pietro broke his leg when he'd encountered another wild boar.

"Next week I'll shoot you some rabbits," Giovanni called as she went to her room to change clothes, as if food would somehow make her life complete.

Minutes later she returned wearing a comfortable housedress. There sat Giovanni in his favorite chair, watching the younger girls lay plates on the table. Gina had changed her clothes and was pouring five glasses of wine.

"I'd better check on the stew," Isabella said on her way to the stove. She lifted the lid and did a quick inventory of the pot's contents. Cato had eaten only what she'd allotted him.

"Bella, bella, your mama smiles like the Mona Lisa," she heard Giovanni say. "That means her stew is cooked to absolute perfection."

*****

Later that evening after Gina was asleep, Isabella carried another napkin of food down to the stable. She pushed the door open and Cato appeared from behind it. The rations slipped from her hand as he kissed the soft spot above her collarbone. She forsook her prayer from the morning when she let him push her against the wall, let him push into her. And when he dropped to his knees and made her shudder; she begged him not to stop.

After they made love that surpassed the night before, she watched him eat with the same passion he'd shown her, caressing the goblet with respect, treating its contents as if fit for the nectar of gods. And when he finished, it was Isabella who led him to the hay.

"Take off your clothes," he said. "All of them."

She obliged. And then took off his before he entered her again. She thought of Pietro, but only once.

Later they lay side by side, too exhausted to speak until he finally asked, "What did you find out about the partigiani?"

"I should have an answer tomorrow, at the market in Pont."

"Which means I could join with them by tomorrow night." He leaned over and brushed hay from her face. "Or, maybe find myself as a pawn being exchanged for an imprisoned comrade, is that what you think?" He laughed in response to her silence. "Not to worry, Signora. My life has so little value, the soldiers would just as soon kill me quickly than feed me for a single day."

*****

The next morning it was Mondo knocking at the Rocca door before sunrise. "Giovanni's big toe hurts," he told Isabella. "He thinks it's that damn gout acting up again."

"I'll take him some tonic later, after the market. Hurry, let's load the wagon."

"He wants me to pick up some tobacco today," Mondo said as lifted the smaller crocks of cheese into her wagon.

"Since when did Giovanni start puffing on his pipe again?" Gina asked.

"Not now, Gina. We'll discuss his bad habits on the way to Pont. Mondo, gather the remaining eggs, please. You know how I hate being late."

"Which means not being first," Gina told Mondo as he walked away to check out the henhouse. She put her arm around Isabella. "You look tired, Mama. Did you not sleep well?"

Isabella shrugged. "The sausages kept talking back to me."

"Is that why I heard you come in from the cold night?"

"Mi dispiace, I didn't mean to wake you. Sometimes a brief walk aids my unpredictable indigestion."

"Be careful, Mama. One never knows the dangers a woman alone might encounter, especially on a cold night. Isn't that what you always tell me?"

*****

Later that morning in Pont Isabella waited until the sales tampered off before telling Mondo he could run his errands. While he limped across the piazza to the tobacco shop, Gina stayed with the wagon so Isabella could wander through the aisles with her notebook. She hadn't gone far when one of the farmers nodded for her to join him and two others. She held her pencil to the paper and listened to their words.

"This friend of yours, can you vouch for him?" one man asked.

"He is intelligent, strong but hungry, and speaks many dialects in addition to formal Italian. Also French, some German and English," Isabella said as she wrote her made-up names. "He experienced the pain of watching loved ones board the Nazi death trains. He yearns for the freedom his ancestors knew."

"But can we trust him?"

"A cunning man makes a better friend than your worst enemy."

"But can we trust him?"

"If my Riccardo were a partigiano, I wouldn't hesitate to send this man to fight beside him. What more can I say?"

"His name."

"Cato. That's all I know."

"Come back when the market closes. We'll give you our answer."

When Isabella returned to her wagon, Mondo was sorting through his purchases: tobacco, a newspaper, and two periodicals—all for Giovanni.

"Did I see soldiers in the tobacco shop?" Gina asked him.

"Si," Mondo replied. "Here they come now."

Capitano Sergio Davito made his way along the aisle, followed by two privates who were accepting donations of food from the farmers. He stopped at the Rocca wagon and tipped his cap to Gina.

"Buon giorno, Signorina, are you and your sister still bicycling?"

"Not up to Ceresole until next spring," Gina said. "Do you still have roadblocks along the way?"

"Si, whenever there is a need, which seems to be increasing with each passing day." He turned to Isabella, tipped his cap again. "Buon giorno, Signora …"

"Rocca … Isabella Rocca."

He looked from her to Gina. "Ah-h, but of course, I should've surmised as much."

"Would you like some cheese for your men?" Isabella asked. "Or perhaps some eggs?"

"Grazie, but not this morning, Signora Rocca. Your generosity is well-known throughout the area but I already have what I need for today."

He tipped his cap again and left with the other two soldiers. Isabella waited until they turned the corner before she pulled Mondo aside. "When you were buying Giovanni's tobacco, did the capitano talk to you?"

Mondo shook his head.

"What about the other two?" Gina asked.

Again he shook his head.

"Did you talk to anyone, other than the proprietor?"

"Well sure, I talk to everybody. What do you expect? We talk about the weather, the market, the dead and the dying. We talk about—"

"Basta. I need to take another walk."

The market was on the verge of closing when Isabella strolled down the aisle and stopped to pet a friendly dog. "The capitano who lingered at your wagon, does he suspect anything?" asked its owner.

"Not that I could tell but he wouldn't accept my offer of cheese."

"We need to move fast. Ten o'clock tonight, the cemetery behind Santa Caterina's in Faiallo. Tell your friend to come alone with his horse."

"I think he has one but I'm not sure," Isabella said.

"Every gypsy has a horse. If not his own, then someone else's."

*****

That evening while Gina sat in her bedroom, counting to one hundred as she pulled a boar's hair brush through her long hair, Isabella gathered more food and carried it down to the stable. As soon as she closed the door, Cato took her in his arms and lifted her up. She wrapped her legs around his waist and pushed into him.

"Hold tight, Signora. I'll take you on a gypsy ride."

She nestled her head in his shoulder and they danced as one around the stable. "We haven't much time," she murmured. "You'll be pleased to know I vouched for your worthiness."

"Grazie, Signora. I give you my undying gratitude."

When he backed her into a post, she explained about the church cemetery, ending with: "Cut straight down through the wooded area instead of taking the winding road." She waited until he moaned before telling him to arrive before ten o'clock, in case there might be trouble. "Be sure to bring your horse," she said, breaking loose from him and lowering her feet to the ground. "That is, if you have one." He kissed her hard enough to arch her back and make her toes tingle. And after he disappeared into the night, Isabella realized he hadn't said, "Arrivederci."

She spent a few minutes putting her stable in order before going upstairs. The glow from the kerosene lamp made her heart race, more so when she saw Gina sitting at the table, still in her day clothes.

"Did you send your lover away, Mama?"

Her heart slowed to thumping as she sought the right words. "He went of his own accord, to join the partigiani. Please don't hate me for being human."

"What Papa did was despicable, condemning you to the life of a married woman in name only. Do you want to talk about it?"

"Perhaps some day, but not this one. Buona notte, Gina."

Before Isabella crossed the threshold into her room, Due started barking. Loud banging thundered through the house and sent her and Gina scurrying to the door. "Who's there?" she asked in her sternest voice.

"It is I, Capitano Sergio Davito. May we come in, Signora Rocca? I fear for your safety."

Isabella's hand shook so hard she let Gina unlatch the door. Headlights from a military jeep nearly blinded them. A somber soldier sat behind the wheel. Capitano Davis tipped his cap, while three other soldiers stood nearby with their pistols drawn.

"Please quiet your dog before he forces us to shoot him."

Isabella rubbed Due's head until he settled down.

"We have reason to believe gypsies are roaming the hills," the capitano said. "These undesirables may be hiding nearby without the villagers even aware of their presence. As we speak, soldiers have blanketed the area, searching every house and outbuilding, with the owner's permission, of course."

Not waiting for her reply, he snapped his fingers and two men entered the Rocca house. Isabella huddled with Gina on the terrace bench, their wool shawls warding off the cold night as Capitano Davito followed the third man into her henhouse. A fugue of squawking and fluttering and yelling didn't stop until the men backed out quicker than they'd entered.

"Your stable, Signora, please show us the way."

Not one piece of hay was out of place, nor a single particle of food left behind. Capitano Davito sniffed the air. He sniffed again, glanced from Gina to Isabella and back to Gina. He turned on his heels and left the stable. After he and his men searched the remaining outbuildings, Isabella and Gina followed them to the jeep. The capitano was about to climb aboard when a lift of his brow signaled a sudden revelation.

"About your cheese, Signora, I did not see more than a few tomini."

"We store our dairy products in a hillside cave."

The pencil-thin mustache stretched across his upper lip. "Aha! I smell a band of hiding gypsies. Please show me the way, Signora."

"I'll get the lantern," Gina said.

"Men, turn up your flashlights. Andiamo!"

Isabella's mouth went dry, her stomach churned with every step she took. She knew Cato wouldn't be there, but wasn't sure what he might've left behind. When they arrived at the cave, the capitano pulled back the flap and motioned Isabella to enter first. She didn't bother striking a match to the wall lantern. Four military flashlights and Gina's lantern filled the entire area.

"These tunnels, where do they lead to?" the capitano asked.

Isabella lifted her shoulders. "I've never gone beyond a few meters."

With a snap of the capitano's fingers, his three soldiers spent another fifteen minutes exploring the tunnels only to return shaking their heads. "Did you see anything suspicious?" he asked, only to be disappointed by their negative response.

This time it was Capitano Davito who led the way back. He climbed into the jeep and tipped his cap to Isabella and Gina. Hugging their shawls, she and Gina watched the vehicle eased down the road and around the first hairpin curve. They waited another minute before walking toward the house, only to stop when distant shots rang out from the hillside below. Due started barking.

Isabella wanted to run into the bare woods that separated the winding road but her knees started to buckle. She wound up rocking on the bench with Gina's arm around her shoulder. She shivered and prayed, again begged God's forgiveness for her sin of adultery, and added uncontrollable lust to her other failings. Realizing Cato's had purposely omitted his final arrivederci, she prayed for the soul that must've left his body. She heard the methodical clop, clop, of approaching hooves before seeing the horse lean into the curve, headlights from Capitano Davito's jeep illuminating its upward trek.

Isabella ran across the stone-filled yard with Gina and Due at her side. When they reached the road, the brown and white horse stopped before them. The proud animal lifted its front legs into the air to expose a round belly and released the rider slumped over its thick, bloody mane. A man slid to the road, four bullet holes piercing his back, no doubt from the capitano and his men. Isabella bent down to turn him over, braced herself not to display any sign of recognition. She looked into eyes that no longer saw what others didn't. The mouth that sometimes talked out of turn was now but a gaping hole, no doubt silenced by a partigiano bullet. Due whimpered and Gina cursed under her breath while Isabella choked back tears. And when she prayed, it was for the soul of her neighbor Mondo Gotti.

Chapter 34

Latimer Farm—July 1942

"Now aren't you glad I talked you into acquiring those American citizenship papers," Connie said with a slight slur of his words. "Let's see, was that in '36 or '37?"

"Thirty-eight," Pete replied. He sat across from the Kingpin, an overhead fan cooling his den on an early afternoon that promised to sizzle before three o'clock.

Connie poured another scotch, his third in an hour. He raised his thick brows to Pete, who responded with a show of his palm. Two glasses of wine was Pete's limit, and every man who dealt in liquor should know his limitations or find a career with fewer temptations.

"Why if it weren't for me, Pete Montagna would be sucking his spaghetti from a tin can in a trench hole somewhere in Europe, along with the rest of Mussolini's lackeys."

"You could be talking about my Italian son," Pete said.

"It's the liquor talking, my apologies."

"What's more, I don't eat spaghetti and you know it."

"Oh, right. The Piemontese eat from a different trough than their Southern counterparts. I keep forgetting."

Pete allowed the insults to pass. The Kingpin always hit the bottle extra hard around the anniversary of Collinsville Avenue, which was how they both referred to that fatal day when Billie and Fallon sacrificed their lives to rid Pete of Leo the Loser. Damn, all for a few thousand bucks and an unblemished reputation. The idiot shooter simply disappeared, thanks to Connie. As if any of that mattered after the first bullet meant for Leo somehow found Billie, and her careening automobile crashed into his beloved Fallon.

Their son came running into the den, a miniature plane in each hand as he staged an imaginary battle over every inch of floor space before taking on the leather sofa

"That'll be enough, Danny-Boy," Connie said, his eyes closed and head sandwiched between oversized hands.

The blond imp slid down and stomped his foot. He cupped his hands to skinny hips. "How many times do I have to tell you, Connie: my name is Daniel Latimer Montagna. And I'm six, which makes me w-a-y too old to be called Danny-Boy. So be a sport and just call me Dan, OK?"

When Connie didn't respond, the boy climbed onto Pete's lap, leaned his head into the inviting shoulder, and whispered, "What's the matter, Pop? Why isn't Connie giving me any lip?"

"Not today, son, Connie has a headache."

"You mean a hangover, don't you?"

"I heard that, Danny-Boy."

The giggling child slid off Pete's lap and crawled onto Connie's. Their little ping-pong, as Connie often referred to him.

Daniel Latimer Montagna was the tie that bound them as tight as wet leather when it dried—so unforgiving it kept Pete from returning to Italy after Fallon's death. On the day they buried her and Billie, Connie didn't pull any punches.

"If you so much as visit that other family in Italy, it won't be with my grandson. Thanks to your dago friend, Danny-Boy is all I have left. And if you do cross the ocean alone, when you return, I can't guarantee you'll have a job. Or a son who still loves the father who chose to desert him."

Pete had messed up one family; he couldn't do the same to another. At least Gina and Riccardo could depend on Isabella. The American son only had Pete. And Pete didn't want a junior version of Conrad Latimer.

Three short raps on polished walnut brought Pete from his thoughts. There stood Beans in his Hawaiian shirt, creased slacks, and aviator sunglasses. "Excuse me for interrupting your tea party but the first bus just pulled off the highway."

"Then by all means, we must greet out guests, right … Dan?"

"Another party, you bet. I'll race you guys to the door."

Outside in the driveway circle Pete positioned Dan between him and Connie as the first group of Jefferson Barracks Hospital patients stepped off the bus. Next came those with canes and on crutches, helped by nurses in starched white uniforms. Two more busses from across the river drove into the circle with patients in various degrees of recuperation, followed by six military ambulances with personnel to carry those on stretchers. Connie and Pete welcomed every patient, doctor, and nurse with warm handshakes. Beans and Jackie G escorted them to the nearby tent, where Hester and the Mexican workers had set out an array of food prepared by One Eleven's cook: fried chicken, mashed potatoes, hamburgers, hot dogs, coleslaw, baked beans, and desserts galore. The Budweiser beer and Coca-cola were courtesy of local distributors who responded to Pete's request. A five-piece orchestra from the club played the latest Glen Miller hits while those patients who could, played croquet and volleyball on the thick, green lawn. Two comedians, also from the club, promised to provide thirty minutes of belly laughs later in the day.

Connie's extravaganza was one of three summer tributes he would pay to the injured men who fought so bravely to keep America free. Some of those patients would eventually stay in Southern Illinois or St. Louis, and among those who stayed, some would eventually find their way to One Eleven. Pete had already captured the able-bodied airmen stationed nearby at Scott Field, plus any GI on leave in the area who wanted a few hours of entertainment.

The comedians had just pulled a buxom nurse on stage when Pete leaned over to Dan, and said, "Time for me to hit the road, Big Guy."

The boy turned a cheek smeared with mustard for Pete to kiss. "Don't worry, Pop. I'll keep an eye on Connie."

Pete walked over to the front of the buses and found Jackie G leaning against the Buick sedan. "You want I should drive you, Boss?"

"Nah, you'd better stay here and look after the party. Some of those GIs having too much fun might need help boarding the bus."

Pete slid behind the driver's seat, started the engine, and headed for One Eleven. In spite of America's wartime economy, the club thrived on a full range of vices, plus a dinner menu that included the thickest of steaks from his private Black Market. After pulling into his reserved parking spot, Pete went straight to his office. He spent the next hour checking yesterday's receipts:

Gambling, the house take was ninety percent; Liquor, the house took seventy; Women, sixty; Food, a mere thirty—no small accomplishment considering the shortage of quality ingredients. Some restaurants doctored horsemeat, renamed it ground beef. Not One Eleven; Pete ran a high-class operation. He pressed the intercom and called his longtime assistant, Tom Baker.

Within minutes, Tom appeared with more sheets of paper. "Looking good, Boss. We have silk stockings coming out of our kazoos."

"What about those C stickers?" Pete asked, referring to gas rationing privileges the government allotted to those citizens essential to the country's well being: physicians, ministers, mail carriers, and railroad workers.

"In production as we speak." Tom lit a cigarette while Pete looked over the reports. "By the way, your lawyer strolled through the front door right before you buzzed me. He's warming a barstool, but refused my offer for a drink."

Pete shoved the papers in his folder. "Send him in now, and don't bother me until he leaves."

"Whatever you say, Boss." Tom jumped up, left the door ajar on his way out.

Pete poured two small glasses of Courvoisier while waiting for Herman Wasserman, his go-between with the lawyer in Pont Canavese and advisor on all legitimate activities.

"Don't bother getting up," Herman said as he came through the door. He closed it, sat across the desk, and raised his glass to Pete's. He took a long sip, too long.

Pete read the lawyer's face. Didn't like what it said. His own drink for Herman's benefit remained untouched. "How's your family?"

"Good, Pete. Thanks for asking."

"What about mine?"

"Not so good. It's about your son Riccardo."

"Just give it to me straight, Herman."

"He's listed among the dead but Mrs. Rocca thinks otherwise."

Chapter 35

One day in the late summer of 1943 Gina returned from the post office wearing a smile so broad she couldn't contain it. "I'm going to Torino," she said, handing Isabella the letter confirming her announcement. "I've been accepted at the university, to study art restoration."

"Not now with the country at war," Isabella said.

"Especially now, with our men fighting for Italy the university must rely on dedicated women to protect its antiquities."

"Gina, Gina. With Il Duce in power, why undertake such a terrible risk. Our cities will know the pain of destruction before the countryside."

"I leave on Friday, Mama. Be happy and pray for me. I too have a mission to fulfill."

Isabella dropped her shoulders. "In that case bring me a stack of lire. We can't have you living like a pauper."

*****

In Torino Gina made a quick transition into the university life. As a student she excelled, always demanding the more difficult projects that might garner the attention of her professors. During her second year she accepted a paid internship at the Museum of Ancient Art, a short walk from her second floor apartment. The pay was meager but allowed her some financial independence. After all, every lira Mama sent Gina meant that much less for the young men of Canavese. Poor Riccardo, if only Mama had instigated the tangenti arrangement sooner, her brother's life might've taken a different course.

Other than a curfew that curtailed late evening activities, Gina and her friends enjoyed the life of dedicated students. But then the Nazis took control of Torino—Hitler said to protect the city from the Allied Forces; the Italians showed their contempt for him. Gina wept for those now dead in the streets, for Riccardo, who'd left no body for his family to inter. She didn't have Mama's unwavering faith that he still lived. And she wept for the antiquities the *Tedesche* might destroy or claim as protective bounty. But when they posted one of their own at Gina's museum, she had run out of tears.

Tall and fair-haired, Erich Heimberg strutted around the museum in his gray military uniform, the heels of his tight-fitting polished boots clicking against the marble floors. Gina abhorred their sound, yet felt drawn to the arrogant Tedeschi who wore them. Perhaps she had allowed her feelings to surface since one afternoon the museum curator called her into his office. The bespectacled man with a manicured goatee poured thimbles of Tuaco from Tuscany.

"For you, Gina, I have a special assignment," he said, "one that involves your fulltime employment here and is essential to the protection of Torino's priceless assets."

"Of course, I want to help."

"The *Tedeschi*, I've noticed him watching you. Perhaps we can use this interest to our advantage."

"Dottore Strada, I'm a student of the arts, not a seductress."

"I did not mean to insult you, merely to suggest you establish a friendship with the young comandante. A deception born of necessity, if that is more palatable to your tender upbringing." He poured more Tuaco. "Simply convince this German that the inferior works of art our staff takes such care in storing away are reproductions. And not the true masterpieces they indeed are. After all, other than exercising power by annihilation, what do these warmongers know or appreciate?"

*****

Gina initiated the first encounter, an invitation to mid-morning cappuccino at a café across from the museum. She maintained a formal demeanor, to give outsiders the impression she'd been forced to join the comandante. He observed her through eyes the color of aquamarine, leaned back in his chair, and bent one leg to the knee.

"You have family?" he asked in heavily accented Italian.

"Mama and two sisters, my brother died in the war."

"Fighting for Mussolini and our Fuehrer?"

"But of course," she replied, eyes downcast as she clanked her spoon against the cup.

"Your brother died a hero's death." The Tedeschi sat up, and to her horror, reached across the table to lift her chin. "Hold your head with pride, Gina Rocca."

Soon their coffee breaks extended to several times a week, but at various locations. They discussed art, which he admitted to having scant knowledge but wanted to learn more. She only spoke of the great works housed in Southern Italy, not those in Torino or any city north of Rome. Nor did she explain what skill went into determining a legitimate work from a well-defined forgery: the pigmentation, the canvas, the nuances and signature of the artist.

"I wish to take you to dinner sometime," he said one day, "perhaps that restaurant known for wild boar and truffles."

"I don't think an after-hour meeting would be prudent."

He sat back in his chair, stretched out his long legs to their full length, and studied her face. "Then your apartment, yes?"

She agreed but did not tell Dottore Strada.

*****

Gina supplied the most basic of meals: crusty bread, soft cheese, and red wine. "I hunted all over Torino for cinghiale," she said when he arrived that evening, "but I think the last beast must have escaped to the mountains."

"Hopefully to sniff out the partisans hiding under rocks," he said.

Gina regretted her attempt at light humor that prompted his response. She swallowed the words she dared not say, and instead uttered an insipid, "Please, no more talk of war."

"Or, antiquities," he replied. "But just for tonight."

She listened to stories of his childhood in Bavaria, how he hiked deep into the forests but had no desire to kill wild game. His face softened when he brought up his parents and two brothers. "Your siblings, how old are they?" she finally asked.

"Much younger than my twenty-four years, one is fourteen, the other twelve. My *mudder* buried three early babies before my brothers arrived healthy. Each day she prays the war will end before her boys are called to defend … my apologies. We agreed to conversations that bring laughter, not tears. Of course, even the simplest giggle begins with a smile. I've yet to see one of yours."

He clasped his hand over hers, a simple gesture, yet electrifying. At that moment she no longer considered him The Tedeschi. Or even the museum comandante. From now on Gina would think of this man by his rightful name, Erich Heimberg.

*****

Erich Heimberg went away for a week. To confer with his counterpart in Rome, according to Dottore Strada, who worried The Tedeschi might pick up a crumb of worthwhile knowledge. Erich's absence relieved the muscular tension behind her neck but didn't stop Gina from thinking about him. After he returned, she avoided an encounter until he stopped her in the hall one morning. "While in Rome I inspected some wonderful treasures. Perhaps we could discuss them over dinner tonight."

"I haven't shopped in a while. My cupboard …"

"Let me take care of everything."

Such an array of foods he brought, the best Torino could provide during Nazi occupation. Gina ate and laughed, to Erich's delight. She tried not to think of the street urchins, and privately vowed to hand out coins whenever the little beggars approached her.

The next time Erich came, he carried in more food, plus a phonograph and five American records. As soon as the spinning platter sent out its first notes, Gina blinked away tears welling in her eyes. Damn all things American, she wanted to say. Damn Pietro Rocca for making Mama a widow in all but name.

"I did not intend for the music to make you sad," Erich said.

"No, no. it brought memories of my papa. He died many years ago."

"Ah-h, yes, you told me about the tragic accident."

They munched on fat grapes while listening to the mesmerizing orchestras, the phonograph turned low so as not to disturb the neighbors or to incite their curiosity. Then Erich asked her to dance, a pleasure she'd not enjoyed since her sixteenth year. In his arms she felt oddly secure and at the end of the evening, she allowed him a kiss to her cheek. That night she lay awake, remembering the gentle brush of his lips.

The following evening Gina had already kicked off her shoes and slipped into a housedress when Erich knocked on her door. He came in, full of apologies for the unexpected visit.

"I worked late at the museum to prepare for my superior. He will arrive in two days and—"

"You were wondering if I saved yesterday's leftovers," Gina said with a laugh. "But first a proper greeting, please."

She offered her cheek and when he leaned down, she turned her mouth to his. At that moment friendship turned to love. Later, when Erich carried Gina to her bed, she gave as much as she received, and never considered the consequences of taking a road from which there was no return. Afterwards, she cried in his arms for a loss so vague it defied explanation.

She soon fell asleep, for only an hour, and when she awoke, Eric was gone. She rolled over and slept until noon. By the time she arrived at the museum, the door to Dottore Strada's office was closed, and several people were waiting to see him. Strolling past Erich's office, she caught a glimpse of him, head down and pouring over a pile of documents.

The next morning Gina stayed at her desk while Erich strutted around the museum with a somber Tedeschi, thick hands laced from behind. Four of his subordinates brought up the rear, and behind them, Dottore Strada carried a handkerchief to mop his brow. That afternoon she watched from her window as the Tedesche sped away in their car.

"I suspect they'll be back, when I do not know." Dottore Strada said in a low voice. "That I leave up to you, Gina. Do not fail me again."

Gina and Erich's passion was so remarkable it flourished without any thought of the possible consequences. They professed their love, discussed an imaginary future when the war's end would allow them to marry. At the museum Gina assured Dottore Strada that The Tedeschi remained clueless to the true value of so-called reproductions. Out of mixed loyalty, she did suggest ending her charade of distracting him, but Dottore Strada disagreed, citing another surprise visit from the commandante's superior as one reason.

"For the good of the museum, I beg you to continue the harmless friendship," he said. "In time you may be able to secure some information useful to the Resistance."

The Resistance, the partigiani, she'd helped them in Canavese, cheered when they sabotaged, killed and mutilated the Tedesche in retaliation for devastating Italy. But that was before Erich. Gina's Tedeschi had given his heart to her; she had given hers to him. They belonged to each other now.

Chapter 36

Faiallo—October 1944

"Are you sure you want me to do this," Maria asked Isabella.

"I for one do not approve," Giovanni said. "Not that your mama ever listens to the words of a crippled old man."

Isabella shifted in her chair. "Then go sit by the window, Giovanni. I cannot abide your hovering."

"Si," Allegra said. "Before Maria makes a terrible mistake."

Isabella shifted again. "Now, before I lose my patience."

Allegra held up a handful of Isabella's waist-length hair and Maria whacked it off with a pair of sharp scissors. Giovanni sucked in his breath. He limped to his chair and with a grunt eased into it.

"This is not befitting a woman of your stature," he said as Maria made a second cut.

"Joan of Arc wore her hair short," said Allegra.

"Si, they burned her at the stake."

"The woman was a saint."

"And I am not."

"But everybody says—"

"Basta, pay attention to what you're doing please."

Isabella watched her hair drop to the floor covered with last week's newspaper. She closed her eyes to block out the headlines, unsure of what to believe anymore. Mussolini and Hitler were failing, of that she was sure. But how many Italians would die before the war ended, she couldn't bear to contemplate.

"Can I go with you to Pont on Monday?" Maria asked as she took off another section.

"Don't make me decide now. Yesterday you went to Cuorgnè."

"When do I get another turn?" asked Allegra.

"I need both of you at home."

"Si, Mama, to milk the cows, to milk the goats, to send them up the hill."

"And gather the hay, clean out the henhouse, and dig up the root vegetables."

Allegra lifted the last clump of hair. "What we need is another Mondo."

Isabella crossed herself, Maria dropped her scissors, and Allegra whispered, "Mi dispiace."

"What?" Giovanni said.

What. They all knew what no one dared speak. That it was Maria who told Giovanni about the gypsy, Giovanni who convinced Mondo to report the gypsy, and Mondo who paid with his life for what had been Giovanni's betrayal. Isabella had been wrong too, for not listening to Maria when she should have. All this because of the gypsy—for him, she had no regrets.

Maria's hands were still shaking so Allegra picked up the scissors and made the final cut. She patted down Isabella's hair, circled around her, snipping here and there. *"Fini,"* she said at last. "Go look in the mirror before we clean up this mess."

Isabella left the silent three for the sanctity of her bedroom. The mirror reflected a woman with high cheekbones, tired eyes, and shoulder-length hair. Where had the years gone? Those years when Pietro used to sit on the bed, watching her weave her hair into one long braid. After he left, her cheeks didn't blush again until Cato. And then no one noticed except her. And Gina.

Returning to the kitchen, Isabella found Maria waiting with the broom, in case a few hairs had strayed from the paper.

"Already she looks like an Americano," Giovanni said, shaking his head.

"More like a movie star," said Allegra.

"Shorter, Maria, and this time no holding back."

*****

That evening when Isabella was alone, she picked up the broom and danced around the room, conjuring up feelings she usually kept buried. Two soft raps from outside stopped her dreaming. She stood motionless, until she heard the knocking again, no louder than the first set.

She went to the door, whispered. "Who's there?"

"Let me in, please. I'm freezing my balli."

Blessed Mother! That voice could only mean one person. She flung open the door to the one person she never doubted would return. He stepped in quickly, along with Due, closed the door, and took her in his arms. They hugged and kissed, and then some more.

"My prayers have been answered, Riccardo," she finally said in his ear. "God sent you back to me."

"Mi dispiace, Mama. For all the grief I caused you, forgive me. I would've come soon but—"

"You're with the partigiani, right?"

"But how did you know?"

"If you weren't with them, it meant you were dead. And that I refused to believe."

She stepped back to look at him, his face too old for his twenty-one years. "My God, you're so thin. You must be starving. I'll warm up the soup."

"Would you have enough for a few of my comrades?"

"But of course, where are they?"

He went to the door and whistled once. From out of the dark, four men appeared and hurried inside before the door quickly closed. Like Riccardo, they had rifles slung across their backs; they needed shaves and hot, soapy baths. They didn't remove their coats or caps when she motioned them to sit around her table. "I'd introduce you, Mama, but better you don't know their names."

"But we know about you," one of them said. "Your name is legendary."

"Riccardo didn't say you were so young."

"Or so beautiful."

Such nonsense, they reminded her of Cato. Isabella lit a fire under the soup and a second one under a skillet with butter. She set out cheese, salami, and bread. The men ate and talked while Riccardo opened bottles of wine. She cut yesterday's polenta into squares and added them to the hot skillet. While ladling soup into bowls, she felt Riccardo's eyes on her.

"Your hair, Mama, what did you do to it?"

"Maria chopped it off this afternoon."

He distributed the bowls of soup. "Ah-h-h, sweet Maria, how is she?"

Isabella put the warm polenta on a platter, sprinkled it with grated cheese before passing it to a waiting hand. "She talks about you every day and uses her own money to light candles."

"Don't ever tell her I was here."

"Of course not. Nor would I tell Giovanni," Especially Giovanni, she wanted to add. "Or Allegra, she misses you too. They're not little girls anymore, Riccardo."

"So I noticed from a distance today." He poured two glasses of wine; they clicked and drank. "I see Giovanni still leans on them."

"Harder than he ever leaned on you and Gina." Riccardo shoved a polenta square in his mouth.

Did he have to eat so fast? "Your sister's in Torino, studying art restoration."

"I know, Mama." He drained his glass, filled it again.

"You saw her there?"

"Gina must never know."

"Of course not," Isabella said. "How long can you stay? I mean your friends too. There's your bedroom, plus the stable. I have plenty of warm blankets."

Riccardo checked his wristwatch, the one she gave him before he left with Mussolini's army. He walked around the table, talked with his burping comrades until they pushed back their chairs and stood up. One by one, they kissed Isabella's hand and said, "Grazie, Signora Rocca."

The last man added, "Regrettably, we must decline your kind invitation to stay longer. A night such as this is perfect for traveling—no moon, no stars, and no snow."

They went into the dark, leaving Riccardo to say his goodbye in private, just as he had greeted her an hour before. They kissed and hugged three times before she released her hold on him. His hand was on the doorknob when he said, "Oh, I almost forgot this." He fumbled in his coat pocket, took out a tiny envelope, and closed it in her palm. "I regret not bringing my own gift, but this comes from one of your many admirers. Do you remember the day those gypsies came to Pont, the boy with one blue eye, and one brown? He's with the partigiani now—the best of the best, in fact."

Riccardo left before she realized he hadn't asked about Pietro, not that Isabella had anything new to report. She cleaned up kitchen before sitting down. Only then did she shake out the contents of Cato's envelope. A pair of gold earrings fell into her palm, the finest filigreed hoops she'd ever seen.

Chapter 37

Torino—April 1945

For Gina, the passing months had been glorious because they brought her closer to Erich. She lived for those nights he held her, those delicious moments during the day when he glimpsed in her direction. But in the past week she developed the uncomfortable feeling of being watched, on her way to the museum and in the shadows of her early evening return. She often turned around, but saw no one following her. In her apartment she kept the shades drawn and the lights turned low. When she and Erich made love, the bed felt crowded. Too many unresolved issues cluttered her past.

One evening a knock at the door interrupted her meal with Erich. Gina covered the dishes with napkins; he went into the bedroom. She cracked the door open, saw a bearded man dressed in scruffy trousers and a vest over his shirt in need of laundering. A soft cap covered his hair and forehead but a second glance at his face prompted Gina to muffle a scream. She sank to the floor, sobbing. The Erich appeared, his Luger aimed at the scowling man who had yet to cross her threshold.

Gina scrambled to her feet. She stood between the two men glaring at each other. "Erich, please, put your pistol away. This is

Riccardo, my brother."

She pulled him inside, closed the door, and covered his face with tears and kisses. "Mama was right. She said you were still alive, but I was the doubting Tommaso who didn't believe. Oh my God, Riccardo, it really is a miracle. You've come back from the grave."

Riccardo returned her affection, but with a reserve Gina knew he wanted her to feel. She pulled back to savor his lean, muscular physique. His roguish face showed no visible scars but it displayed a myriad of emotions, primarily anger directed at Erich who had holstered the Luger.

"We must celebrate. Erich, will you open another bottle of wine."

"None for me," Riccardo said.

Erich didn't move.

"Then have something to eat." She pulled back the napkins to reveal a display of rolls, sausages, éclairs, and fresh fruit tumbling from the platter.

Riccardo curled his lip. "I don't eat what is denied the rest of Torino."

"Riccardo, please, don't ruin this moment by insulting my hospitality. When I learned you were dead, part of me died too. After all, we shared Mama's womb."

"And her nourishing milk. Now you've disgraced Mama and our family." He jerked his head toward Erich but his eyes never left Gina. "So this is how you aid our cause and the museum, by sleeping with a Tedesche."

"Your cause? Does this mean you contacted Dottore Strada? Told him to promote me in exchange for ..."

"Distracting me from my duties," Erich said, whirling Gina around by her shoulders. Anger distorted the aquamarine of his eyes. "Your brother is with the Resistance and you whored for them in order to destroy me."

"No, no. It wasn't like that. You must believe me."

"And that unctuous pimp, the curator?"

"He asked me to befriend the lonely officer assigned to his museum. That was all he asked. You made me fall in love with you. What we have together, I don't ever want to end."

Erich turned his back to her. He ran his hand over the precision haircut befitting his rank and slapped on his peak cap, the eagle perfectly centered. "I must leave now," he said. "Do not speak another damning word to me. When we pass each other in the museum halls, cast your eyes to the floor. If you attempt any reconciliation whatsoever, I shall report your partisan activities and have you shot. Your brother too."

As soon as the door slammed behind Erich, Riccardo uncorked the wine he'd earlier refused. He poured two glasses, gulped one down, and poured another. Gina ignored hers.

"So, now it's your turn to be angry," Riccardo said. He plopped onto the sofa and rubbed his eyes. "Before the war your lover may have been a good man, but no Tedeschi is worthy to breathe the same air that fills your lungs or mine."

"What do you know of love?"

"Enough to know it comes in many forms. But none can exceed the love of country and cherished freedom."

"And what about Mama? Every day she lights a candle for you. Does she even know that her prayers were answered long ago?"

Riccardo cracked a smile, his first of the evening. "Gina, Gina, who do you think sent me here?"

"Then you did know about Dottore Strada."

He patted the cushion and Gina sat beside him. She rested her head against his shoulder. "You've been following me."

"Only this past week," Riccardo said. "Soon we will liberate Torino and when that day comes, Tedeschi blood will flow in the gutters. And that stronzodi merda Il Duce we will slaughter for allowing the rape of his country"

A single tear trickled down her cheek. Riccardo wiped it away with his thumb.

"We'd planned to marry after the war," she said. "Now, Erich hates me."

"Then heed the Tedeschi's warning: stay away from him."

The curfew whistle blew and Gina hopped up. "You can sleep on the sofa tonight. I'll get a pillow and blanket. Tomorrow we'll have coffee and talk some more."

To her relief, Riccardo agreed. He even soaked in the hot bath she prepared. But in the early morning when she put on the coffee, he was already gone.

*****

Riccardo's loyalty to his partigiani took precedence over any concern for Gina's broken heart. He and Flavio had joined the Resistance the day they crashed in Sicily. After learning guerilla warfare, they both traveled north, enlisting and training more Freedom Fighters along with way. City by city, they worked with the Allies to reclaim Italy. Now the Allied troops were advancing on Torino. And the Nazis were preparing to destroy the city's power stations, communication networks, and main factories.

As members of the Committee for National Liberation, he and Flavio spent the next week helping to organize a citywide general strike. Its success left the city in turmoil, the Nazis on the defensive. And the Resistance primed to liberate Torino before the Allies arrived.

Early one morning in the heart of Torino Riccardo and Flavio were holed up in on the second floor of an abandoned building, along with ten of their comrades. To a man, they all had rifles slung over their backs, ammunition strapped to their chests. Silence filled the room, each Freedom Fighter absorbed in his own thoughts. For the second time in an hour Riccardo watched Flavio sharpen their six knives. He held each one to a candle, turned the blade to inspect it. Only then, did he return Riccardo's three and slip one into the sheath at his waist, the other two down his boots. Riccardo did the same.

"Are you ready, my brother?" Flavio asked, a smile crinkling his freckled face.

Riccardo held that face between his hands and kissed both cheeks, hard. Indeed, they were brothers. They'd fought together, shared the same bottle, the same bed, and the same women.

Their grizzly leader moved away from his watch at the window, and said, "Andiamo."

Riccardo and his eleven comrades hurried down to the street, joined with more of their partigiani. And civilians armed with shovels, boards, chains, and more knives. Their numbers grew as they marched through Torino, determined to destroy every Tedesche who dared show his face. Within hours the CNL mobile forces entered the city as the fighting continued. Bodies littered the streets. Women and children wailed. Sporadic gunfire erupted.

Burning structures belched thick smoke that blurred vision and tested every man's endurance.

Riccardo and Flavio were chasing two Tedeschi when a third stepped out from a doorway. He jumped Riccardo, knocking him to the pavement. They wrestled like two unleashed logs rolling into the scattered embers and debris. When they bumped against a curb, the damn Tedesche wound up on top of Riccardo. He felt the horrible sensation of a vile thumb being jammed into his eye, the pressure so intense he could only think of pulp being extracted from a grape. He nearly passed out from the pain before he allowed an agonizing scream to erupt from his throat. Only then did he focus his good eye on the man straddling him. Horror registered on both their faces. Then disbelief—right after Flavio came from behind and slit the Tedesche's throat. A volley of bullets whizzed through the air, one searing a hole in Flavio's forehead. United in death, he and the Tedesche fell over Riccardo, who screamed again, this time from Flavio's sharp blade digging into his flesh.

*****

Not daring to venture out, Gina had watched some of the bloody skirmishes from her apartment window. By nightfall the streets were quiet and she went to bed with thoughts of the war ending. When Erich was no longer tied to Hitler, he'd have to forgive her.

Early the next morning, she awoke to a loud banging at her door. She threw on her robe and unbolted the door, expecting to open it to Riccardo. Instead, four partigiani pushed their way in without being invited. Three had their rifles drawn, the fourth kept his slung over his shoulder. He looked at her through narrowed eyes, and said, "Gina Rocca, you've been reported as collaborating with the Tedesche."

"There must be some mistake …."

"You deny knowing Erich Heimberg?"

"He is the Nazi comandante at the Museum of Antiquities where I work."

"You'll need to come to headquarters and clear yourself."

"Wait! My brother is with the Resistance. Perhaps you know him: Riccardo Rocca."

The men looked at each other and shook their heads.

"He's in Torino now."

"In that case, put on your prettiest dress and highest heels."

Thirty minutes later she found herself locked in the damp cellar of a government building, along eight women accused of collaborating with the Tedesche. Four of the women were soon dragged away, screaming their innocence. Gina's heart pounded in her ears. She threw up bile in the only available container, a bucket reeking of feces and urine. Afterwards, she slid down the wall, circled her arms around her legs, and did what Mama would've done. She prayed.

When Gina's turn came, two angry women dressed in men's clothing pushed her up three flights of stairs to an office with no windows. They forced her onto a high stool.

"Your hair, it's very pretty," one of them said, grabbing a handful and twisting hard. "Did your Tedeschi run his fingers through it?"

Gina didn't answer.

The other one punched Gina in the face, so hard it made her cheekbone throb. She wanted to rub it but refused to display any sign of weakness. The women had one pair of scissors between them and took turns chopping away at her hair until it barely grazed her scalp.

"Bella, bella," one of them said, holding Gina's face to a cracked mirror. "Do you know what the partigiani do with pretty women who collaborate with the enemy? They shoot them in the face or against the wall."

Later a one-armed man brought Gina some broth and stale bread. He called it her last supper.

*****

The next day the partigiani marched her and five other women around the Piazza della Repubblica. Each of them had a sign hanging the neck that read *Tedeschi Whores of Torino*. Gina saw Dottore Strada standing off to the side, a pained expression on his face. At least he didn't join the rowdy onlookers shouting vile insults. Rotting food started flying. An egg splattered Gina's face. Such a waste, Mama would've made better use of food past its prime. A stoic man jabbed his rifle in her ribs. He told her to lick the balls of the brass bull embedded in the terrazzo walkway. She prostrated herself and obeyed, glad for an excuse to rest her aching feet.

With each passing minute the crowd grew rowdier. Gina heard talk of a stoning, murmurs of an early morning firing squad. She clenched her teeth to keep from crying out for Riccardo, or Mama. She dared not think of Erich, or of the precious gift of love he'd given her.

Book Five—Chapter 38

Illinois—1957

"I'm inclined to think Connie woulda been proud," Beans said.

Pete nodded. "He couldn't have picked a better exit—scotch in one hand, cigar in the other."

The two men still wore their dark suits displaying black armbands as they sat on cushioned wicker gracing the Latimer porch. Beans gulped the last of his Stag Beer and licked foam from his lips. "D'ya ever encounter so many mourners attend one man's funeral?"

"Not everyone was mourning," Pete said, pouring another glass of fine red wine.

"Ain't that the truth. I caught more than one whiff of plain clothes and the press. Did you see that gaggle of nosy matrons and retirees trying to gather juicy tidbits in order to impress their friends. According to Jackie G, the procession stretched for five blocks. Not even what's-his-name got that much homage—you know, Mr. Big Shot Union Boss who met His Maker last year."

"Connie would've appreciated that too."

"Come again?"

"Your loyal optimism—that he actually made it to heaven and met His Maker."

"Sure as hell Connie did. After all, he took care of me for many a year."

"And a lot of other people, in more ways than one."

"Yeah, I know what you mean. The man dealt out his own kind of justice, but he also had a soft side." Beans opened another Stag from the chilled bucket. "You never did forgive him, did you, Pete?"

"As much as I could. Besides, what happened nineteen years ago was more my fault than his. I dragged my feet instead of taking care of Leo, one way or another."

"The sonofabitch had it coming."

"Sure, Leo was a lowlife but he didn't deserve to die. Neither did Fallon and Billie."

Beans took a deep breath and cleared his throat, signs Pete recognized as preparation for cleansing of the soul. "You know, Pete, There's something I've wanted to tell you for a long time, something that should've come from Connie but—"

"Whatever you've been holding back, will it change a single thing?"

"Maybe your mind, but only you can be the judge of that."

Pete fell back to the old habit of checking his watch, except time had not been an issue for several years. Not since the new brand of politicians wanting a squeaky clean image had run their campaign on doing away with gambling and prostitution. Their election resulted in the One Eleven property being sold to the local Moose Lodge. "What the hell," Pete said, motioning him to continue.

Beans lit a cigarette and leaned forward, bony elbows to knobby knees. "The whole mess on Collinsville Avenue started with me. It was yours truly who told Connie and Billie about Leo putting the squeeze on you."

"Hell, Beans. You're not telling me anything I don't already know. You did what Connie paid you to do."

"Wait, there's more. All these years you've been blaming the wrong person. Connie never put out a hit on Leo. He said the weasel was your doing and he trusted you to take care of the problem, however you saw fit. I guess Billie thought otherwise 'cause she took matters into her own hands."

"Wait a minute. You're telling me Billie hired the gunman?"

Beans bent his arm in an oath-swearing position. "The fuckin' bastard confessed as much, right before Connie put him out of his misery. Finger chopping couldn't compare to the butchering Connie performed that day."

Pete didn't flinch. Bean's acknowledgment was the first he'd heard of Connie's role as executioner. In fact, the body had ever been found. Leo's hit man had simply disappeared, just as Giovanni's Dog had years before.

Beans expelled a belch through puffed cheeks before he continued. "This guy was a two-bit amateur. A pro woulda known better than to stage a kill on Collinsville Avenue at ten in the morning. Sure as hell Billie didn't expect such stupidity, or she woulda never showed up to witness the act."

"La Bianca, who could do no wrong. The one time she goes

against Connie, she winds up hiring a bungler."

"La Bianca, that's what you called her? You Eye-talians sure got a way with words. Anyway, that morning Billie was doing Connie's bidding—checking up on Fallon—not knowing their paths were destined to intersect with Leo's. What more can I say, Pete? The rest you already know."

All too well, if only Pete had given Leo what he asked for, when he asked, maybe Leo wouldn't have squeezed Fallon for more. If only Pete had shown up five minutes earlier that day. If only—

"I guess you wannabe alone," Beans said, directing his words to a face gone blank. Without waiting for Pete's reply, he made himself scarce with a walk in the yard.

Pete sat for a few minutes before deciding to shake off the gruesome images of his past. He went upstairs to his study, unlocked the bottom drawer of his desk, and took out a manila envelope. Sitting in his club chair, feet propped up, he pulled out the photograph. He'd not looked at Pietro's family for some time, a self-imposed mental flagellation for having denied their existence. But with no one looking over his shoulder, Pete indulged himself. Slowly, he traced one finger over the faces of Isabella, Riccardo, and Gina as if to extract their forgiveness.

He still sent money every month but maintained no control over its use. Not that he needed any control, not with Isabella's frugal management. Had she found another man to warm her bed, to share the burdens of the farm? And Riccardo, did he grow into a strong, and above all else, honorable man? Gina, his sweet girl, did her eyes still dance when she talked of what made her happy?

A firm hand to Pete's shoulder pulled him back to the Midwest. He started to shove the photograph into the envelope, but

Dan's hand proved quicker than his.

"Not so fast, Pop. I don't remember seeing this old photo before." Dan displayed few physical characteristics of his mother but was every bit as mouthy as she had been, a trait which endeared him all the more to Pete. The young man had topped out at six feet, not as tall as Connie had anticipated, but nothing pleased Pete more than being able to look up to his son.

Dan sat down in the smaller chair Pete kept as a reminder of Fallon. She'd often sat there and rested her feet on his lap, demanding that he rub them. He complied, mostly to keep her quiet while he read. If only he had known then how little time remained for such simple pleasures.

Dan furrowed his brow as he studied the photograph. Then his face lit up. "Like father, like son," he said, tapping his finger above the little boy's image. "I always thought you and I looked alike, even though Connie swore I took after the Latimer side. The little girl comes as a surprise though. I didn't know you had a sister."

Pete sighed. Beans would not be the only one to cleanse his soul on Connie's funeral day. "She's not my sister, Dan. She's my daughter. The boy is her twin."

"No shit. Then the father has to be …"

"Me as a young man, not much older than you right now," Pete said. "This was my first family, before I met your mother."

"Wow, I'm really sorry, Pop. It must've been tough, losing such a nice family."

Pete dropped his eyelids.

"So, Pop, if you don't mind my asking, how'd they die?"

"They didn't. They still live in Italy."

"You're shitting me. No, I guess you're not. And you never went back, or sent for them? Why?"

If Pete had still been a smoker, he would've lit a cigarette. If he'd been sitting at Connie's desk, he would've poured himself a scotch—and one for Dan. Instead, he got up and went to the window.

"You won't find the answer out there, Pop."

"Shut up. I'm thinking." He'd been preparing for this day for years, and still couldn't come up with an explanation that made him anything less than a heel. He held his gaze on two squirrels scampering up a tree. When they were out of sight, he cleared his throat, and said what seemed reasonable, "Lack of money, lack of honor, and too much ambition."

"Nah, I'm not buying those flimsy excuses. Stupid, I'm not."

"My son, the college graduate, not exactly a top student but still you make me proud."

"Even with such mediocre grades?"

"At least you came by them honestly."

"You bet I did. All those contributions Connie poured into the university couldn't buy me one stinking A. So, enough with the buttering up—what's the story on this other family?"

Pete smiled. He returned to his comfortable chair, ready to face his son. "I came to America in a hurry, not planning to stay. But then I fell, really hard for your mother and later you came along. The rest you already know."

Dan's eyes drifted from Pete to the photograph and back to Pete. "All these years I thought of myself as an only child."

"You're the child of my Fallon and the life we shared in America. The Italian family belongs to my youth."

"Like hell. What you're really saying is: if it hadn't been for me, you'd have gone back long ago." Dan shook his head. The years had turned his crew cut from blonde to the color of pinecones. "Me with a brother and sister I've never met."

"Don't keep rubbing my nose in what I already know."

"I'm not letting you off that easy. What about their mother?"

"A good woman who deserved better."

"What a crock of bullshit. No wonder you ran out on her."

With that, Pete jumped up. Heart pounding in his temples, he grabbed the closest object, a vase he sent flying across the room. Porcelain crashed into the wall, its shattered remains sprinkling the carpet.

"Dammit! That's not the way it happened. I loved her, as God is my witness I did. We both adored our children." Holding out his empty palms, Pete leaned over to the son who sat motionless. "They were my life, Dan. *They were my life.*"

He collapsed in the chair and stared at wallpaper until Dan found his voice.

"OK, that's what I needed to hear. What the hell, you should go back. Pablo could handle the farm for a while." He referred to Sebastian's son, a reliable employee who continued the tradition of importing relatives from Mexico.

"Going back wouldn't be right, not after all these years."

"Then take me with you."

"As I recall, you promised to spend this summer landing the ideal job, with a company worthy of your expectations."

"The job can wait 'til fall. It's not like I'll starve without working. Besides, these people, they're my family too."

"They don't even know you exist."

"All the more reason for my going too," Dan said. "Look, when the chips were down, you had to make a choice, them or me. I mean no disrespect for the recent dead but Connie did live up to his reputation. And if only half the stories I've heard about him are true, I hope he managed to squeeze out a good act of contrition before he hit the floor. The man was an enigma and he covered all bases: remarkable, relentless, and ruthless."

"That's some eulogy. A lot more honest than any I heard at his wake."

"I loved Connie as much as he loved me, but I have no intentions of following in his footsteps. God only knows how I'd have turned out if you'd left me behind."

"Connie never would've let me take you."

"That's for sure. But nothing's holding you back now."

Chapter 39

Italy—July 1957

"Come on, Pop. I think we should go with something a little flashier."

Pete ignored Dan's comment as they followed a nattily dressed salesman around the Fiat showroom in Milan.

Franco Negri stopped at a solid, six-passenger vehicle, black with minimal trim. With a broad sweep of his arm, he bowed slightly and spoke in precise Italian.

"Signore Rocca, allow me to present the Multipla, our *seicentro* model, one of the most desirable. It has a four-cylinder engine and rear wheel drive. A practical family machine I highly recommend."

"What'd he say, Pop?"

"That it will handle hairpin curves."

Franco opened the Multipla's door, invited them to peer inside.

"I don't think we should rule out the Ferrari," Dan said, referring to a demo drive they'd taken the day before. "That sweet machine purred like a kitten."

"As long as you're dreaming, why not reach for the moon and ask for a Bugatti?"

"Even I know where to draw the line."

Pete slid onto the driver seat, gripped his hand around the steering wheel. Dan entered from the passenger side, ran his hand over the dashboard.

"No offense intended, but I say Connie would've gone for the Ferrari."

"And if he could rise from the dead, he'd have it imported to Illinois—just to keep you under his thumb, which means you and I wouldn't be having this conversation in Italy. We're not here to put on a show and don't you forget it. The seicentro model will do fine."

"This from a man who drives nothing but top-of-the-line Lincolns," Dan said.

As an extra caveat, Franco assured Pete there would be minimal loss on the Multipla if it were resold before he returned to America. Pete nodded but thought he might leave the car with Riccardo, a decision subject to the kind of welcome awaiting him in Faiallo.

*****

The next day Pete sat with Dan at a small table on Pont Canavese's main piazza and outside the hotel they'd checked into an hour earlier. He stirred three sugar cubes into a small cup of steaming espresso and trickled the thick brew down his throat.

"So that's how you make that mud slide," Dan said, reaching for the sugar bowl to follow his father's lead, a practice that had accelerated ever since they stepped off the plane in Milan, and one which amused and flattered Pete. Quite a few years had passed since Dan relied on him for much of anything besides money.

"See anybody you know, Pop?"

Pete heard the question but chose not to answer.

Dan repeated his words.

"We agreed to speak Piemontese," Pete said. "That's the only way you'll learn the dialect. These people have no use for a snot-nosed Americano who won't honor them by at least attempting to speak their language."

"Si, Papa," said Dan, repeating his question in Piemontese.

Pete gestured a negative response.

"Now Papa speaks with his head, the universal language," Dan said with a grin. "OK, from now on we communicate in the native language but show some mercy. I've only been working on this for four weeks."

"All the more reason you should've stayed behind."

Dan struggled for the correct words and finally came out with a fractured version of "Not on your life."

Pete held up his hand. "Basta! With me, speak English; but with everybody else …"

"Thanks and grazie." Dan cocked his head to their hotel. "Now, how soon can we ditch these crummy digs?"

"Spoken like a Latimer, but I told you not to expect the Waldorf. We share a bath in the two best rooms of the best hotel in the best village. The sheets are clean and the towels—"

"Are the size of handkerchiefs. Not that I'm complaining."

"Sure as hell you better not."

"I only meant: when are we going to the old homestead. I can't wait to meet the family."

"All in due time," Pete said. "Now take a walk or check out the shops. I need time alone to think."

Pete watched his son walk away. Dan's long stride carried him across the cobblestone piazza where elderly men with drooping mustaches had congregated. The mustachios bantered and gossiped and opined on every subject from sex to politics—a scene familiar to Pete and one transcending centuries. He ordered a second espresso and tried to create a plan for returning to a family of strangers and having to explain an unexpected member. To open with "meet my son from America" would translate into *bastardo*. Dan didn't know he was the child of an unlawful union and now in a country that didn't recognize divorce. Although Connie's lawyer assured Pete the matter had been quietly resolved in America, Pete never saw the legal papers. Nor had he asked for them. Not that the question of legality ever compromised Dan's status. A lifetime of wealth and acceptance had insulated him from insecurities that plagued the have-nots.

A commotion developing across the piazza jolted Pete from one of his many concerns. He hurried toward a crowd gathering in a narrow street to watch a brawling sideshow. No surprises here, just Dan scraping with two young Italians. He caught a punch to his jaw and slid down the stone facade of a panetteria displaying an array of breads and pastries. One of the men grabbed a pretty girl's hand, and all three hurried off, leaving Dan to the curious mustachios.

"*Non ospedale,*" the old men murmured, determining the Americano had not shed enough blood to warrant a trip to the hospital.

"What happened?" Pete asked in Piemontese.

"Who can say?" one replied with a shrug.

"The girl, she is engaged," another said. "Perhaps this Americano—"

Moving aside for Pete, they hung around for the finale. He leaned over for a closer inspection of Dan's cut lip and bruised cheekbone before pulling him up. Satisfied his son had received nothing worse than an embarrassing introduction to village protocol, Pete gave him a playful nudge to the chin.

"Already you forgot one of my first lessons."

"You mean about leading with my left?"

"Pay attention," Pete said, steering him back across the piazza. "Do nothing to provoke a fight."

"I never saw the bozos until one of them punched me."

"This is not Rome, where a man compliments a woman by pinching her behind."

"I only asked her name."

"Around here, a gentleman first makes inquiries. If no one has spoken for the signorina, he enlists a go-between to arrange a proper introduction."

"No doubt for a price."

"Easy words coming from someone who never scrambled for a dollar."

"What do you mean? I worked on the farm every summer since my fourteenth birthday."

"Only because I insisted. Why if I had let Connie have his way—"

"Hey, Pop, look at us. We didn't need to travel seven thousand miles just to replay the same argument we could've had in Illinois."

"You're right. So, what about that banged-up face? I won't be embarrassed by taking some shitty scrapper to meet my family."

"Hester always used a hunk of beef to reduce the swelling," Dan said. "Not that I would know from personal experience."

"Like hell, you don't. Who do you think told Hester to use steak on that battered face you got after the Senior Prom?"

*****

In the early morning before the fog had lifted, Pete and Dan were back in the piazza, enjoying bowl-size cups of cappuccino and fresh bread Pete requested from the panetteria. After an earlier application of raw meat, Dan's face showed scant effect from the previous day's encounter.

It was market day and across the piazza farmers were setting out their produce and the venders, their assorted wares. Time had done little to change the scene Pete remembered from earlier years, except for the addition of a few automobiles, pre-war vintage. And more females: the young and not so young, their bare arms and legs soaking up the warm sun.

"You think she'll show up?" Dan asked.

"Coming from a farm, you can ask such a question? It's peak harvest season."

"Give me a little credit, will you? I thought she'd send one of her kids."

"She has a name—Isabella. And Riccardo and Gina are no longer kids." He spoke their names the Italian way, taking extra care to enunciate the vowels, emphasize the double consonants, and roll the letter r.

"Cut me some slack, will you, Pop? This whole business with your first family is a mouthful for me to swallow."

"Mi dispiace, sometimes I forget. By the way, just so there's no confusion, around here the name Pete Montagna means zero—*niente*." He paused, waiting for his latest revelation to register with Dan. "To these people I am Pietro Rocca."

"Hells bells, then who am I?"

"My son … and don't you forget it."

"Just so you don't. Anything else you want to tell me?"

"Not now." Pete's voice trailed off as he glanced toward the market. "Look, over there to your right. I told you Isabella would come."

"Oh yeah? Well after all these years and from way over here, how can you tell that particular woman is Isabella?"

"Hers is the only booth set up and making sales." Pete welcomed the momentary relief of Dan's distraction with bread and coffee. Sometimes his son surprised him by knowing when to keep quiet instead of arguing.

Had it not been for the distinctive fluid motions and unyielding posture, Pete could not have identified Isabella so readily. Gone was her familiar peasant attire: the long dark skirt skimming sturdy shoes and babushka protecting her hair. This middle-aged Isabella wore a straw hat, white blouse and brightly colored skirt, so full he could almost hear it swish around the calves of her legs. Had her clothes not been the current style, Pete might have mistaken Isabella for a gypsy. Except, no gypsy worth her tarot cards would be caught wearing the floppy sun hat.

"What about the other one?" Dan asked after wiping his mouth. "Could she be Gina?"

Inwardly, Pete chastised himself for not being more observant. He squinted for a better look. "Perhaps a neighbor; Gina has dark hair, almost black."

"Well, are we just going to sit here? Or do we go over and say hello."

"To interrupt before the end of market would violate the sacrosanctity of good business."

"And I thought only in America. As with the almighty dollar, in Italy the lira reigns supreme."

Pete imparted his sternest look, which had worked in Dan's early years but now conveyed little more than exasperation. "After yesterday, I hesitate to suggest you take another walk, but—"

"Good idea." Dan stood up. "I'm going for a casual look-see, and this time I promise: no talking to females under the age of forty."

"Stay away from Isabella's booth. I decide when the time is right."

"Give me some credit, Pop. All this market stuff may be old hat to you, but for me it's an opportunity to experience the Italian way and to explore my heritage."

Experience the Italian way, explore his heritage. Where did Dan dream up such bullshit? For a rich kid with a college degree, when it came to everyday life, Dan possessed the smarts of a just-weaned pup. With a lift of his finger to the hotel waiter, Pete switched from cappuccino to espresso. He settled back to while away the morning observing Isabella and her helper. Something about the younger woman seemed familiar. Perhaps a neighbor Gina once played with, perhaps Maria from next door, the bald-headed baby who used to ride on the hip of Giovanni's wife. All this had started because of Serina. All this he'd left behind because of Serina.

Pete rubbed his thumb over the faint line faded into the deep crease of his cheek. The scar belonged to his face, so unremarkable no one ever asked about the circumstances of its origin. Not even Dan, who displayed an insatiable curiosity about everything.

If only Giovanni hadn't come home early that Sunday. If only Giovanni hadn't found him humping his wife. Poor cuckold, so distraught he whipped himself into a stroke while beating the two of them. Pete figured she got the hell out after Giovanni quit clinging to a life not worth living. God rest his soul.

"Well, what do think, Pop?" Dan had returned with his face flushed from having viewed everyday life from a foreigner's perspective.

"I see you didn't pick up any new bruises."

"You'd have been proud of me. I even used my Piemontese. No talking, just some pointing and listening." He held out a bag of apricots, Pete's favorite fruit. "Try one."

Pete made a face. His stomach had been churning for an hour. Too much espresso, he wanted to believe, refusing to consider a case of nerves over the impending reunion.

Dan motioned his head toward Isabella's booth. "Maybe we should go over and say hello before she—I mean, Isabella—packs up and leaves."

"This day is not the appropriate one.

"Oh no you don't, we didn't come all this way for you to chicken out now."

"I'm no coward, but perhaps I should approach Isabella on my own, just the first time, so as not to alarm her."

"I get it. The errant husband returns from America. But will his deserted family accept the bastardo who tags along?"

"What the hell are you talking about?"

"Just repeating what I heard. It seems the two of us are the talk of the market place. But your pseudonym has thrown a monkey wrench into the equations since no one can place the Montagna family. Whether Isabella suspects, I couldn't make out."

"In that case, we'll sit tight. I don't want to create a scene that would embarrass her. Isabella has been through enough."

"Don't tell me we're holding off 'til the next market day in … what's that other village?"

"Cuorgnè," Pete said. "Actually, that's not a bad idea, one I'd consider if I were here by myself. But I don't think I can put up with your insolence much longer."

"Look, Pop. I hate to admit this, but maybe you were right after all. You're pedaling uphill, and I'm the broken spoke getting in your way."

"First things first, the hotel has a decent mid-day meal. Seven courses, I think."

"How can you think about eating? Back in Illinois the sun's not even up yet."

"I think better on an empty bladder and a full stomach. Now quit your bitching and let's take a leak before we eat."

They sat down in a dining room of crisp white linens and aromas Pete had not savored since his days in Butte. Garlic and olive oil were the prevailing odors, mingled with basil and oregano and sage. The owner brought out crusty bread and plates of antipasto. "The mushrooms are superb," he said. "I gathered them myself, early this morning."

Pete's thoughts drifted to the last time he went hunting for mushrooms: the day he clashed with a wild boar, the broken leg that changed his life forever—and that of his family.

"Don't fill up on bread," he cautioned Dan.

"Sorry, I'm hungrier than I first thought."

"It's the mountain air."

"And the good food. Here comes the next course."

The creamy risotto with three different cheeses reminded Pete of Isabella's. So did the thin, vertical slices of zucchini topped with a generous ladling of *bagna caôda*. The combination of anchovies and garlic sautéed in olive oil permeated their senses with ambrosia, a gift from the gods capable of clearing sinus-clogged passages. By now, Pete and Dan were on their second bottle of Barbaresco, the region's premier red.

Dan held up his glass to admire the wine's clarity. "Is it my imagination, or does this grape juice go down smoother than any we get back home?"

"It's all in the fermentation."

"That's what you said about the bread."

"Si, the same goes for both."

"Go on, you're shitting me."

"Would a father lie to his son?"

"Not any more I hope."

"Then shut up and mangia."

After Dan insisted he'd eaten his weight, the waiter brought plates of roast beef sliced thin and small new potatoes still in their jackets. "This meat's as tender as butter," he raved. "Remember Hester's?"

"Like a bad dream. Leave room for the insalata mista."

"I know, I know. Greens and olive oil make for a healthy evacuation."

"You're a quick learner. One more bottle of wine?"

"Why not, the bottled water's too salty."

"Try some fruit, to cleanse the palate."

"Maybe a fig or two."

"Um-m, did you ever eat a juicier pear?"

"I'm stuffed to the gills."

"In that case, something to aid the digestion. Waiter! Limoncello for me and my brother, I mean, my … my…"

"My head hurts."

"Don't blame the wine. It's the altitude."

"A nap sounds good, before we tackle Faiallo."

"Tomorrow. Better we should go tomorrow, after our morning coffee."

Chapter 40

The next morning found Pete and Dan traveling the two-lane road to Faiallo, after an earlier discourse on each man's driving merits in which Pete had reluctantly assumed the position of co-pilot, navigator, and instructor. Dan provided him little reason to criticize or to offer worthwhile suggestions so Pete leaned back, inwardly pleased with his son's expertise in handling the winding roads as he alternated between second and third gears. They ascended higher into the foothills, leaving Pont behind to bask in a picture postcard panorama of lush forests and blue lakes surrounded by the looming snow-capped mountains

"You know, Pop, I can't remember the last time I ate as much as that meal yesterday."

"Such gluttony, but it gave us a few good laughs, si?"

"Si, Papa."

"A lot of years have passed since I last heard someone call me Papa.

"I don't ever remember calling you ... oh, you mean the twins. Sorry, I keep forgetting."

"No need to apologize."

"Good, then you won't mind my asking if you loved them more than me?"

"Spoken like a man with no children. After you've had more than one, I'll ask you that same question."

"Point taken," Dan said. "Anyway, back to yesterday: what you said about a father not lying to his son."

"In other words, you want to know why I left Italy."

"I'm a grown-up, Pop. Just give me the straight and skinny."

"You're right. That much I owe you so here's the Reader's Digest version. My neighbor—an old but good friend—had a massive stroke when he caught me cheating with his wife."

"Funny, I never pictured you as the type. His wife must've been some dish."

"Sweet enough to suck music from an out-of-tune mandolin, not that it says much for me," Pete said. "Isabella witnessed the same ugly scene as my old friend did. She sent me away, just until the gossip died down. Instead, I followed my childhood dream and went to America with Leo Arnetti."

"You mean Leo the dickhead from Collinsville Avenue?"

"The same. We spent two years in Butte, working the copper mines and gambling away more than we saved. After a while, I wised up and caught a train for East Saint Louis."

"Come on. What man in his right mind would leave the Wild West for the Midwest?"

"One he thought he was on the run, that's who. My cuckold neighbor must've survived, at least long enough to sic some hound with a switchblade on me."

"And I thought Connie was the only …"

"Hey, this dago never killed anybody," Pete answered in the street talk that kept popping into his conversations with Dan. "Nor did I ever hire some goomba to murder on my behalf."

"Damn! It all sounds so …"

"Sordid? You right. Had you thought otherwise, I'd have failed you as a parent. And your mother, God rest her soul, would've haunted me from her grave." As soon as the word 'grave' exited Pete's mouth, he noticed the stone chapel of Santa Caterina's. "Pull over to the side," he told Dan. "It's time you met the other side."

They walked through the cemetery, passed the graves with stone markers displaying encased photographs of the deceased—young and old, children and parents. When they came to the concrete walls of more photographs, Pete searched every face as he continued walking.

"What's with the wall?" Dan finally asked.

"After the bodies stay in the ground for so many years, the remains are moved up there—to make room for the newly deceased."

"Why don't they just extend the cemetery?"

"This is not America. The Old Country has limited space and steeper traditions." Pete stopped. He pressed his fingertips to the image of Riccardo Pietro Rocca. *"Mio Padre."*

"Ciao, Nonno," Dan said, placing his fingers next to Pete's

Pete crossed himself and touched the image of Madelena Trono Rocca. *"Mia Madre."*

"Ciao, Nonna." Dan kissed his fingertips, pressed them to her photograph.

"I left without saying goodbye to them in their final resting place," Pete said. "Never did I think a lifetime would pass before my return. They died within days of each other, from the Influenza of 1918. Their love carried them into the next life."

"I'll leave the three of you alone for awhile, Pop."

Ten minutes later, Pete slid onto his side of the car and Dan started the engine. He shifted into first, then second, and finally third as they climbed higher and higher. Knowing Dan better than he knew himself, Pete was not surprised when Dan hit him with another question.

"Did you love her? I mean my mother."

"With all my heart."

"More than Isabella?"

"Another way of asking a father to choose his favorite child."

"Ouch. I still want to believe your world revolves around me and mine."

"Since the day you were born, but maybe it's time I cut you loose."

"Thanks, but not here. Don't leave me stranded in the enemy camp, OK?"

"You know better than to ask such a fool question."

"Just testing your love; anything else I should know?"

"Nothing that can't wait," Pete said. "Besides we've run out of time, and road. Turn here."

They left the pavement and rumbled over a decades-old road of stone and dirt leading to clustered farmhouses. Rows of white bed linens flapped against the blue sky with the intensity of birds in flight. Pete also considered taking flight, anything to relieve the knots gripping his stomach. "Over there," he said, motioning to the left. He'd expected his former home to look smaller than he remembered. Instead the house projected an appearance of modest prosperity, especially with the addition of a single-story wing. At least the family had made good use of the monthly offerings he'd increased to comply with the club's profitability. Money well spent and never missed, he'd often rationalized. When the path disappeared into a stony meadow, Dan slowed to a stop and turned off the ignition.

"From here we walk," Pete said. They exited the car and were greeted by cool air and the distant voices of females having fun. At the crest of the hill Isabella and her companion from the market came into view, their arms laden with baskets of garden produce. On seeing Pete and Dan, they stopped chattering and abandoned their words mid-sentence.

Time suspended for a quick scrutinizing from both sides. Pete couldn't take his eyes off Isabella—same silly hat and another modern outfit, but she still wore the same dignity that characterized her from the day they first met. If only he could snap his fingers and produce Gina and Riccardo as they once were: six-year old moppets, their curly ringlets bouncing with every step that brought them closer to him. Pete couldn't rid himself of the lump crowding his throat. For the first time in twenty-nine years, he heard Isabella's voice, issuing a set of rapid-fire instructions to the young woman who kept nodding. She took Isabella's basket and hurried into the house.

"You think it's safe, Pop?" Dan asked, his voice bordering between sarcasm and concern.

"Unless they plan on barricading the house and opening fire on us."

"As if anyone around here would stop them."

"The way I see it, you can either take your chances with me, or get back in the Fiat and keep the motor running," Pete said as he started walking toward Isabella.

Dan soon caught up with him. "Look, if this homecoming doesn't work out, you can always say we have important business in Pont."

"You've been watching too many B movies. Now put on your best manners and don't embarrass me."

As the distance separating Pete and Isabella narrowed, Pete called out her name.

"I've been expecting you, Pietro," she answered in Piemontese, "ever since the market yesterday."

"I wasn't sure if you heard about the strangers from America."

"How could I not, with the whole place buzzing."

"Didn't I tell you," Dan murmured.

As Pete outpaced Dan in those final steps, he left him behind in more than one way. At last he and Isabella came face to face. After the momentary awkwardness of lost years, Isabella tossed her floppy hat aside and leaned forward to kiss in the Italian way, a greeting Pete hadn't used since Butte. Strands of her contrary hair tickled his nose, and Pete closed his eyes. Feeling a little dizzy, he steadied himself with a light grasp to her shoulders before folding her into his arms. As they clung together, their swaying bodies melded into one. A sob erupted from Pete's throat, choking off words of regret better left for another time.

Isabella pulled away first. Hand-in-hand with arms outstretched, they examined each other. She was thinner than he remembered but her almond eyes had not changed, except for the age lines creasing their far corners. Gray peppered her chestnut hair, cropped short and left to curl on its own.

"Don't look too closely or too long, Pietro. What little beauty I once possessed faded long ago."

"Not in my eyes. In fact, you're lovelier than ever."

"So many years, Pietro."

"I was a fool."

"I should never have sent you away."

"U-hum." Dan clearing his throat ended the magic.

"And who is this?" Isabella asked, her eyes shifting back and forth between the two men.

"Mi dispiace." Already Pete regretted starting out with an apology. "This is …"

"Dan Montagna," Dan said, offering a charismatic smile along with his hand. "So nice to meet you, Signora Rocca."

Isabella's smile reverted to sadness mixed with resignation. Her eyes remained on Dan while she directed her words to Pete. "He reminds me of Riccardo at that age."

The mention of Pete's eldest son overrode any immediate explanation of the younger one. "How is Riccardo?"

"Married and soon to be a father," she replied with a smile that warmed Pietro's heart. "Their first bambino after many failed attempts."

"The young woman who went into the house is his wife?"

"No, no. Riccardo married Giovanni's daughter. You remember her, don't you?"

"Si, Maria." Pete could never forget the baby who played on the floor while he made love to her mother. Hopefully, Maria made a better wife than her mother had. And Riccardo, a better husband than Pete.

"And Gina, she's married too?"

"Not Gina, she lives in her own world."

While Pete and Isabella were getting reacquainted, the younger woman came back from the house. She flipped a green and white-checkered cloth over the outdoor table and set out the contents of a linen-covered tray.

"Come, sit down." Isabella said, slipping her arm through Pete's. "Allegra has set a fine table of our best cheese and wine."

Introductions followed, which consisted of little more than an exchange of given names and polite nods serving to evade any explanation of Dan's relationship, or of Allegra's.

Allegra, Allegra. Pete searched his memory: after he went to America, Isabella's sister must've added another pup to her litter. This one did seem familiar, a new face emerging from an old photograph. Still, he didn't remember any redheads on the brother-in-law's side.

The young woman walked around the table with a clay jug, pouring wine before she sat down next to Isabella. They all raised their glasses and clicked.

"*Salute!*"

"*Il familia.*"

They clicked again, and paused to savor the full-bodied aroma before drinking. The wine lifted Pete's spirits, enticing him to believe its power capable of cleansing away a multitude of sins, those of commission as well as omission. If only life could be so simple. "Every bit as good as I remembered," he said.

"Our grapes from 1952," Isabella replied while cutting wedges from a round of tomino. "Allegra made the cheese, a duty I turned over to her several years ago." She passed the plate to Pete and smiled again. "Now our customers ask for Allegra's cheese instead of Isabella's. I'd be lying if I didn't admit to being a little disheartened at first."

"Oh, Mama, I only took over the cheese because you said you were tired of making it." Allegra reached over to pat Isabella's hand.

Allegra's kind words were the first Pete had heard her speak. The respect she showed Isabella intrigued him. So did her term of endearment. A single word rolled from his lips before he considered its implications. "Mama?"

"Allegra is my adopted daughter, Pietro."

"The only Mama I've ever known." Allegra squeezed Isabella's hand before letting go.

"My mother died when I was two," Dan chimed in, his first contribution to a conversation which had ignored his presence. He'd spoken in his native tongue, his words out of place until Allegra replied in English.

"Mine deserted me," she said, showing no emotion, "and Maria, my sister."

Pete poured more wine.

"She speaks of Serina Martino, Giovanni's wife," Isabella said.

"How sad for all of you," Pete said. "I'm sorry your mama did not stay."

Allegra opened her palms outward and projected a smile sweeter than honey. "The loss was hers, not ours. Neither Maria nor I feel any regret for what we cannot remember. Quite the contrary, we have been blessed. No other woman could ever equal Mama *Seconda*, the one God chose to look after us."

"And your papa? How long has he been dead?"

"Sh-h-h." Her finger tapped rosy lips. "Do not speak of Death before it knocks at our door. Our papa is very much alive."

"Bene, bene," Pete said, trying to cover his embarrassment. "I apologize for my ignorance. Your papa was not well when I left."

"Nor is he now. But his will to live outshines that of Methuselah." Again Allegra smiled, as much with her eyes as her mouth, an expression Pete recognized as similar to Serina's. Except Serina's eyes were the bluest of blue, and Allegra's, the darkest of chocolate.

"Papa has spoiled me," Allegra said. "So rotten in fact that Mama says no man will ever dare to compete with him. Is it any wonder I have not married yet?"

Nor had the Isabella that Allegra referred to as Mama, Pete thought If Allegra considered Isabella her mother, then how did Giovanni regard Isabella? Surely, the mother of Pete's children would not have allowed the old cuckold sexual privileges. She still answered to Signora Rocca when Dan introduced himself. The ring on her finger was the one Pete had put there, even though he'd lost any claim on her.

"But Allegra, you're still young," said Dan, returning a smile that rivaled hers. "I'm twenty-one, and you don't look much older than me."

"Grazie, the face can deceive but never the calendar. Next February mark my twenty-ninth year."

Although the morning was cool, beads of sweat broke across Pete's forehead. He needed to escape, if only for a while, to sort the clutter crowding his brain. With a nudge to Dan's arm, he stood up. "We should be going. I have business in Pont."

"Won't you stay and eat with us?" Isabella asked. "Riccardo will soon return from the field."

Riccardo! How could Pete have been so thoughtless, again. "I, uh …"

"Can't our business in Pont wait?" Dan asked. "After all, we came all this way to see your family."

"Then it's settled," Allegra said, not waiting for Pete's response. "I'll start dinner." She hopped up and started clearing away the dishes.

"Scusi," Dan said, "the *toilette*?"

"Ours is in the house," Allegra said. "Come, I'll show you,"

As soon as they were gone, Pete turned his eyes to Isabella's.

"Si, Pietro. Allegra's birth date does not lie. Nor do those calculations spinning in your head."

"You always could read my mind."

"Not always, not when I should have: those months your leg was on the mend. Does it still bother you?"

"More than ever."

"I meant your leg."

"I know what you meant. Does Allegra know?"

"She knows the papa who wiped her nose and dried her tears, the one who told her stories from long ago."

"Forgive my stupidity. I don't know what to say."

"In time, I'm sure you'll think of something. But for now, let's not let it ruin this day."

Pete kept up his end of small talk about the neighbors and the crops and the weather while his thoughts raced back to the last morning with Serina, when she stuck out her taut, naked belly, and told Giovanni it held another man's baby, just as it had when she carried Maria. Later, Serina denied the pregnancy to Pete. And he believed her because he didn't want to believe otherwise.

When Dan came out of the house, Isabella stood and wiped her hands on her apron. "I must help Allegra. She's such a perfectionist."

"With you as her teacher, I'm not surprised. Can't we talk some more?"

"We'll have many opportunities, unless you're planning to leave soon. But for now, perhaps you should have time alone with …"

"Dan, Signora Rocca," he said before Isabella even hesitated on his name. "My name is Dan Montagna."

"Si, your name is one I would not easily forget. And you must call me … Isabella."

She walked away, leaving Dan to mouth the syllables of her name. Neither he nor Pete spoke for several minutes, the silence reflecting their level of comfort.

"Phew-w!" Dan said at last, blowing the sound through his

slack lips. "That was some bathroom, all marble with a flush toilet, shower, and ceramic hand bowl."

"Don't be patronizing," Pete said. "Around here marble is as common as coal in Illinois."

"Around here? Well, around here I could've used a little patronizing."

"Blame me for leaving you out. I kept waiting for the right moment to explain."

"As if they didn't already know, judging from the look on their faces. You should've just come right out and said, 'Meet my son, Dan.'"

"This is a delicate situation and your kind of help I don't need."

"How well I know. Compared to you, I really did lead the life of an altar boy. You must've been some swinger."

"More like some fool."

"And that redhead," Dan said as he bounced his open palm. "Mama mia, what a beauty."

"Forget Allegra."

"I made an observation, Pop. Not a proposition."

"We shouldn't have come."

"Like hell. You can say that after the way you and Isabella greeted each other?"

"Basta! I have this splitting headache."

"It's called a conscience."

Pete called a truce with his hand. Any attempt to excuse his past would've been hypocritical. "About Allegra—"

"Look, Pop, I was only joking. Sure she's pretty but older women aren't my type. I like being in charge."

"He likes being in charge!" Pete slapped his hand on the table and let out a hardy laugh, the perfect catharsis to clear his head, at least for a while. "Listen, my son, if I never teach you another thing about the Italian woman, know this: regardless of her age, not you or any other man will ever be in charge."

"Is that why you left?"

"Maybe," Pete said, chewing on his lower lip, "although it's a reason I never considered until now."

"Feeling better?"

"Not until I finish what I started to say earlier. And this time, no interrupting." He took a deep breath, his preparation for an impromptu confession. "The mother who deserted Allegra is the same woman I had the affair with. Unless Giovanni's wife had someone besides me, which I doubt, Allegra is my daughter."

"Ho-o-l-y shit. This sounds like one of Hester's soap operas. But aren't you jumping the gun, taking credit for sowing another man's seed. What about this Giovanni?"

"An old soldier with a worn-out pecker," Pete said.

"How old was he?"

"Younger then than I am now."

Pete's comment produced another laugh, one both he and Dan shared, unaware of the farmer heading in their direction. Taller than most Italians, he carried himself in a proud, almost defiant manner.

Suspenders held up his dark work trousers and the rolled up sleeves of a white shirt exposed muscular arms tanned to an olive hue.

"Papa?" His solitary word revealed a bittersweet greeting choked with emotion.

Pete jumped up. "Oh my god, Riccardo!"

Locked in a bear hug and with smooth-shaven faces cheek to cheek, they muffled words in Piemontese, discernable only to each other. Pete pulled away, expecting to savor the handsome features of his adult son. What he saw produced a stifled gasp and pooling tears. A black patch covered Riccardo's left eye and under it an ugly scar zigzagged from cheekbone to jawbone. Pete traced his finger over the raised blemish, worse than his had ever been. "The war?"

"Against the fascist Duce and his pigs."

"Perhaps with plastic surgery …"

"My scars I wear with pride, a tribute to my fallen partigiani." Riccardo tore off his cap, releasing a mass of unruly curls. "What about you, Papa? Did you fight with the Allies?"

"Only in my heart, Uncle Sam did not want me." Nor did Pete want Uncle Sam. "So, I hear you're going to be a papa."

"God willing. Bella, bella, wait 'til you see my wife." With fingers laced, Riccardo stretched his arms out front to simulate a grand belly, at the same time glancing in Dan's direction. "You'll see her soon. We always take our noon meal together: Mama, Allegra, Maria, and me. And, of course, my godfather."

"How is Giovanni?"

"Not long for this world," Riccardo replied with a smile. "At least that's what he's been telling us for almost three decades."

When the conversation paused for words that excluded Dan, he stood up and extended his hand. *"Buon giorno, Riccardo! Io sono Dan Montagna, il Americano fratello."*

"What!" Riccardo said, backing away. "This is true, Papa?"

"Si, his mother died many years ago."

"Her name was Fallon," Dan said. "Fallon Latimer Montagna. She was married to our papa—yours and mine. And they were crazy in love, right, Pop?"

"Not now, Dan," Pete said, shaking his head.

"Listen to the wisdom of your papa," Riccardo said. "This moment belongs to my papa and me. Already I can tell you are a spoiled rich boy. You spent an entire lifetime with the papa I only had for five years."

"Sorry, but I don't enjoy being regarded as a fresh pimple sprouting on the end of a sorry dick."

"Dan! Watch your mouth."

"It's OK, Papa," Riccardo said. "I understand the Queen's English and also what passes for American slang."

"Cool it, Riccardo. Maybe we should start over," Dan said. "I didn't come here to make trouble. I just thought we should all get acquainted."

"Then show respect for your elders and be quiet for a while," Riccardo said. "Your time will come later. For now let me tell about our family so you will better understand why I might not appreciate yours."

They sat down, Riccardo and Pete on one side and Dan across the table. Riccardo filled his glass and passed the jug.

"The wine, it's good," Dan said, raising his glass. "In fact, the best I've ever tasted."

Riccardo acknowledged the compliment with a gruff nod. After the customary *salute*, they emptied their glasses before Riccardo turned his attention back to Pete.

"Did you ever think of us, Papa?"

"Every day of my life ... well, at least in the beginning.

"Mama never cried in front of Gina and me; but when she went to bed, her muffled sounds came through the closed door. Worse than not having our Papa with us was Mama's not wanting us to see her tears. That's when we cried too."

"Mi dispiace, Riccardo, I—"

Riccardo showed his palm. "Wait, let me finish. What I have to tell you, Mama would never say. But you should know how life compromised us when you were in America. Soon we quit praying for your return and started praying for Giovanni's death. You so understand, don't you? We could not burden God with too many requests."

"My God, Riccardo, I ..."

"Life did get better. So did Giovanni." He finished off the last of the wine, and narrowed his eyes to Dan. "And what about this one, what year were you born?"

"Nineteen thirty-six."

Riccardo thought before answering. "For the Rocca wine, it was a good year, one measure of our success. But then the damn war came, changing our lives and those of every paesano forever. But that's another story, one I'll save for later."

Dan opened his mouth but before he could speak, Riccardo came back with, "I think better on an empty bladder and full stomach." He stood up and set the cap back on his head. "Scusi, Papa, I must wash up before we eat."

Pete felt a swell of pride as he watched Riccardo walk toward the rocky incline that separated the two houses but would forever link the families occupying them. "Maria! Giovanni!" his son called out. Pete shifted his gaze to Riccardo's wife, her hair as red as Allegra's and just as he remembered Serina's. The pregnant Maria wore a blue dress wrapped around a belly so full of life it seemed to lead the way for both her and the old man clutching her arm. They walked with care, each step accommodating his stooped posture.

"Can this get much worse?" Dan whispered, as much to himself as to Pete.

"Only if you fail to remember your place."

"Highly unlikely with so many tormented Italians to remind me," Dan said, his eyes riveted to where he'd managed to distract Pete's. "Get a load of your number one son. He just gave his wife the latest newsflash: prodigal papa returns."

Pete and Dan stood up to acknowledge the approaching couple.

Disengaging her arm from Giovanni's, Maria smiled shyly and offered her cheek to Pete. They exchanged greetings with the formality of strangers sharing a common bond.

"Scusi," she said with a polite nod in Dan's direction.

"Buon giorno," he replied. "Io sono Dan."

Maria studied his face, and then Pete's, before leaving to help Allegra and Isabella bring out the food. Meanwhile Giovanni and

Pete appraised each other through watery eyes: one man middle-aged and healthy, the other, old and frail. Giovanni made the first move, opening his arms wide to encircle Pete, a gesture Pete returned.

"Can you ever forgive me, Giovanni?"

"What's to forgive? The years since Serina left have been the happiest of my life," he replied in a voice high-pitched and cracking. Stretching a mouthful of broken teeth into a grin, Giovanni shook his head, and laid another set of kisses on Pete's cheeks. Then he shuffled back two steps and pointed the tip of his bent cane to the young stranger. "Who is this?"

"My son Dan."

Dan held out his hand and wound up steadying Giovanni. "Dan Montagna," he said.

"Montagna? Of course, a bastardo would take his mother's name."

Although Giovanni had spoken in Piemontese, Dan's face indicated he understood the words. "The name belongs to my father," he said. "And I'm no bastard."

"In Italy you are. So, Pietro, did you also abandon the family name of Rocca?" Giovanni answered his own question with a feeble laugh erupting from a belly loose and sagging. "No wonder my good friend … uh. Isabella!" he called out, straining his voice. "What was his name … my soldier friend in America? You know, the one I hired to bring Pietro home."

"Nunzio Drago," she answered. "Now stop talking long enough to take your place at the table. Everybody, before the food gets cold."

Nunzio Drago, Isabella knew about him? Giovanni said he'd sent Nunzio to bring Pete home. How could Pete have been so stupid, allowing Leo's panic to determine a course of action from which there was no retreating, one that changed his life forever, and that of his family.

"Pop, are you OK? They're waiting for us."

"I must apologize for Giovanni's poor manners."

"What the hell," Dan said. "He's an old fart with an old ax to grind. If you can stomach him, so can I."

"What's this?" Giovanni asked. Instead of serving the meal in traditional courses, the women had set out a full spread of bread, antipasto, risotto, roasted chicken, sautéed green beans, insalata mista, chestnuts, and pears. Jugs of wine anchored each end of the table. He eased into the master chair, the only one with arms and situated at the head of the table. "Does this mean we must hurry to make indigestion?"

"No, Papa, it means we don't want to keep running back to the kitchen." Allegra said. "Today we will eat in the style of Americans. Am I right, Dan?"

"Well … I guess. Sometimes it depends on the family." Dan looked at Pete seated across the table and to Giovanni's right.

"Picnics, Dan means picnics and barbecues," Pete said. "In America the Midwesterners usually take their meals indoors unless it's for special occasions in the summer."

"And what about the other times," Maria asked, "the everyday life?"

"The rich eat in big dining rooms," Riccardo said. "They pay servants to bring their food and clean their plates. Right, Dan?"

"So I've heard."

"And what about you and Papa," Riccardo asked. "Did you have servants?"

"A woman helped out," Dan replied. "Like I told you before, my mother died when I was very young. Someone had to keep house and cook meals, same as here in Italy."

"Basta. Enough with who serves the food and where it's served," Isabella said. "Here we eat when I say it's time. And so it is: *mangiamo!*"

Hardy appetites were quenched, and conversation centered on grapes and wine, goats and cheese, the marketplace, and the weather. When it turned to the politics of Italy, Pete and Dan had little to offer since neither had followed the ever-changing and unpredictable government. After a stretch of more eating and less talking, Pete used a bread heel to clean up the last morsels from his plate. As did everyone else, including Dan after he gave in to Isabella's urging to finish the last of the risotto.

"Riccardo, you promised to tell us about the war," he said.

As if on cue, Isabella stood up and began scraping plates. "Maria, Allegra, help me clean up. War stories, we'll leave for the men. Not because we don't care, Pietro. God knows for years we prayed every day for Riccardo."

"This woman did more than pray," Giovanni said. "To all of Canavese and the partigiani she is still revered as a saint."

"I did what had to be done," Isabella said.

"And then some," Maria said.

"More than most women," Allegra said.

"But not all women, I did not give my life. Nor that of my son."

"We should stay and listen to Riccardo," Maria said, moving behind her husband's chair. She wrapped her arms around his shoulders and rubbed her flawless cheek against his scar. The tender gesture endeared her to Pete. Indeed, Riccardo had been blessed with the love of a good woman; what more could any man desire.

"We've heard his stories many times," Isabella said.

"I know, I know. And who will do the woman's work, if not the women," Maria said, moving away from Riccardo. She balanced a stack of plates on the natural shelve her round belly had created, and walked toward the house.

After pouring another round of wine, Riccardo held out his cigarette pack to Pete and Dan. Both refused. "A habit I picked up during the war," Riccardo said. "Too many days spent alone in the mountains."

"You were a Freedom Fighter?"

"The best," Giovanni answered, his voice fading off as he settled into the chair.

"My godfather exaggerates," Riccardo said. "I got caught in a fiery ambush. Amidst the confusion my friend Flavio and I hopped on a motorcycle and escaped into the woods. An explosion nearly sent us to the moon. We came back to earth as two deserters with one choice. We offered our services to the partigiani standing over us, with rifles pointed at our heads.

"The Resistance could've shot us. Instead they taught us guerrilla warfare. Later I traveled north to enlist and train more Freedom Fighters, and finally hugged Mama—three years after I first went missing. In the beginning my survival was a secret the two of us shared. With the fascist pigs, the family of a dead soldier would be honored, but the family of a known partisan suffered disgrace—property confiscated, imprisonment, sometimes worse."

"My God, Riccardo. I didn't know. Only after the war was I able to contact the lawyer. Only then did I learn all of you were safe."

Riccardo continued his report. "We set up a radio operation in the foothills where we could observe the Tedeschi coming in with their supplies. Some of our fair-skinned men, those like Flavio who spoke fluent German, infiltrated the enemy's positions and reported back so we could keep the Allies posted. We won their respect and without us the Allies could not have stayed ahead of the Tedeschi."

"Tell them about Torino," Maria said as she and Allegra took their places at the table.

"I was honored to be among those fighting in the streets to retake Torino."

"And where he lost his eye," Giovanni said. "Squeezed out by the thumb a Tedesche, but not before Flavio died while saving him."

Riccardo's face turned white, a sharp contrast to the jagged scar and vein pulsing on his forehead.

"Maybe you should finish your story another time," Pete said again.

"No Papa, I'll tell it now. So I never have to repeat these words." Riccardo filled his glass and quickly emptied it before pouring more. "The blood of the Tedesche and of Flavio's mixed with my own, even as I screamed for God not to forsake me. For weeks after that day I could still taste the good mixed with the evil, unable to distinguish one from the other. Even now I …" Turning away from the table, Riccardo ejected a wad of saliva onto a rock and scrutinized the clarity of his discharge.

"Please, Riccardo," said Pete, hoping to distract him. "Go on."

Riccardo settled back into his chair. "I was mending in the hospital that day my comrades found Mussolini near Dongo. The fallen Duce, his mistress Claretta, and a small band of loyal followers had been traveling with a Tedesche convoy attempting an escape to Switzerland. In the back of an SS truck hid Mussolini, still filled with his own importance but not for long, not after the Tedesche traded him and the others to ensure their own safe passage out of Italy. I regret not standing with the execution squad in Mazzagra."

"But Lucca Sasso did," Isabella said, having returned with more wine. "Do you remember him, Pietro?"

"Si, he used to play the ocarina."

"He still does, at Il Sole è la Luna."

"My God, is that place still in business?" Lucca, a hero; Leo Arnetti, dead, Pete thought. "Please, Riccardo, go on."

"From my bed and in my heart I took aim and killed the fascist pig. For the disgrace he brought on Italy and for those who died on behalf of his idiotic dreams: the soldiers, the partigiani, the civilians. As for the whore who died beside him, what's done is done. But had the decision been mine, and not that of my comrade Audisio, I'd have sent Claretta back to her parents."

"Claretta was a fool."

"She loved the wrong man."

"So did my sister."

"You mean Gina? What happened?"

"Gina's story is not mine to tell."

"Then tell them about the *Piazzale Loreto*," said Giovanni, having awoken from a short, but loud snooze.

Riccardo emptied the jug into his glass before he continued. "The year before we sent Mussolini to hell, his Milanese fascists executed fifteen partigiani—brave men I once fought beside. In retribution for this cowardly abomination, fifteen of the fascists hiding with Mussolini in his final hours were executed in Dongo. The bodies from Mezzagra and those from Dongo were tossed into the back of a truck and brought to Milano. There, in that same Piazzale Loreto where the fascists murdered our partigiani, Mussolini drew his last cheering crowd at a forsaken benzino station. His bloody corpse hung upside down, along with those of Claretta and four other Fascists—like slaughtered animals swinging from meat hooks. When I heard the news from my hospital bed, I wept tears of joy, as did every wounded man in the ward."

Riccardo wiped away more tears; the gesture reminded Pete of his son as a child and the perfect face he once possessed. If only he had known to worry for Riccardo's safety, to pray for his return, to cry for his pain.

"More wine?" Isabella asked. She filled to accommodate the number of fingers held to the glass.

Giovanni had dozed through most of Riccardo's story but Isabella's offer alerted him to show three fingers. When she poured no more than two, he tapped until she filled to another finger. "Riccardo needs to rest his voice," he said. "Isabella, tell Pietro how you fought the war."

"Why relive nightmares," she said. "Besides, I did nothing heroic."

"You are too modest, Mama," Allegra said.

"What about Gina?" Pete asked, his question directed to Isabella.

The table went silent. Riccardo poured more wine before passing the jug. Giovanni honked into his handkerchief. The two younger women exchanged glances. And Isabella focused on a wayward ant, allowing it free reign over a few crumbs.

"Yeah, when are we going to see Gina?" asked Dan.

"Gina lives in Milano," Isabella said.

"Tell him, Mama," Riccardo said. "Even now my heart breaks when I think of my twin."

"Please, Isabella. I haven't been much of a father, but she's my daughter too. If Gina is troubled, I want to help."

Isabella explained how Gina went to Torino as a student and later worked at the museum. "When the war moved northward, I pleaded with her to come home. Remember how stubborn she was, Pietro?"

He nodded with thoughts of the carefree little girl who chased butterflies because she loved beautiful things and couldn't sit still.

"Only later did I learn she loved more than art. Gina fell under the spell of a young officer assigned to the museum. For one so smart, she should have known better. But when the thunderbolt strikes ..." Isabella paused. "Well, it cuts through barriers no sane person would ever consider crossing. Turning back becomes all but impossible. Right, Pietro?"

"You know me better than I knew myself. But I did return."

"Si, after twenty-nine years, I should be so grateful."

"Mama, please, finish Gina's story."

Isabella's eyes left Pete's. She cleared her throat and sipped more wine. "From Gina's own mouth, I learned how much she loved this man. Kind and good were the words she used to describe him. I'm sure his mama and papa agreed with her assessment, as would any loving parents. I wanted to think Gina knew better, but the war compromised all of us in some way. Besides, how can love be condemned and killing, glorified? When Torino fell to the CNL, Gina's Tedeschi … he—"

"He died a soldier's death," Riccardo said. "And for that I forgive him."

"All of us did. But how can we ever forget," Isabella said. "Not with a daily reminder as certain as the rising sun."

"What are you saying?"

"Oh, Pietro, the soldier who gouged Riccardo's eye from its socket was Gina's Tedeschi."

"Sweet Jesus!"

"Holy shit!"

Riccardo crossed his heart. "I swear on the souls of my unborn children: in the confusion of battle neither of us knew we were fighting the other." He released more saliva and examined the moist earth.

"God rest the souls of those who died that day," Isabella said, "even those of the Tedesche."

"Gina's Tedeschi had a name?" Dan asked.

"Erich something."

"The partigiani learned about her collaboration with the Tedeschi."

"From you?"

"On my life, I did not betray her." Riccardo crossed himself again. "Because of Mama and me, Gina's life was spared. Instead of putting my sister in front of a wall, the partigiani cut her hair. They marched her around Torino's grand piazza. People yelled, *Bocchinara. Stronza. Cagata.*"

"Basta, basta," Pete said, recalling the newsreel and written stories of how women were punished for collaborating with the enemy. With fingertips to ears, he pressed hard to drown out what he could not bear to hear. A gentle tug from Riccardo opened his ears.

"Those words came from the mouths of her tormentors," Riccardo said, "But your ears should hear what Gina's heard. Your heart should know the way hers ached. Thank God I was still hospitalized and didn't witness her humiliation, but others told me. We haven't seen each other since before the liberation."

After Riccardo left to relieve himself, Maria took over. "We went to Torina, Mama and I, to bring Gina home. The short hair branded her a shamed woman, but not in our eyes. 'I cannot go home now' she said. 'The whole village will know.' We agreed to return without her, just until she grew back a decent head of hair."

"Three months later we received Gina's letter," Allegra said. "She had moved to Milano."

"She still won't come home," Isabella said. "No one around here knows what happened in Torino. And even if they did, no one would dare to condemn her. Time heals most indiscretions." Isabella offered Pete the same subtle smile she used to give. "I've written Gina, called from the telephone in Pont. Each time I beg her to come home. Once a year I go to Milano, by myself and only after Gina has invited me. Maria and Allegra visited twice, again on Gina's terms."

"She says she forgives Riccardo."

"And God knows Riccardo does not blame Gina. Yet neither can bear the thought of hurting the other again."

"If only I'd come back sooner."

"It's not too late, Pietro," Isabella said. "In America you were a good businessman. At least that's what the money you sent told me. You must've practiced the art of persuasion, si?"

"Take it from me, he's one of the best," Dan said.

Where Dan came up with that, Pete had no idea.

"Then go to Gina," Isabella said. "She works as a museum docent. Maybe you can convince her to come home, if only for a little while."

Chapter 41

After listening to the family's war stories, Pete had no intention of revealing the success of his black market profiteering during the corresponding years. Nor was he prepared to talk about the years before and after, not until he could take time to selectively glean the worst years, although none could compare to those his family had endured. While Dan captivated his siblings with the inside scope on Cardinal baseball, Pete looked for an excuse to get away. He asked Isabella to show him the house.

"Your house, Pietro, it was yours when I came into the marriage and your name is still on the deed."

"At least some of the money went for comfort," he said, viewing the remodeled kitchen with modern plumbing to replace the hand pump and pail. A large wooden hutch filled with everyday dishes occupied most of one wall, along with a six-burner cooking range and oven. The table and chairs handed down from his parents had been replaced by chrome and upholstered vinyl, smarter than any he'd seen in America. "Nice," he said, rubbing his hand across the table surface.

"From Milano, where all the best designers work," she said. "Gina picked it out."

Pete smiled, his way of acknowledging their daughter of the city. The pressure between his eyes had returned and he forced himself to concentrate on Isabella's kitchen, the crown jewel of her modest palace. Only the leaded windows and fireplace remained unchanged but he could still recall every detail of the old kitchen. Closing his eyes, he tried to resurrect visions of his youthful family and the happy hours spent around the wooden table.

"Don't cling to the past, Pietro," Isabella said, her words bringing him back. "Tend to those who need you now." She took his hand and led him over a threshold he'd not crossed before. The new section boasted a comfortable room comparable to an American living room, but unusual for small Italian homes with a few upholstered pieces relegated to the perimeter of the dining area. He admired the marble bathroom, true to Dan's description, as well as two more bedrooms—one for Riccardo and Maria, the other destined for their baby.

When they returned to the kitchen, Pete prepared to leave but Isabella had not finished the tour.

"The twins' bedroom has been updated too," she said, pulling aside a flowered drapery to show another room of new furniture. "For Gina when you bring her back." She took his hand again and pulled him to the one area his mind had been avoiding. "I almost forgot the room which becomes more important with each passing year."

The bedroom came as no surprise to Pete, unchanged since the day he left. There on the wall to his right hung the photograph that matched his: two beautiful children peering out from lumps of coal; their mama, serene as the Madonna; their papa, smug with the confidence of youth.

"Pietro's family," he whispered, more to himself than to Isabella although she heard his words.

"Our family, Pietro, yours and mine."

*****

Later that afternoon Pete left with a recent photograph of Gina and her address tucked in his breast pocket. Confident with Dan behind the wheel, Pete allowed himself to slump down into the seat and close his eyes. "Just give me a few minutes."

"Sure, Pop. I could use a little soft time myself."

"You keep your eyes on the road. I'll do the thinking for both of us."

No amount of money could ever make up for Pete's absence, or for pains his children still endured. Riccardo, a soon-to-be father, was nursing wounds in his heart worse than the scars on his face. Gina, nursing demons Pete had yet to meet. Isabella, who lived the life he gave up in search for a better one. Isabella, who always made the world right, now looked to him to resolve what had escaped her wisdom. And Allegra, the child of Pete's lust, who didn't even know he had fathered her. No wonder she was so happy.

"When do you want to leave for Milan?" Dan asked.

"Tomorrow morning. Why put off another day of misery."

"Misery? For me the day actually improved. I even squeezed a few chuckles from the siblings. But then, what do I know about the Italian way. Maybe they were just being polite. 'Course you had to deal with the same people from a much tougher perspective. Opening those old wounds had to sting worse than lancing a carbuncle."

"Don't read more into my words than I said. What I meant was: I don't expect Gina to come back with me."

"Us, I'm going to."

"This is one mission I plan to undertake on my own."

"Are you kidding? Not after today. Listen, Pop. I know you're older and wiser, but take some advice from an outsider … yeah, I said outsider 'cause that's how I feel. Even though I want like hell to belong, the rest of them don't think I deserve a place. There's no way my life could ever compare to what your first family's been through, and for that, I thank God. Jeez, just listen to me. Already, I'm talking like them. Anyway, back to your current challenge with the black sheep … as in a ewe that's gone astray. More than ever, you need me: an objective bystander, and the best friend you'll ever have."

"Like I said, we'll leave tomorrow morning," Pete said, "after our breakfast."

"Hell yes, after breakfast. No way would I miss dunking fresh pané into a cup of steaming hot coffee and milk."

Dan's best friend, what greater honor could any grown son bestow on his father. At least Pete had done right by Dan: one out of four, not an impressive record.

*****

The following afternoon Pete couldn't help but feel edgy when Dan drove into Milan. Their first stop was the only address Isabella knew, a run-down apartment building they discovered Gina had moved from three months earlier without leaving a forwarding address.

"I'm not surprised," Dan said. "Isabella made this whole venture seem way too easy."

"So don't make it seem way too difficult. Two to one, we find her by the end of today."

"You're on, Pop. But finding Gina doesn't mean bringing her home."

They checked into quiet accommodations on Milan's Via Spirito Santo. Once the palazzo of an industrialist, the elegant hotel was an easy walk to the Piazza del Duomo where Isabella said Gina conducted tours in the centuries-old Gothic cathedral.

"If we hurry, maybe we can catch Gina on her way back to work," Pete said as they walked toward the piazza.

"Oh, yeah, I keep forgetting about these three-hour midday meals, especially the one we just skipped in favor of spinach and cream cheese sandwiches. I thought you said no more American meals, the gobble and swallow variety."

"Consider today an exception. But from now on we will eat the Italian way."

"Well, the Italian way sure makes for one helluva long business day."

"But allows the family to enjoy the best of their day together," Pete reminded him. "Now let's quit talking about food and start looking into the face of every attractive female in her mid-thirties."

"Picking out a chiseled nose would be a helluva lot easier. These Italian women all look good and after my faux pas with Allegra, I'm no judge of age. Anyway, back to Gina. You have her photo?"

"Imprinted in my brain," Pete said. *And my heart*, mentally patting his breast pocket.

"Since she's already in your head, how about letting me carry her picture."

"Here, but don't mess it up."

Dan studied her image with the same regard he'd given to the likeness of Pietro's young family. "Dark-haired, wide-eyed, and gorgeous, just as I figured," Dan said, "and dressed to the nines."

"Of course, she's a sophisticate now."

"I'd say a chip off the old block—more your daughter than Isabella's. Maybe a rebel, you think?"

"Riccardo was the rebel."

"Not when it came to family. Sorry, I didn't mean to bring up the past."

"How can I argue with the truth? Anyway, I … we are going to bring Gina back. This much I owe Isabella. And Riccardo."

"What makes you think she'll jump at the chance? As I said before, she sounds an awful lot like you."

"I had my reasons."

"So you told me: shame, money, love, responsibility. Maybe she has her reasons."

Pete glanced over to Gina's photograph. "I wish she had smiled. Surely, after all this time something brings her happiness."

"Or someone."

"Dan Montagna, the romantic."

"Can't help myself, Pop, it's in my … wow! Get a load of this."

Dan stopped; Pete bumped into him. They took in the vast Piazza del Duomo swarming with pedestrians, mostly tourists photographing each other and locals using the vast area as a thoroughfare to their next destination. Beyond the bustle of everyday life stood Milan's crowning glory, its architectural tribute to God. Spires and statues formed the

Duomo's expansive profile, soaring to the heavens like legions of spear-toting warriors guarding a symmetrical fortress.

Pete crisscrossed the piazza twice with Dan before he wiped sweat from his brow and moistened his lips "Maybe Gina didn't leave the Duomo today, or maybe she came back early. Let's check out the barn."

"You're talking the Duomo, right?" Dan used both hands to open the heavy bronze door and motioned Pete to take the lead. They entered a bygone era where architects and craftsman had dedicated their entire lives to create a monument they wouldn't live long enough to see completed. The interior of marble presented a cool sanctuary, complemented by rays of sun forcing a collage of brilliant colors through massive stained glass windows. Following the lead of the awestruck tourists they had now become, Pete and Dan leaned their heads back. Slowly they turned to view the remarkable ceiling before lowering their gaze to the marble saints and hovering gargoyles that co-existed in a state of gothic harmony.

"Even Connie would've been impressed," Dan said, performing a series of gyrations to loosen the kinks in his neck. "You know, Pop, while we were heaven bound, I'd have sworn I heard angels."

"You did." Pete motioned to a group of giggling children, no older than five and sandwiched between two nuns dressed in swooping white habits appropriate to the Middle Ages.

"Only in Italy," Dan said, amused by their wide-eyed innocence, "a school of midget tourists."

"More like poor little orphans, signore," projected a voice from under the winged headdress of the nun bringing up the rear. "Their continuing care depends on the generosity of those more fortunate."

Pete padded the nun's open palm with a stack of lire, which disappeared into the confines of her bell-shaped sleeves, a gesture reminiscent of his night in the Chinese Underground years earlier. But this time the money belonged to him and not to a dead man.

The nun spoke with downcast eyes. "God will bless you."

"Please, Sister, a moment of your time." Dan whipped out Gina's photograph. "Have you seen this woman?"

She held the picture between slender fingers before returning it. "The lady is not a member of our order, signore. Perhaps you should inquire at the docent office."

"She knows Gina," Pete whispered after the nun walked away.

"What do you mean? Nuns aren't supposed to lie."

"They just don't give straight answers. You never said anything about Gina being a docent."

Dan banged the heel of his palm to his forehead. "Damn!"

"Watch your language. We're in a place of reverence. Now come on, let's find that office."

One flight of stairs down to the mustiness of the underground level and a rap to the opaque glass door brought them into the docent office.

"Scusi, signora," Pete said to a woman with gray hair pulled back in a severe chignon, "You have a certain tour guide. The best I've been told by more than one person."

"All of our docents are very good, signore. We only accept those who have years of training and an extensive knowledge of art history."

"The guide I refer to is in her mid-thirties: dark, slender, and well-groomed."

"Signore, you describe half my staff," she said with a pleasant smile. "The rest are men."

"Perhaps this would help," Dan said, holding out Gina's photograph.

"You have a photograph but no name?"

"Please, signora," Dan said.

She took the picture and smiled at the ten thousand lire accompanying it. "H-m-m," she mused. "I cannot be sure, you understand, but I think this might be ... Gina Rocca."

"She's a good tour guide?"

"One of my best, signore, and proficient in several languages. I could keep her busy every day if only she would honor me with her presence." She returned the photograph. "Alas, the address I have for her is no longer valid."

After they left the office, Pete needed to use the toilet so Dan went back to the hectic piazza. While looking at Gina's photograph, he heard a woman's voice from behind. She spoke English, but with a heavy accent.

"The picture, Signore, please let me see it."

He turned to look into the bluest eyes he'd ever seen. Odd, for a gypsy, he thought they all had black piercing eyes. What little he saw of her hair under the long colorful scarf had faded to the color of sand. It might've been red at one time.

Gold bracelets on her wrists jingled when the old gal opened her hand. "Put the picture here. You do need her address, right?"

"Well, yeah but … OK, how much will it cost me?"

"First, the picture."

He set it on her palm, with Gina's face showing.

"No, the other way."

He turned it over. She spit on the back, three times, rubbed her saliva into it.

"Hey, watch it. That's my only photo."

"Sh-h." She closed her eyes; opened them fifteen seconds later. "First, the money, how much you got?"

He wiggled his finger. "No, no, no."

"This is Gina Rocca, right?"

Dan didn't hesitate. He yanked a wad of money from his pocket. "First the address."

She snapped her fingers. "Pencil."

He gave her his engraved ballpoint pen, a pricey gift from Connie.

She wrote on the back of the photo and returned it to him.

"How do I know this address is for real?" he asked.

"Silly Americano, you go there." She smiled for the first time. "Here comes your papa."

"You know him?"

"From long ago, God has treated him well."

She disappeared into the crowd, along with his prized pen.

"Since when do you talk to gypsies?" Pete said. "I told you they're nothing but trouble."

"Not this one. She gave me Gina's address."

"You fell for that? How much did she take you for?"

"She knew Gina's name, said she once knew you."

"Me?" Pete's fingertips went to his chest, a gesture he hadn't used in years. "I don't know any gypsies."

"This one had the bluest eyes I've ever seen."

The bluest of blue could only mean Serina. "Quick, where'd she go?" Pete asked.

Dan extended his arm and forefinger. "Maybe that way but I wouldn't swear to it."

"Just make sure we head in the opposite direction." He lowered Dan's arm. "And no more pointing."

"Right, it shows a lack of good breeding."

Pete whiled away another hour with Dan, window shopping the enclosed glass archway of the Galleria Vittorio Emanuele, an arcade of extravagant shops, trattorias, and coffee bars linking the piazzas of La Scala Theater and the Duomo. When their feet rebelled against the unforgiving terrazzo pavement, they leaned against a stand-up counter and drank espresso.

"I wonder if the Galleria in Butte still attracts customers," Pete said, bringing up a topic unfamiliar to Dan.

"No way could Butte's merchandise compete with what I've seen here."

"Depends on what you're buying," Pete said as a classy blonde strolled by.

"Stick to the plan, Pop. Look, we have Gina's address."

"Maybe so, maybe not, that gypsy could've been stalking us."

"You're stalling."

"I hoped to first see Gina, away from where she lived. Know a little more before we approach her."

"What you're really saying is you don't expect her to welcome you with open arms."

"Can you blame her?"

"Enough with the guilt, OK? Here's the rundown as I see it. After moving to a decent area, Gina only works when the mood suits her. She's not too proud to take Isabella's money and she doesn't like unexpected company."

"You're right. Already I know more than enough. Let's try the gypsy's address."

Gina's supposed residence was located about six blocks from the Duomo, in an area of tree-lined streets and handsome buildings renovated after the war to their former splendor. Pete and Dan climbed four long flights of marble stairs before knocking on the polished wood of *appartamento quattro*.

A lump formed in Pete's throat. He ran his finger under his shirt collar.

"Easy Pop. Remember your mission."

Some mission, Pete thought. Isabella had to have known more than she let on, sending him to catch Gina off guard, to uncover her secrets. Some secrets were better left buried.

"*Uno momento!*" a female voice called out.

At the sound of footsteps padding to the door, Pete's stomach rolled and churned with a digestive disruption unfit to share with his son. Already Dan seemed to know more about him than he knew about himself.

"What do you want?" the woman asked in Italian.

"I'm looking for Gina Rocca," he said, trying not to sound like the *polizia*.

"Who are you?"

"Her papa, Pietro Rocca."

The door opened to the width of the chain securing it. "Gina doesn't live here anymore."

"Please, could we just talk with you," Dan said, holding up the photograph. "We need to find Gina Rocca."

"Scusi." Pete searched her face for any sign of warmth. Niente, he found nothing. Words spilled from his mouth. "I thought you were the daughter I foolishly deserted for America. I came back to beg the forgiveness of my family who still lives in Faiallo. That is, everybody except my beloved Gina. She resides somewhere in Milan and her mother prays every day for her safe return."

"Who is it, Mama?" a child called out.

The voice belonged to a young boy whose face came into view. He looked to be twelve or so, with blonde curly hair and eyes the color and shape of shelled almonds.

The door closed long enough for the chain to be unlatched. "Come in," she said, opening the door wide. "Why hide what you already suspect." She stepped back, wrapped her arms around the boy like his protective shield. He stood as tall as her shoulders and from the length of his gangly arms, had the potential of soon reaching six feet.

"Are you the strangers Sister Francesca saw at the Duomo?" the boy asked.

"How do you know Sister?"

"She used to take care of me, before—"

"Antonio, this is the papa I told you about."

"You mean the one who left you, only in a different way from the one who left me?"

"Buon giorno," Pete said, bending to extend his hand. "I am very pleased to meet such a fine young man." After they shook hands, Pete straightened up and touched Dan's arm. "And this is my son, Dan Montagna."

"Oh, Papa," Gina said with a sly laugh, "another one?"

"I knew it, I knew it," Dan said. "Didn't I say you and Gina were from the same mold?"

Emotional rounds of hugging and kissing absorbed another ten minutes before Gina invited Dan and Pete to sit around her table. She uncorked a bottle of Lugana, a dry white to accompany the Sicilian figs and chocolate-covered lacey discs from Florence. While Dan and Antonio listened, Pete and Gina tried to cram in years of highlights and sorrows. Her story of the early years mimicked Riccardo's and included the detailed description of Giovanni's amazing recovery, painful reminders which obligated Pete to listen attentively and understand the bitterness simmering under her pleasant exterior. Dan seemed more comfortable around her than he had with Riccardo, and she readily accepted him without demanding an accounting of his privileged life. Pete thought the competitive edge might be greater between two brothers than between sister and brother, perhaps a throwback to a time when brothers fought over land and power.

Pete talked too, mostly about his early years out West, which intrigued Antonio who asked for more and more. When Pete ran out of escapades suitable for a young boy's ears, Dan took over with endless publicity stories about John Wayne and other cowboy stars. After early evening drifted into night, the boy stifled a yawn, but not from boredom. "Do you have to go out," he asked his mother.

She glanced at her watch, a slender white gold bracelet Pete recognized as similar to one he'd seen in a tony Galleria shop.

"I really should," Gina said. Antonio's face went sad and then brightened once more when she added, "but special evenings justify occasional exceptions."

Antonio grinned like a Cheshire cat. "For me too?"

"You can stay up a while longer, but in your bedroom. With that book you read by flashlight when you're supposed to be sleeping." He kissed Pete and Dan, his youthful warmth touching them to blink away tears.

"Nice," Pete said, scanning the room after Gina left to get Antonio settled.

"Way better than nice," Dan said, "considering the price of hotel rooms around here. Gina had to parade a lot of tourists around the Duomo in order to pay for these plush chairs. And don't get me started on the sofa."

"Those tapestries don't come cheap either."

"Nor do I," Gina said from the doorway, "nor does Antonio's schooling. That's why I go out every night, not that I walk the streets you understand. I entertain considerate gentlemen, but only in the finest establishments."

"Dammit Gina, if only I had known—"

"Dammit, Papa, if only I had known."

"OK, both of you. Now that Gina's more lucrative occupation has been exposed, maybe you should spend time on the topics too sensitive for Antonio."

"Of course, my son comes before all else. But I make no excuse for the other life I've chosen."

"And who am I to find fault. My own is nothing but a series of mishaps and detours." Pete gave Gina the more detailed version of his American life, including Fallon and Dan. Gina shook her head, cried a little when Pete explained the circumstances of Fallon's death.

"I was too young to remember my mother," Dan said. "Pop and my grandfather kept her memory alive for me."

"As I do with Antonio, although I leave out the parts he is too young to understand. Someday he will know the full story. I suppose Mama and Riccardo told you about Erich. The Tedesche, they call him, spitting out the words as if they were cacca."

"So you never told them about Antonio?" Dan asked.

"And bring them further shame. I was bad enough have the partigiani brand me a collaborator."

"Sh-h, don't torture yourself with such bad memories, Gina. The family already told us."

"But they didn't tell you what I'd just begun to suspect, that deep within me the tiniest seed of Erich Heimberg had taken root. Knowing this, I could not attempt a futile escape, or force the partigiani to shoot me. And then I learned how Erich died."

"All of which happened over twelve years ago," Pete said. "What about all the pleasure lost since then? For you and Antonio, for the family? Your mama has a grandchild she doesn't even know exists."

Gina laughed. "Mama knows. That's why she comes alone to visit me. She also has a ... friend who often travels to Milan."

"What kind of friend."

"An old one ... from long ago but not so far away."

"That sounds familiar," Dan said.

"Hush, Dan. Your mama didn't have this address."

"I only moved recently. How did you come by it?"

Dan smiled. "Would you believe I bought it from a gypsy?"

She shrugged. "I know many people; they know me."

"Forget the gypsies," Pete said. "The family should know Antonio."

"One more wound to accentuate the scars on Riccardo's face. That beautiful face, Papa, that face I cannot bear to see. Nor can I expect him look into the face of my son, the child whose father committed such a hideous assault. Riccardo and Erich: the two great loves of my life." She wiped away a trickle of tears, a gesture reminiscent of her twin. "Not only did Riccardo and I share the same womb, but we shared the youthful awakenings of twins, in ways no one else could understand."

"Basta! Such secrets should remain between you and your brother."

"I did not mean to offend your delicate sensibilities. But how else can you understand the pain I knew Riccardo felt then. And what he feels now."

"In all the confusion neither man knew he was fighting the other," Pete said. "That's what Riccardo told me and I believe him. If you love your brother as much as you say you do, then believe and forgive. Riccardo said he forgives Erich. And he begs your forgiveness."

"He actually referred to Erich by name?"

"Both first and last, I heard him too," Dan chimed in. "Riccardo's words were 'Erich Heimberg died a soldier's death.'"

Pete had taught him well. Dan's small but comforting lie carried no dishonor if it brought Gina some peace.

"Look, Gina. Why not come back to Faiallo with us," Dan continued. "You and Antonio could spend the month of August."

"A busy season for the tourists," Gina said. "But not for the Milanese. Those who can afford to escape the heat go on holiday."

"What better holiday for Antonio, fresh air and freedom to roam the hills."

"But would the family accept Erich's son?"

"They would love Antonio. Already Pop and I do, that's for sure."

"And Riccardo?"

"Your brother has fought his last battle. And now he wants to make peace so you can share in his happiness.

Chapter 42

On Sunday afternoon in Faiallo Pete and Isabella relaxed in yard chairs woven from tree branches and basked in the nearby scene of siblings reuniting over jugs of wine and boxes of family photographs.

"Just as we did long ago," Isabella said.

"How well I remember."

When the photographs lost their appeal, Dan took Antonio aside to show him how to play stickball with a wooden board and tin can while Gina and Riccardo cheered arm in arm from the sidelines, all of them waiting for Allegra and Maria to bring more wine.

"You knew about Antonio long before I went to Milan," Pete told Isabella. "Why didn't you tell me?"

"I could not betray Gina. At first she swore me to secrecy, a secret harder to keep than any covert activity I performed during the war. Later, after Riccardo put aside his anger, Gina's stubbornness kept them from reconciling. And then you offered to intervene."

Not exactly, but who was Pete to argue. "Without Dan's help, I couldn't have succeeded in bringing Gina home."

"Don't be so hard on yourself, Pietro."

"I wasn't here for my children when they needed me."

"Pray they will not make the same mistake with their own."

"Riccardo has three women who will make sure he's a good father. But I worry about Gina."

Isabella creased her brow. "The way she lives in Milano, impossible on the salary of a museum guide, and that was before she moved. I'm no fool, Pietro. I know her source of money and I will use every ploy within my power to keep her here as long as I can."

"We both know that will not be long enough."

"Nor do I expect you to stay forever."

"Right now I'm in no hurry to leave."

"But when the time comes, I want Gina and Antonio to go with you."

"And Allegra?"

"Allegra makes her own decisions. But until Giovanni passes from this earth, she will remain here."

Pietro laughed. "So much for Allegra's independence, does she know about me?"

"She suspects but says nothing."

"Between the two of us, we seem to have plotted everyone's life except our own."

"Nor do I intend to start now. Besides, Giovanni has asked to see you this afternoon."

Pete looked around, only now realizing Giovanni had not stayed after the noonday meal.

"He insisted on going home so he would not burden us," Isabella said. "But I know better. He is failing, Pietro. Sometimes I think he hung on all these years waiting for you."

Pete had one more showdown, one more chance to make amends. He took the familiar route to Giovanni's house, a rocky path worn to bare earth. He knocked once before pushing on the half-open door.

"Come in, paesano," Giovanni called out from his chair. The old man lifted his cane and pointed to the cabinet. "Before you sit down, get the wine and glasses."

The room looked as Pete remembered: stone floor, stucco walls, and leaded glass casement windows. His current interest did not extend beyond the kitchen. He poured a measure of three fingers into each squat glass, took the chair next to Giovanni, and leaned forward.

"Salute." They clicked and drank.

Giovanni cupped his gnarled fingers around the dribbles of wine beading his chin stubble and let out an appreciative smack. "Thank God for my Maria and Allegra. When I am gone, they will share a generous inheritance with Riccardo and Gina. Isabella I have already provided for—every day since you left."

"From what I've been told, she earned every lire. Still I ought to thank you, Giovanni. You're a better man than I ever was, and considering my sin against you, a more forgiving one."

"Don't be so generous with your flattery, my friend. Perhaps it is I who should be asking your forgiveness."

Pete shook his head. "You are too kind. Because of me, you nearly died."

"Si, and many times from my bed I prayed for God to take me. But then Serina pushed your flesh and blood into Isabella's waiting hands." He snapped his fingers. "And just like that, I had another beautiful daughter. Me, Giovanni Martino the cornuto, had again become a father. Not one ounce of my blood flows through Allegra's veins, or Maria's, but they both carry my name. And every day I thank God for the love they bring into my life."

Giovanni wagged his finger at Pete, a throwback to the mentoring years. "Ah-h, Pietro, I was not the fool you took me for. For months I suspected some *cazzo* was bedding Serina, but I ignored what was too painful to accept. Even an old fool knows better than to compete with a young one. Then I overhead your friend—what was his name, the one with the loopy nose?"

"You mean Leo Arnetti?"

"That's the one, joking about you and a certain *patacca*. My heart ached with thoughts of you and Serina together. Still, I had to know for certain. I planned my return from Ivrea to coincide with the Sunday morning church bells. Finding Isabella and the twins on their way to Mass without you confirmed my suspicions. Isabella balked about going back with me. But had she not seen with her own eyes …"

Giovanni tapped three fingers to his empty glass and Pete obliged him. Pete anticipated a long and grim afternoon; after all the old fart had earned his say.

"Later from my sick bed I learned from Serina how raging

anger nearly killed me. Never before had I raised my hand to another, except in time of war. To this day I have no recollection of the incident, only her words describing the magic of your *pistolotto*. Confined to my bed, I listened to Serina curse me. She wished me dead for being an invalid while her belly grew bigger with your child. Ah-h, how sweet the irony of it all: her misery feeding on mine.

"Only after Serina left with the gypsies did I take my first steps into a better life, one your wife breathed into me with her undying devotion. Remember when I first took you to meet Isabella, encouraged you to marry her?"

Pete nodded, feeling less sympathetic and more annoyed as he listened to Giovanni drone on in his raspy voice, drawing on a reserve of energy he looked too frail to possess. Duty bound, he returned to the Giovanni saga.

"Looking back, I think Isabella would've made a better wife for me than you, Pietro. I pushed you to marry her because I wanted the pleasure of her friendship. But after you left and then Serina, Isabella became my wife in every sense except *montare*. She cooked my meals, cleaned my house, and planted my garden. Until I got stronger spectacles, she read to me. If I could have lifted my fallen soldier, I like to think she'd have let me enter her. Your twins became mine too." He paused to shake his head. "Such a burden I put on children so young. I loved them as much as the daughters that bore my name. And I believe they cared for me. At last I had a real family—yours, Pietro."

Giovanni's last words stung far worse than his lashing years earlier. Pete resisted the urge to rub his scar, a habit he broke after leaving Butte. His jaw tightened, barely allowing his words to pass through clenched teeth. "And the man you sent looking for me?"

"To please Isabella," Giovanni said with a chuckle. "Nunzio

Drago had *cacca* for brains. More than once I saved his life during the Austrian war. I took a chance by asking the impossible of him. He accepted my challenge. I sent Nunzio just enough money to finance a search through Montana and for your return to Italy. Even that damn photograph Nunzio made me send didn't bring him success. My gamble paid off when Isabella finally quit looking for the letters I prayed you would never send."

Giovanni tapped his glass again.

As Pete was pouring more wine, he said, "The cagata had the misfortune of finding me. But we never had a chance to talk. Two Chinese murdered him right before my eyes."

"Merda! Then he was not such a *cagata* after all. No wonder I never heard from him again."

Pete stood up, pulled out an envelope, and threw it on the table. "Here's the money your *cagata* tried to give me before he died. Had I known then what it was for, I'd have put my shame aside and returned home." More money came from his money clip. "This should cover part of Allegra's expenses. I'll arrange for the rest when I return to America."

Giovanni's bloodshot eyes watered up. "What choice did I have, Pietro? You nearly destroyed my family, so I took the family you deserted."

Pete stuck his face in Giovanni's, so close he caught the nauseous odor of decrepit organs. "Old man, I could kill you right now. Snuff the stinking merda from your stinking body and blame your death on a heart attack."

Giovanni raised his cane and was ready to strike when he glanced over Pete's shoulder. The cane slipped from his hand, and Pete turned to see Isabella wearing a pained expression that tugged at his heart.

"You should go now, Pietro," she said. "Giovanni's medicine and his nap are long overdue."

Pete brushed past her and then came back. Taking her face between his hands, he kissed her with a passion he'd not felt since Fallon's death. "Put your devious *cazzo* to sleep. He gave as good as he got. What's more, the old goat was right about me. I was never worthy of you, Isabella."

Before she could answer, Pete left. He headed across the field to his partying family. When Dan saw him, he broke away from the group.

"Everything OK, Pop? You don't look so hot."

"I'm fine, but I need to get away for awhile."

"What? Just when my siblings and I have learned to communicate? A little Italian, a little English, and a lot of this," Dan said with a series of hand gestures. "In fact, I think Riccardo might be on the verge of almost liking me. We've been comparing the merits of baseball over what he calls *fútbol*, not that soccer could ever hold a candle to America's number one pastime."

"You're right. I have no business pulling you away from a good time. You stay, and I'll pick you up later."

"This evening?"

"Tomorrow." Pete walked over to Allegra and put his arm around her shoulder. "I have business in Pont that cannot wait. Can you make room for Dan tonight?"

"Si, si …" She'd hesitated, awkward with the proper way to address him.

"Pietro, call me Pietro." He kissed her cheeks, wondering how much she'd figured out on her own. After a quick round of farewells, he walked to where Dan had parked the Multipla and with one more vigorous wave he called out, *"Domani!"*

Navigating the narrow winding road slowed Pete's reactions. He wanted to douse himself in sympathy but the steep drop-offs demanded his attention. If he drove off the hairpin, no one would care except his American son. Dan would be madder'n hell for not being able to complete his own mission: to charm Pietro's family into accepting him. Pete needed to clear his head, but all these revelations were coming at a speed faster than his brain could accommodate. Right now he hated Giovanni for being so damn self-righteous, for hanging around long enough to gloat over his own clever deceptions.

*****

By the time Pete arrived in Pont, the sun had washed an array of orange-red colors across the brooding mountains. He took the last table in the crowded piazza and ordered a bottle of Barolo. It remained untouched while he stared into space, nursing his wounded pride.

"May I sit with you?" he heard a familiar voice say.

"Isabella!" He almost tipped his chair over as he stood to pull one out for her. "How did you get here?"

"We own an automobile too. Not as nice as your Multipla, but an old Fiat Riccardo brought back to life with his gifted hands. We are not so backward, Pietro. The war pushed us into the modern world. And like my daughters, I insisted on learning to drive."

"Knowing you, I'm not surprised."

"I don't think you ever really knew me, Pietro. Nor did I know you. Only after you went away did I long for what I once took for granted."

Before he could call for another glass, the hotel proprietor appeared with one. "Grazie, Signore ..." Pete said, unable to remember the man's name.

"Prego, Signore Rocca," the proprietor answered, although he had been referring to Pete as Montagna. He turned to Isabella and smiled. "Buona sera, Isabella."

"Buona sera, Silvio."

Pete waited for Silvio to leave before he spoke. "By tomorrow everyone in Pont will know the true identity of the wayward husband from America."

She laughed. "The Rocca family has always intrigued my market customers and competitors, here and in Cuorgnè."

"You work too hard, Isabella."

"I don't know how to stop."

"The stipend was supposed to make life easier."

"Easier, no; better, yes. The war you already our story; the improvements on the house, you saw for yourself. And Gina receives a monthly check, mailed to a post office box in Milan. I want to send more, anything to keep her from ... well, you know, but she insists on leading her own life. So much of life, good or bad, revolves around money."

He nodded. "And always has."

She reached into her purse. "About this afternoon, the money you gave to Giovanni."

Closing his hand over hers, Pete shook his head. "How much did you hear?"

"More than I ever knew or even suspected. His words took me back twenty-nine years: Giovanni in the throes of a stroke, you and Serina."

"You had every right to send me away but I was stupid to give in so easily. To hell with the wagging tongues of nosy neighbors, I should never have left."

"The fault was as much mine, Pietro. I was such a testa dura, every bit as stubborn as Gina. When you begged my forgiveness, I should've taken you in my arms, made you forget Serina."

"Serina was not about love."

"I understood that later, but at the time pride stood in the way of reasoning. I sent you away without shedding a single tear. My tears came later, after seeing Gina and Riccardo so miserable. And then I had to contend with Serina. I made her take care of Giovanni, closed my ears to her constant whining. Had she not been growing a baby—yours or any other man's—I would have killed her. How I wanted to feed her bleating tongue to Tobi!"

"When Allegra was born, I cut the cord that nourished her. Three months later, Serina cut another cord—the one connecting her to the rest of us. Serina's freedom became my confinement. I inherited a bedridden man and two babies."

Pete put his hand on her shoulder. "Isabella, I—"

"Let me finish, please. Above all else this you must believe: no matter how Giovanni regarded me, I did not return those feelings. To Giovanni, your family may have become his. But to Gina and Riccardo and me, we were and still remain Pietro's family."

Pete blinked away the hint of a tear. "All those years wasted. If only I could turn back the clock."

"No, Pietro. Then there would be no Dan. And if you turned the clock back even further, there would be no Allegra."

Voices from the nearby diners had diminished to bare whispers. A discreet glance of the surrounding arc of tables revealed every patron caught up in the scene he and Isabella had been playing out. Pete got up. With a slight bow to Isabella, he extended his hand for her to join him.

"Silvio, please send a bottle of your best wine to my room," he said in a voice projected as much for the hovering proprietor as for the empathetic audience they had garnered. "And more towels. My wife will stay the night."

Arm in arm they took a leisure walk around the piazza. "Never have I seen the moon so clear and bright," Pete said.

"The same one shines on Illinois."

"But through a clouded atmosphere."

"And what about Montana?"

"Sometimes the stars were so bright they reminded me of home."

"You were there with Leo Arnetti?"

"Si, he caught up with me again in Illinois, and died soon after."

"So that's why he never came back. Did he know Dan's mother?"

"Only for a few days," Pete replied. Memories of Fallon didn't belong in this precious moment, but Isabella pressed on.

"You loved her?"

"I'd be lying if I said I didn't."

"And I would know. She was *bellamissimo*?"

"She gave me a handsome son."

"Ah, but Dan's features are yours. I think his ways must be those of his mother. One look told me he grew up with money."

"His grandfather's, I worked long and hard for mine."

"You always did. Dan said she died in an accident, but that you were not driving the automobile."

"Sometime Dan talks too much."

"More than you ever did. But he also listens. At first I was hurt to learn a pampered child had been nourished by your love while ours did without. But you did well by Dan, and I am growing fond of him. That special relationship the two of you share touches my heart. In time perhaps it will be the same between you and Riccardo."

"I already gave Riccardo my father's watch. When I leave, he can have the Multipla. And—"

"Not things! He needs—"

"Will you let me finish? After our grandchild arrives, I'm taking Riccardo to a plastic surgeon in Bologna, one who specializes in facial injuries. Gina already made the arrangements before we left Milan."

The sound of Isabella softly crying marked another milestone for Pete. One he hoped would not be repeated soon. They came full circle around the piazza, her body shivering against his. "It's getting cold," he said. "We should go inside."

Upstairs in the hotel Isabella gave the accommodations a thorough inspection. A gentle breeze moved gauze curtains covering the amber-colored casement windows. The double bed wrapped in white linens sat high off the floor of polished hardwood set in a herringbone design. On the bureau lemon-scented ivy geraniums tumbled from their metal container, a nice touch Silvio had provided along with the extra linens.

"I always wondered about the best room in Pont's best hotel," Isabella said. "Are you comfortable here?"

"The mattress is firm and the pillows soft. But I can't abide the alley cats. They keep me awake with their damn screeching."

She sat on the bed, bounced three times. "For me it's still the roosters and their crowing."

Pete sat beside her. He ran one finger under the wide neckline of her blouse, slipping it over her shoulder. Moving his finger to the filigreed hoop dangling from her ear, he whispered, "How many?"

"Roosters?" she asked with her Mona Lisa smile. "In my chicken coop there's only room for one."

"One at a time or just mine?"

"Why, Pietro, you of all people should know better than to ask such a question."

###

About the Author

Loretta Giacoletto divides her time between the St. Louis Metropolitan area and Missouri's Lake of the Ozarks where she writes fiction while her husband Dominic cruises the waters for bass and crappie. An avid traveler, Loretta has written several sagas inspired by her frequent visits to the Piedmont region of Italy, a soccer mystery that takes place in St. Louis, and an edgy novel about a young drifter searching for the father who doesn't know he exists. Her short fiction has appeared in numerous publications including *Literary Mama*, which nominated her story "Tom" for Dzanc's 2010 Best of the Web.

Connect with Loretta Online:

http://www.lorettagiacoletto.com/

Or mail to:loretta@lorettagiacoletto.com

A note from the author:

My thanks to Caren Schlossberg-Wood of Lost Marbles Design for the cover design; to The Museum of Mining and the Orphan Girl Express; Ellen Crain of the Butte-Silver Bow Archives, and Rudy Geicek of the Dumas Brothel Museum—all located in Butte, Montana; to Bill Nunes and to the late Rube Yelvington for their published histories of East St. Louis, Illinois; to the late Clifford Ahlert for his recollections of the East St. Louis Stockyards; to Esther Gherna and Joseph Bertot for their recollections of Italy and the Italian culture; to Scott Giacoletto and Steve Giacoletto for their input on the poker scene, to beta reader, proofreader, and marketing consultant Diane Giacoletto Lambert; and to my husband Dominic Giacoletto for his help with the Piemontese dialect and his continuing patience and unwavering support.

**Fiction
By
Loretta Giacoletto**

Family Deceptions

The Family Angel

Free Danner

Lethal Play

A Collection of Givers and Takers

Chicago's Headmistress

Added Bonus for Your Reading Pleasure

Opening Chapters of THE FAMILY ANGEL

Current available as an eBook on Amazon.com

Coming soon as a paperback on Amazon.com

A paranormal 60-year saga of romance, conflict, and crime revealing the Americanization of an Italian family, from immigrant bootleggers and coalminers to proud winemakers and ambitious priests, but only a chosen few will encounter the chameleon-like Black Angel who shows up when least expected, to offer advice or merely observe. After all, there's only so much one arrogant angel can do.

Loretta Giacoletto

BOOK ONE

Chapter 1—Chicago 1925

"Another day, another dollar," the young Italian with precision sideburns mumbled to himself, "Another day ... another lesson." Or not, depending on his mood and if he felt like going to Night School after supper.

What Carlo Baggio needed now was a drink—his kind, not the illegal beer he'd been loading into crates all day at Becker's Brewery. Or the near beer the brewery produced as a front for its more lucrative ventures. After flipping the last of his cigarillo into the gutter, Carlo ran one hand through his dark, slicked-back hair and stepped into a Southside saloon geared to immigrants and native Chicagoans who came for the cheap liquor and decent food. He exchanged nods with two regulars, slid onto a barstool, and raised his forefinger to Vincenzo Valenza, a man cursed with a large hooked nose and the scars of adolescent acne.

"Ah-h, *paesano, uno momento!*" the bartender and co-proprietor of Fabiola's called out. While Vincenzo drew five beers and poured as many grappas, Carlo drummed his fingers and sucked in the hazy air thick with tobacco smoke married to the aromas of beer, wine, tomato sauce, salami, garlic, and cheeses. When Vincenzo finally got around to Carlo, he wiped a wet ring from the golden oak bar, filled a teacup with wine, and served it with an unctuous smile. "*Vino rosa*, paesano, from my private stock."

Carlo laid down thirty-five cents. Holding the cup to his nose, he took in the full-bodied bouquet to conjure up memories of Pont Canavese, his village in the foothills of the Italian Alps. Only after this savoring ritual did he allow himself to pleasure the wine, even before water his drink of choice. He spoke in halting English that had improved considerably since his two years in America. "So, about this sister you got back in Locana."

"Ah-h, you mean *bella Luigia*." Vincenzo cupped a handful of fingertips to his puckered lips and smacked a kiss. "As God is my witness, she has the temperament of an angel."

Carlo took more wine and waited for the next words to roll from Vincenzo's tongue.

"Look, Carlo, you want an Italian bride, a quiet one who will give you many sons? This, I can do for you."

"But can she cook?"

"Wait 'til you taste her rabbit and polenta," Vincenzo said as he started back down the bar.

Polenta, sweet Mother of Jesus. Carlo salivated at the mention of peasant food fit for kings. In Carlo's Italy, life had moved slower, on less money. But after his parents died, Carlo and his younger brother wanted a different life, one that didn't require never-ending work just to survive. While still in their teens they sold the family home to finance a new beginning in America.

Vincenzo had only covered half the bar length before he came back to Carlo. He leaned across the glistening wood and spoke through breath reeking of garlic. "Listen, paesano, with my sister the Baggio name will live on, long after you have turned to dust. Our ma bore seven sons, four who lived and three under the ground, and only one girl, the lastborn. Louisa took care of Ma 'til the day she died."

"A nursemaid I don't need."

"Maybe not today but think about *domani*."

Carlo checked his pocket watch. He drained the last of the wine from his glass.

Vincenzo poured more and held up his palm when Carlo attempted to pay. "You know, Carlo, bringing relation over ain't so easy. Not like before the Great War."

"Me and Giacomo made it here."

"Consider yourselves lucky. They say America has too many Italians."

"So who's counting?"

"Immigration." Vincenzo smiled like a dog with a fresh bone. "All you have to pay is my sister's passage plus a little extra." He rolled his eyes, opened his palms to the ceiling. "Paesano, for our trouble, be reasonable. Massimo and me, we make all the arrangements."

Inwardly, Carlo bristled at Vincenzo's reference to Massimo, the older brother and saloon partner, a hard-nosed *padrone* known for exploiting Italian immigrants in need of employment and housing.

Carlo felt a pointy elbow jabbing his ribcage. Without looking to his right, he returned the gesture.

"Ah-h, another Baggio blesses our humble saloon with his presence," Vincenzo said, pouring a second teacup, also his best, for Carlo's brother, Giacomo.

Both young men were slight in stature, with chiseled profiles and dark hair; but Carlo's was poker straight, his eyes as round as chocolate malt balls. Cowlicks ruled Giacomo's wavy hair; amber drops floated in slate eyes too vain for glasses. The brothers wore their clothes with the confidence of window mannequins although a trained eye could distinguish the hand tailoring of Carlo's suit from Giacomo's off-the-rack.

Giacomo waited until the bartender left before he spoke, "Vincenzo still pushing to bring the sister over?"

Carlo shrugged. "I hear she cooks pretty good."

Giacomo shifted his eyes in Vincenzo's direction. "But does she take after the two *brutes*?"

"Only if God played a cruel joke on their mama."

"Just remember: with the Valenzas you pay and then you pay some more, whether the deal works out or gets flushed down the drain. Same goes for a wife, so pick one who's already here. In the long run she'll be a helluva lot cheaper. And if you're lucky, less trouble."

"Sh-h," Carlo mumbled, "not so loud."

"People are gonna find out—from the Valenzas 'cause that's the way they are. Let the ugly bastards pay to bring their own sister over, just like everybody else. Knowing them, they'll probably want you to kick in extra just for marrying into their family."

Carlo's discussion with Giacomo came to a quick end with the arrival of Hildie Kramer. The brewmeister's daughter slipped her arm through Giacomo's in a way that Giacomo ignored and Carlo resented.

"You know I can't sit here, Honey Bun, not on a stool like some common barfly." Hildie pursed her lips into a pout. "Besides, I am positively starving."

"You two go ahead and eat," Carlo said. "I'm not that hungry."

Hildie exchanged the pout for a smile. "Well, if you insist—"

"No way," his brother said. "We'll eat together, just like we do every night."

After getting their teacups refilled, and a root beer for Hildie, the threesome decided on a table near the blackboard menu and sat down. Giacomo moved his chair closer to Hildie's. He rubbed his leg against hers and squeezed her plump thigh. Hildie's blonde bob bounced with the lift of her head. She bunny wiggled her nose and cut through the air with the wave of her pudgy hand.

"Goodness gracious," she said, "how can you tolerate this putrid smell?"

"It sure as hell beats that of cabbage," Carlo said.

She shifted her round face to Giacomo. "Chicago has plenty of good eating establishments. Decent ones, if you know what I mean. Even better, how about some old-fashioned home cooking for a change? I could fix you some wonderful potato pancakes and sausages, just like my *mutter* taught me."

Carlo's nostrils flared. He kicked Giacomo under the table. Hildie's previous cooking efforts had produced gaseous eruptions and heartburn that kept both of them awake all night.

This time Giacomo squared his shoulders but avoided Hildie's eyes when he said, "We're staying here."

"Whatever you say, Sweetie." She kissed his cheek and pushed her chair back. "Now if you'll excuse me, I have to dust my knees."

"Now, when we're just about ready to order?"

"As if I didn't already know what you like. I'll have the same."

While Hildie sashayed to the powder room, Carlo reviewed the evening fare with Giacomo. They vetoed meatballs and spaghetti as only fit for the Southern Italians their papa called Mezzogiorno, as in hot sun and hot tempers. Chicken and risotto tempted the brothers but the rice often came undercooked or too dry, either way, unacceptable. Beef could be tough unless simmered slowly in its juices. Veal spelled disaster if overcooked. In the end they ordered the usual Wednesday special—ravioli with a side of the *insalata mista*.

Two tables over a skinny flapper decked out in a burgundy chemise twirled a half-eaten grissini between her teeth, and exchanged sultry expressions with Giacomo.

"Better not let Miss Hoity-toity catch you," Carlo said.

"Looking ain't a crime and Hildie ain't my keeper."

"Neither is Papa Gus but we still salute him every time he signs our payroll sheets."

"*Basta*, enough, okay? Here she comes."

Hildie cozied up to Giacomo. She slipped her hand into the front pocket of his trousers. And to the burgundy flapper, she puckered her lips. Hildie's competition responded with a flash of pink tongue and returned to the conversation at her own table.

"You know, Sweetie, I've been thinking," Hildie said, directing her words to Giacomo but her eyes to Carlo. "Maybe you should change your name to something not so foreign. According to Papa, all the Southern Italians at the brewery are switching to names that sound more ... well, American."

"As if me and Giacomo care what those damn *Terroni* are doing."

"Yeah, yeah, I know." She lifted her chin, lowered her lashes. "You and Giacomo are *Piemontese* Italians. Papa says the Terroni call your kind *Mangiapolenta*."

"Better to be called polenta eaters than clumsy yokels. At least, we ain't ashamed of our own names."

Giacomo leaned over the table. "Hold on, Carlo. Maybe Hildie's right, I mean about the name 'cause I been thinking the same thing."

Hildie rubbed her leg against Giacomo's. "Yeah, Honey. You could switch from Giacomo to Jake. Hm-m, maybe something like Jake Rhodes."

"Jake ... yeah, I like Jake. Reminds me of Big Jake Garrity from the Fourth Ward. 'Course, in America Giacomo means Jim," he mused. "But, I ain't going with Rhodes." He nudged Carlo. "So, what do you think, brother? What about Jake?"

Carlo didn't answer.

"Come on, say something."

"Just like that," Carlo said with a snap of his fingers, "You wanna go from Giacomo to Jake?"

"To fit in, be more American. What the hell."

"Like those damn Terroni?"

"They ain't the only ones, Carlo. Some things should stay in the Old Country."

"Jake—Jim—Giacomo." Carlo shrugged. "Take your pick. Just don't turn your back on Baggio. Without the family name, we are…" He blew his next word away from the fingertips of one hand. "… *niente*."

"Then Jake Baggio it is." Giacomo held up his cup to Hildie's root beer.

Carlo followed with an unenthusiastic toast. "To Giacomo's new name."

"*Salute!*" the trio said with a click of their vessels.

Hildie sniffed a few times to show her soft side.

While she searched her cluttered pocketbook for a hankie, Carlo leaned over to his brother and whispered in Piemontese. "Tonight she got you to change your first name. Tomorrow, she'll get you to change her last name."

"Do I look like I just got off of the boat? I'm—"

"Hey, you two, that's not fair," Hildie said. "When you're with me, either talk like Americans or keep quiet."

"Well I ain't about to keep quiet." The immigrant with a new name stood. He stepped from his chair to the top of the table and spread his arms like a Chicago politician. "Listen up, everybody!"

Hildie clattered a spoon against her glass and the room went quiet.

Giacomo tapped his fingertips to his chest. "You all know me as Giacomo Baggio. Well, tonight you're looking at a new man. From this day on I am Jake … Jake Baggio."

The patrons of Fabiola's applauded as Jake lifted his arms and moved to the music of a nearby ocarina. And in an uncharacteristic display of generosity, Vincenzo Valenza banged the side of his fist on the bar before yelling out, "A round of drinks, in honor of Giacomo's rebirth as Jake."

Carlo did the right thing. He bought the next round and his brother the one after that. After the hoopla died down, he watched Jake shake every extended hand and then leave with Hildie, just as he did every Wednesday evening.

*****

After a twenty-minute stroll through sidewalks crowded with pedestrians, Jake and Hildie entered a brick tenement on Taylor Street. As they climbed the open well of creaking stairs, Hildie was giddy with excitement, all the while oblivious to air thick with the stench of fermenting mash and bootleg brew seeping through the apartment walls. When they reached the second level, Jake slid his hand down Hildie's back and stopped at the crease of her round buttocks, prompting a seesaw of giggles and protests from her. On the third level they stopped at the door of a furnished studio Jake shared with Carlo. While Jake fumbled with the key, Hildie unbuttoned the fly of his trousers. Clinging to each other, they moved inside and Jake kicked the door shut. Neither spoke as they flung off their clothes and tumbled onto the lumpy horsehair mattress.

"Oh Jake, do what you did to me the last time."

What? He tried a couple places before finding one that made her purr like a kitten.

"Jake, Jake. I just love the sound of your new name. See, I have good ideas every so often, don't I?"

Jake didn't answer. He was concentrating on the small of her back.

"Wherever did you learn all those wonderful moves? Ooh-h, Jake, you and me are so good for each other. Jake and Hildie, Hildie and Jake. Such sweet music to my ears."

Within minutes a simpler melody played from the worn spiral bedsprings. In the next apartment their aged Russian neighbor took her cue and joined in the mating ritual, using her cane to bang out a rhythmic accompaniment on the thin wall separating her bed from theirs. Jake pictured a gummy grin erupting to expose the lone eyetooth left in the woman's mouth. Her own sexual escapades, some sixty years earlier, were legendary and usually involved more than two people. At least, that's what she'd told him more than once.

Jake waited for Miss Clarissa Spencer, one floor below. She worked in the notions department at Woolworth's Five and Dime, and was always complaining to him about her overhead light rattling and loose plaster spraying her face. A broom handle to the ceiling usually got his attention and tonight was no exception.

"Quiet!" he heard Miss Spencer scream.

More plaster fell.

"Filthy, disgusting Eye-talian!" This time her voice cracked.

Maybe if she gargled with salt water...

Jake forged ahead with a swell of perspiration and did the right thing, making Hildie squeal before he yelled. Afterwards they lay side-by-side, half-listening to the Chicago night, its screeching taxis and irritating police sirens competing with wailing infants and drunken revelers.

Hildie cleared her throat. "Not that I'm in any hurry, you understand, but I have been giving serious thought to my ... our future, you and me in a long-term arrangement. You know, as in marriage."

He shifted, causing the bed to let out a groan. As did Jake, but his didn't reach Hildie's ears. "Uh, right now I can't afford marriage."

"I'll talk to Papa about promoting you. That is, as soon as something comes up."

He pushed her determined hand away. "Not yet, I need time to recoup." He stretched his arms overhead, folded them to cushion his head. "It's different with Carlo. He's a year older than me and still thinks in Italian."

"Well, don't you be thinking about buying yourself an Italian bride, Jake Baggio. 'Cause if you do, you'd better leave Chicago before I find out. Why, if it wasn't for Papa hiring you and Carlo, you couldn't even afford this dump." Hildie screwed up her face, tried to squeeze tears from her dry eyes. Having failed, she heaved a few deep sighs instead.

Jake knew what was expected of him; he reached for her snatch. "Yeah, Hildie, we owe all our success to the Kramer family."

This time she pushed him away. "Well, you can forget about that special dessert I promised. It's reserved for engaged couples."

With that, their evening ended. Hildie wiggled into her wrinkled clothes and slammed the door on her way out. She stomped down the stairs, and before her patent leather pumps hit the honeycombed tiles of the entryway, Jake was already sawing logs.

Chapter 2—Night School

After assuring Vincenzo he would consider the arranged courtship, Carlo moved on to Pané, a twenty-four-hour bakery that catered to a steady stream of customers. Flipping a quarter on the linoleum countertop, he requested the specialty.

"*Foccacio*," Patsy replied. But instead of a round flatbread, the clerk selected a five-cent loaf of crusty bread from the case and did not return any change. "So Carlo, you want I should keep the pané 'til later?"

"*Grazie*, Patsy. Me and Giacomo will eat it for breakfast." *Giacomo*. Would Carlo ever get used to him as Jake.

"Your brother still dating that little Kraut?" Patsy asked.

"For now but not forever."

"Si, better he should stick with his own kind."

Carlo circled his thumb and forefinger. He went outside, to the side entrance of the three-story brick building where he knocked twice. A little door within the larger one slid open. "Foccacio," he said, the password gaining him access to an inner sanctum.

Two well-heeled couples staggered through a set of swinging doors that led to The Playground, Chicago's most glamorous speakeasy. For the right price flowed the best liquors: Canadian whiskey, French and Italian wines, imported and real domestic beers. Direct from New Orleans a quartet of black musicians played sweet jazz on piano, drums, trumpet, and clarinet. Revolving lights created a hyperkinetic distortion of tuxedos and flappers, their fingers splayed across knees scissoring in and out, in and out. Arms went up, heels jutted outward as they gave their all to the Charleston, a dance Carlo had never attempted.

He stayed long enough to acknowledge one of the bartenders and two waiters from Italy's Piemonte region before returning to the stairs, taking two at a time to the next level. On the landing stood a somber man whose bulging eyes lacked any visible lashes.

"*Bona sera,* Frog," Carlo said. "She's expecting me?"

Ugo Sapone responded with a single nod from a thick neck partially retracted into his round stooped body. With some men words weren't necessary, just mutual respect.

Carlo strode down the hall to a door marked private. One knock clicked it open to the office of Night School's headmistress, sitting behind a gold-inlaid desk cluttered with stacks of paperwork. Giulietta Bracca looked up with a smile. She positioned a cigarette into her rhinestone holder and slipped it between ruby lips that sang to Carlo. After giving her a light, he sank into the plush sofa, crossed an ankle over his knee, and let his eyes caress her fine features. Henna spit curls circled her rouge-painted face, and pencil-thin eyebrows arched over thick false lashes framed her emerald eyes in perpetual wonderment.

"Why so quiet, my pet?" Giulietta asked.

"It's my brother, again."

"Sweet Giacomo?" She closed her eyes for a moment and blew out more smoke. "How I miss our weekly sessions. What has he done this time?"

"Changed his name, just like that." Carlo snapped his fingers. "To Jake."

"To please the little Kraut, no doubt."

"Not according to him."

"Don't be so hard on … Jake, is it? He's all you have besides me."

"Maybe that's not enough. I'm thinking about getting married."

"At twenty-one? You're barely out of knickers."

"I was man enough for you."

Giulietta cocked her head to study him through half-lowered lashes. "Surely you're not considering one of my teachers."

"Chicago's best don't make the best wives."

"Ah-h, my very words. I taught you well." Dragging from a rhinestone cigarette holder, she deliberated before speaking through puffs of exhaled smoke. "So who's the lucky girl?"

"Someone from the Old Country, someone like my mama."

"How quaint. In other words, someone you have yet to meet."

She walked over to the sofa and sat beside him. He leaned over to nestle his head against her breast, felt it rise and fall with a gentle rhythm.

"Of course I wish you well, my pet," she said, playing with his hair. "But this bride, must she come from the mountains?"

"More like the foothills."

"Oh, you Piemontese and your Alps."

"And you Genoese and your Ligurian Sea."

"Piss on Genoa and the childhood I never had. This idyllic life you imagine may not survive the reality of Chicago."

"I'll take my chances," he murmured, his forefinger tracing the outline of her slender hip. "I want a woman who thinks like me. One who cooks good food and will give me a houseful of bambini."

She lifted his head, pressed her lips to his, and opened his mouth, her tongue making its familiar journey before gently exiting. Soft laughter bespoke their former intimacy. "Feels like old times, doesn't it?"

"Did you have to graduate me?"

"You left me no choice."

"Says you, I had no say-so in the matter."

"And now you talk of food and babies. First, look for a woman who will share your passions. The rest will either happen or no longer be important." She left the plump cushion and returned to the chair behind her desk. With a wave of enameled nails, she dismissed him. "Now go. You know how my teachers abhor tardiness."

*****

Down another hallway and in the doorway of the Anatomy Classroom waited the honey blond Miss Molly, her arms folded and foot tapping. She wore a pink and white gingham pinafore with ruffles circling her shoulders and knee-length skirt baring her backside. "Naughty boy, you're late again. Whatever shall I do with you?"

Carlo hung his head, held back the smile he could barely contain. "I'm sorry, Teacher."

"Apology accepted. Just don't let it happen again. Now let's put our heads together and decide on an appropriate lesson for this evening."

Miss Molly often said her classroom was designed to fulfill a schoolboy's fantasy, but none Carlo could've imagined in Italy. Erotic chalk drawings, those artistic expressions by the more talented students, decorated three blackboard walls. On the fourth wall, green shades covered tall windows. An imposing well-padded desk occupied the center area, along with an upholstered chair. Big enough for two, it swiveled and rolled on heavy casters suitable for navigating the length of the room, or to a low stool and wooden paddle in the corner designated Playful Punishments.

"I just love our sessions," Miss Molly said, "but already you know so much. Perhaps we should concentrate on honing some of your skills."

"Honing?"

"As in practice makes perfect."

Carlo rested his chin on his knuckles, as if to consider her suggestion. "Maybe this time I could examine you."

"Oh-h! Playing doctor sounds like the perfect test." She turned around and looked over her shoulder. "Could you help me untie this silly bow?"

Fifteen minutes later they were conjoined on the desk, oblivious to a hallway commotion until two uniforms and a vice squad detective barged into their room.

"Enough with the copulating, this teacher's heading for the pokey," snorted a pudgy cop while jabbing his nightstick in Carlo's ribs. "Extinguish the smoking pecker, dago boy. Night School's no place for the likes of a greaser such as yourself."

The insult brought a rush of blood to Carlo's face but he knew better than to trade insults with Chicago's finest. Instead, he rolled off Miss Molly and picked up his trail of scattered clothes.

"Oh, dear," Miss Molly said, transforming her lips into a soulful pout. She covered her luscious breasts with one hand, her manicured fluff with the other. "I've never been arrested before. Whatever will my friends think?"

"If your friends work here, they oughta be thinking about a good lawyer," replied the detective. "Come on, Leroy," he said to the older cop. "Connor can handle this."

Carlo recognized the rookie patrolman whose freckles were competing with his blush but said nothing when Connor handed the naked teacher her costume, and said, "Here, ma'am, you'd better put this on."

"Thank you, Johnny-Boy," Miss Molly replied with a wink and a curtsy before tossing aside the pinafore he handed her. "I've missed our corner chats." She twisted her hair into a schoolmarm knot, turned her backside to Connor, and bent over to retrieve her lace panties.

Carlo was already dressed when he walked into the hallway that formed a square around Night School. It was there he witnessed the scene of naked or nearly naked men of all ages, shapes, and sizes scramble from classrooms labeled Literature, Music, Mythology, Painting, and Sculpture. Slowest to vacate was Physical Education since its extensive workouts accommodated groups instead of individuals. Unlike Giulietta's teachers, her students were considered victims of enticement. The police ordered them to dress and get the hell out.

Carlo left first but after crossing the street he stopped to linger in the shadows. He lit a cigarillo, leaned against the wall, and watched the mucky mucks of Chicago politics, business, and high society exit the brick building. They disappeared into the night. But what about the hoodlums, those high rollers who wore spats and bowlers, and weren't afraid to flash their money rolls around Night School. Not one of them in sight. They must've got wind of the raid and went elsewhere. Next came the vice squad, herding Giulietta's teachers. Carlo knew them all, especially Bonnie Bodacious, Fanny Bright, Medusa, Twins 1 and 2, Sister Mary Agatha, and, of course, Miss Molly. One by one the teachers lifted their skirts and climbed into the waiting paddy wagons. Last to board was Night School's headmistress. Not wanting Giulietta to see him, Carlo moved further into the shadows and waited until the wagons turned the corner before he left. The evening was still young, but with any luck, by the time he made it home, the sheets on his side of the bed would've cooled off.

****

At the police station Giulietta and her teachers were booked and moved to a holding cell. Within the hour her lawyer Bernie Shoeman arranged bail for everyone and a fleet of cabs for transportation back to Night School. Leading the caravan was a green Pierce Arrow, Giulietta's prized vehicle. Ugo Sapone had positioned his bulky body behind the wheel; Giulietta and Bernie sat like Chicago royalty in the back seat.

Bernie held his gold lighter to her cigarette, and then lit his own. He cracked the window before he spoke. "Giuli, Giuli, talk to me. I've represented you in civil matters for the past seventeen years. Advanced you the money to buy your own building. Watched you grow Night School into Chicago's most innovative venture. Advised you on collecting a share of profits from the bakery and speakeasy, even though you're no more than their landlady. But until tonight, I have never crawled out of my bed to bail you out of jail."

"Would you believe, the precinct captain and I go back a long way," Giulietta said. "Last year he brought his son to me, a delightful young man I taught with the utmost sensitivity. At a fifty percent discount, I might add. Good will creates more business and I'm all about business."

"Just give it to me straight, Giuli. What the hell is going on?"

She leaned back, peeled off her false eyelashes, and after cracking the window, sent them into the night. "I suspect a payback from Mr. Capone."

"The Big Fellow? Hells fire, I don't have to tell you how brutal the man can be. Johnny Torrio he most definitely is not."

"There was a time when Johnny had a thing for me."

"Well, Johnny's out of the picture and Capone only thinks of Capone."

"His bagman accused me of skimming the gross profits."

"Holy shit, you mean Fingers Bellini, who once blinded a poor schmuck he accused of cheating?"

"Please, don't remind me. He came in on Monday, flipped through the c-notes in Capone's envelope, and claimed the take was short. I told him business was slow, that I personally recorded every transaction."

"Giuli, Giuli."

"You know my word's good as gold, Bernie. For that, I sacrificed tonight's profits. Capone has put a stain on my reputation."

"Will you please heed my advice one more time: do not mess with The Big Fellow. Call me a self-serving bastard but I'd rather represent the flesh-and-blood Giulietta Bracca than whatever's left of her estate."

Chapter 3—Night Run

Monday on Becker's docks started out as grueling as every other summer day with Carlo alongside Jake, both stripped down to their undershirts and trousers while unloading crates. Then the crew chief showed up, which could've meant anything from a lay-off to unexpected overtime. This day it was, "Gus wants to see you boys in his office."

"Now?" Carlo said, wiping sweat from his brow.

"You got it. Right away, pronto. Or whatever 'hurry up' means in your lingo."

"What'd we do wrong?" Jake asked, stretching his arms overhead.

"As far as I know, nothing," the crew chief said. "But I ain't the brewmeister."

"And we don't mix the beer," Carlo muttered as the boss walked away.

"I guess we oughta put on our shirts," Jake said, tossing Carlo his.

"Yeah, show Heidi's papa some respect."

After making themselves presentable, they took the freight elevator up one floor and circled through a maze of bubbling vats before reaching Gus Kramer's office. He met them in the doorway, this stocky man with a pipe clenched between clunky false teeth and pale hair receding from a pink forehead. He pointed to two chairs but Carlo and Jake didn't sit until Gus had settled into his behind the desk.

"So, boys, for you Chicago's finest brewery is going well?"

Jake looked at Carlo, as if waiting for his okay before they both nodded.

"Good, good." Gus sucked on the pipe, sending a sliver of spit out the corner of his mouth. "My Hildie this morning got up early and made coffee." He cleared his throat. "Better she should leave that to her mother. With me she wanted to talk about the name change."

Jake gulped, Carlo figured to calm the bobbing adam's apple so he nudged him with his foot.

The old man spoke between puffs. "Jake she said I should now call you, right?"

Jake nodded. With Gus, the less said the better.

"Maybe a new last name you'd like. Something easy, as in B-r-o-w-n—Jake Brown."

"No," Carlo answered for his brother. "A man without—"

"Thanks, Gus, but I'm sticking with Baggio. Just like Carlo."

For a long moment beady eyes flickered behind Gus's bifocals. "To me it makes no never mind," he said, "but for my Hildie ... well, another story that is, for another time. Anyways, that's not why I invited you boys into my office. Can you handle an outside job? It pays good."

Carlo leaned forward. "How good?"

"One night, just one." Gus held up a stubby finger, as if they couldn't count. "Twenty-five bucks each."

Lifting his brow, Carlo turned to Jake. Jake blinked once. "That depends," Carlo said. "We ain't into killing or beatings."

"And no setting fires, scaring old ladies or little kids," Jake added.

"Don't forget, you're talking to Gustav Kramer. A man of violence I'm not." He stood, went into the hall, and bellowed, "Harold! Come!"

Merda! Carlo slumped in his chair. Not Hildie's brother, anybody but that stupido. He whispered to Jake. "It's not too late to back out."

"Like hell. Gus will say, 'no problem.' For him, that is, to lay us off. I'm talking forever."

They stood up when he came back with Harold. The son could've passed for a young Gus, but with more hair covering a thicker head and duller brain.

"Harold, meet your Friday night team." Gus moved back to his chair, but was the only one who sat down. "Hildie's beau you already know but now he goes by Jake."

"Yeah, so I hear." Harold cocked his head toward Carlo. "I know the brother too. So, here's the deal, I'm in charge. Either one of you drive? I didn't think so."

"This I already explained, Harold. Another driver the man don't need."

The man, did Gus mean Capone? Damn, another Siciliano he and Jake could do without.

"Now out of my office with the details," Gus said. "Five minutes I give. Then back to work, all of you."

Harold went first, stumbling across the threshold as he spoke from over his shoulder. "You two're still grunting on the dock, right. That's what I figured. Well, I need privacy to conduct business."

They followed Harold into the toilet facility where he checked the stalls to make sure no one else was there. At the long urinal Carlo stood to one side of him and Jake, the other. An unspoken pissing contest began, with Harold no match for brothers who'd been out-pissing each other for years.

Harold stepped back and made a show of tucking in his balls before buttoning his fly. "Friday night, ten o'clock, meet at the dock to quick load some beer. We'll be running the barrels to Michigan in exchange for some prime Canadian liquor."

"I don't know," Carlo said, crossing streams with Jake. "Loading illegal beer from a dock is one thing, but rumrunners we ain't."

"Me either." Harold wiped his hands on the seat of his trousers. "I'm doing somebody a favor. Just like Pop did Hildie a favor by giving you dagos this chance."

Dagos, some nerve coming from a clumsy Kraut, even if he was Hildie's brother. Carlo wanted to bust him. Instead he tried easing out. "Maybe you should get somebody else."

"And disappoint Pop and Hildie—no way. So what's it gonna take to please them?"

Before Carlo could answer, Jake jumped in with, "Fifty bucks for me and fifty for my brother. Okay, Carlo?"

*****

The next day after putting in ten hours on Becker's dock, Carlo returned with Jack to load more beer for the night run. While they moved barrel after barrel into one panel truck and then another, Harold and a burly man called Otis watched from the comfort of folding chairs, all the while sipping beer and growing a pile of cigarette butts around their feet.

At midnight two groaning trucks rumbled onto the street, with Harold taking the lead and Jake at his side. Otis followed with Carlo riding shotgun, not that he carried one but that's what Otis had called the passenger side. At least Carlo didn't have to put up with Harold. Poor Jake, that's what he got for putting up with Hildie.

Otis didn't have much to say but he knew how to belt a song. His robust baritone voice kept both of them awake, along with endless miles of streetlights and sporadic strings of neon signs illuminating their way. As they drove further east, the lights grew dimmer and eventually faded into night along with the city boundaries. Carlo felt his eyelids dropping, only to snap them open whenever the truck rolled over a bump or deep rut. At some point he realized the singing had stopped. Then Otis yawned. Once, twice, three times.

"You all right, Otis?"

"Sure, but if you're chomping to take the wheel, I might consider it." He spoke his next words through another yawn. "You do drive, don't you?"

"Not so good."

"Hey, I was just kidding." Otis took a deep breath. "We got a long ways to go before Michigan and it's all about making time 'cause making time is making money. Hold on, I feel another song about to spring from my throat."

He belted out an aria from a familiar Italian opera, which prompted Carlo to sit back and relax the muscles tightening across his shoulders. Soon the taillights from Harold's truck started bouncing and weaving from side to side. Were they supposed to do that? Day or night, this over- the-road-trip was a first for Carlo. Jake too, since whatever they did, they did together. Except for the women … and even that when the occasion demanded. Their jobs at Becker's may've been on the shady side but the brothers earned every dime, alongside other immigrants struggling for a fresh start, family men trying to feed their families, here or in the Old Country. This one-time job from Gus paid better but came with a greater risk. Rumrunners, that's what they were tonight, regardless of the cargo—beer, whiskey, or rum.

Somewhere along the deserted Indiana route, baritone serenading stopped again and Harold's taillights grew bigger as Otis moved their truck closer. Carlo looked over to see the driver's head bobbing on his chest.

"Dammit, Otis, wake up!" Carlo jabbed his finger into the man's meaty ribs.

Otis snorted, rustled his head like a staggering bull. But when the truck up ahead swerved to the left, Otis forged theirs straight ahead. Carlo yelled for him to slow down. Too late, they rolled into a gaping hole. Merda! The only word Carlo could manage when the nose of the truck plunged forward, throwing him and Otis against the windshield. From behind came the sound of clashing barrels, followed by an expected sloshing of the best illegal beer money could buy. At least that's what Harold had called the cargo as he tugged open the driver's door. Carlo looked through blurred eyes, expecting to see Harold yank Otis out. Instead, the singer rammed his fist into Harold's face. Otis's next words were music to Carlo's ears.

"Shut your trap, cabbage head."

Harold reeled, fell to the ground, and let out a groan. Otis stepped out of the truck, reached down for Harold's hand, and pulled him upright. "This here's your fault, Harold. Blinding me with them damn taillights just 'cause you couldn't drive a straight line."

"But you wrecked the truck, not me."

"Tell that to The Man and I'll make sure you never drive so much as a tricycle."

They were still exchanging words when Carlo heard tapping on the passenger window. He pushed open the door, climbed out, and stumbled into Jake's open arms.

"You two, over here," Otis yelled. "There's a mess that needs cleaning up."

"You think he means Harold too?" Jake asked.

"Nah, no such luck. Besides we're better off without that turd."

A bent axle and steam hissing from the radiator had crippled the truck but some of the barrels had managed to survive. This time Otis sat alone on a tree stump, surprising Carlo when he sent Harold to grunt alongside him and Jake as they transferred salvaged beer into the other truck.

"Not one word of this to my pop or Hildie. Understand, dagos?"

"Sure thing, Harold. Me and Carlo ain't telling a soul."

Carlo poked Jake to keep him from snickering. Under the light of a quarter-moon the three men worked in silence, finishing thirty minutes later with a slam of the panel doors. The brothers leaned against the truck, waiting for Harold to catch his breath.

"Hey, you rummies, rest on your own time," Otis said. "I want that bum truck pushed to the side of the road. Nosy cops asking questions we don't need."

At that moment Harold developed a convenient coughing spell, so jarring it doubled him over, which left Otis to take over the wheel.

"Damn, this better not give me a hernia," Carlo grumbled to Jake as they pushed from behind.

After they moved the truck off the road, Otis hopped out and slipped Carlo two twenties. "For you and Jake, my friend," Otis said. "In case anybody should ask, it was an unavoidable accident."

"You bet. That's the way we saw it," Carlo said. "Now, about the broken truck..."

"Damn." Otis peeled five more twenties from his money roll. "You, I'm leaving here to take care of the damn thing, but don't spend all of this unless you have to." He pointed to an open field stretching into the black of night. "About a quarter mile off this road, there's a farmer with a team of horses."

"You know this for sure?"

"The yokel helped me out before. What's more, his son's a decent mechanic. I swear, between the two of them, they must be digging these potholes in the road."

"We better get a move on," Harold said, tapping his pocket watch.

"Yeah, but with me doing the driving," Otis said. "Jake, you climb in the cab with us. We'll stop for your brother on our way back."

"You gonna be okay," Jake asked with a look that told Carlo he didn't want to leave without him.

"Yeah, sure. Now get out of here."

Carlo watched the swaying taillights disappear before he started up the lonely dirt road. The quarter mile Otis had described soon quadrupled into a twenty-minute walk, complemented by a serenade of hooting owls and chirping crickets that reminded him of nightly strolls over the foothills of his youth. Three mutts came from nowhere, barking and baring their teeth as they escorted him to their master's domain. A light flickered outside the house.

As he approached the porch, a silhouetted man held up his kerosene lamp and called out, "Who goes there?"

"Carlo's my name. My truck broke down on the hard road. I was hoping to get it towed."

"Before dawn, no doubt, I ain't no mule. You from Chicago?" The voice teemed with suspicion. The man still hadn't shown himself.

"Just passing through. I'll help with the horses, whatever it takes."

"Damn right you will. But it's still going to cost you. I suppose you'll need a mechanic too."

"He's good and fast?"

"Amen, but he don't come cheap."

"I'll need a place to lay my head too. Forty bucks, that's all I have so don't make me beg, okay?"

Twelve hours later Carlo marked time on the farmhouse porch as his stomach wrestled the ham hocks and beans he'd eaten at noon to please the farmer's wife. And to fill his empty stomach since he had no other choice. Living in Chicago had blurred his vision for the country life, an America not unlike rural Italy and one he could adjust to again. If he had to, that is. He'd been watching the distant hard road, at last felt relief on spotting a cloud of dust building in the wake of the rumrunner's truck that eventually barreled into the dirt yard. A flurry of chickens scattered in all directions. With the mutts yipping at his heels, he strolled out to meet his cohorts, not expecting to find Otis and Harold as passengers and behind the wheel Jake, a grin crossing his whiskered face that reminded Carlo of his own stubble.

Jake climbed out of the cab and they traded punches instead of the usual hugging. Looking over Jake's shoulder, Carlo saw Harold, frowning as he slid over to the window seat Otis had been warming before he stepped out.

"Otis thought I needed some practice driving," Jake said, "just in case the other truck ain't fixed yet."

"According to the farmer, it won't be ready 'til dark."

"That's what I figured," Otis said. "What about the money?"

"I didn't have much choice. The man drove a hard bargain."

Otis curled his lip and spit a wad into the ground. He lifted his thick body into the driver's seat. "I'm leaving Jake behind with you. We still have to deliver our pricey return load, which will arrive in St. Louis on time I might add, thanks to you boys." He shifted into first gear and rattled off, sending the chickens into another uproar.

"How'd it go?" Carlo asked.

"Couldn't have been better, even with Harold pouting, which

me and Otis ignored. He said I should let you drive part way back. You know, just in case he needs us again."

Chapter 4—Negotiating

On Tuesday evening the overhead lights at Fabiola's had already dimmed, urging the last of their customers to leave with no hard feelings. Outside, Carlo leaned against the building with Jake at his side, both smoking cigarillos that exceeded their daily allotment.

"You really want to go through with this?" Jake asked.

"I'm here, ain't I?"

"That's what scares me. A Chicago bride would be a helluva lot cheaper."

"And a know-it-all, need I say more?"

"If you mean Hildie, we ain't tying the knot."

"Says you, she has other ideas."

"Look, this ain't about me. You got hit with a bad week. First the Night School raid, then our trip into the countryside."

"For which Harold reneged on the fifty bucks Gus promised. What a bastardo, giving us each a lousy twenty-five."

"Otis pitched in some extra, even though he didn't know it."

"That extra shrunk when the farmer's wife took her share."

"Yeah, thanks for covering my supper. There's only so much liquor one man can

put in an empty stomach."

Carlo peered through the window. The saloon appeared empty so he opened the door and motioned Jake inside.

Jake moved but stopped short of stepping over the threshold. "Did I tell you there ain't enough reasons in hell for marrying some stranger?"

"So we get acquainted first," Carlo said. "Right now, I just need to know you're with me."

"All the way, brother." He put his hand on Carlo's shoulder. "Just go slow with these Valenza bastards. I keep thinking how we paid Massimo for those apprentice jobs."

"Come on, Jake. Was it Massimo's fault the bricklayers went on strike a week later."

"What about the job with Sieben's. We paid Massimo for that one too. Then a midnight raid closed the brewery."

Carlo shook himself loose and pulled Jake inside with him. "Just for tonight, forget Johnny Torrio and all that shit."

"*Basta, basta*, I've said enough. Look at Massimo, waving us over like—"

"Remember, Jake, no wine tonight."

"Right, to keep our heads clear."

Carlo watched Massimo tug at a waistcoat challenging his expanding girth. He had three years on Vincenzo's thirty-seven, and an extra thirty pounds. Still, the Valenza brothers couldn't deny their resemblance: same hooked beak, same pitted skin, same unctuous smile.

"Ah, paesani," Massimo called out. "Come, we sit."

While Vincenzo locked the door and pulled the shades, Massimo offered wine from a carafe. Carlo and Jake said no with their fingers. Sitting around a table, the four men exchanged pleasantries in their Piemontese dialect before Massimo eased into the negotiations.

"So Carlo, Vincenzo tells me you desire to meet our Louisa, a woman whose beauty erupts from the very depths of her soul."

"You have a photograph?" Jake asked.

Vincenzo shrugged. "Only as a child."

"Let me assure you, she takes after our ma's side," Massimo said. "Now about the arrangements—"

"Perhaps we should wait," Carlo said in response to Jake's nudge.

"For what, another year to pass?" Vincenzo asked. "As we speak our sister grows older."

"How old?" Jake asked. A question Carlo hadn't thought to bring up.

"Paesani … please." Massimo tapped two hands of fingers to his chest. "What my brother meant was time lost, pleasure lost."

"Maybe we should come back later."

"Of course, but I must caution you: waiting could result in disappointment," Vincenzo said. "A widower from our village is pursuing Louisa. He possesses land, a big empty house."

"And no children to carry his name." Massimo leaned forward. "Perhaps Louisa should stay put. Italy needs more sons; so many perished in The War to End All Wars. The Old Country, it's not like America with its damn immigration quotas."

Carlo leaned even closer. He knew what he wanted and had played the game long enough. "How much did you say?"

"One hundred dollars for Louisa's travel expenses, another hundred for me and Vincenzo."

Jake snorted. He pushed his chair back.

"That's pretty steep," Carlo said.

Massimo shrugged. "It depends on how long you want to wait. We're not just talking the cost of boat and train fares. There's paper work, the usual greasing of palms. It's the Italian way, in case you've forgotten."

Carlo could never forget.

"New clothes for our sister," Vincenzo added. "Naturally, you'll want to show her off for the courtship."

"So what if she and Carlo don't connect?" Jake asked. "Who pays her return passage?"

"Carlo, of course," Massimo replied.

"And if she refuses to go back?" Carlo asked, although he couldn't imagine this happening.

Evidently, neither could Massimo. "Paesani ... please, an unlikely situation such if ever there was." Narrowing his beady eyes, he stuck his nose inches from Carlo's, and spoke with a breath of wine and garlic. "But should this happen, trust my words: it would be a matter for Vincenzo and me to resolve. After all, we Valenzas are men of honor."

(End of Excerpt)